HUNTING BLOODLINES

BOOK III IN THE FALLING NIGHT SERIES

LEE LARSEN

For Lincoln and Lucas, who inspire me to give more time to the rising generation. They are the future.

PROLOGUE

Isaac felt a twinge of pain as he slapped himself across the cheek with his right hand. The stinging dissipated almost as quickly as it had come, as his body instantly healed itself. Though the pain was brief, it was enough to prop his drooping eyelids back open. He had been driving all night, trying to put as much distance as he could between himself and the carnage that had occurred back in Harrisburg. After all the healing his body had been through during the fighting, his exhaustion was overwhelming. He knew if he didn't pull over soon, his fatigue would consume him. The last thing he wanted was to total the car or draw attention to himself by wrecking. When his faltering eyes suddenly spotted the rectangular blue rest area sign on the side of the freeway, Isaac was relieved.

The rest area was large enough to hold at least two dozen cars, but there was only one semi-truck parked on the North side of the parking lot. A small patch of grass rested in front of the small structure he guessed held bathrooms in the middle of the rest area. Isaac pulled into the last spot on the far south side of the lot, farthest from the truck. The semi appeared to be unoccupied, but the rear portion of the vehicle looked to double as a sleeping pod, so Isaac assumed that the driver must be getting some rest. Considering that there was likely only a couple hours of twilight left, Isaac had every intention of following suit.

Before leaning back to rest, Isaac decided to check on Liz's wounds. She was still sleeping, so he pulled the collar portion of her shirt down just enough to expose the gunshot wound below her clavicle. He was surprised by what he saw. The wound that had still been oozing blood a few hours before, was now completely scabbed over. It looked like what he would expect the wound to look like, after four or five days of healing. Only Liz had only been shot a little over ten hours before.

His curiosity piqued, Isaac gently leaned Liz over enough so that her back was facing towards him. He then slowly lifted up the back of her shirt, exposing the other two gunshot wounds. These ones had barely been bleeding before when he had checked them, as the bullets had lodged only halfway into the skin before stopping. Both wounds were already mostly healed. They also appeared to have been healing for days… not hours.

Liz stirred slightly as Isaac pulled her shirt down to normal and laid her back in her seat, but her eyes remained closed. Her significant progress in healing was intriguing. While it wasn't as fast as members of the bloodline healed, it was significantly faster than a normal person. Isaac felt relieved to know that Liz was healing so quickly, as it meant the odds of her survival were now looking quite favorable.

Isaac leaned down to press the recline button on the side of his seat and noticed another car exiting the freeway. Even in his exhausted state, Isaac was alarmed. He couldn't imagine it was any kind of coincidence that another vehicle had decided to pull off the remote Washington highway immediately after he had.

As the vehicle approached the parking lot, Isaac noticed that it was a newer white four door sedan. It pulled into a parking spot halfway between where Isaac and the truck were parked. With the dark tint on the windows, Isaac couldn't see how many occupants were in the car. He knew that in his exhausted state, he wouldn't be able to put up much of a fight. He glanced over at Liz as he tapped her on the arm and was surprised to see that she was awake.

Elizabeth Scott had tears streaming down both of her cheeks, and her colorful green eyes screamed devastation. Her stare was unbreakable, as she appeared to gaze through the dashboard in front of her, trapped in some lonely abyss. Her brown hair hanging just past her shoulders was mostly straight, but more matted than normal. Isaac couldn't blame her for her sadness. The wrenching pain in his own chest from losing Leuken was still fresh, but whether he wanted to deal with it or not, they were still in danger, and he needed to focus on keeping Liz alive for now. There would be time for mourning later, but only if they stayed alive.

"Liz." Isaac said softly as he tapped her arm again. She did not respond, so he gently shook her arm, while glancing back at the car to make sure no one had exited. "Liz, I need you to focus."

Elizabeth's tear-filled eyes shifted to Isaac, but her expression didn't change. Isaac felt like she was looking more through him then at him. He could understand her depressed state, because he felt similar, but this was no time for feelings.

"We are being followed Liz." Isaac explained. "And in my weakened state, I am not sure how well I can protect you." Liz said nothing. It was difficult for Isaac to tell if she had even heard what he said.

"Did you hear me, Liz?" Isaac said, growing more frustrated.

Liz nodded slowly, and she seemed to focus on him momentarily. "It's okay Isaac." She said softly. "I don't care if I die."

"Liz!" Isaac said sternly as he grabbed her shoulder firmly with one hand. "Get a hold of yourself. Whether Luke is alive or not doesn't matter right now. What matters is that your father and your little brother are waiting to meet up with us, and if we don't meet them then they will suffer the same agony that you are going through right now. Is that what you want for them?"

Elizabeth stared at Isaac for a long moment, before slowly shaking her head.

"Then I need you to help me." Isaac continued, softening his voice. "That car that is following us is probably occupied by bloodline members. If it is, I will need your help to fight them. I know you are injured, but with the sun still down you can't be harmed unless they get my sword from me. I will do my best to fight them off, but in my current state I can barely function. Until I get some rest, I will be virtually useless. Between the two of us though, we might stand a chance."

Isaac hoped that Liz would be able to put up some kind of a fight, because he knew that he couldn't. If there was even one bloodline in that car that possessed the skill with a blade that the taller Latino back in Harrisburg had, Isaac knew they were in trouble. He could only hope to end the fighting quickly, with the little strength he still possessed. The driver door of the white car opened slowly, and a man stepped out.

"Can I count on you Elizabeth?" Isaac asked, glancing briefly at her while directing most of his attention at the man emerging from the car.

"Yes." Elizabeth said calmly. Fresh tears streamed from her eyes. "I will help you fight…Because that is what Luke would want me to do." She opened her door as she finished speaking and stood up.

As Isaac exited the car, he slung his sword over his back, with the hilt pointed skyward. The man who had stepped out of the car across the lot slowly closed the door and began walking towards them at a hurried pace.

Isaac was relieved that the man was alone, but something just didn't feel right about him. The man was walking with one arm tucked behind his back, likely concealing a weapon, but Isaac felt a strange calming sensation wash over him. For some reason, only the light could explain, Isaac felt like he shouldn't kill the man.

As the man grew closer Isaac recognized his face. It was the same one he had fought with only hours before in Harrisburg. The same one who had almost beaten him. Isaac drew his sword the moment he recognized his foe. The heat of the glowing terralium blade flooded the air in front of him, as he brought the sword forward in a ready stance.

No sooner had Isaac drawn his sword, than the Latino raised both arms over his head. There was nothing in the man's left hand, not a weapon or anything. The other arm was halfway missing, the same as it had been since Isaac cut it off. This man, who only hours before had tried to kill him and Elizabeth, was now approaching unarmed. The logical part of Isaac's brain told him to kill the man quickly before he produced a weapon, but the light prompted him not to, so he hesitated.

"I no want to hurt you." The man said in a heavy South American accent. "I sorry for what we did to you family." Isaac could tell that the man was struggling to find the words in English to communicate.

"What do you want?" Isaac asked in Spanish, assuming that to be the man's native tongue.

"My Spanish is no very good either." The man replied in English. "You speak Portuguese?"

"I do, but it's been a while so speak slowly, please." Isaac replied in Portuguese. He had spent almost a decade in Brazil back in his eighties and nineties but had rarely spoken it in recent years. "What do you want?"

"I know this might sound crazy, but I need your help." The man said slowly in Portuguese.

"You just killed one of my family." Isaac said through clenched teeth, trying to suppress the rage he felt welling up inside. "And now you dare to ask my help?"

"I am sorry for your loss." The man actually sounded sincere. "But I do not ask your help for myself. You see the Chosen Ones made us do what we did back there. They have our families… our wives, our children. If we do not do what they demand, they will kill them."

Isaac could see tears forming in the man's eyes, and his anger quickly turned to disbelief.
"What do you mean?" He asked the man.

"There are dozens of us, over a hundred." The man continued, speaking more rapidly now. "The Chosen Ones keep us locked up and hold our wives and children as ransom. My name is Royce Romero, and my wife, my son, and my daughter Isabel are being held in a compound in Brazil. It is just outside of Campo Belo, a couple hours northwest from Rio De Jannero." The man pulled a folded piece of paper from his pocket, stepped closer, and handed it to Isaac. "Those are the coordinates."

"When you say, "Chosen ones", what do you mean?" Isaac asked as he looked down at the folded paper. "How many of them are there?"

"There are only two, but they are invincible." Royce explained. "Nothing can kill them. Some of us have tried, on several different occasions, but every time the rebels were killed. None of the weapons we used so much as scratched them, and every time someone tries to fight them, not only are they killed, but their families are publicly executed as well. That is why we hunt you and the others like us..." The man hung his head in shame. "It is not because we want to, but because we have no other choice. By not reporting back in, they will kill me soon, but I had to tell you. You are the first group we have encountered with more than a couple bloodlines who actually seem to know how to fight. I already lost my son yesterday, while fighting you... and I am done being their weapon. Someone needs to stand up to them... Please... you have to help my family. There must be some way to kill them and free my people."

"What do these chosen ones look like?" Isaac asked, while looking around. The talk of someone coming to kill Royce was making the hair on his neck stand up. "And how will they kill you? Are you being tracked?"

"They look like ordinary people. Silas and Priscilla are the names they call each other, but there is nothing ordinary about them. They are ruthless and cruel. I know they sometimes track us, but I am not sure how, they might be tracking me now for all I know, which is why I must leave, in case they decide to come and get me instead of killing me from a distance."

"How would they do that?" Isaac was still perplexed. "Kill you from a distance that is?"

"They have a magical necklace, with a mechanical device attached. If they press the button on the device, they can kill anyone they choose no matter how far away they are. They can also do it by..." Royce's sentence was cut off suddenly and unexpectedly as his head exploded.

Isaac jumped back in alarm, looking for threats as he scanned the countryside around them. Liz screamed momentarily, also jumping back and covering her mouth in surprise. It took her a moment longer before she looked around, and when she did her eyes seemed drawn continually back to Royce's headless corpse, lying on the ground in front of them.

The semi-truck was the only other thing in sight besides them, and Isaac was alarmed at what possibly could have killed the man. He had heard no sounds, seen no projectiles prior to Royce's head exploding, and yet, something had caused the damage. "What could it be?" Isaac thought out loud as he studied what was left of the bloody body in front of him.

Only Royce's head appeared to be damaged, as the rest of his body was still completely intact and unharmed. As Isaac leaned over the body, he could smell a combination of burnt flesh and something else. Something almost... sulfur smelling, but somehow different.

There had been no sound other than the small explosion... which meant that the blast must have come from inside the man's head. It was the only logical explanation he could think of. Isaac stepped over to the corpse and began to examine the remains. The tissue in the middle part of the head appeared blackened and scorched. A small piece of metal was lodged into the back of the neck, so Isaac retrieved it.

The metal looked like what could have been part of a metal case, with a small wire connected to it.

"What is it?" Liz asked curiously, still keeping her distance from the carnage.

"I'm not entirely sure." Isaac said as he finished examining it. He shifted his attention back to the paper in his other hand, and as he unfolded it, there were two series of numbers with decimals interspersed. Isaac recognized the numbers to be latitude and longitude co-ordinates. While he didn't want to believe Royce, it was hard not to when he had just watched the man sacrifice himself to warn Isaac.

"But I think the others will want to know about this." Isaac continued as he turned back towards his own vehicle. "We should leave though Liz. Now!" He didn't try to hide the urgency in his voice. He wasn't sure if the man had been followed or not, but he wasn't about to stick around and say hello to whoever or whatever came to collect the corpse. Sleep would just have to wait for a while longer. Death was not an appealing alternative.

*　　　*　　　*

"Can you please forbear killing them unless they actually deserve it this time?" Silas said casually from the gilded chair he was seated on at the front of the antechamber. "They do take so terribly long to grow."

"Of course. I won't kill them unless they actually deserve it." Priscilla nearly snarled at Silas through gritted teeth as she paced back and forth in front of him, her black heeled shoes echoing on the marble floors with each step. Her long dark hair flowed down her back, a sharp contrast to the form fitting yellow dress she wore. Her piercing brown eyes were even darker than her hair, and were it not for her hawkish nose, she would have been beautiful.

"Okay." Silas sighed loudly. "The last time you said something similar you killed three of them... Alastair will not be pleased if we can't deliver the quota each cycle, and the next two are due next year. If what they said on the phone is true, we already lost most of our best hunting party. We don't need to lose any more."

"You think I'm unaware of that?" Priscilla shouted as her eyes locked on him and she stopped pacing. "Whoever did this will pay... mark my words!"

"I am sure they will my dear..." Silas said cautiously. "I was only saying we may need every able-bodied bloodline we have to hunt down this group. They are obviously a threat and must be disposed of."

"You think every able body?" Priscilla asked nervously, the ice in her voice being replaced by cautious disbelief. "Even from the retreat?"

"Not all of them." Silas explained. "But we may need to form another party from that crop to make up for the ones we lost. Alastair will never be the wiser, and we will have enough to operate 3 full hunting parties. We can send two to search out and destroy this crew, while still having one party free to search out other bloodlines."

"You are assuming we will need two crews to finish off these animals…" Priscilla sniffed.

"Considering we just lost several of ours and some of them got away, I think it certainly wouldn't hurt to send in two teams. At least then we will have an overwhelming advantage. I doubt there could be more than half a dozen of them if that, but we will know soon enough when this party reports in. They should be here soon." Silas found himself surprisingly interested in what had happened up there in the United States. It had been nearly a year since they had lost a single person from one of their hunting parties, and they had never lost more than three. To think that seven had been killed on this trip was infuriating… but it had piqued his curiosity.

Several loud taps at the door suddenly echoed through the chamber.

"Enter." Priscilla said loudly in Portuguese. The servants opened the doors, and behind them entered two bloodlines. "It's about time!" Priscilla said loudly as they approached.

Silas was indeed surprised by what he saw next. Hugo entered the hall first, followed by another skinny even younger looking bloodline that Silas vaguely recognized. The absence of the tall companion that usually accompanied Hugo was strange, but the fact that Hugo was missing his right arm at the elbow was even more peculiar.

"I am sorry my lady." Hugo said quickly, his voice quivering. "We were met with more resistance than usual. They were... highly trained... and there were more than just the two we thought. A lot more. Probably at least eight to ten of these bloodlines. They attacked my surveillance team before my whole crew could assemble... Picked us off one or two at a time. One of them was older, probably at least two hundred, he killed three of my men himself, and I lost my arm trying to stop him."

"Enough!" Priscilla shouted and the man actually jumped.

The consistently arrogant little man was more nervous than Silas had before seen him. After re-gaining his composure, Hugo bowed himself down even further on the floor in apologetic fashion but didn't say another word until after Priscilla spoke. If the pathetic sop bowed any lower, his face would be going through the floor. As it was his nose seemed rather uncomfortable squished against the marble flooring in such a fashion.

"Stop your pathetic stammering!" Priscilla said loudly and impatiently. "I want you to answer my questions exactly, and you had better not say a word otherwise. Do you understand?"

"Yes, my lady." Hugo replied, not lifting his eyes from the ground.

"How many bloodlines did you see?" Priscilla asked.

"Personally, my lady, I only saw two. I think, but others from my crew saw three more."

"What do you mean you think?!" Priscilla snapped. "Either you saw two bloodlines, or you didn't. Which is it?"

"My lady I apologize, but it is hard to say exactly what I saw." Hugo was visibly shaking now, appearing more nervous than ever. "One of them was definitely a bloodline, he even had the scar from getting the mark of the bloodline removed. The other one I saw though seemed different. She had no scar or mark, but something was different about her. When I tried to cut off her head, my sword barely scratched the surface of her skin. She was unconscious, and yet somehow indestructible. I even struck her more than once, and it did virtually nothing. My sword even bent when it hit her. My sword has never bent before this my lady."

Priscilla looked up at Silas, and Silas stood from his chair as their eyes met. *Could it possibly be?* He thought to himself. It seemed impossible that there would have been another Auserwhalt with these bloodlines, but he didn't know what else would explain what he described.

"Continue." Priscilla said as she walked to her throne and sat down.

"The other bloodline who was with her, the old one, was very skilled with the sword. He even beat my best blade, Royce in one-on-one combat, and he fought with a white-hot glowing blade. I'd never seen anything like it." Hugo glanced up just enough to look at their feet, but no further.

"The other members of my crew that survived said that they encountered another three bloodlines during the fighting, but I never saw them myself my lady." Hugo continued.

Priscilla's eyes met Silas' again, when Hugo mentioned the blade, but she quickly recovered. "So, these five killed seven of your crew, and incapacitated you?" Priscilla's tone was still harsh.

"Yes, my lady. Eight actually. I am sorry I have failed you."

"What do you mean eight?" Silas asked. His database showed that there were still five left over from the crew, including the two that were in front of him. There were two still in Oregon, and another further north in Washington State by himself. The numbers Hugo provided weren't adding up.

"I am sorry my Lord, I was only saying that we lost eight. We survived," He gestured towards himself and his companion. "And so did the two I have doing recon back in Oregon. Everyone else was killed."

"You told me there were five left?" Priscilla nearly snarled at Silas now. He was immediately annoyed by her unabashed petulance. It was one thing for her to disrespect the slaves so, but he was not a slave. The engraved bracelet on his left wrist might have implied otherwise, but he had an arrangement with Priscilla. She was supposed to be merely first among equals... not his master.

"There are five." Silas pulled the digital tablet from under his chair that had the program he used to control the chips implanted in the bloodline slaves. As he opened the program and selected the first hunting party, 5 names lit up. He was surprised to see Royce's name on there, with the big man not being present. That one was nearly inseparable from Hugo.

"Where is Royce?" Silas asked, as Hugo's eyes raised just enough to glance at him. Just enough for Silas to see the dread in his pupils.

"My lord he is dead." Hugo offered, timid and nervously.

"Are you certain?" Priscilla's tone was ice again.

"I am my lady." Hugo said, swallowing loudly.

Pricilla glanced at Silas, who slowly shook his head. Before he had finished motioning with his head, Priscilla moved in a blur, pulling Hugo's sword from the sheath and using it to strike off his only good arm. Hugo cried out in pain as he jumped to his feet, quickly turning to run. Before he had even taken a step, she struck from behind, severing his leg at the calf. Hugo hit the ground hard, again crying out in pain.

"How dare you lie to me you pathetic fool!" She snarled as she grabbed what was left of his other arm, pulling him over to face her.

"I'm sorry." Hugo spoke frantically now. "I really thought… he was dead." His pain must have been excruciating, for the man could barely speak.

It was difficult to tell if the tears streaming down Hugo's face were from pain or pure cowardice. Either way seeing the weasel crying so pathetically was strangely… satisfying. Silas was also angered by Hugo's treachery. Suddenly the idea of Priscilla finishing off the pitiful man seemed like it wouldn't be such a bad idea after all. The chump was nearly worthless without that arm anyways.

"And exactly why would you assume that? Oh, please do tell Hugo." Priscilla's feigned smile looked more like another snarl as she finished speaking. She held the sword at his throat, as she bent down to look him in the eyes.

"Because… because…" Hugo was stammering, still in tears, obviously trying to think of what to say next. "Because the bloodline Royce was fighting when I ran… was just too talented. Even Royce… never stood a chance against… someone that good with a sword." The man's labored breaths between words annoyed Silas. Then something the man said stood out to him.

"When you what?" Each word was ice as it left Priscilla's lips. "You mean you ran away from the fighting?"

"Well, you see…" Hugo's futile attempt to explain was cut short, as Priscilla quickly raised and lowered the sword, decapitating him.

Silas smiled, until Priscilla turned, and her eyes met his.

"I'm sorry, I know I promised not to kill them, but that one was practically begging for it with his lies and cowardice."

"Oh no." Silas smiled briefly at her. "No apology needed. That was well deserved darling. I would have done the same thing. You merely beat me to it."

"Okay good." Priscilla was walking back towards Silas, but stopped as she passed the other bloodline, who was still groveling on the floor. She turned to face him, raising the blade above her head as if she might strike him down. "And you. Did you know Royce was alive?"

"No, my lady." The man said, still keeping his eyes focused on the ground.

"Look at me when I'm talking to you!" Priscilla shrieked.

The man flinched, and then quickly looked up at Priscilla.

"I'm going to ask you again… and for your sake I hope you tell the truth. You know how we respond to lies." She gestured towards Hugo's lifeless body with her free hand.

"My lady I would not dare to lie to you." The olive-skinned youth said subserviently. "I was still searching in Eugene with one of the others when this fight broke out. By the time I arrived, I found Hugo with his car and his arm missing. He told me that Royce and the other seven had all been killed, and we immediately decided to get back here. I swear it is the truth."

"So did you even see any of these bloodlines?" Priscilla asked.

"No, my lady. I did not." The boy's voice was quivering as he spoke, and his clasped hands were visibly shaking.

"And did you see or hear from Royce after you met back up with Hugo, or hear any mention of him?" Silas inquired.

"No, my lord. Other than Hugo saying he was dead; I didn't see or hear of him."

"So, then he must have run away." Silas said disappointedly as he held the tablet up to look at Royce's icon on the screen. "That really is too bad. He was quite talented with a sword." Silas had seen on more than one occasion the man sparing with two or three other bloodlines at a time and winning.

"Well, we know what happens to traitors!" Priscilla snarled again, looking at Silas expectantly.

Silas reluctantly clicked on Royce's name and then the command execute on the screen. After confirming the execution by re-typing his password, the man's green icon turned red momentarily, and then black. Priscilla dismissed the young bloodline, who left as fast as humanly possible without running from the room.

The moment the door closed Priscilla turned to Silas. "Should we tell Alastair?" He could see by the look in her eyes that she was nervous. The bulging veins that had showed in her temples moments before were gone, replaced by a ghostly expression.

"What would we tell him?" Silas was thinking out loud now, his mind moving quickly as he thoughtfully considered the outcome of either telling or not telling Alastair. "If there are other Auserwhalt using bloodlines... but wait... Hugo said that the female was unconscious, yet the bloodline was still protecting her. That sounds more like an alliance than subservience."

"What do you mean?" Priscilla asked, obviously not following him completely.

"I mean it sounds like either Tobias or Jareth has been killed, and the new Auserwhalt has allied herself with a pack of bloodlines." Silas was contemplating the implications of such an alliance. "To tell Alastair might give him an excuse to break our little agreement. Failing to provide bloodlines or failing to properly keep the wild bloodline population under control, both give him the excuse he needs to void our contract and kill us. I for one... would rather not have to deal with that."

"Perhaps we could ally ourselves with this new Auserwhalt, and between the three of us and all the bloodlines, we might be able to kill Alastair himself." Priscilla said excitedly.

"Perhaps we could." Silas knew the very idea was idiotic. No free bloodlines would willingly partner with them as long as they enslaved and controlled other bloodlines. The very thought was laughable, but Silas had too much on his mind to worry about explaining Priscilla's idiocy to her. No... their best option would still be to hunt down and kill this other Auserwhalt, and her bloodline friends.

CHAPTER I

My eyes were closed, but slumber was unattainable. I pretended to be asleep, but it was only so that I could avoid talking to Isaac. Everything felt like a dream... a horrific nightmare I couldn't wait to end... but I knew that it wasn't. After driving for nearly 6 hours straight while the man slept, it was nice not to be behind the wheel anymore. Of course, the short conversation that had followed him waking was not one I cared to repeat.

I had mentioned the futile hope... I knew it was futile, but it was the only hope I had... that Luke might still be alive. He had assured that not even one of the bloodlines could have survived the explosion that Luke was in, but I was firm in my denial that he was dead. The tears that streamed down Isaac's face had been unaccompanied by words... yet spoke volumes.

Even still, it was a truth I wasn't ready to accept. So, I held on to the dream that Luke had somehow miraculously survived and would be waiting with open arms at the rendezvous point for me. The pain and emptiness I felt was so overwhelming, that the only way I felt I could survive was to hold on to hope that he would somehow show up at the mansion.

And so, I kept my eyes closed, only peeking out the right one from time to time to see if we were close to the mansion yet. I didn't want to talk to anyone, let alone Isaac. I would speak again when I saw Leuken Bennett, or when I had to. For now, though... I waited. And waited... and waited some more.

We had passed the state line into Idaho over an hour before, which meant we should be arriving at the mansion any minute. The problem was that each minute seemed to last for an hour or more. And the closer we got to the mansion, the more the possibility of Luke's certain death became a reality. The very thought again brought tears streaming down my cheeks, but I didn't bother to wipe them. I didn't want Isaac to see my faltering hope. Leuken Bennett had to be alive. There was no other alternative that I could bear to fathom.

I was surprised when Isaac suddenly turned off of the main highway. Looking around, I realized that we had arrived at the turn off towards the mansion. I had been so lost in thought, that I hadn't even seen it coming.

"Elizabeth you might want to be ready." Isaac said cautiously. "There's a chance we could be walking into a trap if the others beat us here and were followed. Who knows how many of those bloodline hunters there are."

"I know. I'm ready." I replied nervously. At the present moment I cared about one thing... and one thing only. It would only be moments before I discovered if my world had truly been destroyed or not... If the only man I would ever love was still alive. I could feel my stomach knotting in anticipation.

"How is your chest feeling?" Isaac inquired. "Is there still a lot of pain?"

It took me a moment to realize what he was talking about. I had completely forgotten about the gunshot wounds to my chest and back. They weren't exactly a priority in my mind.

"Honestly." I replied. "I haven't felt them at all." I ran my hand across my upper chest where the wound was just below the neckline of my shirt. Reaching inside, I felt mostly smooth skin. As I looked down at it, the scabbing that had been there was gone, replaced by a large fresh-looking scar. It was no longer tender to the touch either.

"Splendid. It would seem my theory was correct then." Isaac said under his breath. He seemed to be thinking out loud.

"What theory is that?" I asked.

"Well, you see, when you beat Tobias within an inch of his life, I noticed that he healed up completely in a matter of hours. I wasn't sure if that was a fluke or not, but your injury should have taken a couple weeks to heal. The fact that it is completely healed after less than two days makes me fairly certain it is another gift your Verdorben curse gives you. You may not heal as quickly as we do, but you still recover remarkably faster than normal people. That knowledge could prove useful in dealing with other Verdorben.

"Oh." Was all I could think of to say. *Who cares if I heal fast?* All I cared about was seeing Leuken again. After pulling through the gate, I was excited as we rounded the curve in the road and the mansion came into view, with the snowcapped mountains towering above in the distance. My eyes instantly scanned the front of the mansion for Leuken. There were only two vehicles parked in front, the Hummer and my Tahoe. I could see my father and Sara leaning against the Tahoe in the driveway. Ben was also seated on a bench near the front door between two of the columns. He stood and walked towards us as we approached.

It was a relief to see that our families had both made it here safely. As Isaac pulled to a stop at the front of the driveway, I stepped out of the car. Scanning the rest of the surroundings, I saw no sign of Leuken. My father and Sara had joined Ben and were all walking towards us now. As Isaac exited the car, his eyes met Sara's and Ben's.

The look on Sara's face was one of disbelief, mixed with sorrow. I felt the tears begin to flow down my cheeks. It was the look of a mother, who knew she had just lost her son. Tears filled her eyes in an instant, and she walked up to Isaac, who quickly embraced her. I hadn't even thought about the fact that they were holding on to hope that Leuken might have escaped with us.

"He didn't make it... did he?" Sara asked softly. Her eyes closed as she hugged Isaac, and were it not for the tears, one wouldn't have been able to tell the sadness she was feeling. I couldn't understand how she could be so composed at a time like this.

"No." Isaac replied softly. "He went back for the car, and one of the bloodline hunters followed him into the house. He was wearing explosives... ended up taking down the entire house with Luke inside... I'm sorry Sara, but not even one of us could have survived that blast."

Sara's sorrow intensified, as she let go of Isaac and sank to the ground. Sobbing uncontrollably, she curled her arms around her tucked in legs, and began to rock back and forth on the ground as she cried. My father squatted behind her, placing a hand on her back to try and console her, but it was to no avail. Through my tear clouded vision I noticed Ben kneel down in front of her, also trying to comfort her. Isaac stood watching for a moment but turned away as his own tears began to flow again.

I took a step towards Sara, my own grief seeming inconsequential compared to what she must now be feeling. Her eyes glanced up briefly at me as I approached... and stopped me dead in my tracks. The anguish in those eyes was unbearable... and I sunk down to my knees. Suddenly the world around me seemed quite small, as guilt collided with the ocean of grief that had already consumed my soul. Leuken Bennett was dead... and I was to blame.

Had it not been for me, none of this would have happened. The first two Verdorben would have been killed, and the Bennett's would have moved on. Those other bloodlines wouldn't have found them... and Leuken would still be alive. My vision faded even more as the avalanche of guilt buried me. I was no longer looking at Sara, but the look of utter devastation in her eyes was burned into my mind. I wanted to disappear... I wanted to stop existing. The pain and guilt were more than I could bear. It felt hard... hard to breath... hard to see... hard to feel anything... but the pain inside. Someone moved to stand over me, and I felt a hand on my shoulder.

I didn't bother to look up. I was sure whoever it was probably felt the same as I did. Were it not for me, none of this would have happened. It was all... my... fault. The urge to disappear intensified, so I stood up. I did the only thing that seemed logical. I ran. Where to I didn't know. My legs moved faster than I thought possible, as I tried to disappear from the scene of sorrow and devastation that I had created. I vaguely noticed slamming into or through a lot of things as I ran. Trees, bushes, and the grass seemed to whiz by in a blur. Trying to escape... hoping this was still just some nightmare.

At first someone must have followed. It sounded like Ben calling after me, pleading with me to stop, but I didn't dare. Luke's family were all good people. None of them deserved to have to look at me after what I'd done. After who we had all lost.

After some time, I couldn't tell how long, I noticed the blurs around me were mostly white. My running slowed slightly as I ran through the snow. As I crested the top of another hill, and burst out of the trees, I suddenly had the strange sensation that I was flying. I couldn't feel the ground beneath me.

Then I realized I was falling, as I plummeted several hundred feet through the air towards the ground. The snow below had large rocks sticking out in several places. *Finally,* I thought to myself as I plunged towards the boulders below, *I can end this pain and suffering now.*

I closed my eyes and braced for death... but instead was jolted to my senses by shearing pain in my legs and hip as my body slammed into the snow and against the edge of a rock. I barely had time to feel the pain, as I struck rock after rock with my arms, hands and face as I tumbled down the side of the hill I had landed on. It seemed every rock on the mountain had managed to place itself in the path I toppled down. When my body finally came to rest in what must have been a pile of snow, I could feel shooting pain throughout all of it. I opened my eyes slowly...seeing whiteness as the snow fell slowly on me and my surroundings... before they involuntarily shut... and I drifted into nothingness...

*   *   *

"If you remember anything else, or see anything suspicious Misses Fairbanks, please give me a call." Detective Jimenti said politely as he handed the woman he had just finished interviewing his business card.

"I will Detective." The older woman replied nervously, her arms folded across her chest as she peered around Detective Jimenti and his partner. "You be safe now. There are some bad people out there." She closed the door slowly as the men turned to leave.

Michael Jimenti and his partner, FBI special agent Gilberto Valdez, were both assigned to the Joint Terrorism Task Force for the state of Oregon. They had just finished knocking on the last door for their canvass area in the neighborhood. This one was at the end of the street that the two teenagers, now persons of interest for several murders, had lived on.

"Something just doesn't add up here Gil." Jimenti said as they walked back towards where their car was parked a few doors down. He was rubbing the side of his cleanly shaved bald head as he talked, obviously deep in thought. "First you have an active shooter at a school, with only a few dead bodies, in spite of over a dozen people being shot with a high-powered rifle. Some of those victims even had holes in their clothes, with blood all over, but no injuries to show for it."

"You actually believe the kids back at the school Mike?" Valdez asked, shaking his head in disbelief. He was several years older than Jimenti, with graying hair near the temples and a large nose. His tan Guatemalan skin made Jimenti look even more pale. "I told you, I think these kids were in some kind of witness protection program or something, and a cartel or some other hired guns had taken out a hit on their families. Once I hear back from my source at the CIA, this will all make sense."

"Nothing about this makes sense man." Jimenti paused to look at Valdez, who stood a couple inches taller than the thinner detective. "You ever heard of a cartel or other hired guns getting in long drawn-out fights, using swords? For crying out loud, those guys were definitely hired pros, but those curved swords they had were crazy, and it looks like most of them were killed with their own weapons."

Valdez' phone began ringing from his pocket, and he quickly answered. "Valdez here." The person on the other line was not speaking loud enough for Jimenti to hear. But they spoke at length before Valdez replied. "None of the passports or prints came back to anyone?" He said incredulously to whoever was on the other end of the phone. "Okay thanks, please let me know the second you hear back from Interpol. These guys have to be in somebody's system somewhere."

"That was the lab." Valdez explained as he hung up the phone. "They said they ran DNA, fingerprints, and all of the passports on each of the suspects whose bodies we found back there. They are all ghosts, no records or nothing on any of them."

"What about the kids from the school and their families. Does their stuff check out?" Jimenti asked.

"Yeah, birth certificates look legit, and their info checks out. We still haven't made an ID on the uncle, as his info came back to some guy that died back in the 1950s, but the rest of the family is clean. No criminal records on any of them, not even so much as a parking ticket. The girl, Elizabeth, her dad is actually a retired Cop out of Portland. So maybe someone he locked up a while back had a hand in this? Headquarters personnel that came out to help are pulling his personnel file and scrubbing all his old cases to see if anyone has ties to the cartels." Valdez shrugged as he finished explaining.

"Yeah maybe." Jimenti did not sound convinced as he shook his head again.

"Look Mike." Valdez said, putting his hands on Mike's shoulder reassuringly. "Whatever happened, I'm sure you will get to the bottom of it. Do we always get our guy… or do we always get our guy?" He smiled broadly as he finished talking.

"We do… we do." Mike nodded slowly as he turned again to start walking, his black leather jacket swaying slightly in the wind. "But personally, I think our "guys" are actually the good guys. As crazy as it might sound with so many dead bodies, and most with their heads cut off, I think this was a case of self-defense. Nothing else adds up. You don't save a bunch of kids, and then turn around and kill a bunch of well-equipped random mercenaries for no reason."

*　　*　　*

I woke to sharp and aching pain. For an instant I had the false hope that it had all been just a dream. That lasted until I opened my eyes, and saw that I was waist deep in snow, my body twisted sideways. The reality brought back the reason I had ran in the first place. All the shooting pain throughout my body seemed to fade, when compared to the anguish in my soul. I could hear myself crying loudly, wailing like a small child who had just lost everything. I could hear wailing… screaming like a lunatic… but it did no good. The pain was too suffocating to care about anything else. He really was gone…

I wasn't sure how long my lamentations lasted. It could have been mere minutes… or perhaps hours. The sensation of being cold came faintly as I lay there in the snow. Other sounds from the mountainside echoed through my ears. A wolf howled in the distance. The wind wailed intermittently around me as my hair blew back from my face where I lay in the snow. The sound of the wind grew fainter as the wolf's howls seemed to draw closer and more frequent. Other wolves were copying the first now, and there were at least three all howling at the same time. My sobbing stopped as I listened to the animals. Their cries seemed sorrowful as well, and I couldn't help but think that perhaps they were sympathizing with me. That perhaps they were sharing my pain. When the howling suddenly stopped, I was surprised. Perhaps a bear or larger predator was in the area and had quieted their screams.

I opened my eyes when I heard a yell in the distance.

"Liz!" The call sounded faint. Like it was coming from far above me. Something about the voice was familiar though… it sounded almost like…

"Luke!" I shouted as I turned my head to look up the mountainside. I spotted a tall figure a few hundred yards up the mountainside from me, near the place where I had fallen. *It can't be!* I shouted in my head, as I felt hope and excitement wash away the grief I had been feeling. I struggled to move, but it was painful. Every single joint and bone inside of my body was aching and stiff as I tried to sit up.

When I turned my head back to the direction my body was facing… I was met with a growl. A large gray wolf was standing only a few feet away, his teeth snarling as his eyes took me in. There was no pity in this creature's yellow eyes… but rather… hunger. It was looking at me like I was to be his next meal. My excitement was joined by sudden fear, as I realized there was growling coming from all around me. Scanning around me hurt my stiff neck, but the four other wolves around me were more alarming than the pain. There were two large gray ones to my right, and two white and gray wolves behind me to the left.

Without warning the wolf closest to me attacked, and I barely could raise my arm to protect my face when his teeth sunk into me. The creature yelped as he bit down, and I flicked my arm to get him off of me, sending him flying back through the snow. Before I could turn, I felt a pain on the back of my neck, as another creature had attached his teeth to me there. I reached back to pull him off, and another wolf attacked from my right, latching onto my forearm. I pulled my left arm free from the snow as I shifted my body sideways, only to have another creature latch onto it, snarling fiercely in my ears.

This is not happening. I thought to myself as my fear began to be replaced by adrenaline. "I'm not dinner." I grunted as I swung both of my arms together in front of me. The two wolves attached to my arms yelped as their bodies smashed together with a loud crunch. One of the animals didn't move, while the other quickly limped away.

I reached behind and grabbed the wolf on my neck by the hide at the back of his neck and attempted to tug him off and throw him. To my surprise, the wolf stayed locked on me, but snarled in pain as I ripped a large portion of his skin and fur from him. Luckily, I didn't have time to be grossed out, because the animal's sharp teeth were still tearing into me. I reached back again, this time grabbing the top and bottom of the wolf's mouth as I yanked him off of me. Bones snapped as the creature's head ripped in two along his jaw line, and the thing didn't move after I threw him to the side.

Looking around, I could see that there was still another wolf watching me, but as our eyes met, he yelped and scampered away as quickly as they had appeared. After the wolf left, I was disturbed by the animal carnage that lay around me. I painfully pulled myself out of the snow and trudged in the direction of where I had last seen Leuken, running down the mountain. The snow had started to fall again, obscuring my vision.

I had only taken a few steps when I heard him approaching. He was running through the snow towards me. I could barely make out his figure when he slowed to a walk.

"Luke!" I screamed excitedly. "I'm so glad you're a…" I cut off abruptly as the boy's face came into view.

"Liz… are you okay." It was the worst time to realize just how much Ben's voice sounded like Luke's. Their faces were so similar; I hadn't recognized Ben until he was close enough for me to see his eyes, and the blond locks of hair peeking out the front of the hooded sweatshirt he was wearing.

My excitement was crushed. I looked down, not knowing what to say… unable to find words for the hope that had just been decimated inside of me. My hands were covered in blood, though only some of it was mine. I sank back down to my knees, and it felt as though my insides had suddenly turned to ice. There were no tears this time… no crying…just ice… and hardened pain. I curled up on the ground. Unable to move… trying not to feel.

Ben was saying something, but I couldn't pay attention to him. I tried to be cold. To lock out my emotions. If I could just shut out the world around me… perhaps I could end this horrendous pain. I needed to be callous. I needed to be steel.

I could feel my body being moved and had the vague sensation of being carried through the snow. Ben spoke to me as I was carried, but I paid him no attention. My false hope being crushed had confirmed one thing: feelings were just too painful now. I was walling up all of the emotions in my mind… shutting myself off from them. As I did so the pain seemed to grow more distant. Why would I need feelings anymore anyways? Leuken Bennett was dead… and my heart dead with him.

*   *   *

The two young bloodlines moved slowly. Attempting to appear casual as they followed their target through the crowded streets of downtown Salt Lake City. Most of the people in the crowd seemed to be young couples or large families. It was just after sunset, and the steam coming from the passersby's mouths was indicative of the cool temperatures. Neither of the bloodlines were bothered by the cool air, but they wore dark hooded sweatshirts to better blend in with the crowd.

Shops lined either side of the street, and the crowd was mostly moving at a slow pace, with people carrying large shopping bags as they milled to and from between the shops. Occasionally a person or couple could be seen moving quickly through the crowd... obviously on a shopping mission with Christmas fast approaching. Only one of the bloodlines, Fernando, had ever experienced the holiday with his family. That had been decades ago when he wasn't much older than his partner was now. His younger companion had grown up on the plantation in Brazil, where celebrations of any sort were not allowed.

Their target, who appeared around the same age as his hunting partner, also moved slowly through the crowd. The young man had on a dark gray hooded sweatshirt, and for the most part he gave no indication that he knew he was being followed. His only strange behavior was the way he constantly looked side to side, apparently scanning the crowd and buildings around him. To Fernando it seemed that the man was looking for someone.

After trailing him for so long, Fernando hoped that the target would lead them to some other bloodlines. Then the next time they checked in with the plantation they would actually have some good news, instead of another update that the man was still traveling alone. Their instructions had been clear, follow the man until he either tried to run, or met up with others. If he ran, it was to be a quick and quiet execution. On the other hand, if he met others, they were to report in and wait for a full strike team to attack.

Their target disappeared as he passed behind a large food truck in a courtyard between two shops. When he didn't emerge where he should have, Fernando became alarmed, and began to walk quickly to where he had last seen the man. As he approached the food truck, he spotted the target, walking swiftly through the crowd, nearly 100 yards away. The man had used the truck as cover to create more distance between them.

"He doesn't escape alive!" Fernando said under his breath, as the two of them ran after the target. They closed the distance quickly, until the man disappeared around the corner of some shops. When they made it to the corner where the target was last seen, they were about three seconds behind. The side of the building led to a back alley, with two dumpsters on either side of the building. They both ran to the alley, not caring about the old woman with a green apron who was throwing a small trash bag into one of the dumpsters at the opening.

Around this corner Fernando spotted the man, disappearing around another corner to his right. The target was doubling back. If he made it back to the crowd, he would be hard to spot. "This way." He said to his young companion over his shoulder, as he ran as fast as he could after the target. At the next alley crossing he stopped. The man had disappeared when he glanced back over his shoulder, so he wasn't sure if he had gone left down the alley, or back towards the crowd and shopping.

"He went this way." His young companion said excitedly as he ran past Fernando and down the alley to the left. It was a long alley, with wood slotted fences on both sides and barely enough light to see the leaves and debris that lined both sides of the gutter. He and his companion's steps made crunching noises as they ran. The alley was long, and as they ran Fernando realized something. There was no way their target had made it to the end of the alley already. He had to have jumped over the fence or hidden somewhere.

"Stop!" He shouted to his young companion as he approached a couch on the side of the alley that had been tilted up on its side, but it was too late.   As his partner passed the couch, still running, a blade flashed out from behind the couch, as the target emerged. He sliced his young companions head off in a single stroke.

Fernando pulled his own curved blade out and charged to strike the man before he could move. The man was fast though, quickly flashing his blade up to block Fernando's strike, as he pivoted and shoved Fernando from the back. Between his own momentum, and the man's shove, Fernando flew about 30 feet forward, landing sideways as he struck the side of a wooden fence and hit the ground hard.

He jumped back to his feet, with his sword up in a defensive stance, but the target was only walking slowly towards him. The dark-haired man's hooded face looked angry as he scowled at Fernando.

"Why are you following me?" The man asked as he stopped, about ten feet from Fernando. His ornate blade was held down at his side. The weapon was unlike anything Fernando had ever seen, with decorative symbols on the hilt and etched into the side of the blade. "How could you betray the bloodlines, and hunt your own people?"

"You wouldn't understand." Fernando replied, taking a small step towards the man. With the blade down at his side, Fernando just needed to get a little closer before he could strike the careless man. The man obviously had little training fighting bloodlines, or else he wouldn't stand so unprepared. "I have no choice!" Fernando finished with a snarl as he flashed his sword at the man's head.

The man moved surprisingly quick, ducking under Fernando's strike as he flashed his glowing blade up in a sweeping motion.

"Aagh!" Fernando screamed as his sword hand was severed at the wrist. Before he had time to react, the man kicked him in the stomach, knocking him backwards through the wooden fence. He hit something hard and realized that he had struck a large tree. Fernando landed slumped in front of it, in a large residential back yard. The man stood there looking at him, but did not move, he must have been waiting for Fernando to attack again.

In the blink of an eye Fernando was on his feet, jumping high over the side fence as he turned and ran for his life. He knew if he could just make it back to the crowd, he might survive. He could hear the man chasing after him, so he ran as fast as he could, jumping over two more fences, and on to a commercial building. He ran across the top of the building, jumping down into an opening in the crowd. An older woman screamed in surprise as he landed right in front of her, and a few people stepped back from him, but most of the crowd was going on about their business, completely unaware that Fernando had just lost his partner, his hand... and nearly his life.

As Fernando walked quickly through the crowd, he glanced back at the building he had just jumped down from. On the roof he could see the outline of the man who had just bested him in combat. The man still held the sword in his right hand at his side. The other hand held a much smaller object that was hard to make out. After a few more steps Fernando realized what had been in the man's other hand. He looked back again, but the man had vanished from the rooftop.

Fernando looked down at the nub he had tucked in his right pocket, painfully aware of what the man had taken from him. How quickly his world had been turned upside down. Mere minutes before he had been hunting that man... and now... he was trying desperately to escape with his own life. While he did not look forward to what might happen to him when he reported back to the compound in Brazil, at the moment he was more concerned about surviving through the night.

CHAPTER II

"Oh no!" Sara shouted with obvious concern as Ben approached the front of the mansion from the forest. "Is she…?" She didn't finish the sentence, but glanced over her shoulder at Dan, who was walking up quickly from the front door.

"No but she's lost… a lot of blood… we might need to… get her to a hospital." Ben had been running for the last few minutes and was breathing heavily as he spoke.

"What happened to her?" Liz's father asked, a mix of anger and concern showing in his voice. "Who did this?" He reached down and put a hand on the side of Liz's face.

"Let me see her." Jazmine said as she came running up behind Dan. She put two fingers from her right hand on Liz's neck, obviously feeling for a pulse, and she used her other hand to quickly move Liz's dark hair out of the way, as she searched for additional wounds.

As Ben watched Jazmine examine Liz, he realized that all of the blood on her had dried, and she didn't appear to be bleeding anymore. She had several large puncture wounds on both sides of her neck, which was where most of the blood on her face and clothes had come from, and one of her legs had a large gash from where he assumed she had landed on the rocks after falling from the mountain. Her jacket was also torn and bloody on both sleeves, additional wounds that must have been inflicted by those wolves when they had attacked her. Ben only had one concern, and that was Liz's survival. He couldn't let anything happen to her. Now that Luke was gone, he would have to look after Liz. The mere thought of Luke brought back the sharp pain that he had felt since the moment he heard the news of his brother's death.

"Tobias, go grab me some towels or rags from inside the kitchen. They are in the pantry near the rear door." Jazmine said quickly to the man. He started to move. "Hurry please!" She shouted urgently, and he sped off into the house in a blur.

"Let's get her inside." Jazmine said as she pulled her hand away from Liz's neck. "I can barely feel her pulse."

"She's lost too much blood, grab the hummer keys, I'm taking her to the nearest hospital." Ben interjected, not bothering to hide the concern from his voice. He knew she might need advanced medical care to survive, and with Luke gone, he didn't care if others knew of his feelings for her.

In a blur, Tobias re-emerged from the house, holding several folded house towels in his hand. "I'm guessing your healing doesn't work on us?" He asked as he held out the towels to Jazmine.

"No... I've tried before, and I just tried again." Jazmine replied as she began slowly dabbing away the blood from Liz's face and neck with a wet towel. It appeared that most of the wounds were on the sides of Liz's neck. There were a couple puncture wounds on the left side of her jawbone, in addition to at least half a dozen on her neck. "When I try to heal... it feels like I hit a brick wall. We can't risk taking her to a hospital though Ben. You know that will only draw attention."

Ben clenched his jaw as if he might protest but shook his head and continued walking into the house, as Jazmine worked on cleaning up the wounds. A couple of the deeper ones on Liz's neck appeared to still be bleeding and oozing slowly as Jazmine wiped, but it was less compared to how bad it had been bleeding when Ben had first found her. They made it into the formal living room, and Ben set Liz down on one of the large couches.

"Her pulse is still faint." Jazmine said concerned, as she felt at Liz's neck again. "We might need to take her somewhere to get help."

"No offense intended. But exactly where would you take her?" Tobias interjected. He reached down gently towards Liz's neck.

The thought of that monster touching Liz's wounds made Ben cringe, and he moved to pull the man back. Before he had a chance though, Daniel grabbed Tobias from behind by the throat, forcibly pulling him back from Liz.

"What are you doing!?" Daniel snapped at Tobias.

"Whoa… relax." Tobias said calmly as he put his hands up in the air, defensively. He pointed at the elaborate bracelet attached to his wrist. "I was just going to check her pulse. Besides, this prevents me from harming her… even if I wanted to."

"Allow me." Isaac said as he appeared from the hallway leading into the kitchen. In a flash he moved to Liz's side and placed two fingers on Liz's neck. Ben was growing impatient. He knew he had to get Liz to a hospital. There was no way he could just stand by and watch her die.

"Isaac, she needs a doctor!" Ben blurted. Isaac looked calmly up at him but said nothing at first. *Why isn't he saying anything?!* Ben thought to himself exasperatedly.

"She is fine." Isaac finally stated, after what seemed like an eternity for Ben. "Her pulse feels normal."

"How can you say that?" Jazmine asked, pulling her dark hair away from her face. She leaned in again to feel Liz's neck. "She barely has a pulse."

"For us that is normal." Tobias stated as he stepped back from Dan. Dan had released him, but still glared mistrusting at the tainted one. "Our normal pulse is about one beat every 6 to 10 seconds."

"I also noticed," Isaac began, "after Liz was shot back at the Harrisburg house that she heals remarkably fast."

"What do you mean after she was shot? She was shot?" Dan's ire turned from Tobias to Isaac, as his eyes shifted. He took a couple of steps towards Isaac; his voice growing louder as he spoke. "When? How did that happen!?"

"It happened after Luke was killed." Isaac replied, his voice was calm, but with a noticeable edge to it. Ben recognized that tone. It was the tone Isaac used when he was trying to be patient but was ready to snap. Ben had seen it a few times in the past, usually during intense training sessions. "Liz began digging through the burning debris, trying to find Luke."

"I was fighting off another one of the bloodline hunters who had arrived, when another one showed up and began shooting Liz with a high-powered rifle. I was able to kill that one too, but not until after he had shot Liz a couple of times. The first round struck as the sun was setting, going through her upper chest. The next couple of rounds were seconds later, and barely broke the skin." Isaac's eyes began to water as he spoke. "After Liz went down… I had to make a decision. I could either search for Luke and hope that he had somehow survived, all the while hoping no more of those bloodline hunters showed up. Or… I could try and save Liz and escape. Knowing he was probably already dead… I abandoned Leuken… so that I could save your daughter. That is how she was shot." Isaac finished with a teary glare back at Dan.

Liz's father's expression softened, as he clearly hadn't expected that response. "I am sorry Isaac... I didn't realize what had happened..." Dan looked down, appearing embarrassed. "You saved my daughter... so thank you. I'm sorry for blaming you. I was out of line."

"No apology needed. Luke chose your daughter, and because of us you were all dragged into this mess." Isaac replied, looking slowly around the room as he spoke. "As far as I'm concerned you are all family now... that's what Luke wanted all along... it just took me a little longer to learn to trust you... that's all. It is I who am sorry. Your lives will never be the same because of us."

Isaac paused for a long time before continuing, clearing his throat loudly. "Anyhow... as I was saying. I noticed when we were driving that Liz was healing exceptionally fast. Within a few hours her wounds looked like they had been healing for days. It was a good thing too because we were followed from Harrisburg."

"What do you mean?" Ben interjected as Isaac opened his mouth to continue. "You were followed, and you still came here?" Ben and Jazmine both looked around the room at the windows and doors, scanning for any threats.

"I wasn't finished." Isaac continued. "I was saying it's a good thing Liz healed quickly, because one of the bloodlines ended up catching up to us, and I was too exhausted to fight. Her ability to heal herself proved quite useful since she was capable of helping me fight if needed. However... this brings me to my next subject, something we all need to discuss."

"What is it?" Jazmine asked, her eyes were still fixed on Liz and filled with concern.

"The bloodline hunter who followed us, he didn't attack." Isaac paused again, clearly contemplating what to say next. "Instead, he apologized for attacking us, and explained that he is being controlled by two other Verdorben. He and dozens of others are being held captive at a compound in southern Brazil. The tainted ones use their wives and children as ransom to get them to hunt and kill other bloodlines."

"That's terrible!" Sara interjected, her expression shocked.

"The man's name was Royce. He said that his wife and small daughter are still being held captive by these Verdorben. At first, I thought he might be trying to lure us into some kind of trap, but his last few words before he died seemed like a pretty sincere plea for help. He gave me some co-ordinates for where the compound is that the other bloodlines are being held in just before they killed him."

"Just before who killed him?" Dan asked.

"I don't know for sure, but I would guess it was the same Verdorben that were controlling him. We were in the middle of talking when his head suddenly and most unexpectedly exploded."

"Another sniper?" Tobias asked.

"No." Isaac continued. "I think whoever was controlling him had implanted something into his head. It exploded while we were talking, and afterwards I found a few small metallic fragments in what was left of his cranium." There was a long silence as Isaac paused and looked around.

"Like I said, at first I didn't believe him. After his head exploded though... I think he was telling the truth." Isaac shook his head slowly in thought before continuing. "I know this might sound a little bit crazy... but I think we should call for a Council of the Bloodlines."

"A council?" Jazmine seemed surprised. "But you said that all the other clans ever do anymore is bicker. And besides, the next one isn't scheduled for another 2 years."

Ben opened his mouth to speak but didn't know what to say. Isaac had taught all of them about the clans, and the council that was held every 20 years… but he had never heard of calling one early. *How would that even work?* He thought to himself.

"I know it is not supposed to be for another two years, but there is also a provision for any clan leader to call for an early or emergency meeting, if there is ever a threat of extinction." Isaac's tone grew graver as he spoke. "Most of the clans have at least one terralium weapon and are capable of spotting and running from Verdorben. These bloodline hunting parties though. I'd never even heard of them. It places all of the bloodlines in immediate danger, and the council must be convened so that we can warn all of the others."

"I don't know…" Jazmine was biting her lower lip as she paused. Something she only did when she was extremely nervous. "How do we know that they haven't captured any bloodlines who know about the council? We could end up leading everyone to a trap."

"That's true." Isaac retorted. "But if they do already know about the council, then that means in two years everyone will be going like lambs to the slaughter. If I give the signal now, with a meeting scheduled for three days, it gives these bloodline hunters less time to prepare, and it gives them less time to capture someone who might know about the meeting. Besides… considering the way they immediately tried to kill us… without even trying to ask any questions, it makes me think they don't take a lot of prisoners."

"I don't know Isaac…" Jazmine said. "What if that man was acting? It could be a trap. For all we know those coordinates could be the Verdorben's headquarters. If they also have bloodlines with them... we would be slaughtered."

"I know that." Isaac replied. "But I don't think that man was acting. I am nearly certain of it. And besides, just because we call a meeting doesn't mean we have to try and rescue those bloodlines. We will leave it up to the council. If enough clans are willing to help, we can try a rescue. If none of them do, then at least we will have warned the other clans. I don't want anyone else's blood on my hands."

"This absolutely sounds like a trap." Tobias said, sounding afraid. "You would be risking all of our lives if you go after the others."

"Okay, then I'm going with you." Jazmine still sounded unsure if she liked the plan, ignoring Tobias' objections. "If there are bloodline hunting parties all over, you need someone to watch your back. Though we cannot leave until Liz is more stable. I want to make sure she is good to go before we leave."

"No. I need you here to help look after everyone. It will be easier if I travel alone. A plain old man is less conspicuous than a stunning young lady." Isaac grinned slightly. "After lighting the signal, I will need to be cautious getting to the meeting place, so I'll need you to lead our group south and meet me just outside Las Vegas. If any of the other clans sense these three," Isaac gestured at Dan and Tobias "they might panic, and it could jeopardize the entire meeting."

Ben was confused as he listened to them speak. Why risk everything to warn some people he had never even met? All he cared about was Liz. As he looked back down at her, he was relieved to see her chest rise slightly as she took a long breath. Ben smiled. He was sad that Luke was gone... but excited about the opportunity to have more time with Liz.

*　　*　　*

When my eyes first opened, I felt like I was dreaming. Benjamin Bennett was sitting next to my bed, his light blue eyes anxiously studying me. His blond hair seemed even more disheveled than normal, and he looked exhausted. Ben smiled uncertainly at me as I lifted my head to look around the room. It was a large room, with a fancy dark cherry wood bed frame forming a canopy above me. Another dark brown Victorian looking couch sat against the wall near the foot of my bed, with two more chairs sitting next to the one Ben occupied at my side. One was empty, and the other one was occupied by a chubby-cheeked familiar face.

"Izzy you're awake!" Alex smiled excitedly at me as he jumped up from his chair and threw his arms around me from the side of the bed. "I'm so cusited you are okay."

His smile always brought warmth with it, and I smiled slightly as I put an arm around him. "Hey little buddy." I replied. "Of course, I'm okay. Why wouldn't I be silly?"

"Daddy told me about the wolf biting your neck." Alex explained. "That's why you have all that white stuff on you neck silly."

"Oh… I had forgotten about the wolves." I said as I brought one hand up to my neck. I could feel what felt like gauze wrapped around my neck almost to my chin. I glanced at Ben, and the sight of his face brought me back to reality. He looked so much like…his brother. The thought of Leuken instantly brought back the pain and hopelessness I had somehow managed to forget while sleeping. I sat up in bed, suddenly wishing that I was alone.

"What's wrong Izzy?" Alex asked as I stepped out of the bed. I realized the sweatshirt and pants I was wearing were different then what I had been wearing when the wolves attacked me. Jazmine or Sara must have changed my clothes while I was unconscious. Normally I would have been embarrassed at the thought... but I wasn't in the mood to care. It wasn't the first time I had been dressed by the Bennett family after being attacked.

"Oh, nothing Alex, I just need some fresh air." I said over my shoulder as I walked from the room.

"Liz, I don't think you should move too much." Ben began to protest as I walked away.

"I'm fine Ben." I replied quickly, not letting him finish whatever else he had meant to say to stop me from leaving. Pulling open the heavy door, I found myself in a wide hallway with marble floors. To my right were two more doors and a large window facing out into snow. I decided to turn left. After passing another set of doors across from each other, the hallway turned and opened up into a large room, which connected to the main ballroom of the mansion. I heard Alex and Ben's footsteps behind me, but I kept walking till I made it to the front door.

As I opened the door to step outside, I heard Ben say softly from the other room: "I think Liz just needs to be alone..." His sentence was cut off as I closed the front door behind me. The air felt cold as I breathed it in, but it didn't chill me like it would have before I had changed. Even the cold stone floor barely registered on my feet, though I was sure it was probably freezing. There was a flurry of thoughts running through my mind, much like the snow that swirled in front of the mansion. As I neared the edge of the covered driveway, I decided to sit down on a small stone bench. Both sides of the long bench curved up to form stone carved lion heads, with yellow jewels affixed to where the eyes should have been.

I pulled my legs up to my stomach, wrapping my arms around them as I looked out into the snow. I wasn't sure how long I had been sleeping, but most of the pain in my leg and neck were gone, so my guess was it had been a while. There was enough light to know it was daytime, but the snow and clouds were too thick to tell what time of day it was. I thought about going back inside to apologize to Alex for walking out so abruptly… but Ben was right. I did need to be alone. A part of me was disappointed… disappointed that the wolves hadn't finished me off. It was the second time recently that I had been disappointed to be alive after thinking I was a goner. With Leuken gone… being alive just felt… empty. Everything felt wrong… and I now knew this wasn't just a bad dream. I wasn't going to wake up from this…

I watched the snow fall for a long time. Sara came out once with some food and shoes. I put on the shoes, but I told her I wasn't hungry. A few minutes later Alex came and gave me a long hug, but then he went back inside without saying a word. I tried not to think. Thinking inevitably brought me back to Leuken each time, which made me feel saddened. I didn't want to feel anything... So, I just sat there, with my legs tucked in front of me on the bench, looking out into the snow.

Every so often the flakes would speed up or become thicker. After a while they would slow again. It wasn't until I noticed the light beginning to fade, that I realized I must have been sitting there for a long time. I could smell something pleasant cooking from inside the mansion, and the sound of my stomach growling told me my body wanted food… but I just couldn't see myself eating. Every once in a while, I had the false hope that Luke would miraculously appear walking through the snow, but I knew that was nothing more than wishful thinking.

Ben appeared with a plate of steaming food. His hair looked like he had actually run a comb through it now, and he came and sat next to me, holding the plate out in front of me.

"Hey Liz." He said casually. "I know you want to be alone…
but I just wanted to bring you something to eat in case you were
hungry."

I was hungry, but just didn't feel like eating. "Thanks Ben,
but I'm not hungry." I lied, glancing down at the plate. The plate had
grilled chicken, mashed potatoes with gravy, and steamed carrots on
it, and looked almost as good as it smelled.

"Okay." Ben replied. "Well why don't I just leave this here
in case you change your mind." Ben stood and set the plate down on
the bench next to me. Then reached out and gently touched the side
of my face in a comforting fashion. The warmth of his touch was
soothing. "And just so you know Liz… if you need anything… I'm
here for you."

"Thanks Ben." I managed to say after he turned and was
already walking away.

"You're welcome, Liz." He stopped and turned back as he
spoke. A moment later he walked back into the house, leaving me
with the cool wind and snow.

It didn't take long of me smelling the delicious food, before I
finally picked the plate up. It tasted even better than it had smelled,
and I scarfed the whole thing down in a couple of minutes. My
appetite had been the biggest since transforming. It made me wonder
if my body healing so much had something to do with it. After a
couple more hours of staring off into the snow, I realized that I was
being foolish. With my enhanced vision, I could see some of the
individual flakes drifting slowly towards the ground, but I was not
sitting there because I liked watching the snow. I realized that there
was still a part of me that was waiting for something. There was a
longing that somehow… magically… Leuken Bennett would
suddenly emerge from the swirling snow, with his heart-warming
smile and deep blue eyes, and rescue me from the cold depression I

was sinking further into by the minute. It was utter nonsense… and I knew it.

Ben came back outside. He said nothing as he quietly grabbed the empty plate I had left sitting on the bench.

"Thank you." I managed to mumble as he turned to go.

"No problem." Ben replied as he went back inside the house. Less than a minute later, he re-emerged. He came and sat next to me on the bench.

When I glanced over at him, he seemed to possess none of his usual mirth. His expression was concerned. Something was obviously troubling him.

He said nothing as we sat there, so neither did I. The snow continued to swirl in front of us, but I was too wrapped up in my own despair to worry about Ben's feelings. Sometimes silence was preferable to small talk… and this was one of those times.

After several minutes I glanced back over at Ben. His expression had changed to one of nervousness. He was visibly worried about something. "What is it, Ben?" I asked casually.

"There's something I need to ask you." Ben blurted as he suddenly rose to his feet and turned to face me. "Can you stand?" He asked as he held both hands out, offering to help me up. His nervous expression had been replaced with one of resolve. Like he had decided something and was ready to act on it.

"What is it…?" I began to ask as I slowly stood. Something my eyes caught through the snow made me stop mid-sentence. On the other side of the rounded driveway, just inside the clearing from the trees, I could see a man, who appeared to be walking towards us. I didn't need to see the face to recognize the figure that was approaching. The upright gait with purposeful stride was something I had come to adore over the past few months, and the dark hair only confirmed my suspicions. *Leuken!* My mind shouted as the figure drew nearer, and my heart leapt.

Before I had a chance to move, Ben suddenly grabbed my face with both of his hands, pulling it towards himself as he bent down and awkwardly kissed me. His grip was firm, and obnoxiously forceful. I tried to turn my head and quickly pull away, as I could see out of the corner of my eye that Luke had stopped approaching. Ben's grip was stronger than expected though, and I had to step back and forcibly push him to escape his grasp on the side of my head. *I don't have time for this. Luke's alive!* I thought to myself as Ben staggered backwards from my shove. "What are you doing?" I asked annoyed as I pushed him away.

I turned towards Luke and my heart sank. The place at the edge of the driveway where his dark figure had been standing less than a second ago was suddenly empty. Only swirling snow was there now, which fell thicker as I scanned in both directions for Luke.

"I'm sorry Liz! I don't know what got into me." Ben said exasperatedly as he turned to walk quickly back towards the house. "Stupid! You're so stupid man!" I could hear him mutter to himself under his breath as he stalked away. I didn't say a word as he slammed the door on the way into the house.

My annoyance with Ben barely registered as I thought about the figure I had been sure was Leuken Bennett. I slowly walked towards where I had seen him, but when I arrived where I thought he had been standing, there was no sign of him. Desperation and loss again overpowered me as I re-realized the obvious. Leuken Bennett was dead… and I was starting to go crazy from it.

"Great." I mumbled to myself "Now I'm seeing things." I could feel tears sliding down my face as I sank to my knees in the snow. I was kneeling in the same place I had thought I saw Luke. Only I knew he wasn't there. He had never been there. I fell forward into the snow and sobbed. I barely noticed the feel of the frozen snow on my face as I laid there crying. The ice in my heart had shattered, even if only briefly, and the floodgates opened as I cried. It was a long time before I finally got my sobbing under control. *Crying doesn't help anything.* I thought to myself, embarrassed by my pathetic sobbing. I needed to close off my emotions again. I needed to be cold, like the snow around me. The frostbite on my heart returned as I gathered my emotions, and then began to spread, consuming me… again.

*   *   *

Grady Johnson slammed on the brakes as he suddenly saw a man standing in front of him in the middle of the highway. He knew his old Ford pickup truck wouldn't stop in time, but he also didn't have time to swerve. Just before his truck struck the tall figure in the road, the man suddenly leapt out of sight into the snow. As his tires came screeching to a halt, some 80 feet from where he had nearly struck the man, the hair on Grady's arms stood up. He had never seen anyone move so fast… no man or beast could move like that. He quickly backed his truck to the side of the road and put on his emergency flashers. There was no sign of the man in his rear-view mirror as he stopped a little short of where he had last seen him. He got out of his truck and slowly walked towards where the man had been standing, while peering cautiously from right to left all around him.

"You're just seeing things old man." Grady mumbled under his breath as he walked. His eightieth birthday was still a few weeks away, but he already felt older than that. There was no sign of the man anywhere as he peered around, so he resolved he must have imagined him. Perhaps he had fallen asleep while driving and had a bad dream, Grady mused. Or maybe… Grady's mind suddenly stopped contemplating as he reached the place he had imagined the man standing and saw two large footprints in the snow in the middle of the road.

As he knelt down to feel the prints, his nerves began to get the better of him. "No dreams leave footprints." He said aloud as he stood and peered in the direction the man had darted off in. As he stepped out of the highway, for he wasn't about to become roadkill himself, he heard a loud scream. Even with the wind and snow swirling loudly around him, the sound was unmistakable. It was the sound of an anguished soul, the kind of guttural scream you rarely hear from anyone. It came from the top of the mountain hill, and sounded far away, but there was no way that was possible. It had been less than a minute since he nearly struck the man, and no one could run that fast. The eerie feeling that suddenly came over him creeped him out to the core.

Grady felt a rush of adrenaline as mild panic set in, and he moved quickly as he ran back to his truck. His legs didn't move as fast as he wanted them to, but he wasted no time putting his truck in drive as he hurriedly slammed the door shut. His tires squealed as he punched on the gas and pulled back onto the highway. The dark outlines of the Selkirk mountains to the north were not visible through the snowfall, but he had driven this road enough across northern Idaho that he didn't need landmarks to know his way. While he had no idea what in tarnation was going on, he also wasn't about to stick around and find out. Nightmare or not, he was ready to put this evening behind him.

*   *   *

I wasn't sure how long I laid there in the snow, but it was still dark when I finally decided to sit up. As I realized just how foolish my vain hopes were, I noticed my emotion changing. The cold sorrow that had been consuming me seemed to melt away as I felt my temper flaring. Sure, I still felt mostly emptiness, but my hopelessness was slowly turning into bitterness and anger. The memory of that bloodline savage chasing Luke into the house… and my pathetic inability to save him, was painfully burned into my mind; so was the smell of burnt flesh and smoke as my futile attempts to save him from the rubble had failed. At first, I was angry at the one-armed animal that had chased him into the house and ended his life… but then I remembered the other armless bloodline. The one who's fear and hopeless plea was made all the more compelling by his sudden death. I did not doubt that all of these bloodline hunters were being controlled, and while I had no idea about what these other Verdorben looked like, or exactly how they controlled the other bloodlines… I hated them.

In fact, the rage I felt intensified so rapidly, that suddenly I realized I had stood up, and my fists were clenched furiously down at my sides. The icy sorrow in my veins had melted, replaced by a rage and determination than penetrated every fiber of my being. I couldn't bring Leuken back… but that didn't mean his death would go unavenged. The thought suddenly came to me: *Whoever these Verdorben are… I will make them pay.*

CHAPTER III

"I said I want you to teach me to fight." I said stubbornly as I stared Ben in the eyes, with my hands on my hips. His baby blue eyes studied me intently before he answered.

"I don't know… I'm not sure if Isaac wants me teaching you…" Ben trailed off as he looked around the room for support. Sara and my father were sitting on a couch across from us in the hall, speaking a little too friendly with one another in low voices. Tobias stood at the far end of the hall, staring out the window into the snow. His old-fashioned dark tunic with the well-trimmed beard made him look like he belonged in the 16th century. Ben had tried to apologize when I first came inside earlier, but I had quickly brushed his awkward apology aside. I know it was callous, but I didn't have time for his feelings right now.

"Well, what do you think Daniel? You are her father." Sara said as she looked back and forth between my father and me. It was strange to hear someone call him Daniel. No one had called my father by his full name since my mother… to everyone else we knew, he was just Dan.

"Well, it certainly can't hurt anything." My father replied thoughtfully. "Do you still remember any of your lessons from all those years Liz?"

"Of course, Dad. But I need to learn how to fight with weapons. All the training you put me through was either empty hand tactics, Jiu Jitsu, or firearms training. I need to learn how to use the only weapons that can kill us. Because then I can kill the one's responsible for Leuken's death."

* * *

Isaac pulled the small black briefcase from his bag and placed it directly in front of the doors to the main entrance. In it was two million dollars, which should be more than enough to pay for having the torch refinished and painted. He wasn't even sure how much damage the compound he was using to light the blue flames would cause, but his honor wouldn't allow him to not compensate the owners for the damage. He pulled out the note he had written and affixed it to the top of the briefcase with a small piece of tape. It read:

THIS SHOULD COVER THE DAMAGES. I APOLOGIZE FOR THE INCONVENIENCE.

He was sweating profusely from climbing the stairs and ladder so many times to place the compound where he needed, and a few drops of sweat fell from his chin to the paper, creating small wet circles. The time was nearing ten o'clock, and he wanted to make sure the spectacle was ready for the late-night news, so he quickly went out the back window to the visitor's center that he had entered through, making sure to stay far away from the roving security guards that were walking on either side of the building.

He quickly made his way back to where his gear was hidden by the rocks on the shore directly behind the statue. When he got to where the boxes of fireworks were set up, he quickly re-examined them to make sure they were angled right to go off directly over the torch to the Statue of Liberty. As he glanced up at the towering figure, Isaac said a silent prayer that this whole thing would work. He pressed a button on the small control tablet that would begin the fireworks ignition countdown, and then spoke into the com on his wrist.

"Okay Jazmine. The fuse is set, go ahead and start your blaze. We'll rendezvous back at the harbor in three minutes."

"Copy Isaac, I'm starting it now. Don't get eaten by sharks." Jazmine teased through the mic.

Isaac grinned as he put his gear back into the watertight bag, before donning his oxygen tank. Jazmine frequently made Isaac smile. She reminded him of the daughter he wished he could have gotten to know. His own daughter had died before her first birthday. She was slaughtered by Verdorben on the same night they had killed his wife... a day that still brought chills to Isaac's spine when he thought about it. Isaac quickly slipped the large black flippers over the thin shoes on his feet, snapping them into place. The last thing he wanted to think about was that dreadful day.

He jumped into the ocean water and began swimming just under the surface as quickly as he could. The water was dark, and he swam fast, poking up to the top of the water every thirty seconds or so to make sure he was still going the right way. After a couple of minutes, he came up to the surface to finish swimming, figuring he had put enough distance between himself and the statue. He could see the lights of the harbor about half a mile away as he swam. If his plan worked, it would at least make national news, if not international. Hopefully from there the word would spread between the clans that actually still communicated.

Based on what that bloodline had said before he died, they would probably need at least a dozen more bloodline members to try and free the others, preferably closer to thirty. If he could get enough of the other clans to listen… it just might have a chance of working. If not… well then, they would just have to decide if it was worth risking the operation by themselves. Either way… he now had about three days to come up with a plan for how to address the other clans at the meeting. With all the cantankerous bickering and paranoia that usually happened when the clans got together… Isaac knew he had his work cut out for him.

*   *   *

Metemba was seated at the kitchen counter, carving the steak he was preparing to eat, when he heard commotion in the other room. His uncle, sister and six brothers were all sitting in the living room, watching something on the television.

"Metemba come quick. You're not going to believe this." His younger sister Shawnee said excitedly as she appeared in the archway that separated the two rooms.

"What is it?" Metemba said patiently. He was famished, and his nineteen-year-old sister was notorious for getting excited about inconsequential things. Her dark hair was braided to form to her head, coming down in a dark braid to the right side of her neck. She was much paler than Metemba, with a beautiful light brown complexion, as her father was from the Netherlands. Metemba's father had been killed a few years before Shawnee was born.

"You have to see it for yourself." She said as she turned and hurried back to the living room.

Metemba set down his steak knife and fork, rising slowly from his chair. Shawnee seemed even more excited than usual, so he figured he may as well see what the commotion was about.

As he walked into the living room, Shawnee was standing behind the sectional next to his uncle, with both their eyes focused on the television. His brothers, who were all seated throughout the room, were equally fixated on the device. It didn't take long for him to see why. As he looked at the TV, there was a live reporter on the New York City Coastline, with a split scene to an aerial view of the statue of liberty. The statue was brighter than normal, as a bright flame burned from the top of the decorative torch in the statue's hand, a sharp contrast to the night sky. Behind the female reporter, who was speaking on the news, was an empty container ship in the ocean between her and the statue. A large framework was burning, in the shape of a circle with patterned edges on top of the vessel. The outline looked vaguely familiar, but Metemba was not concerned about the outline, so much as the burning statue.

"Everyone pack your bags." He said to the room without taking his eyes off the television. "Tomorrow, we leave for America." He did not know why someone had called for an emergency meeting of the bloodline clans… but he would learn soon enough.

*   *   *

Kezia Shaw glanced up from the book she was reading as her father Sampson swept into the living room in full stride. She pulled back a few strands of her long blonde hair that had fallen in front of her eyes. Her father's dark hair was beginning to gray at the temples, and his dark brown eyes appeared full of concern.

"I think it merits our attendance is all I am saying." Her Uncle Ingram was pacing just behind Sampson, and though Ingram was about a century younger than his brother, you wouldn't know it. He stood nearly a head taller. "When is the last time one of the clans called for an emergency meeting?"

"The last time..." Sampson stopped and turned to face Ingram as he answered, stroking his long mustache as he contemplated.

"It was before the great battle." Ingram continued before Sampson could finish answering.

"You mean the great slaughter." Sampson quipped as he turned to stride off again.

Kezia's father may have been the smaller of the two in terms of physical stature, but she also knew him to be far sharper and more intelligent than her headstrong uncle. Every decision her father made was calculated, with little emotion involved. As a member of the bloodline, you didn't live past two centuries without being somewhat paranoid.

"Please brother just hear me out." Ingram placed his hand on Sampson's shoulder as Sampson opened the front door of the house to leave. Sampson stopped and turned again to look at Ingram.

"Go ahead. Be out with it." Her father said. "But this had better be compelling."

"I think if we approach this cautiously and scout things out ahead of time, there is little risk by attending. The last time a meeting of this sort was held over a hundred from the bloodline attended. If it is a trap, we leave before the meeting even starts. You have the gift of foretelling, and the light is strong in you. If there is danger we will know. But... if we do not go." Kezia's uncle looked down into Sampson's eyes as he finished. "We will never know what this was all about. That ignorance could prove more dangerous than the risk of attendance."

"Very well." Kezia's father replied after a long silence, again stroking his mustache. "But we will scout it out first. If there are any warnings from the light or signs of trouble, we leave immediately. We must think of our family as well."

Her father's eyes turned to Kezia as he finished speaking, and the worry in them was unmasked. Something had her father more concerned than she had ever seen him before, and they had been on the run for as long as she could remember.

Seeing her father's concern made Kezia feel anxious. She was not brave like her older sister Charity. Nor was she strong or fast like her sister. Though her sixteenth birthday had just passed, she still had not snapped, and was beginning to worry she would never get the abilities her father and sister had developed. Unlike Charity, whose mother had died years before Kezia was even born, her mother was just an ordinary person, and did not come from the bloodline. This meant it was quite possible she would never manifest the powers that sometimes came with being part of the bloodline.

*   *   *

Jacob was sipping his morning tea on the back patio, watching the sunrise on the Pacific Ocean to the east. His family had owned this estate for over a century, but this was only his third time staying on the Eastern edge of Australia. He had learned it was best to move every decade or so, and not to return to the same place twice until a half century had gone by. His nearest neighbor was a quarter mile away, and his owning all the land between the two properties guaranteed it would stay that way.

As a cool breeze swept in from the eastern shore, Jacob heard the sound of an automobile approaching from the distance to the west. His property was at the end of the road that came off the main highway, which meant that his home was their intended destination, unless it was another tourist who had gotten lost and meandered out to him. He walked to the back corner of his house, instinctively touching the terralium ring on his left hand. The cool metal reassured him that the visitor was not a true threat.

He recognized Jarvis's old Mercedes as it drew near to the side of his home, coming to a stop about 50 paces away. Jarvis jumped out of his vehicle and approached at a quick pace, holding his spectacles with two fingers as he ran.

"Did you see it?" Jarvis asked excitedly in his heavily accented English voice as he approached Jacob. The man's head was completely bald on top, with the hair wrapping around the sides of his scalp kept neatly short. The man's scholarly unkept appearance in no way gave away his hidden talents. He wasn't great at hand-to-hand combat, but his skill with a blade nearly rivaled Jacob's. Jacob didn't understand why the man insisted on wearing the glasses all the time, as a member of the bloodline, he certainly didn't need them.

"See what my old friend?" Jacob asked as the man neared. Jarvis was holding a folded-up newspaper in one hand.

"See this." Jarvis said in a matter-of-fact tone as he held the newspaper out to Jacob. "There at the bottom."

Jacob quickly read the article about a strange act of vandalism at the Statue of Liberty in New York City. There was also mention of fireworks and a burning ship, but it was the torch on the statue burning and the picture that got Jacob's attention. He could see the lit flame of the statue, and the bloodline symbol burning on the ship.

"Someone has called for an emergency meeting of the clans…" Jacob said under his breath as Jarvis examined him slowly. "Do you recall the designated meeting location Jarvis?"

"Since the torch was lit in America, I believe the meeting location would be the small town of Overton in the state of Nevada." Jarvis mused thoughtfully. "Assuming it is still called that."

"You are correct." Jacob paused, running his fingers slowly through the gray hair on the top of his head. "The question is do we bring the whole clan, or go it without them? If the rumors of the bloodline clan hunting other clans are true, we could be walking into a trap."

"Considering what happened last time one of these meetings was scheduled, and the fact that we only have two terralium swords and the two daggers." Jarvis replied. "I think it best if just we seasoned grandfathers go. My son can look after the clan with your two grandchildren should anything go wrong while we are away."

"Seasoned, eh?" Jacob grinned. "Leave it to a bloomin Englishman to make being old sound like a compliment. My only hope is that the poor fool who called for this meeting doesn't want what I wanted when I called the last one." The very thought of the carnage that had unfolded after the last meeting made Jacob feel a sudden chill come over him. He could only hope that nothing bad would come of this meeting, but he wasn't optimistic.

*   *   *

"That was good." Ben said, breathing heavily as I rested the tip of my short practice stick against his throat. My knee was on his chest, with my other leg on his upper thighs in a side mount. His practice blade was in the hand I had pinned to the ground with my free hand. We had been training for a couple of hours now, and I could tell that Ben was getting tired. The first hour he had landed at least five fatal strikes for every one that I got in, but this was the third time I had bested him in the last ten minutes. While I wanted to think I was quickly improving, I think his fatigue had more to do with it than anything.

"You know." Ben was catching his breath as I let go of him and stood up. "It's almost scary how fast you learn, and how fast you move."

"I think you are just tired." I said, stretching my neck from side to side. It was an old habit from the years of self-defense and mixed martial arts training my father had put me through, but the truth was I didn't need to stretch anymore. My joints hadn't ached since the transformation, and there was never a need to stretch before physical activity. "Do you need to take a break, or can we keep going?"

"Uh…" Ben hesitated as he stood up. "Sure… we can keep going, just let me get a drink of water." Ben walked to the back patio of the mansion at the edge of the snow-covered field. My father and Sara were sitting on the steps to the patio, a few feet from where Ben retrieved his water bottle and began drinking.

The sky was beginning to get darker, and I realized some clouds were moving in from the west, covering the sun that was close to dipping below the trees anyway. I was standing in a patch of grass near the middle of the white field. Several other patches of grass were visible around where I stood, all from parts of our practice where either Ben or I had ended up on the ground and pushed the snow aside.

"I think you should rest Ben." I heard Sara say softly to Ben as he took a swig of water. "You can't keep going like this, and it's almost time for dinner."

"Hey Liz." My dad said loudly as he stood and began to walk towards me. "Why don't you guys be done for today. Ben looks exhausted, and I think your training will be more effective if he is fresh. Try to remember he's not Verdorben like we are. I have to say, I'm glad I had you tutored and in all those MMA classes for those years. It seems like what you learned has helped prepare you for fighting with weapons also."

I was annoyed at Ben needing to take a break. I needed to train harder if I wanted to be able to kill the Verdorben responsible for Luke's death, and with Isaac and Jasmine still coming back from New York, Ben was the only one skilled enough with weapons to train me.

"Okay dad." I said softly under my breath, trying not to let my frustration show in my voice. I walked to where Ben was standing. "Hey Ben, why don't we take a break till after dinner."

"Sounds good." Ben replied. The relief was clear on his face as I approached. "I'm so tired I can barely move, let alone fight."

"Liz, I think he'll need more time to rest than that." My father said as he walked up behind me. "You need to remember that they aren't immune to getting tired like we are sweetheart. Why don't you guys pick back up tomorrow morning."

Sweetheart? I thought to myself. My father hadn't called me sweetheart since before my mom had died. I didn't know what that was all about unless he was just trying to annoy me.

"Jazmine just texted and said they'll be back in less than an hour." Sara was looking at her phone and typing on it as she spoke. "Maybe if Jazmine isn't too tired, she or Isaac will train with you after dinner."

"Okay, thanks." I managed to say, fighting back the annoyance I felt. I couldn't tell why, but I was feeling very impatient to get better at fighting with weapons and didn't like all of these breaks. I needed to remind myself though that Ben had been helping me, and I shouldn't take my frustration out on him. Since he had apologized a second time for kissing me, he had not been weird at all, and was acting completely normal again.

I tried not to think about the awkwardly forceful kiss he had given me. There just weren't words for how strange that whole thing had been. Even if the kid had feelings for me… could he have picked a worse time to let me know, or a worse way to go about it? I know he's only sixteen but come on… boys just didn't make any sense at all.

Tobias arrived back from town where he had picked up pizzas and salad for everyone. I had a slice of pizza, and I had to admit it was as good as Tobias had advertised. Ben took down an entire pizza by himself, which probably shouldn't have surprised me.

I heard the front door open and close, just before Jazmine spoke as she entered the room. "Whatever that is, it smells amazing."

"It might be the best pizza ever." Ben said, putting a hand to his stomach as he sat back in his chair. "And I might have eaten too much."

"Judging by the news coverage." Sara said as Isaac emerged from the main entrance. "I would guess your trip was a success?"

"Only time will tell. But yes, it did go rather smoothly. We didn't even have to put any of the guards to sleep at the statue, thank goodness. I still felt like a criminal in spite of that, but the message had to be sent." Isaac replied. "In two days, we will know how many clans saw the signal."

"Or at least how many of them saw it and cared enough to show up." Jazmine added.

"Oh, I surmise that many of the clans will come. The question is how many of them will want to help free the others in Brazil. While it pains me to admit it, I'm not optimistic about the clans wanting to help. Only the African clan is a sure bet, as those ones dedicate their lives to helping people incapable of helping themselves. I would be shocked if they did not ally themselves to our cause." Isaac grabbed a plate and food as he spoke.

"So… just how many of these clans are there?" My father asked. He was sitting at the end of the table, flanked by Sara on his right, and Ben in the seat to his left.

Tobias was sitting on the opposite side of the long table, as far from my father as he could get. For whatever reason, Tobias still seemed squeamishly uncomfortable around him. I suppose it could have been the fact that he was a creeper who held girls against their will with his compulsion ability, and he knew my father was a retired cop. It was confusing that Tobias simultaneously did that to girls, while he himself hunted down and killed sexual predators in his free time. Maybe in some twisted way it lessened his own guilt? I couldn't pretend to understand the strange man.

I was just grateful that with the ring on my finger and the bracelet on his wrist, he wouldn't be hurting anyone else. The artifacts were also helpful in getting information from the man, who didn't like to say more than he had to. He would help us free the other bloodline members and help me kill the tainted ones responsible for Leuken's death. For now, that was all that mattered.

"There are several dozen clans." Isaac's voice brought me back from my deep thoughts. "At the last emergency meeting, I think fifteen showed up, and there were a handful that chose not to come but asked other clans to pass along the information. Seven clans agreed to help fight the tainted ones, with each sending only their best fighters. They wanted to make sure most of our kind were armed with the terralium weapons needed to kill the Verdorben."

"Is that the 'great battle' I heard you mention?" My father asked. "What actually happened with that?"

Isaac's face seemed to flush with emotion as he spoke. "What happened is a lot of good men and women were slaughtered, and we only managed to kill a couple of the tainted ones." He sounded a mix of angry and sad at the same time.

My father opened his mouth again, probably to ask another question, but shut it without saying a word. Obviously, Isaac didn't want to discuss the topic further. Bringing up the battle got me thinking about the one we could potentially be fighting in the near future.

"Tobias, exactly what can you tell us about these Verdorben in Brazil?" I turned to face him as I asked. "Are you sure this is not the main group?"

"I don't believe they are together." Tobias said thoughtfully, staring out the window as he spoke. "It has been so long since I have seen anyone from Alastair's group, and they were never near the two in Brazil. That being said, I chose this place because I didn't want to be anywhere near other Auserwhalt. This estate is far from any flight paths and major cities, which is the best one can do to avoid others of our kind."

"So, what is the plan for the rendezvous?" Jazmine asked, looking to Isaac.

"I surmise if I go to the meeting with any of the Verdorben, the clans will panic, and we won't have a chance to enlighten them on developments." Isaac appeared deep in thought, looking at the floor as he spoke slowly. "But it will be important for me to bring someone."

Isaac glanced around at the group before continuing. "It makes the most sense to bring Ben. He just lost his brother, and his father Nathan was respected by several of the clans, even if he was young when taken from us. Jazmine will need to stay with Liz and the others to keep the rest of the family safe. If the meeting goes well, we will bring the clans that agree to help to meet up afterwards."

CHAPTER IV

"This is the place." Isaac said matter of fact like as he pulled to a stop in the dirt parking lot. He parked the truck backed in near the curb. As he and Ben exited the car, they went and unlocked the padlock that was on the gate leading into the grass area by the nearest structure. He crossed a greenish brown field with large overgrown ash and oak trees spaced every 30 or so yards. Using the other key on the keychain he had picked up from the fairground's manager, he opened the door to the canopy shaped building. Inside the large warehouse was half concrete, half dirt, with makeshift half-height partitions blocking off corners of the room. Those were likely where they did the petting zoo for the smaller animals during the fair, Isaac thought to himself as he looked around. As he had requested, there were white folding chairs set up in several rows near the center of the room, enough for about 100 people. Although Isaac suspected they probably wouldn't have even half that many, he had prepared for an optimistic showing.

"What's this town called again?" Ben asked while taking the room in, grimacing slightly as he put one hand up to his nose. "It kinda smells like farm animals."

"Logandale, Nevada." Isaac said casually as he walked to the podium just past where all of the chairs were laid out. "During the fair they keep some small animals in this room, that's probably what caused the faint sent. The other clans should be arriving soon. Why don't you go to the front to greet our guests? Remember, no one should come in without the mark, unless they are family of other bloodlines who attend. Our privacy in this matter is of the utmost importance."

"No problem." Ben's smile was a mix of excitement and relief. "As much as I love smelling animal stank, I'll take one for the team and wait outside. Are you sure everyone will be cool with me questioning them?"

"No one should give you grief." Isaac reassured. "As you greet them, just make sure your scar is visible, and introduce yourself as Benjamin Bennett, son of Nathaniel Bennet, rest his soul."

As Ben was walking out the front door, Isaac was only slightly surprised to see a group of people already forming just outside the building on the grass. At least a dozen people stood in three separate groups, with another twenty or so trickling in from the parking lot. Isaac waited inside the room to greet the clans as they came in. The first man through the door was tall and built, a dark complected African man whose face looked strikingly familiar to Isaac. He was followed by three others. One looked to be his brother, while the other boy and tall slender female had a somewhat lighter complexion.

"You must be Metemba?" Isaac said smiling. "You have your father's strong jaw and eyes."

"I must apologize. I do not know your name." The younger man said as he and Isaac's hands clasped. His grip was strong, and he stood a few inches taller than Isaac.

"I am Isaac Bennett." He replied, nodding in respect as he turned to show the mark of the bloodline on his neck. Metemba also angled his head to show the sun symbol on his neck, though it was less obvious with his complexion. "Thank you for coming. I have dire information to share with all the clans."

"It is nice to meet you, Isaac." Metemba's accent was only a slight blend of British mixed with a hint of South African. "I was a young boy when my father gave his life, but I appreciate the compliment." Metemba looked down briefly as he spoke, his eyes watering slightly. "He brought great honor to our family, and I hope to someday be half the man Jafari Adebayo was. This is my sister Shawnee," Metemba turned and gestured to the others as he spoke. "And my brothers Zane and Kwame." The others nodded to Isaac in turn as Metemba introduced them.

*   *   *

"I really don't think this is a good idea." Jazmine said cautiously as she stopped at a red light.

I was sitting next to her in the passenger seat, with Alex, Sarah and my father in the middle row of the Tahoe. Tobias was in the third row by himself. Since the death of Luke, I found it harder to hate the man, even though I knew he was mostly evil. The chilled rage I kept barely under control for the Verdorben who were responsible for sending those who had taken Leuken from me made it difficult to hate anyone else. I knew it was callous... but lately it was hard to think of Tobias as anything other than a useful tool. He did exactly what I told him to do and had useful knowledge as well. He would help me get revenge.

"Whoa! A castle!" Alex exclaimed excitedly from the back seat. Out the window to our left, a massive hotel towered over us.

Multiple colorful spires sat atop white stone walls, and a sign with the word "Excalibur" in front of the hotel gave away its name. Only seconds before we had passed another massive black building, shaped like a pyramid, and Alex had seemed equally excited about that structure.

"You like that buddy?" My father asked, smiling down at Alex from the seat next to him. As I glanced back, I noticed that he was holding Sara's hand. It wasn't the first time I had seen affection between the two, but it didn't make it any less weird. The love of my life had been blown to pieces, and now his mom was dating my dad? *So weird!* I thought to myself.

As we continued driving down the Las Vegas Strip, I had to admit the hotels were pretty impressive. I was in no mood for sightseeing, but I also didn't want to sit bored at the hotel while we waited for the counsel of clans to meet and make a decision. When Isaac mentioned clans from around the world would be gathering to discuss if they were willing to help us or not, I had wanted to go. I thought by explaining the loss of Leuken and the plight of the bloodlines who were being held against their will and used as ruthless assassins, it would sway others to our cause. It wasn't until Isaac explained that my very presence would scare off most bloodline members who were coming, that I saw the reason my father and I needed to stay away. The second everyone's terralium blades and rings began heating up, everyone would have scattered, assuming it was some sort of trap.

And so, I found myself sitting in the passenger seat, taking in the sights with my family, the woman I had hoped would someday be my mother-in-law, a girl I'd hoped would be my sister-in-law, and a psychopathic serial killer of sex offenders who himself used former prostitutes as slaves. Yeah… there was nothing even remotely close to normal about my current situation. At least the demons inside of my father and I were kept at bay thanks to a healthy dose of daily sunlight.

"I'm surprised you didn't want to go to the clan meeting Jazmine." Sara said casually from the back seat. "Perhaps you could have met a nice boy from the bloodline."

"You know that probably wouldn't happen anyways." Jazmine said lowly under her breath. "I need a strong man with a good heart. One that is fearless and thoughtful. Preferably with big muscles too." She paused thoughtfully before continuing. "I know I'm probably too picky, but if he's not perfect I'm not wasting my time."

"Well, I don't know how you will meet Mr. perfect if you aren't even trying." Sara replied.

"How far away did you say you can sense other Verdorben Tobias?" Jazmine asked after a few moments had passed in awkward quiet. We were passing by another hotel with Roman columns near a sign labeled "Caesar's Palace."

"If you are referring to the Auserwhalt my range has not changed." Tobias replied, a somewhat sullen tone in his voice. "My best estimate would be approximately 500 miles, but I haven't exactly had another of the chosen willing to hold still while I drove and measured the coordinates of disappearance from my abilities." I wasn't sure what had gotten into the man, as he had been acting even more disgruntled than normal all morning. He was probably frustrated by having to sit in the third row by himself, but my father had insisted, and I wasn't going to lobby for the sick man. Just because he was a useful tool did not mean he deserved too much respect. Especially considering all the horrible things he had done.

"Thanks Tobias." Jazmine said casting an annoyed look his direction through the rear-view mirror. "You have a gift for explaining things so nicely."

"Well Ms. Bennett, I'm not sure when the last time was that you were held against your will." Tobias began. "But I would guess it was never. So, while I love the whole family outing for you all to sight see, I am presently more concerned with the fact that I have spent hundreds of years staying alive by mostly avoiding large airports and major cities, yet now I find myself a couple miles from an international airport. The thought of Alastair and his cronies finding and killing us is not exactly calming. So, if kindness is what you are looking for in my compulsory answers, you'll have to search elsewhere!" Tobias had raised his voice substantially by the time he finished.

"Will our presence here endanger the meeting?" Sara asked suddenly.

"We should be good." Jazmine replied. "The meeting is starting as we speak, and with it being an hour from town, I think the odds of any bloodlines being near these hotels are pretty slim. Besides, the terralium is only effective up to about a mile, so we should be out of range unless a clan is sleeping on the strip. Which… I think is unlikely."

"Is that a volcano!? Alex asked excitedly, putting his face up against the glass. We were passing another large hotel with a gold and white colored tower. In front of it was a smaller volcano shaped mountain that rose about 50 feet into the air.

Tourists lined the sidewalks and fronts of the hotels on both sides of the street, and an even larger group of people were in front of the small mountain. Many were taking pictures while others just stared in awe. I should have been impressed by the overall grandeur of the buildings and cities, but I felt impatient and restless. I wished I knew if the other clans were agreeing to help or not. *Please let this work.* I thought to myself. *Those people need freeing… and I need revenge…*

"Fellow bloodlines, I would like to start by thanking you and the light that you all came here today." Isaac began after taking his place in front of the group. Nearly 100 people had gathered from various clans, including a group of about 20 people, mostly women and children, from the Romany gypsy clan. "I know it is no small thing to call an emergency meeting of the bloodlines, but I stand before you today to give warning, and a call to action."

"A few days ago, my clan was attacked in the city of Harrisburg, Oregon. I'm sure some of you have seen the video posted online of Leuken Bennett from my clan healing shooting victims at the school there." Isaac continued, trying to keep his emotions from showing. "What you are probably not aware of, is that Leuken Bennett, who I have helped to raise from the time he was just a small boy, was killed just after the shooting.

"You see after stopping the crazed gunman, a group of people came to our home nearby, and attacked us. During the fighting we were able to kill many of the attackers and escape, but not before Leuken was killed in an explosion." Several members in the crowd shook their heads or bowed them in respect, and Isaac heard more than a few people whisper or mumble under their breath.

"While I mourn his passing into the light. I know that everyone here has lost loved ones, and that none of us are strangers to sacrifice or danger." Isaac paused briefly, contemplating the best words to explain the situation. "I am sure it will not surprise you all to learn that this attack was orchestrated by the Verdorben. What was a surprise to me, however, is the fact that none of our attackers were Verdorben. They were members of the bloodline, like each of us." Isaac heard gasps throughout the room as he finished that statement.

"A hunting party of at least 10 bloodlines attacked us at our home in Oregon." Isaac continued. "They were well armed and trained. They attacked first with sniper rifles and blades, and one of them even blew up the house with explosives, which is how Leuken was killed. We were barely able to fight them off to escape and had to kill most of them before we got out. I do not know how many there were total, but we counted ten, with a few more showing up every few minutes until we got out of there. What is even more troubling, is that one of them followed us." The leader of the Romany gypsies stood up and looked around anxiously. "That was a week ago." Isaac added, attempting to console the Romany clan. They were known for their paranoia and almost religious distrust of people.

"The man who followed us was a talented swordsman, and nearly bested me before I took his sword arm in the fighting. He explained that he and dozens of other bloodline members are being held captive in Brazil. He said that unless he does whatever the tainted ones tell him, they beat his wife and children or threaten to kill them. Sometimes they even beat people to the point of death. Some who rebel have even been quickly executed. The man's name was Royce, and he handed me these coordinates for where the bloodlines and their families are being held prisoner. Immediately after giving me this paper," Isaac held the paper up so everyone could see it, even thought it would be difficult to read from where most of them were seated. "He was killed by the remote detonation of an explosive device in his head. The situation was tragic, but I will say that I do believe the man. The light was with him before he died, as strange as that sounds for an assassin who kills his own people."

There were mumbles throughout the crowd, as several people began whispering or speaking softly to one another about the latest news. Isaac's brother Jacob was seated in the back row with his friend Jarvis. They had come all the way from Australia. Jarvis was leaning over and saying something to Jacob, but Jacob stared unshakingly at Isaac.

"Though this news is certainly alarming by itself, I must admit I have much more to say, and this next part is even heavier, as it will weigh into each of your decisions on if you are willing to help us free our enslaved bloodline brothers and sisters." Isaac paused briefly again, looking around the room. "Last year my clan was attacked by one of the Verdorben. A large, bearded, axe-wielding man who called himself Jareth. He also had an apprentice. We killed the apprentice first, and in so doing, young Leuken's girlfriend was cursed with the taint of the Verdorben."

Gasps escaped loudly from some mouths, and the whispering grew louder. So much so, that Isaac was forced to pause again before it began to quiet.

"Her name is Elizabeth Scott, and she is a seventeen-year-old girl. Much to our surprise, she quickly learned how to control the darkness inside of her. After studying her for several days, we learned that she still had full control of all her mental faculties and her body. We don't know how she was turned, as we were careful to fight the Verdorben far away from her, with several others in close proximity. Yet alas... it didn't matter. Somehow the curse entered her body, and after bringing her back to our house, and running some tests, we decided we would release and monitor her."

"Much to our surprise." Isaac spoke louder to be heard over the whispers from the incredulous crowd. His last comment had spurred even more chatter. "The Verdorben's master Jareth, the large man with the red beard, showed up a few days later. Killing him was more work, but when he died, Elizabeth Scott's father, Daniel Scott was turned into Verdorben. Now when Daniel was turned, the curse seemed to affect him more, as over the course of a few days, he grew darker and more sinister. Since we discovered that direct exposure to the sunlight weakened the effect of the taint on him, he has been amicable, and also appears in full control of his body."

"Where are these creatures now?" The same Romany clan leader stood again, looking around the room, while pulling out a terralium dagger to examine the blade. The metal appeared cool, a clear indication that no Verdorben were nearby.

"There's no need to be alarmed." Isaac reassured while raising his hands slowly. "They are miles away and don't even know where we are. I kept them off sight and away from where any of them would be sensed by our terralium. This was to prevent any alarm or panic on your parts, as I know this is a lot of information to take in."

Their voices had grown louder again as Isaac spoke, making it nearly impossible for him to be heard. He paused and looked around the room. Only Jacob and Metemba appeared motionless and thoughtful as he took everyone in. Half of the gypsies were standing now, and a few of the adults were arguing not so quietly about if they should leave immediately or not. The Mexican clans were also arguing, though slightly less loudly, and only the Chinese clan were whispering so quietly Isaac could not make out a word.

"Who else has seen what you speak of?" A young woman from one of the Mexican clans asked loudly over the din. Isaac motioned for Benjamin to come forward and he approached the podium.

"I have seen the Verdorben." Benjamin said loudly in front of the group. "I am Benjamin Bennett, son of Nathaniel Bennett, and by the light I speak the truth. I saw the Verdorben and the bloodlines who attacked us and killed my brother."

As Benjamin spoke, Isaac noticed movement to his side. A tall, hooded figure standing near the entrance suddenly began moving towards the podium. His purposeful stride looked familiar, but Isaac could not see the man's face with his dark hood pulled over his face. *It can't be...* Isaac thought to himself as the man reached the podium, lowering his hood.

To Isaac's utter surprise, Leuken Bennett stood in front of the podium, his face dark with stubble and somewhat dirty. He gently pushed a wide-eyed Benjamin aside before speaking, with Ben's mouth hanging open.

"I am Leuken Bennett, son of Nathaniel Bennett." Leuken began speaking loudly to the group, and everyone momentarily drew quiet. "My uncle and brother speak truth about the Verdorben and these bloodlines, though they were mistaken about my death. I barely survived the attack by the bloodlines that reduced my house to rubble and buried me in the wreckage, but I stand before you today as a third witness that these Verdorben are real, and they are on our side."

"What trickery is this?" A middle-aged man from the gypsy clan stated loudly. "My clan wants no part of this mess. Those cursed creatures will never be on our side. We never should have come here. You are leading us all into some kind of trap." The man was already standing, and he gently pulled on a few young ladies' shoulders seated near him, before heading for the exit. As he walked, the rest of the Romany Gypsies and their children moved to follow. He noticed three teenage girls, and a handful of younger children besides the adults.

"Please don't leave." Leuken said loudly as they moved to exit. "This discovery effects all of the bloodline." The group had reached the front door and were quickly exiting. "Putting your heads in the sand or running from this threat will not make it disappear." Leuken was nearly shouting as the last of the group made it to the door. One of the teenage girls paused and turned before exiting, looking curiously at Leuken and Ben. Someone outside grabbed her arm and pulled her from the room.

CHAPTER V

"I told you we are leaving." Kezia's father said angrily as he pulled her arm. He sounded frightened as he spoke. She had been looking at the two Bennett brothers standing in the center of the room. Both were handsome, but it was the one who had spoken first she was staring at when her father pulled her out. He had been watching her clan as they left, and she couldn't help but think she had felt something when their eyes met, even if it was only for a brief moment. His eyes had been a piercing baby blue.

Kezia Shaw felt a mix of emotion, but beyond the slight excitement from the younger brother, she was angry. Her intrigue had the best of her, and she wanted nothing more than to stay behind and hear what the Bennetts had to say. Instead, her father's paranoia had again forced them to leave in haste. Being around so many others from the bloodline had been comforting to Kezia. Her clan had always been so exclusive and cautious that she rarely saw anyone else with their abilities. Not that she had abilities herself yet, but she had only turned sixteen a few weeks before. It wasn't uncommon for people from her family line to snap in their later teens. Of course,

Charity had snapped a few days after her own fifteenth birthday, but *not every daughter could be perfect,* she thought to herself.

She reluctantly followed her family back to the vehicles they had parked in the dirt near the structure they had met in. While she was angry at her father, she knew better than to argue with him once his mind was set. As her clan quickly loaded into the vehicles, Kezia wanted so badly to hear more about the boy's friends who had been turned Verdorben, and the bloodline traitors who were hunting their own kind. *How could anyone do such a thing?* She thought.

The tires on their truck kicked up dirt as they pulled quickly from the parking lot. The families were spread between five separate vehicles, and they caravanned through the small town as they moved back towards the main highway to the north.

"Why didn't we stay and at least hear them out?" Kezia asked angrily from the back seat, after a couple minutes had passed in silence.

"You know you shouldn't question father on these matters." Charity shot Kezia a disapproving stare as she sounded matter of fact like. "When you are older you will understand."

"Oh please!" Kezia knew she should hold back but couldn't help herself. "You aren't even three years older than me, but you think you know everything don't you?" Kezia scowled at Charity as she spoke.

"Now girls." Kezia's mother chimed in from the front seat, her usually calm voice clearly anxious and distracted. "Now is not the time for you two to fight."

"Stop it!" Her father Sampson said curtly. "I think we are being followed."

Kezia looked back and could see two black cars behind the SUV her uncle was driving in the rear of their caravan. Both were traveling at a high rate of speed but kept just far enough back as to not be too obvious.

She felt herself jerk forward as her father slammed on the brakes, and she turned forward just in time to see a large semi-truck crash into the front of their truck. Everything spun as the front passenger side of the truck was immediately smashed in, and their truck twisted sideways into the air, before landing, bouncing, and sliding at least fifty feet on the ground, coming to rest upside down in the dirt just off the center median.

Kezia was completely dazed by the collision. She could feel pain in her legs and head, and the only thing that had kept her from landing on her head was the seatbelt holding her somewhat suspended upside down. As her surroundings came into focus, she noticed the part of the truck where her mother and sister had been sitting was completely gone, and her sister Charity was lying motionless in a crumpled heap on the road at least 30 feet away. She could hear shouting in the distance, and the sound of gunfire from fairly close.

"Kezia are you okay?" Her father's voice was cracking as she saw him rip her door open from the outside. She hadn't even seen him leave his seat, but he was now pulling her sideways as her seatbelt clicked off and he scooped her up to her feet. His frenzied eyes were full of concern as he held her face in one hand while looking her over quickly.

Her face felt wet, and she realized that she couldn't see out her right eye as it was covered in blood. Her father was ripping his own shirt sleeve off and began tying it around her right leg. Only then did she see the large metal piece protruding from her leg. It was a twisted piece of metal about 6 inches long, and by the searing pain she felt, it had gone most of the way through her leg just above the knee before stopping.

"This is going to hurt." He said as he wrapped the shirt piece around her leg and pulled it tight, tying the end into a knot. She winced as he tightened it but noticed the blood flow slow from the wound in her leg. "I need to check on Charity." He turned and said over his shoulder as he was already running towards where her sister lay in the street. He moved so fast she could barely see him.

Charity was lying motionless on her back, her forehead soaked with blood, and she appeared to be missing her right leg. There were several large chunks of metal and glass strewn between where Charity was in the road, and where what was left of their truck had come to a rest.

As her father got to Charity and began to shake her, she heard screaming coming from further back on the road. She spotted her four-year-old niece Trinity running as fast as she could towards Kezia's father, as another high-pitched scream escaped her tiny mouth. There was someone shooting from behind her, but the gunshots barely registered in Kezia's ears. All she could focus on was her little niece's terror, and what was happening behind her.

Two slender Hispanic men in dark clothing wielding long swords were attacking Trinity's father Ingram. He moved quickly to defend himself, parrying their strikes with a long dagger in one hand. He was able to land occasional strikes with his free hand and feet on the men, and he even cut one in the arm as the three seemed to dance between one another while fighting. The moves were so quick that she could barely follow them with her eyes, but in a matter of seconds the two men overpowered her uncle, severing his right leg at the knee as he stabbed one of them in the stomach. That man, the shorter of the two with a short dark beard, seemed unfazed by the wound, and quickly jumped back as he swung his sword down, striking off the arm Ingram's dagger was clutched in.

Kezia's niece had just reached her father as Ingram was cut down by the two men. He was frivolously attempting to wake Destiny when Trinity pulled on his arm from behind screaming.

"Help uncie Sam!" Trinity screeched as she drew his attention. Her pink dress had blood on one sleeve and on the front, and the tears covering her face only added to the look of desperation on her face.

"Trinity." Sampson said as he quickly picked her up off the ground and hugged her. "You and Kezia need to get out of here now." He gave her a quick squeeze before setting her back down. "Now go to your cousin and both of you run!" He pointed at Kezia, giving her a light shove towards her.

Trinity did as she was told, running quickly towards Kezia. As Kezia bent down to hug Trinity, she noticed a stabbing pain in her leg from where the metal was protruding. The metal was lodged deep and prevented her leg from bending properly. She knew she could not run with the metal in, but she needed to get Trinity to safety. "Hold on a sec." She said as she pulled back from Trinity.

As she grabbed the metal piece with both hands, Kezia knew it would be hard to get out, so she pulled hard away from her body, trying not to do more damage as she ripped the bloody object from her leg. "Ahh!" She shouted. Excruciating pain in her thigh almost caused her to fall over. The object had moved but was still lodged deep. Giving another shout, she tugged her hardest, pulling the object free from her leg. She instantly noticed the bleeding got worse, but she didn't have time to think about that now. The two men that had just killed her uncle were moving cautiously towards her father and Charity. She knew she needed to run now if her and Trinity wanted any chance to survive.

"Run Trinity!" She said firmly as she grabbed her niece by the wrist and began to run across the median to the other side of the road. Trinity was not very fast, but Kezia did not think she had the strength the carry her niece. As it was, each step caused a shooting pain from her injured leg. The pain would have been unbearable were she not so focused on helping her niece.

*　　*　　*

Behind Kezia, the two Hispanic men had been joined by a third, and they all attacked Sampson at once. As the first man swung wildly for Sampson's head, he ducked, striking the man in the groin with a closed fist as his other hand ripped the sword from the attacker. In a quick motion he swung around and through the man's leg, causing him to fall. Sampson quickly pivoted and slashed the man's head off where he had landed on the ground. He turned just in time to see the taller man slashing at his left arm. He twisted and tried to bring his sword up to block, but it was too late as the other man's blade tore through his flesh.

Sampson grimaced, slicing the other man's leg near the calf, as the third attacker sliced him in the back from behind. He felt searing pain as the blade slid partway through his torso, jumping forward to escape the follow up stroke that was meant for his head. The blade nicked his hair as it failed to land on target. Somersaulting forward, Sampson rolled back to his feet, turning with his blade raised, the pain in his back beginning to subside as his body healed itself.

He was standing a few feet from Charity, who was beginning to moan as her body slowly moved. Sampson would have been excited at his daughter's sign of life, but movement to his side made him realize that two more attackers were approaching from the side. With the training these attackers clearly had, he knew he would not be able to take on four of them, especially with his offhand already missing. He glanced at where the bloody hand was sitting, about ten feet away on the ground near the corpse of the first attacker he had felled. While he was tempted to move to grab and re-attach his hand, he knew that doing so would give his attackers the opportunity to kill him easily while distracted.

The two men approaching from the side ran towards where Charity was laying and moaning on the ground, so Sampson moved to intercept. As he swung at the closer man, who looked to be a young teenager at best, the boy quickly turned, parrying Sampson's strike as he turned towards him, slicing at him repeatedly. Sampson parried and blocked, moving quickly to keep his back away from the other two attackers who were moving up from behind. While they fought, Sampson saw the fourth attacker standing over Charity's body as she slowly leaned up, her blood-soaked face confused. Before she had a chance to move, the man quickly raised his sword and struck down, slicing her head from her shoulders as her body fell limp again.

"No!" Sampson shouted as he watched his eldest daughter cut down, helpless to stop her. In a rage, he parried another strike from the young attacker, rolling and sliding sideways as he cut the boy's sword arm off at the forearm. He spun and sliced the body in half, already moving quickly towards the man who had just killed Charity. This man was older, with a soulless grin on his face as he turned to face Sampson, quickly blocking the strike towards his neck. The man's beard was dripping in sweat, and Sampson threw blow after blow at him. The man's smile quickly faded, and after a few quicks exchanged with their blades, he finally sliced the man's right foot in half as he ducked from another attempted head swipe.

The man reached down to clutch his injured foot, and Sampson saw the perfect opening. He quickly raised his blade high, and dropped it down at an angle, cutting through the man's head and a shoulder as he screamed. The slight satisfaction he felt at avenging his daughter's killer was short lived, as he no sooner began to turn and raise his blade when he was stuck from behind again. This time another attacker's sword found his neck, and everything went black for Sampson.

*　　　*　　　*

Kezia ran, curving back towards the city on the other half of the highway from where the carnage was taking place behind and beside her. She could see some of her family fighting to the left as she ran holding Trinity's hand. Haysom appeared to have stolen a sword from one of the men in all black, and he was swinging the dark curved blade quickly while trying to fend off two attackers at once. There were several other bodies on the ground, including another man in black, and some of her cousins. Kezia realized that they were running too slow, as another man in black off to her side shouted something in another language as he pointed at her.

The man started running, and Kezia knew they were not moving fast enough, so she quickly reached down and scooped Trinity up with both arms, turning and running from the man as fast as she could. *I can't let them get Trinity!* She thought to herself as she ran, pushing as hard as she could to run faster, ignoring the brutal throbbing pain in her leg with each step. At first, she could hear the man quickly closing in behind her, and then all the sudden, everything changed. The pain in her leg was instantly gone, replaced by a warm sensation as it faded. The ground beneath and around her seemed to speed up as she ran, with the desert and bushes to either side of the road seeming to zip by.

The footsteps that had been closing in quickly were now trailing further behind. Ahead of her on the other side of the highway, Kezia could see several vehicles approaching from the distance, appearing at a high rate of speed. *The other clans!* Kezia thought with relief as she saw the vehicles getting closer. She turned slightly to glance back over her shoulder, and somehow tripped over her own feet. She was not accustomed to running so fast. As she fell, she pulled Trinity in close, trying to shield her niece as she fell and rolled on the ground. As she came to a stop that she realized she barely felt any pain from falling.

The excitement she felt as she realized she must have snapped to be able to run so fast, and the only thing that would explain the nasty hole in her leg suddenly healing, was short lived. As she quickly stood up, the man that had been chasing them caught up. With a full beard and darkened tan skin, the man looked old enough to be her father's age. The sinister look in his eyes, however, was unlike any she had ever seen.

"Please don't hurt us. She's just a child." Kezia pleaded frantically as she set Trinity down behind her, standing between the man and her niece in a protective fashion.

"I no have a choice." The man said in broken English. He scowled as he suddenly lunged at her, raising his sword above his head.

Kezia jumped to the side to avoid being struck, and the blade cut through her shirt sleeve on her left arm, barely missing her flesh. "Run Trinity!" She yelled at her niece, moving sideways while trying to keep the man's attention. It didn't work.

As Trinity turned and began to run, the man lunged after her. While the man moved fast, Kezia moved faster, throwing herself into the air between the man and her niece as he slashed at Trinity with his sword. In the air she turned, putting her arm up to try and shield her niece from the strike of the blade.

She felt a flash of pain in her arm and chest, realizing the sword had cut through her wrist and into her chest as her body hit the ground. She quickly jumped to her feet, prepared to sacrifice the rest of herself to keep her niece alive longer. As she clenched her teeth to jump again, she suddenly heard screaming from behind Trinity. The attacker who had appeared to be about to strike the young girl down suddenly stopped, turned and raised the blade in a fighting stance, while Trinity continued to run.

Kezia turned just in time to see two men charge at the attacker. She was surprised to see that the first was the younger Bennett boy who had spoken at the clan meeting just minutes before, while the other was an older man with graying temples. Both of them held large silver swords, though these were not curved like the men in black's blades had been. The younger of the two reached the attacker first, slashing at his torso while the man parried, countering to slash at the Bennett boy's arm. Just as the blade appeared to connect, the boy moved in a flash, blocking the strike quickly and after knocking the curved blade to the side, in a continuing motion he swung the blade back down, cutting through the man's shoulder and arm. As the clang of the metal hit the ground, the Bennett boy struck again, this time taking off the man's head in one smooth motion.

"I told you we need to work together Ben." The older man scolded as he reached the younger. "If that one had more skill, he could have killed you in your sloppy haste."

"I'm sorry Isaac, but I couldn't let him kill her or the little girl." The boy turned to face Kezia. "Are you okay?"

The boy's light blue eyes seemed so full of concern as he looked at her, that Kezia suddenly felt self-conscious about her blood-soaked clothes and missing hand. He was even more adorable up close than he had been from across the room, she thought to herself.

"I…" Kezia struggled to find the right words. "I think so… just need to get my niece so we can get out of here." She stammered, noticing that Trinity has stopped running and was looking back towards her. "Come back Trinity!" She called to her niece.

"We aren't going anywhere till we stop these guys." The older man, Isaac said calmly. "Ben, you tend to these two and help her heal her hand, I will go to help Luke and Metemba finish the other's off and rescue any other survivors." He sped off at a full sprint, running towards the smoking cars.

"Where is your hand?" Ben asked, looking down compassionately at Kezia.

"It got cut off." She said embarrassingly, keeping her bloody wrist behind her back. It had already stopped hurting, but she didn't want Ben to view her as a gimpy one-handed girl.

"I know, but if you want it back on, the sooner the better." Ben said while looking around at the ground. "Ah… there it is." He said as he moved quickly over, grabbing her bloody hand from where it lay in the dirt.

"What do you mean back on?" Kezia asked bewildered. "Is there a hospital or a surgeon close by?"

"No silly. You are going to heal it back on. You are a bloodline, right? You must be to move that fast" His smile was very calming.

"Yes I am. But I only just snapped while I was running." She said. "This is my first time with abilities, so I don't really know what I am doing."

"Well, you did a bang-up job saving your little sister or niece or whoever that is." He said smiling and pointing at Trinity, who was cautiously walking back towards them. "And with how fast you moved keeping her alive, I'm sure you will heal pretty quick. Now hold your wrist out in front of you and let's see what we are working with please. Unless you would like to spend the rest of your life with a hand missing that is?" He grinned sheepishly as he finished speaking.

Kezia slowly stretched her arm out in front of her, the flesh had surprisingly healed with fresh skin at the end of her wrist where the nub ended. "How do I heal it though? I thought arms and legs can't grow back."

"Well, I am not going to lie, this will hurt a bit." Ben said while brushing dirt off the tip of the hand. "But I will give you a hand..." The boy paused smirking after that comment before continuing. Kezia would have laughed at the joke, but she was too nervous. "I think it will be best if you just hold your arm very still and close your eyes." Ben gently grabbed her wrist near the end, moving to take a position at her side.

"What are you going to do?" Kezia asked nervously. For some reason she couldn't stop worrying about how bad she looked with her gimpy nub right in front of Ben's face.

"It's probably better if I don't tell you and just fix it." Ben looked down and got closer to Kezia, his face only inches from hers. "By the way, my name is Benjamin Bennett. What's yours?"

"Kezia...Kezia Shaw." She said softly, nervous about what he was planning on doing with her wrist.

"Well Kezia, do you trust me?" His eyes were locked on hers, and at this distance she couldn't stop thinking about how much she was enjoying looking at him. His face was skinny and tan, with slight rosiness to his cheeks, but his jawline appeared strong. Blonde messy hair and the slight split in his chin perfectly finished his near flawless face.

"Yes." She found herself meaning it as she said it. Everything about this boy was just... special. She had been taken by boys before and had several crushes that never lasted long with how her family had always been on the move. Yet even her strongest crush was nothing compared to what she already felt for this boy. *Was it possible to be so happy during such a tragedy?* She thought to herself.

"Then I need you to close your eyes and don't open them until I say. Okay?" He smiled again.

"Okay, I promise." She replied, closing her eyes tightly. Ben was still holding her wrist gently, and she felt his weight shift somewhat as his grip tightened.

"Ahh!" Trinity screamed as Kezia she felt a sharp pain at the end of her wrist. Her niece's cry caused her eyes to open, and she saw Ben drop his sword as he pressed her detached hand against her freshly bleeding wrist. It appeared he had only sliced the very end off, re-exposing the flesh and bones to press against the hand. As she watched, the warming sensation returned to her wrist, and she could feel the tissues somehow reconnecting to each other before her eyes. In a matter of seconds, her hand was back, and she was surprised to see that she could feel it again.

"Sorry about that." Ben said as he gently rubbed her wrist and hand with his hand. "I know that had to have hurt like a mother, but it was the only way to fix your hand for good." His touch was calming, and he gently traced one finger up and down her palm. "Can you feel that okay?"

"Yes." She replied smiling sheepishly. "It feels good." *Feels good? You idiot.* She thought to herself, worrying she sounded as smitten as she felt.

"Can you feel each of these as I touch them?" He was gently rubbing up each finger with his thumbs as he held her hand in his.

"Yes." She said, slowly wiggling her fingers. "And they are moving just fine too."

"Okay great. I am glad that worked. Would have been a terrible first impression otherwise." He grinned childishly. "Perhaps you should check on your niece?"

"Oh yeah." She realized he had let go of her hand, but she was still holding it out in front of him. "Of course. Trinity, come here." She said, walking towards where her niece was frozen, the look on her face a mix between utter disbelief and bewilderment.

Kezia bent down as she reached her niece, picking her up and hugging her on one shoulder. It was strange how light she was, it almost felt like Kezia was holding up a balloon with no weight. "It's okay Trinity. I have you and you are safe."

"I'm so scared." Trinity said, crying softly. "I just want my mommy."

As she heard Trinity say that the weight of everything that had just happened hit Kezia like a brick in the chest. Her own mother was gone, her sister was dead, and she doubted her father had survived the attack. To the best of her knowledge, her and her niece were all that were left of the Romany clan. Trinity would never see her mom again, but Kezia didn't have the heart to tell her. Tears suddenly flooded her eyes and dripped down her face, but she tried to be strong. She had to be, for her niece's sake.

*   *   *

"You two save the girls!" Leuken shouted as he slammed on the brakes. "Me and the others will help the group." Isaac and Ben jumped from the car as it slowed, running towards where one of the men in all black with a sword was attacking a woman and her small child. Leuken slammed back on the gas, waving out the window for the vehicles behind him to follow as he drove on towards where the burning cars were at.

Members of the African clan had followed in two other vehicles, and another car behind that held two people from another clan, one of them had sounded like he had an Australian accent as they had offered to help Leuken back at the meeting grounds. In less than a minute they reached the carnage. At least that was the best way that Leuken could think of to describe it. A semi-truck was turned on its side with a large portion of the front missing, smoke rising from what was left of the engine block. Four other smashed vehicles were on or beside the road. With the furthest one appearing to have been ripped in half and then crumpled beyond recognition. Broken glass and various sized chunks of metal and other debris were strewn around the vehicles.

Only the two closest SUV's, which were flanked by a mid-sized SUV and a couple of sedans, appeared undamaged. Several bodies, including women and children were spread between the wrecked and otherwise unoccupied vehicles. Both of the women were missing their heads. As Leuken jumped out and drew his terralium dagger, he noticed a very short man fighting desperately for his life against four other men. The four attackers were all dressed in black. The lone man was parrying and retreating from their blows, weaving quickly from side to side and between vehicles as the others advanced again and again towards him.

Glancing over his shoulder, Leuken saw Metemba and his sister running towards the fight, while the two Australians ran into the desert towards two black clad figures a few hundred yards away. Turning his attention back to the short man, Leuken noticed he was running around a car from two of the men about thirty feet away, so Leuken joined the two African clan members to intercept the closest attackers. Both of these men appeared Latino, with dark tan skin and large curved swords. The leader of the African clan pulled an even larger curved sword from his back, breathing out loud and controlled through gritted teeth as he lunged at the front attacker.

The man seemed surprised by the newcomers joining the fight, and as he turned to block Metemba, the second attacker raised his sword to strike the African clan chief. Leuken noticed the sister side-stepped to block the attack with a terralium sword, so Leuken stabbed his dagger into the man's throat from the side as their bodies collided. Both he and the shorter man crashed into the car, and Leuken pulled his dagger out sideways, widening the hole he had cut as he pulled his weapon free. From his peripheral vision Leuken could see Metemba hacking at the first attacker, who had fallen to the ground, cutting several limbs before beheading him.

Leuken did not want to give his man a chance to heal, and he knew the other two attackers would come to their companion's aid, so he quickly struck again, stabbing his dagger through the eye cavity of the man who was clutching his throat while staggering sideways against the car. While the man fell to the earth, Leuken grabbed his sword as it clanged on the ground.

"Look out!" Metemba's sister yelled as she jumped towards Leuken, blocking a strike that would have taken Leuken's arm had he not moved sideways with her warning. The other two men were attacking together, and while the girl blocked the strike intended for Leuken, the other attacker slashed at her leg. Leuken was able to get his sword down to block the strike, but not before it tore partway into the side of her calf.

Pivoting sideways as the girl grimaced in pain, Leuken quickly sliced the fourth attacker's sword arm, cutting it off at the elbow. He would have finished the man with a follow through strike, but the third attacker kicked the girl back as he swung at Leuken's arm. Leuken brought his sword up just in time to deflect but had to direct a series of parries to prevent from being hacked by the third man. It was obvious as they danced and he blocked, that this man knew how to wield a sword effectively.

To Leuken's side, Metemba had reached the man with a missing hand, who had grabbed the sword with his other arm and was about to ambush Leuken from behind. Metemba cut off the man's movement, slashing repeatedly as the man's blocks became less and less effective against the strong clan chief's powerful blows. Metemba sliced the man's other arm off at the shoulder, then kicked him in the chest, knocking him backwards into the desert.

As Leuken found the opening to counter strike his attacker, he landed a slice on the man's hip, then another on his thigh. Both blows would heal quickly, but with each strike Leuken landed, the man began to slow. Leuken parried another strike intended for his leg, and as he raised the blade to strike the man's arm, the African girl jumped up from behind the man, flashing her blade clean through his neck.

"Thanks." Leuken said, breathing heavy as the man's body slumped to the earth. "I am Luke by the way."

"I know who you are. I am Shawnee." The girl replied, reaching down to wipe the blood from her sword on the body of the third attacker. Her accent was heavy and sounded almost British, but she was still easy to understand. "I must thank you though. You saved my leg Mr. Bennett."

Leuken opened his mouth to reply but was stunned to silence as a body flew through the air, slamming into the car he was standing next to while barely missing him. It was the fourth attacker, missing half of one arm and all of another. As the man struggled to rise to his feet, pushing his half arm against the ground for leverage, Metemba quickly ran up to him. Grabbing the man by his throat, Metemba raised him into the air while looking sideways at Leuken.

"I am sorry Leuken Bennett. I did not mean to almost strike you with this heathen." He said calmly and politely, as if he was not actively strangling another man while holding him a foot off the ground with one hand, his large sword still clutched in his other.

"No apology needed Chief." Leuken said respectfully as he stepped back to give Metemba more space.

"Now, I am only going to give you one chance to answer before I subject you to more pain that you can imagine." Metemba said slowly to the man. His voice was so calm that it made him seem even more imposing than his tall muscular frame alone did. "I want you to tell me who sent you and why."

"She is called Priscilla." The man said, only seeming somewhat afraid. "I am already a dead man for failing, so do what you must. There is no torture you can give, that I do not already deserve for hunting my own people."

"Why... why does this Priscilla hunt her own kind?" Metemba asked.

"She is not of our kind." The man replied. "She is a monster with the mark of the moon on her neck. She will kill me with her magic as soon as she learns I have been captured though. For my family's sake, you must kill me now, please. If they knew I had talked, they might kill my woman and my two young boys."

"What if I agree to help free your boys?" Metemba asked thoughtfully. "Where can I find them?"

Leuken saw movement from a way off, behind one of the smoking vehicles in the desert. Another man in black was ducked down and appeared to be talking on some sort of cell phone or radio device. "They are being held prisoner in Brazil, in a compound just outside of..." A loud popping sound cut him off, as the man's head suddenly exploded from the inside. Liquid splatted all over

Metemba's face, and the man's body had fallen to the earth. A whisp of smoke was rising from where the man's head should have been.

"There's another one behind that car." Leuken said as he pointed to the wreckage about 30 yards away just off the side of the road. Without speaking, the three quickly ran towards the vehicle where the man was hiding. As they got close, the last man in black quickly darted from behind the vehicle, running directly away from them. Metemba was the closest, and he gripped his sword in both hands as he ran, hurling it violently at the escapee. The sword flew with precision, striking the man directly between the shoulder blades as it caused him to fall forwards, sliding on the dirt.

Just then the man with the Australian accent came running from the side, striking off the man's head just before Leuken, Metemba and Shawnee reached him. The man turned to look at them as he wiped the blood from his sword. It appeared he had killed another attacker, as he carried the same dark blade that they had used in the ambush on the Romany clan.

"Why did you kill him?" Metemba asked as he reached down to grab the handle on his sword. Putting one foot on the man's back, he quickly wrenched his blade free, and then proceeded to wipe it off on the corpse of the dead man at his feet.

"Well, aren't you quite civilized." The man replied haughtily. "I took off the bloke's head because he was deadly. I did not, however, desecrate his corpse by wiping my bloody sword on the man." It was difficult for Leuken to tell if the man was just being sarcastic, or really was so pompous.

"I only asked because I wanted to interrogate him." Metemba replied patiently. He seemed unfazed by the other man's air of superiority. "If what Mr. Bennett and the others have said is true, he might have had valuable information on how to find and free the others. As to being civilized." Metemba scowled down at the man.

"There is no honor in a man who would ambush and kill innocent women and children, simply because of the way they were born. He deserved no respect, so I showed him none."

"Perhaps you are right." The man replied, pulling off his glasses to wipe condensation from them. "Either way, we had better leave before the police show up and this gets even more messy."

Isaac emerged from behind another of the cars. The short man, who had barely escaped with his life because they had showed up when they did, walked next to him, tears streaming from his face. "There are only the three survivors." Isaac said somberly. "Now we should go."

Isaac ran quickly to the car where the last man had been crouched down and picked up the large black phone the man had been talking on.

As a group they ran back to the cars, where Ben was waiting with the other woman and child. As they got closer, Leuken realized that she was not a woman at all. She was just a girl and didn't appear any older than Ben. Her eyes and face were covered with blood, sweat and tears, and the young girl, who too had obviously been crying, had a stunned, wide eyed look of shock as she held the hand of the teenage girl. She couldn't have been older than four or five but was too old to be the teenage girl's daughter.

"Hop in." Leuken said as he stepped back into his vehicle. "We need to get out of here now."

"But my father…" The older girl said, looking around and taking in the group. "Did anyone else survive besides Haysom?"

"I'm sorry but no." Leuken replied, closing his door as he put the car in drive. "We checked the wreckage. Everyone else was killed. They decapitated every victim. Whoever did this, they knew you had bloodlines, and didn't take any chances with survivors. Now please get in. We need to go before police show up and things get more complicated."

Isaac got in the front seat next to Leuken. "I need to call Jazmine." He said. "We will have them meet us at the Arizona rendezvous location. Hopefully most of the other clans will show up, but after this..." Isaac paused thoughtfully before continuing. "We can't be certain of anything."

CHAPTER VI

It was surprisingly warm for winter, probably one of the reasons there were so many tourists walking the streets as we made our way through the crowds. We had parked in the parking garage at the Bellagio Hotel and seen Alex scream in delight as we watched what he had called the "big waters". An enormous man-made lake in front of the hotel had massive fountains that shot nearly a hundred feet into the air in multiple directions, set to fire on and off while music played loudly on multiple speakers. Had I not felt anxious to know what was happening at the clan meeting, I might have actually enjoyed the show.

That had been 20 minutes ago before we had started walking south on Las Vegas Boulevard. Now we were approaching the Excalibur hotel about half a mile away. Crowds of people walked with and against us on the large sidewalks, the smell of alcohol and occasional marijuana flooding my nose as we walked through the crowd. There were people from all over the world mixed up on the sidewalk. I heard at least four different foreign languages as we walked, in addition to southern and New York accents from people talking nearby.

While the streets and sidewalks appeared mostly clean, I couldn't help but notice homeless people sitting in the shade of trees or sleeping in bushes every so often as we walked. Sadly, most of them did not look that old, as they sat or lay hopelessly. Some of them were even talking quietly to themselves. I couldn't help but feel bad for them, regardless of the countless times my father had said "They are homeless by choice, because the drugs and alcohol are more important than anything else to them" when I was growing up. There were definitely less homeless people here in Vegas than there had been in Portland growing up.

"That's the biggest castle I've ever seen!" Alex shouted excitedly as we arrived directly in front of the hotel. The large white building was shaped like a castle, with colorful spires sticking above each corner and edge of the building. The hotel must have been large enough to hold thousands of people. In front of us to the right, near the intersection was a large structure. The front of it had the Excalibur sign, with four large spires on top of it. The rear part of the building looked like it had a monorail stop, and steps leading up to the middle connected with a pedestrian bridge to cross the large and busy intersection to the other side.

"That is pretty cool huh buddy?" My father said, putting his hands gently on Alex's shoulders. He smiled down at Sara who was giving him an approving grin for Alex's excitement. Even though their relationship kinda bugged, I did like that my father had engaged more with Alex since him and Sara became a thing. I also liked how sweet she always was with my little brother.

"Should we go inside the castle little man?" Jazmine asked excitedly.

"Totally we should!" Alex replied smiling. "I wanna see inside the castle."

As we started to walk, I heard several loud bangs from the distance. At first, I thought perhaps a car had backfired or there were fireworks, but as I looked to the South where they had come from, all I could see were people and the large black pyramid shaped hotel that was a few hundred yards from the Excalibur.

"Did you hear those?" My father asked, looking the same direction that I just had. "I think those were gunshots." His furrowed brows showed the same concern that I was starting to feel inside.

Crack, crack, crack, crack! I heard additional loud bangs, and this time the sound reverberated off of the hotels as the sound echoed slightly. They were clearly gunshots. From a way up the road, people began to scream. I could barely hear it above the music coming from the hotel, the bustle of people talking, and the sound of traffic on the road behind me, but the gunshots were clear. I could tell others around us did not notice, as none of them seemed at all alarmed by the firing. Without my enhanced hearing, I wouldn't have noticed either.

"Sound like gunshots to me." Tobias said casually.

"Liz. Take Alex and the girls and get back to the car now." My father said, suddenly focusing on something to the south. My eyes followed his, and as more shots rang out in the distance, I could see people running from a large open area in front of the pyramid hotel. Several people in that area were also down There was only one reason they wouldn't be running. *Someone is killing people!* My mind almost shouted the thought as it hit me.

"I can help dad!" I said instantly, and as I was about to start running, my dad grabbed my arm.

"Those people need healing." Jazmine said, concern oozing through each word.

"Liz!" His eyes were daggers as he looked down at me. "Let Jazmine and I take care of the shooter. You get your brother and Sara to safety."

I looked down at my little brother Alex, whose wide eyes looked absolutely terrified, and at the same time I felt something inside of me say *Stay with your brother*. It was such a strange, yet distinct impression in my mind, that it stopped me cold.

"Okay dad, go get him." I said, grabbing Alex's hand. "Come on you guys, we need to run now before we get stuck in the crowd."

"We will meet you back at the car." My father said as he turned to run. "If we are not back in 15 minutes, leave without us." Him and Jazmine took off at a sprint through the crowd, quickly disappearing into the throng of people.

"Be careful!" Sara called after them.

As we began to run, I heard some screams from behind us. The people who had first been shot at must have been getting close to us. I glanced back and noticed that about fifty yards away there were more and more loud screams forming as additional people began to run. Beyond the scream of the crowd, more gun shots rang out, usually sounding off in bursts of three to four shots at a time. We hadn't gone more than fifty feet, when suddenly I heard additional gun shots. These were not in the distance though. The sound was almost deafening in my ears with my enhanced hearing.

Looking towards the cracking sounds, I spotted the shooters. There were two men standing on top of the structure with the Excalibur sign and stairs. The men were wearing camouflage and tan shirts, holding assault rifles of some sort as they fired quickly down at the crowd. The crowd that was fleeing right towards the shooters. I quickly realized they were shooting in a planned fashion to try and turn the crowd back the other way. This was a coordinated attack.

"Sara, I need you to take Alex please. I have to stop those guys." I said, shouting loud enough to be heard over the other screams. Sara nodded knowingly as she reached down to grab Alex's hand. "Alex, do not let go of Sara's hand." I said as I looked him in the eyes. "I will meet you back at the car. Tobias, protect them, if anyone else starts shooting before you get to the car, you can do whatever you need to stop them."

"It's too dangerous Liz. You will draw attention to yourself, and Alastair will come for us." Tobias objected.

"Seriously Tobias? People are dying." I said, frustrated by the man's paranoia at a time like this. "Just do as I ask, please."

Tobias nodded, seeming like he actually didn't mind staying with the others, since he knew he couldn't talk me out of helping. For having superhuman strength, the man's cowardice was inexplicable to me.

Pulling the spare keys from my pocket, I handed them to Sara. "Now run!" The crowd was beginning to move quicker around me as more people realized what was happening, causing a panic. Turning from her, Tobias, and my brother, as they ran with the crowd back to the north, I focused on the two closest shooters.

One of them wore a camouflaged shirt with tans and browns, while I realized the other one was wearing a tan uniform. From this distance, I couldn't tell if it was a janitor's outfit or something else, but I didn't care. Running through the crowd, I accidentally knocked a few people over in my haste. I would have felt bad, but with innocent people being killed by the second, I knew that nothing was more important than me stopping the shooters.

As I got closer, I noticed people were thronging down the stairs by the droves, and it became difficult to push against the crowd without knocking everyone over. Glancing to my side, I saw a large, angled support beam, about fifteen feet above my head that connected to the tall structure the shooters were on. I jumped instinctively up onto the beam, grabbing it with both hands as I landed to avoid falling over the front of it. I could see the railing near the pedestrian bridge, so I jumped the extra ten feet up onto that. Gunshots continued to ring out above me as I looked around for a way up. A train car for the monorail was parked at the stop a few yards away, sitting offset slightly from the building in the open air above the track. I quickly jumped onto it, and from there I could see the top of the structure where the shooters were at. It couldn't have been more than fifteen feet above the train car, so I jumped as hard as I could, grabbing the edge of the roof with both hands and arms as I was just short of clearing the building.

Pulling myself up quickly, I saw the two men about 30 feet away. They stood side by side, turning slightly back and forth as they shot intermittently down at the crowd. Loud gunshots overpowered the sound of the screaming crowd below. I was behind them, so they didn't even see me as I quickly ran to the first shooter. The man was wearing a camouflage-colored long sleeve shirt and pants, with a beard. Without thinking, I punched him hard in the side of the head. A loud cracking sound came from his neck as he crumpled over, dropping the gun.

The noise drew the attention of the other shooter, and as he turned towards me, he began firing. Luckily, I was only about five feet away, so I lunged quickly forward as I ducked, grabbing the barrel of his gun as the shots went over my head. From my crouched position with the gun clutched, I jumped over his head, ripping the gun from his grasp. As I landed with the gun, the man pulled a knife from his waist and stabbed at me. I was still holding the gun by the barrel, so I quickly swung it sideways at the arm he was attacking with. I could hear his arm crunch as the gun slammed into his elbow, instantly breaking the arm just before the knife would have struck me.

"Aagh!" The man screamed; his face twisted in pain. He looked like he was middle eastern, with a hawkish nose and small brown eyes. Before he had time to do anything else, I grabbed his head in a Muay Thai clinch, with both forearms against his neck as I kneed him twice in the stomach. Ignoring his grunts, I let go of the clinch, and quickly kicked one leg, breaking it at the knee. He began to fall sideways, so I kicked him one more time in the head as he fell, snapping his neck.

I noticed that he was wearing a police uniform. The gold badge on his chest, with police badges on both shoulders gave it away. For a split second I panicked, thinking that perhaps he was an officer. Then I reminded myself that he had been actively shooting innocent people, so there was no way he could have been a real cop. When I looked down at his gun belt, he did not even have a radio anywhere on it, only the gun and handcuffs. *What a phony.* I thought to myself as I turned to check on the first shooter I had punched.

This man was lying motionless, and his skin was paler than his friends, but he also had a middle eastern appearance. As I reached down to check for a pulse, I couldn't find one. His eyes were closed, but I couldn't help but notice how young this man's face looked even with the beard. He probably was only a couple years older than me. I know I should have felt bad for killing him, as that wasn't my intent... but I honestly didn't. Looking over the edge of the structure, I could see at least half a dozen people down on the ground. Some were moving slowly, while others were clearly dead.

These people I did feel sorry for. These poor innocent tourists were simply trying to enjoy the sightseeing with their friends and family, when these evil men had decided to kill them. I could feel anger welling up as I thought about the victims and their families. Looking back down at the suspects, I was glad they were dead.

I noticed that the gunshots to the South had stopped, so I was guessing my father had stopped the other shooter or shooters. Either way, I knew I needed to get back to Alex and Sara, so I jumped back down onto the monorail car and onto the landing. It was strange to feel no pain when jumping down from such heights. While running, I tried to mostly blend in with the crowd of screaming people as I hurried to catch up to them. *Hopefully there aren't any more shooters.* I thought to myself as I moved through the crowd.

*   *   *

Daniel Scott ran quickly through and against the crowd. While he and Jazmine mostly weaved between the running people, it seemed like every couple of seconds they knocked one over. Jazmine was smaller than Daniel, so she ran directly behind him, moving through the path he made as he meandered through everyone. They were approaching the front of the Pyramid hotel, and Danial noticed a "Luxor" sign in large black letters on the front of the entrance to the building. The crowd thinned off to their right, so they ran that direction, coming into an opening in the people. From there they stopped, taking in the surroundings. Daniel could see several people down on the ground, at least two dozen were either barely moving or completely still, with each of them bleeding from somewhere on their bodies.

Jazmine went quickly to the closest two. A man was sitting with his back against a black bench, cradling a young child in his arms. The girl could not have been older than five, and it struck Daniel as he realized the entire front of her shirt was covered in blood. It appeared she had been shot in the stomach. The man was also bleeding from his upper arm. Crouching down, Jazmine put her hands to the girls' neck to feel for a pulse.

"It's okay sir, I can help. She's still alive.'"" Jazmine said reassuringly. Sparing a quick glance up at Daniel, she concentrated, and her body seemed to stiffen slightly. "Find the shooter Dan. I can't heal all of them, and until he is stopped, he will keep killing."

Daniel heard more gunshots and turned to see that they were coming from a broken window about halfway up the pyramid. He could see the silhouette of a man who was firing with some type of long gun from a room inside the broken glass. The rounds impacted all around Daniel on the ground, and Jazmine screamed briefly in surprise when her leg was struck by one of the shots.

"She will be fine now." Jazmine reassured the man as she gripped her own leg where she had been hit. "But you need to get her out of here now before you get shot again." She sprung back to her feet and turned to Daniel, the wound on her leg healing itself. "A lot of people here need healing or more will die. Can you take him out alone?"

"Yes. I'll deal with this guy. You help the injured." Daniel replied as he sprang into motion. Running forward, he noticed that the angled glass that ran up the entire hotel started about twenty feet up off the ground. He spotted a large dumpster enclosure a few feet from one side of the hotel, so he jumped up on that before jumping up onto the roof of the building.

The man continued shooting as Daniel ran up the side of the black glass. He could feel the heat of the glass underneath his feet as he ran up, surprising himself that he was able to run up the steep incline of the pyramid. Before his transformation, he thought to himself, there was no way he would have been able to run up the surface without falling backwards. His feet made a distinct sliding sound as he made his way up the building towards the shooter. As

Daniel got closer, he could see that the man was wearing some type of head covering as he fired down at people. It covered everything but his eyes.

When he was about 100 feet from the room, the man saw him and turned his rifle towards Daniel. It only took him a couple more seconds to reach him, but in that time, the man fired several shots. Daniel felt a round tear through his left shin and his left shoulder. Luckily his momentum carried him forward and he crashed into the man with the rifle, knocking both of them backwards into the man's room.

As Daniel stood up, the pain in his shin was sharp, but he was only focused on the man he had just knocked over. The man had dropped the rifle, and as he slowly stood, Daniel's eyes were still adjusting to the darkness of the room. Near the window where the man had been shooting from, several more rifles lay on the ground next to him, with stacks and stacks of magazines that appeared to be for an AR-15. The room was surprisingly clean besides the broken glass and arsenal of firearms.

The man wearing the hijab was wide eyed as he reached down to pull a handgun from a holster attached to the belt he wore over his black pants. Daniel moved quickly to avoid being shot again, lunging at the man. He was able to grab the man's gun as he pulled it from the holster. Using both hands, Daniel pushed the barrel of the gun violently up and forward, hearing the man's trigger finger snap. He pulled the gun free from the man's now disfigured hand.

The man screamed incoherently while reaching for the gun with his free hand, and Daniel jumped backwards as he shot the man several times in the torso. Stumbling backwards, the man surprisingly did not fall down, but instead moved forwards again to grab the gun from Daniel's grasp. *Of course,* Daniel thought to himself. *He's wearing a bullet proof vest.* Raising his gun higher as he stepped back, Daniel lined up the front site of his gun with the space between the man's eyes and fired one more time. This time, the man fell instantly to the ground, where his body came to rest.

Daniel looked around the room for any signs of additional attackers. There was clearly no one else inside. The bathroom and closet were both empty, but he did notice that there were at least six large suitcases inside. While he couldn't be certain if the man was working alone, he also didn't want to stick around long enough for the police to show up. There was no logical explanation for what he had just done, and he would probably be arrested as a suspect if police showed up.

He walked out the door to the room, which opened into a long hallway. Running towards the elevator, he saw a sign for a stairwell and decided to go that way instead. As the door shut behind him, he ran quickly down over a dozen flights of stairs before he made it out onto the casino floor. Inside the casino, it was a strange mix of behavior from tourists.

Several security guards and other employees were running in various directions, and a few bloody people who had clearly been shot were sitting near the exit doors with medical personnel attending to them. What caught Daniel's attention were several people, some at slot machines, and some at a poker table near the middle of the room, who were playing their games as if nothing was going on around them. As one security guard ran by, a heavyset pale man in his forties, he heard the man speaking loudly into his radio. "I have had two guests now say that he is shooting from the Luxor pyramid, not the main tower." The man sounded completely out of breath.

Daniel ran out the exit where the two people were being treated for their gunshot wounds. Both of them appeared to have minor injuries, as they were sitting up talking to the paramedics. As he came outside, his eyes had to adjust to the bright sunlight. He spotted Jazmine about 30 yards away near the opening where he had left her. She was leaning over an elderly woman, with both hands on the woman's stomach. As Daniel got closer, she stood and began staggering towards another man who was lying on the ground a few feet away. She looked like she was so tired she could barely stand.

"You look exhausted." Daniel said as he approached her.

"Did you get him?" Jazmine's dark eyes were flittering open and closed as if she could barely stay conscious. "I saved eleven of them, but it was too late for the other five." She said somberly.

"Yes, he is dead." Daniel bent down to put his arm on her reassuringly but realized as he did that, he had blood dripping slowly from his arm. It wasn't gushing out like it should have been from a rifle blast, but the wound was bleeding.

Jazmine's body stiffened as she put her hands on the unconscious man's back, where blood was slowly soaking the ground from his body. A moment later she relaxed and fell down on the ground.

"That's twelve." Jazmine mumbled as she rolled slowly onto her back and sat up. Her eyes opened slowly. Suddenly concern registered on them as she looked up at Daniel. "Oh no... you're bleeding." She put her hands on Daniel's leg and stiffened, but he felt nothing as she tried to heal him.

"I don't think we can be healed." Daniel explained, his concern for her showing in his voice. "And besides, you look like you are in worse shape than me."

"Sorry" she said. "I had to try, but when I try to heal... it's like I can't even feel your injury to push my energy to it." She looked around the courtyard. "I'm sorry I'm so tired. Most of those I healed were critical, and those nasty wounds take a lot more out of me than healing small ones. I didn't even try healing those who... looked like they would… live anyways." As she finished talking, she laid back down on the ground, her eyes closing again.

In the distance, Daniel heard police sirens getting closer. From the middle of the crowd, two police officers wearing tan uniforms emerged, running into the clearing with their guns drawn but pointed to the ground. One of them was short, stout and tan and appeared completely out of breath. The taller one was slender, with a young-looking pale face and mustache. Daniel picked Jazmine up off the ground, her body was completely limp.

"Officers, there is one shooter!" Daniel called loudly to the two young policemen. "He was shooting from halfway up the pyramid, from that broken window. For some reason he stopped about two minutes ago, but I saw him look out the window just before you showed up. It looks like he is about 17 floors up. Please stop him." Daniel tried to sound scared as he remembered which floor he had come from, but it was difficult with how much adrenaline he had coursing through him.

"Thanks!" The tall officer shouted before turning the grab the chubby officer's arm. "Let's go inside and take the elevator up." The two ran into the entrance Daniel had just come out of. The taller one was talking into his shoulder mic to provide updates as they ran.

Daniel felt the pain in his left bicep where he had been shot as he ran with Jazmine in his arms. He quickly realized, after knocking several people over in the crowd, that he couldn't go very fast while carrying her in both arms, so he adjusted her body to carry her over his shoulder with her legs in front of him and his right arm holding her. With Jazmine unconscious, he wasn't worried about her complaining about being caried like a sack of potatoes. This was less painful, and with her body more on top then sideways, he knocked over less people as he moved quickly north through the crowd towards where they were parked. *Hopefully Sara and the kids are okay.* He thought to himself as he ran, trying to ignore the stabbing pain in his leg.

CHAPTER VII

I reached Sara, Tobias, and Alex at the front corner of the Bellagio property. The crowds were not moving as fast down here, probably because no one this far north had been able to hear the shooting. Coming from behind, I scooped Alex up into my arms. Sara turned with a startled expression on her face before she realized it was me and let go of Alex's hand.

"Izzie!" Alex sounded relieved as he saw it was me who grabbed him. "You're okay! Did you stop the bad man?"

"Yeah buddy." I replied, hoping he wouldn't notice the blood on my lower pant leg and shoe. "I stopped them. They won't hurt anyone else any time soon."

"Oh Liz, I am so glad you are okay." Sara squeezed my shoulder affectionately as she smiled. Her deep blue eyes painfully reminded me of Luke. I felt an unexpected jolt of sadness as I thought about the boy of my dreams. But there was no time for sadness now.

We moved quickly through the crowd. Well… not quick for me, but quick for Sara anyways. It felt almost painful slowing down enough for her to keep up. Knowing that my father and Jazmine had much more ground to cover to catch up though, I wasn't too concerned with our pace. I just hoped that they were both okay. Tobias moved alongside me, knocking over the occasional person who thought they could shove past him as we moved. Every time someone bumped into him, he didn't budge while they sometimes fell over.

As we got to the front entrance to the casino near valet, I noticed extra security personnel standing at the front doors. Several of them were talking on their radios, and they even had some armed officers with a k-9 unit from security standing off to the side. From the way they were talking on their radios, it was obvious that they knew about the shooters, even if most others around us were completely oblivious. We made our way through the crowded casino, passing a massive garden display of some sort off to one side of the casino. We had told Alex he could look at it on the way back, but that was clearly out of the question now. Flowers and plants were shaped into gargantuan objects in an artistic fashion. Some looked like tigers, foxes, or various birds. The animals were easily fifteen to twenty feet tall.

While it caught my attention as we walked, I was in no mood to enjoy the sights. The fight with the shooters still had me on edge, and I couldn't help but worry about my father. Jazmine could heal herself from just about any injury. My father though was a different story. As invincible as we were indoors or during the night, I had learned the hard way that daylight brought back our mortality.

We exited the elevator and walked over to where we had parked on the roof of the parking garage. The sound of dozens of police sirens to the South and others heading in that direction was no surprise. I set Alex in his car seat and buckled him in, to make sure we were ready to leave the moment the others arrived. Tobias climbed into the back of the car without complaining or saying a word. Sara was standing with her door open, no doubt scanning the area around us for her daughter and my father. It was remarkable to me how Sara seemed to care for Jazmine just as deeply as she did her own boys.

When I had first realized how genuine and loving she was towards her adopted daughter, it had seemed strange. But... over time I realized that sincere affection was simply a part of Sara. Luke had told me once that he thought it was her way of coping with losing her husband when he and Ben were just small children. All growing up he said that she had sang to him every night and would always tell them that she would forever love them double since they didn't have a dad.

"Are you okay Liz?" Sara said suddenly. Just then... I realized that I had tears flowing down my face.

"Yeah, I'm fine." I lied, realizing that the pain I still felt for losing Leuken Bennett was not as gone as I pretended. Wiping my tears away with my sleeves, I decided I needed to stop thinking about the boy. Even if deep down a childish part of me just hoped that he would somehow magically reappear. I knew that would never happen, so I needed to check my feelings.

"Are you hurt?" Sara asked, looking down at the blood on my pants and shoe. She took a step closer to me and softly rested a hand on my shoulder.

"No... It's not my blood" I shook my head, trying to get the tears to stop. "It's from the second attacker. I think I kicked him too hard and... well let's just say he's never going to hurt anyone again."

"Oh, you poor thing." Sara said, wrapping her arms around me as she squeezed me tight. She then pulled back slightly and put her hands on both sides of my face, looking me straight in the eyes. "You do not need to feel bad for killing one of those monsters. Taking a life to save others is not a bad thing, especially when you are saving innocent people. What you did… that makes you a hero… and you should never feel bad for that."

"This might sound bad." I said, feeling my emotions coming back strong as the tears flowed again. "But I don't even feel bad about killing those guys. It's just… I'm trying not to think about him… but I really miss him so much." I held back the uncontrollable sobbing, but I could feel my body shaking slightly as I cried quietly. Sara's eyes watered as well, and she embraced me again.

"I know Liz." I could feel her crying as well now. "I miss him too. More than anything."

We stood there hugging and crying for a good minute or so. Neither one of us saying a word… and neither one of us needing to. When she finally pulled back to let me go, I had stopped crying. Somehow… and it didn't make any sense how… I felt a little better. Maybe holding back my feelings was not the right way to heal and move on.

"Dan!" Sara suddenly shouted. I turned and saw my father running quickly across the parking lot towards us. He seemed to be limping slightly as he ran, and even more concerning was the fact that he was carrying Jazmine in his arms, her body completely limp. "Is she…" Sara trailed off without finishing as my father got close, a look of pure terror on her face.

"She's okay." He said reassuringly. "She healed a lot of people, and it took a lot out of her. But she is just sleeping."

"Oh my gosh! You're bleeding." The concern on Sara's face was palpable. "What happened?"

"I'm fine." My father said, moving to the open door and setting Jazmine down in the front passenger seat. "I just took a couple rounds when I charged at the shooter, but he only got me in the shin and arm. The bleeding has already slowed down."

I could see that his pant leg was covered in blood by the ankle, with his shoe also soaked in blood. Dried blood was visible from his hand up to just above his elbow on his left arm. A small trail of fresher red blood was also on his hand, dripping slowly to the ground.

"Let me see." Sara said, looking at the wound on his arm first. She grabbed his arm delicately just above the wound and twisted it to examine both sides. "It looks like it went clean through, judging by the two holes. We need to get you to a hospital." She gently caressed one of his cheeks with one hand as she let go of his arm, raising up on her toes to kiss him.

"No, I'm good." My dad reassured again. "But we probably should get out of here now. If anyone saw me running up the building or took a picture, the police might be looking for me and thinking that Jazmine or I are somehow involved. The sooner we get out of here the better."

"Okay but first." I said, reaching back into the car to grab out my light sweater from the front seat. "Let me put some pressure on those wounds." I ripped both sleeves off the sweater with ease, tying the first one on his arm tight, with the knot just on his wound to keep extra pressure on it. *Hopefully that will slow the bleeding.* I thought. Bending down, I rolled up his pant leg halfway up the shin, and saw the holes on the front, and in the back of his calf. As I tied my other sleeve on this wound, I noticed that this shot too appeared to have missed the bones and only hit skin and calf muscle.

After finishing his makeshift dressings, Sara helped him into the car next to Alex before stepping in herself. Without hesitation. I jumped in the front seat, noticing that there was a vibrating sound coming from Jazmine's purse that was wrapped carefully around her shoulders to her back. It must have been her phone ringing. Sara reached forward from the back seat, pulling the phone out of Jazmine's purse.

"Hello." I heard Sara say as I started to drive out of the parking garage and down the ramp.

"What do you mean don't go back to the hotel?" Sara continued after a long pause. "Isn't your truck still there?" I drove out of the parking garage exit and could see that traffic was backed up to turn right, so I decided to go left and take the north way back to the freeway. I could only imagine how bad the traffic was to the south.

"Who? Who would do such a thing?" Sara sounded extremely concerned as she asked. "The entire Romany gypsy clan?" Whoever was on the other end of the phone spoke at length before Sara replied again.

"So only the three survived? How old are the girls?" I could see Sara shaking her head in disbelief through the rear-view mirror as she spoke.

"Well, I hope they know they are welcome to stay with us." Sara continued. "Okay, well then, we will get your truck and meet you at the hotel in Arizona. Thanks Isaac. I am glad you are all okay." Sara hung up the phone and reached forward to put it back in Jazmine's purse.

"Isaac said that the Romany gypsy clan was attacked by more of the same people that killed Luke." Sara said, her eyes watering with grief. "They were ambushed while driving, and they killed almost all of them. Even the women and children... were brutally murdered. Luckily Isaac, Ben, the African clan and some of the Australian clan were warned by the light, so they were able to get there in time to save a man and two children."

"I'm sorry Sara." My father tried to comfort her. "Did you know them?"

"No... I had never met them, but I know they were a decent sized clan, with nearly a dozen bloodlines besides other normal family members. It is so sad." Sara turned back to my father. "How are you feeling?" She asked after a long pause.

"I'm okay." My father replied. "Just glad we were in town today to be able to stop that shooter."

"Do you know who it was?" Sara asked. "The shooter that is. Was it just some crazy person or what?"

"Judging by my shooter looking Persian and wearing a Hijab, I think this must have been a coordinated terrorist attack." My father said convincingly. "I heard there was another shooter at another hotel, so the police must have taken that one out."

"The two shooters I took out were middle eastern as well." I said, glancing in the rear-view mirror as I turned on the main road, barely moving as traffic seemed to inch along. At least it was moving. That was more than I could say about the other side of the road. Loud honks gave away the frustration of people who were stuck in the opposing lanes of traffic, completely stopped.

"What shooters that you took out?" My father raised his voice and went into his disapproving parent mode. "I told you to get them straight back to the car! What happened?"

"I was taking them straight back to the car." I answered defensively. "But when two guys started killing people right in front of me, what was I supposed to do? Run away and let them die?" I was not at all in the mood for a lecture from my father. If anything, I deserved a high five more than a scolding.

"She was incredible." Sara chimed in. "Alex was safe with me and Tobias while she stopped them."

"Look dad. I only left Sara and Alex for about a minute to stop those guys, and if I hadn't, a lot more people would be dead right now." I continued. "I caught back up in a couple of minutes, and I have stayed with them since. I ordered Tobias to protect them."

"I'm sorry Liz." My dad said thoughtfully. "I'm proud of you kid. I just worry about you sometimes, that's all. Sounds like it was some kind of Mumbai style attack. We used to train for those active shooter scenarios when I was still a cop back in Portland. The kind where multiple shooters work together to cause more chaos and death."

"Must be the bloodline curse." I added. "Luke said that just being a bloodline makes it more likely that bad people will do bad things when you are around."

"Isaac said he thinks it is the light's way of putting bloodlines in the right place to stop bad things from happening, but who knows. I'm just glad everyone from our families is okay." Sara said, wrapping one of her arms around my father to pull him in close for a kiss on the cheek. "Now let's get back to the hotel. Once we get Isaac's truck, we will head to Arizona for the new rendezvous spot."

*   *   *

Detective Jimenti hit rewind again on the computer so that he could play the surveillance footage from the school lunchroom again. It was difficult to make out the kid's face with this camera, but he watched as the kid moved superhumanly fast from person to person, putting his hands on each of them as he went. He had already interviewed all the kids involved whose parents would let them talk. While many of them said they only remember being shot and then passing out, the strange part was, none of those ones had any injuries at all. Their clothes had had holes in them, and they had all been bloody, but none of them had any indication from looking at their skin that they had even been shot. "I think he somehow healed them." He mused quietly to himself, as he watched the video again for the sixth time. "That's the only thing that explains everything, even if it doesn't make logical sense."

"Hey Mike." Agent Valdez said as he poked his head in the office. "Stop talking to yourself and get out here. This news is crazy. You gotta see this."

Mike stood up quickly as he paused the video, walking out of his office and into the bull pen area in the middle of the building. About a dozen people were huddled in small groups in front of the large TV, watching the news. The caption on the screen said *Terror in Nevada: Strip shooting leaves 7 dead, dozens injured.* At the bottom of the screen another line read: *Vehicle accident and road rage incident kills 26 people near Overton, Nevada.*

"Someone hit pause." Detective Jimenti said loudly as he studied the video that was playing. It was being shot from above a desert highway, likely by the news helicopter and the scene looked like something right out of a horror movie. Multiple cars were smashed or parked scattered throughout the road, with several dozen bodies spread around the vehicles. It appeared that police had thrown yellow blankets over some of the bodies but ran out before they were able to cover everyone.

"What is it, Mike?" Agent Valdez said as he hit pause on the TV remote.

Detective Jimenti walked up to the television, pointing at two of the bodies that were uncovered. It was difficult to make out the figures, but from this close to the TV two things were clear. "Notice what's missing from those guys dressed in all black?" He said, looking Valdez in the eyes before scanning the rest of the room. Some of the other Agents and Task Force Officers seemed mildly annoyed, but others were clearly interested as they nodded. "They got no heads. And it's hard to make out in the video, but I bet if we could zoom in more, those little black curved objects next to them are probably swords."

Holy crap!" Valdez said loudly. "You think this is related to our case from Harrisburg?"

"It's gotta be." Jimenti replied. "How fast can we all be on a plane to Vegas?"

*   *   *

"What do you mean they are all dead?" Priscilla asked, her eyes so full of the fury that she barely kept it from her voice. "You told me the family they were tracking only had six to eight bloodlines at most? With the ambush tactics they were going to use on the road, there is no reason they should not have easily dealt with that clan!" Her voice had raised to almost a screech as she finished.

"Our last man, before he was killed, he said that someone else had come to help. Other clans ambushed their ambush." Silas tried to keep his voice calm, but it was difficult when he too was so upset. He stroked his beard without thinking as he continued. "He said at least half a dozen more had come, from at least two different clans. These were skilled fighters too, each of them as talented with the sword as our best."

"How... is this possible?" Priscilla said as she sat down and ran her hands anxiously through her hair. Silas knew she didn't usually do that when she was angry. She did that when she was afraid. She must have come to the same conclusion that Silas had.

"If Alastair thinks that we cannot tame the bloodlines with our crews." Silas mused out loud. "Then he will likely nullify our deal and have us killed." He was only standing about six feet from Priscilla, but when he looked down at her, he could see the fear in her eyes. She was actually much more pretty when scared than during her frequent angered expression, Silas thought to himself. It almost made him want to help her, in spite of the bracelet forcing him to.

"We need to pull another crew from the offsite. Let's go heavy and pull a couple of our best trainers with the fighters who are most competent. I want eighteen from there to supplement a twelve-person crew." Her fear was turning to determined resolve as she spoke her plan out loud. "If they were able to defeat our men with only half a dozen people, we must overwhelm them with numbers. We will crush these bloodlines and restore balance before Alastair or his cronies are forced to move against us."

"As you command my lady." Silas said, turning to pick up his phone from where he had left it sitting on the dais near his chair. "I will have them on a chartered flight within the hour. They can do their tactical brief in the air. I will also divert the Colorado crew. They were supposed to fly back tonight anyways, so I will fly them to meet our other group instead."

"Was there any mention of the other Auserwhalt?" Priscilla asked suddenly.

"No." Silas replied. He didn't think these crews were related, but it was strange to have two separate crews defeated in a matter of weeks. Prior to these incidents, the most they had ever lost in a single raid from one of their crews was five. Now they had lost ten and twelve, respectively. "I see no reason to believe these groups are related."

"Good." Priscilla nodded and stood back up. "Do you think we can find them again?"

"Oh, I certainly think we can." Silas added. "They made a crucial error after dispatching our crew. We will make sure they pay for it." Priscilla smiled mischievously, her dark eyes glistening from the reflection of the fireplace.

CHAPTER VIII

"Is it this exit or the next one?" I asked Jazmine as we passed by the green sign on the freeway. I had never even heard of Prescott Arizona, but after driving for several hours, I was happy to have almost reached our destination.

"It's this one coming up." Jazmine replied while looking at the GPS on her phone. She still looked tired, but after sleeping for the last few hours while I drove, the color in her face was back. She had also taken down several granola bars and trail mix packs when she first woke up. It was weird that her and Ben could eat so much and stay so skinny. "Sorry that you had to drive. I was just exhausted from healing all those people. And I always get so hungry after healing."

Alex was asleep in the back seat, and through the rear-view mirror, I could see my father and Sara following a few car lengths back in Isaac's truck. As I pulled off the highway into the small town, I was impressed by how green everything was. For some reason, in my mind I had always pictured Arizona as being nothing but desert. The last few towns we had passed through on the highway had proven me wrong. Various green trees and other vegetation covered the hilly countryside, and I had spotted several dears and other wildlife while driving.

Jazmine guided me a couple of miles from the highway towards the edge of town. The small hotel we parked in front of could not have held more than twenty rooms, but it was far enough from the freeway so as not to alarm any bloodlines with terralium weapons or rings who would show up for round two of the clan meeting. The motel had a brown and green log shaped exterior, and was set towards the bottom of a small, wooded hill. While small, the paint on the buildings appeared fresh, and the landscaping around the building was well kept.

As I pulled into the parking lot of the motel, I observed the Bennett's silver hummer, as well as a few other cars that I did not recognize. Parking next to their hummer, I put the car in park.

"Time to wake up Alex." I said loudly as I turned to look back at my younger brother. Alex was sitting with his head laying sideways against the seat, his stuffed animal clutched in both arms while he breathed heavily.

"Oh." Jazmine said, looking back at Alex as well. "Poor little guy must be tired. He's out cold."

At this point we might as well let him sleep. I thought to myself. As I stepped out of the car to get Alex, I saw movement off to my right. It couldn't possibly be, I thought as my eyes settled on the people emerging from the motel. Isaac and Ben were standing next to a short man, a teenage girl, and another young girl even smaller than Alex, but it wasn't they who had my attention.

"Luke!?" I heard Jazmine shout incredulously as she shut her door. "Oh my gosh is that really you?!" She was still shouting excitedly as she ran up to her adopted brother and gave him a big hug, lifting him slightly off the ground. Luke smiled as they embraced, but I noticed that he was staring directly at me. His eyes were actually watering for some reason.

My mind almost shut down. How could this be? Less than twenty feet away, the man of my dreams, who I was sure had died in the explosion back in Harrisburg, was somehow standing. I pinched myself intentionally as I took in his dark hair and ridiculously blue eyes. His strong jaw and dimpled cheeks as he smiled… although he looked sad for some reason, despite the smile he spared for Jazmine. His long-sleeved blue sweater only accentuated his broad shoulders and muscular chest and arms. I couldn't help but notice his hair was longer than usual, and the stubble on his chin and cheeks made it appear that he had not shaved in a few days.

"Luke?" I said out loud as my body came unfrozen. "Luke." I ran without thinking up to him, reaching him just as Jazmine set him down. As I grabbed around his waist to embrace him and pulled him in close, I couldn't help but notice the hesitation in the way he hugged me. It felt like he was holding back somewhat. Like he didn't even want to hug me.

"Hey Liz." He said casually as he tried to let go of me. I kept hugging, feeling the tears coming down my face. It made no sense that I would have tears, as I could not remember ever feeling such overwhelming joy and relief in my entire life. He was really here this time! Not just my imagination.

"I can't believe you are alive." I said as I buried my head in his chest. He pulled back suddenly, surprising me.

"What's wrong?" I asked looking up at him.

"You are really going to act like nothing happened?" Luke replied. He glanced briefly down at me, but mostly looked away as he spoke. A couple of tears rolled down his cheeks, but they did not look like happy tears.

"What are you talking about?" I said confused, trying to keep the concern out of my voice. "I'm just happy you are alive. I thought for sure I had lost you."

"Maybe we should talk privately." Luke replied, looking around at all the people in proximity. He motioned towards the other side of the motel, away from everyone and began walking that way.

"Okay… sure." I started to follow him as my father and Sara pulled into a parking spot next to my Tahoe.

"What is wrong Luke?" I asked as we reached the other side of the motel, out of earshot from the others. There were a thousand other things spinning through my mind. Like how did he survive? Where had he been? How come he wasn't at the rendezvous spot? Before we could get to any of that though, I had to know why he was so upset with me.

"You think I don't know?" Luke said condescendingly.

"Don't know what Luke?" I replied, utterly confused. "I honestly have no idea what you are talking about. Why are you mad at me?"

"I saw you two kissing Liz." Luke looked away from me, but I could see tears flowing from his eyes and dripping off his chin. "I wasn't even gone three days and you were already kissing my little brother. How could you do something so messed up?"

"What are you…" I trailed off as I realized what he meant. It hit me suddenly, memories flashing back from a week before. The snowstorm when Ben had tried to kiss me on the front porch at the mansion in Idaho. At the time I thought for sure I had seen Leuken Bennett walking towards me in the snowstorm. So, I hadn't been hallucinating… Luke was really there. "Oh my gosh, it was you! I thought that I had just imagined seeing you, but you came to the mansion, didn't you?"

"Yes." Leuken replied. "I mean I knew you were too good to be true... but I just... I guess I was dumb enough to think you were as into me as I was you. I mean I know I was a jerk when you first got changed, but in my defense, I thought you were possessed by some evil demon. I thought we were past that and happily in love... Obviously, I was wrong."

I laughed suddenly, as I realized how wrong Luke was. Just not in the way he thought. He thought that I was romantic with his little brother Ben? The thought was funny, in spite of how upsetting it was. I smiled up at him, as he glanced quickly down at me, his sad expression turning to surprise.

"Are you laughing at me now?" He sounded confused.

"Oh my gosh, Leuken Bennett. You know I love you." I said, grabbing his face as I stopped laughing. "I didn't kiss Ben. He..."

"Liz, I saw you kissing. You can't..." Luke interjected, but his anger seemed to already be dissipating. His stubborn side was showing through.

"No." I cut him off, putting one finger up to his lips. I wasn't going to let this silly boy being confused ruin the fact that the love of my life was still alive. "Hear me out and then you can talk. You saw Ben kiss me. If you had kept watching, you would have also seen me push him away so hard that he almost fell over. I didn't kiss back. In fact, had he not been holding my head in place, his lips wouldn't have even got to mine. The whole thing was a complete surprise, which is why my guard was down. I thought I had seen you in the snow and was distracted. After pushing him away, I went to where you had been standing. When you weren't there, I thought I had been hallucinating or something.

"Later that night Ben apologized for forcing a kiss on me, and I told him to never do that again. Since then, we have been good. He knows I don't care for him in that way, and he has not even tried to get fresh with me again. There is no way he would have tried that if he had known you were still alive. Okay?" I moved my hand to caress the side of his face. His facial hair was just long enough to not be rough, but I still wasn't a huge fan. Now was not the time to tell him that though, so I bit my tongue. "So why don't you worry less about your silly little brother and kiss me already?"

"Luke!" Sara's voice interrupted what was about the be the perfect moment. I guess it wouldn't be fair to fault a mom for being excited to see her son that she thought was dead, but I was still slightly annoyed. "You're alive!" She shouted as I heard her running up behind me.

"Mom!" Luke smiled at his mother, obviously still processing what I had said. I stepped to the side so he could hug her. I wasn't about to get in the way of a mom and her kid, even if I wanted to kiss the boy so bad it hurt. The relief and joy at seeing him alive still felt surreal. I worried that any moment I would wake back up to the cold dark reality that he was still dead.

Luke picked his mom up in the air as they hugged. "I am so glad you're okay!" Sara said excitedly. Her eyes watered as well. The relief and happiness on her face was unmasked as they embraced. After a long moment Sara spoke again. "Why didn't you meet us at the rendezvous spot?"

"I would have mom, but unfortunately, I was buried underneath the rubble below the house. When I finally escaped as they dug it out with the excavator, I was followed by a couple of those guys in all black. They followed me for hours, so I led them to a crowded city in Utah, just to be sure there were only two of them. I was able to ambush and kill one, while injuring the other, but by then it had already been almost two days. Once I saw the sign for the clan meeting on the news, I decided to play it safe and avoid attention until the meet in Logandale." Luke explained.

"Well, I'm just happy to see you alive." Sara pulled back slightly, smiling up at her son. He was almost a full foot taller than her, as she was slightly shorter than me. "Oh, and whatever this thing is about you thinking there is something going on between Liz and Ben, you need to stop. Liz has been heartbroken since she thought you died, and Ben even told me he felt stupid for hitting on her when he knows she doesn't like him. Believe me son, you are the only one she cares about in that way."

Luke looked at me and smiled, then looked back at his mother. He seemed to have processed everything that we had said and was coming to grips with the fact that I was not a cheating hussy who jumped into his brother's arms at the first hint that he was gone. I found it curious that he left out the part about coming to the mansion and seeing me in Idaho, but it seemed like he was just saving face.

"Now you know I don't like to be too bossy. I raised you good enough that I don't have to micromanage every little thing you do." She smiled again, stepping back and gently pulling his arm so that his body turned to face me. "But if you don't stop worrying and kiss that girl, you are gonna be in big trouble. Now I'll leave you two alone."

She turned to walk away, and Luke stared at me again. His smile faded slightly to include a look of sheepishness. From the redness that suddenly flushed his cheeks, I could tell that he felt stupid. I thought about saying something funny to mess with him, but instead I just walked up to him until I was less than a foot from his face.

"I'm sorry for doubting you." He said, nervously looking down at his feet as he hung his head slightly. "It's just, when I saw you kiss, I thought that…"

I cut him off as I reached up and pulled his lips down to mine. All of the coldness that had built up in my heart over the past few days suddenly melted away. The ice replaced by a burning fire I could only describe as pure joy. As we kissed, knowing that his and my family were all watching us, I probably enjoyed it a little too much, but I didn't care. Leuken was back. He was really back. Nothing else in the world mattered to me in that moment. At some point while we kissed, he picked me up and held me closer. After several more seconds went by, and I started feeling like I needed to get him somewhere private, Luke reluctantly set me down and pulled his lips from mine.

"Isn't that better?" I said, smiling mischievously as I leaned in for another hug, burying my head in his chest.

"Yes ma'am. Much better." He held me close, and a long while went by with us just holding each other in silence. It felt so good. I almost worried I was dreaming, but this was too real.

"Ahumm." My father cleared his throat loudly as he approached with Alex. "Luke, I'm glad to see you're okay kid." He moved forward and extended his hand to shake it. "As much as I sometimes don't like Liz having a boyfriend, I'm not gonna lie. She scared me a bit when she thought she lost you."

"Thank you, Mr. Scott." Luke replied with a smile, shaking my father's hand. "It's good to be back with the family and you guys. As much as I sometimes don't like you dating my mom. I'm glad you make her happy." Luke's smile broadened as he finished.

My dad let go of Luke's hand with a somewhat surprised expression. Nodding thoughtfully. "Not bad kid. You got some balls on you... but I like that. You're gonna need those if you wanna survive my daughter. She's a strong-willed kid."

"Luke!" Alex interrupted, running in between my father and Luke. He wrapped his arms around his legs, squeezing tightly as Luke reached down to hug him back with one arm. "I thought the bad mans died you, but I'm glad you okay."

"Hey buddy." Luke smiled, glancing between my father and me. The happy glint I was used to seeing was back in his eyes. "It would take a lot more than a silly bomb to kill me."

"So, what's with the midget and the two girls?" My father asked, turning back to face the group.

"Dad, you aren't supposed to call them midgets. It's rude." I chided with my voice lowered.

"Sorry." He shrugged defensively. "What's with the short guy and the two girls then? Is that better?" I shook my head as he finished.

We all started walking back towards the others. As we approached, I noticed that the shorter man my father had called a midget was a few inches shorter than me. He was probably only a couple inches shy of five feet, with a broad build for how short he was. His skin was a darker complexion than the two girls, but they had some similar features.

The girls on the other hand, were both pale and skinny, with high cheekbones that framed pretty faces. The first was a couple of inches taller than me, with long blonde hair and beautiful brown eyes. She wore a pink sweater pulled overtop a black silky dress with fancy strips of dark cloth hanging from the bottom hem just above the knees. The younger girl had dark hair, with big brown eyes, and wore a yellow dress. While she only stood a couple inches shorter than Alex, she had more of a baby face.

The older girl was standing very close to Ben, their elbows touching slightly as if she was scared to leave his side. She grinned cautiously as I approached. The younger girl was clinging to the short man and turned to bury her head against his leg as we got closer. As I studied him further, he looked almost Dominican, but with lighter skin than other Dominicans I had met. My father's old partner Saul, who used to come over for barbeques back in Portland had been Dominican as well. His skin had been much darker than this man's.

"Hey everyone, this is Liz Scott, her father Daniel and her little brother Alex. I don't want you to have a 'tainted' opinion of any of them, so I wanted to let you know they are good people." Ben said grinning. He gave me a quick hug before continuing. "Liz this is Haysom Fitch, Kezia Shaw, and Trinity Shaw." He pointed first to the short man, then the teenage girl, and lastly the young one.

We took turns shaking each other's hands and exchanging pleasantries, but Trinity was too shy to shake anyone's hand. It wasn't until Alex walked up to her and started talking that she finally loosened her grip on Haysom.

"Let's head inside. I reserved us the entire motel besides the two rooms an older couple had already occupied and booked us the banquet hall for a private party all weekend." Isaac said after a couple of minutes had passed with us talking. Everyone seemed excited about Luke being back, but it was awkward and somewhat heartbreaking to know that the three newcomers had just lost almost everyone they knew and loved. Their entire family had been wiped out in a matter of minutes.

We all walked inside, with Isaac handing out several room keys. In short order, I learned that Haysom and the Shaw's were sharing a room, an idea that became less weird when I learned that he was Trinity's half-brother and Kezia's cousin. I was also surprised to learn that he was in his fifties. He didn't look a day older than 25 at the most.

My father and I were sharing a room with Alex. Sara and Jazmine had a room, and Luke was staying with Ben. Hopefully that would be less awkward now that Luke knew Ben had not stolen me away from him. The very thought of it was still hilarious to me… and kind of gross.

CHAPTER IX

Detective Jimenti stood on the side of the highway with his flashlight, examining the body on the ground in front of him. He felt a slight chill whenever the cool breeze picked up, even with his black coat and pants on. The body, dressed in all black like most of the others they had seen, was unremarkable for the most part. Another younger Hispanic male with no driver's license or other identification. Unlike the others, who had all been decapitated for unknown reasons, this one was different. His head was still missing, but instead of a clean cut through the neck, this man's head had been completely obliterated.

Jimenti had seen victims with their heads blown off before, but never anything like this. Most of the time, when someone was shot in the head and killed, even with a high-powered rifle, it was easy to see where the round had impacted the head, and the destruction was through the middle and back where the round and force of the impact had blown that portion of the head to pieces. In the case of this man, the head appeared completely exploded, as if it had been blown up from the inside.

As he knelt to examine what remained of the neck, he was struck by two observations. The first was that there was some flesh in the upper neck that appeared to have been burnt somehow, with blackened residue consistent with an explosive of some sort being used. The second was that on the right side of the man's neck was a small yet very clear tattoo of a sun. Jimenti had been a gangs detective for several years before joining the Joint Terrorism Task Force, also referred to as the JTTF. He had never seen a sun tattoo on the neck like this one before, except on one of the bodies back in Harrisburg. That one had also had a sun tattoo, identical in size, on the same portion of the neck.

"Hey Gil!" Mike called to Special Agent Valdez, who was examining another body about thirty feet away in the dirt. As Valdez got closer, he continued. "Take a look at this. This guy has the same tattoo as the one back in Harrisburg. Have you ever seen this kind before?"

"Nope." Valdez responded shrugging. "Except on that guy right there." He pointed to the body he had just been looking at.

Jimenti shined his light back on the neck. "What the heck do you think caused this?" He thought out loud to his partner. "At first, I thought he had been shot in the head, but I don't see an entry or exit wound. It looks like this guy's head was exploded from the inside. This whole thing just keeps getting crazier and crazier."

"Oh yeah." Valdez bent down to look closer at the remains. "You can see the burnt portions of the flesh. I think you are right."

"That analyst team you said was set up in the command post in Vegas." Jimenti added. "Can you send them a picture of the tattoo's and have them do a workup? See if they can find any gangs or other criminal enterprises with these specific tattoos?"

"Yeah, no problem. I'll call my girl right now." Valdez replied, pulling out his phone.

Jimenti walked over to the body off the side of the road that his partner had pointed to. As he got closer, he noticed that this one had not just been decapitated like most of the rest. Whoever had cut this man up, had done a brutal job of it. The man's head and part of his neck was attached to a shoulder and arm lying next to the rest of the body, but a part of one leg had been sliced off, and the other arm was also cut off just below the shoulder, lying a couple feet away on the other side of the body.

He could not decide if the man had been tortured to death, or if this was just the result of some brutal sword fight. Remembering the scene from Harrisburg, he had seen an unknown person's arm lying in the road next to one of the cars. That arm had not belonged to any of the other bodies they had found, at least not according to the DNA comparisons that had been rushed through the lab. At the time he had thought perhaps it had belonged to one of the Bennett boys or the Liz girl's father, but it had the same long sleeve black material that the other attackers had worn.

"Hey Mike. You're not gonna believe this." Valdez said as he hung up the phone and walked back towards him. He was holding up his black cell phone, which had a picture pulled up on the front. "I just got this from my analyst at the CP. It's a still shot from surveillance footage of the unknown person who we think killed two of the shooters in Las Vegas. Look familiar to you?"

Mike looked closely at the phone as Valdez stopped. The picture quality on the phone was a little blurry, but it wasn't hard for Mike to recognize the girl in the picture.

"What the..." Mike trailed off as his brain began turning quickly. He was struggling badly to make sense of any of this. "What the heck is Elizabeth Scott doing in downtown Las Vegas, and who are those men?"

The picture showed a girl that looked just like the girl from Harrisburg who had stopped the shooter at the school. She was standing on the roof of a structure, with two men lying on the ground near her. Both appeared dead. Neither of them were wearing the black clothes that the bodies in front of him all had on though.

"Hey Gil. I thought that shooting and this massacre happened at roughly the same time?" Jimenti asked.

"Yeah, they were within minutes according to surveillance on the strip and the 9-1-1 call we received from the first driver on this scene." Valdez replied.

"And it's about an hour drive from here to there, right?"

"Yeah." Valdez replied. "Give or take."

"Was the boy from the school with the girl?" Jimenti was rubbing his bald forehead with one hand as he thought.

"You mean the Luke Bennett kid? No. I asked the analyst. She said the only ones seen with the Scott girl before she took out those shooters bare handed, was a young kid, her father, the Bennett mom, and an Asian girl described similar to the one who was living with the Bennetts." Valdez explained. "And to make matters worse, you probably won't believe this, but my girl said surveillance showed the girl jumping a solid fifteen feet in the air, getting up to the shooters on the roof in Vegas. I don't think we are dealing with a normal teenager here."

*   *   *

"I was somewhat disheartened that only four of the clans wanted to help." Isaac began as he entered the large conference room we were sitting in at the motel. "Considering half a dozen clans from Overton didn't even come to Arizona after the ambush on the Gypsies, I shouldn't be surprised. But two other clans said that they would think on it and reach out once they talked to the rest of their people. I am optimistic that the Danish clan will help, but not so much for the Boston clan or the French. Based on their questioning, they are not convinced that we will win. The French have always had their own best interests at heart."

"Did they say how many they will bring?" Ben asked. He was sitting at the large dining table on the other side of Luke from me. Kezia was seated next to him. After cleaning up and putting fresh clothes on that Jazmine had let her have, I was surprised at how pretty the Romany girl was. Though pale and even skinnier than I was, her large eyes, long eyelashes and high cheek bones framed her face quite nicely. She still had a stunned expression on her face. Little Trinity was sitting on her lap, her head draped over one shoulder as she had fallen asleep. The meeting had gone slightly longer than expected, as they had started at noon, and it was almost dinner time now.

"Why don't you ask them yourselves?" Isaac replied to Ben smiling. He turned to the open doorway behind him, as others filed into the room. The first was a tall black man, with a strong jaw and muscular build. He was followed by a tall, pretty girl, with lighter skin, perfect complexion but similar features, and two other men. One was short and muscular with darker skin, while the other was as tall as Metemba, but with light brown skin and a skinny build like the girl.

"Hello." The first man said with a South African accent. "I am Metemba, son of Juma, of the Abedayo clan. This is my sister Shawnee, and my brothers Kwame and Zane." He gestured first at the girl, followed by the short stocky man, and finished with the tall skinny boy. Metemba smiled, but it appeared somewhat forced as he looked slowly around the room. When he looked at Jazmine, his smile faded for a split second, before returning as he continued taking everyone in.

Kwame had a serious and somewhat mistrusting expression on his face, while Zane and Shawnee both smiled broadly. Behind the African clan, several other people entered the room. The second group was from Australia. Jacob, their leader, who looked suspiciously similar to Isaac, was not surprisingly introduced as his brother. His companion, a pale English man named Jarvis, carried himself as somewhat stuck up, but was polite and formal in his introductions.

The next group, who introduced themselves as the Shinzu clan, were from Japan. Their clan leader, Hinata, was only a few inches taller than me, and about the same height as his two sons. He introduced them as Akira and Akari, while Akira's son Hiroshi was introduced last. He appeared much younger than the others. Only Akira and Hiroshi smiled when they were introduced. Akari only nodded with a cautious expression on his face. As he looked around the room, he seemed to pause for a bit longer when his eyes took me and my father in. Hinata's face showed signs of aging, and his grayish white hair certainly didn't make him look any younger. The others in his party all had dark hair and brown eyes.

As their introductions were concluding, the fourth clan that had agreed to help filed in behind the others. Devansh introduced himself first. He was average height and build, with a heavy Indian accent that made him somewhat difficult to understand. Next, he introduced his two sons, Darsh and Aurush. Darsh had the same dark tan as his father, with a large forehead and wide nose. He was certainly the less handsome of the two brothers, and his already balding scalp didn't help in that arena. Aurush was mildly handsome, with normal features that only slightly resembled his brother. As they spoke, I noticed that their English was much easier to understand than when their father spoke.

Isaac then went around the room introducing everyone. I noticed that when my father was introduced, several of the bloodlines looked at him like he had some kind of disease. It was obvious that they had reservations about the three of us Verdorben. After Jazmine's introduction I noticed that Metemba's eyes kept lingering back over to her, even as others were introduced. I waved and smiled when Isaac said my name, feeling awkward when everyone's eyes seemed to stay on me longer than they had the others.

Considering that many of them had lost loved ones to our kind, I suppose it was reasonable why they would be skeptical of us. If I were in their shoes, I would probably feel the same way. Maybe it was just because I had been raised by a Cop, but I felt generally skeptical of most people until I got to know them. I suddenly noticed Luke was smiling at me again, and I squeezed his hand softly as I smiled back.

"What is it?" People had begun mingling and shaking hands, so I had to lean close to his ear and speak up to be heard over the moderate clamor of voices.

"Nothing." He said, his smile broadening as we just stared into each other's eyes. "Am I not allowed to check out my amazingly beautiful girlfriend?"

"You are." I said smiling. "But don't think you can foist those gorgeous blue eyes on me and not kiss me." I moved my lips towards his but stopped a couple inches short. He closed the gap, and it was a few seconds before I reluctantly pulled away. My blood felt warm as my heart was pounding. "I wish none of these people were here." I added.

"Me too." He said as he looked back around the room. "But I am glad we will be stopping the people who almost killed me. Our people should not have to live in fear of being killed by their own kind. The Verdorben are bad enough."

I raised my eyes questioningly, and Luke quickly corrected himself. "I mean the bad ones. Obviously not you or your father." He reassured.

"Good." I smiled again, tapping one finger on his chest playfully as I spoke. "Because you are not allowed to be mean to me ever again Leuken Bennett. Okay?"

"You have my word, Elizabeth Scott. I really am sorry for being an idiot" He said placing his right hand over his heart. His smile was so contagious. We kissed again, and I stood up, grabbing his hand to pull him away from the crowd. We stepped past Ben and Kezia, and I noticed she was laughing softly at something he had said, her younger cousin still sleeping on her shoulder. If I didn't know better, I would say the two appeared smitten with each other. It was the first time I had seen the girl laugh. But then again, Ben did have a way with helping people feel comfortable. If it wasn't his cheesy jokes, there was just something about the boy that made everyone feel at ease.

I was happy to see Kezia laugh. The girl had said very little when I tried talking to her earlier, but I couldn't even imagine what she must be going through. I had been devastated when I lost my mother in a tragic car accident. Had I lost both parents at the same time, it would have been too much to bear. I was proud of the girl for keeping it together like she had so far.

"Where are you two lovebirds going?" Haysom Fitch said suddenly. I hadn't noticed him slip in between Luke and me. He was standing very close. "Something tells me your pops wouldn't be too happy if he knew you were sneaking off to his room, eh?" He smiled while raising his eyebrows.

"What are you talking about?" I said defensively as I noticed myself blush. "We were just going out for some fresh air."

"Right." The short man rolled his eyes, and then chuckled. "I was just messing with ya. Oh, young love." He laughed again loudly, before turning and walking the other way through the room. I found it peculiar that the man could be so jovial and boisterous when his entire family, besides his half-sister, had all been slaughtered. I also found it strange that Haysom seemed barely interested in the wellbeing of his little sister. Perhaps he just wasn't a kid person.

I saw Jazmine standing on the other end of the room, in the direction Haysom was walking. She had the taller Asian boy and the better-looking Indian man talking to her, but did not appear overly interested in either, judging by the expression on her face. I smiled at her, and she shot me a quick look that said *help me* but continued talking to the boys. Just before Luke and I made it to the exit, I heard an English sounding voice from just behind me and turned.

"You must be Elizabeth Scott." The man who had introduced himself as Jarvis was standing next to Isaac's brother, the two studying me intently.

"Yes I am." I replied, smiling. It was hard not to show my annoyance. I didn't particularly like large crowds, and it was especially awkward when I could tell that half of the room just wanted to study me. I couldn't tell if they viewed me as some kind of Frankenstein like monster, or perhaps an endangered species of some sort they were curious to learn more about. Either way, it was more attention than I liked, so I was anxious to get outside with Luke where we could talk more without the loudness and distractions of the room. "And you must be… it was Jarvis, right?" I asked.

"Yes, yes I am." He replied. "Jacob and I were just talking about you, and I was wondering if you would oblige us by answering a few quick questions?"

"Certainly." I spared a quick glance at Luke, who had stopped next to me and was quietly observing the two men as they spoke. He must not have been quite as anxious as I was to leave, as he didn't seem the least annoyed by the two men. "What is it you wanted to know?"

"Well, you see." Jarvis continued. "Isaac told us about your intriguing ability to sense the other Verdorben. He said you can sense them long before our terralium metal heats up, from miles away. I was curious, do you know exactly how far you can sense them from?"

"To be honest I have never tested it, but before we captured Tobias, I could sense him from several hundred miles away." I paused thoughtfully. "I imagine my range is about that."

"Very well." Jarvis continued. "I was also told that when you are exposed to sunlight, you are not impenetrable. That even simple bullets or common metal can pierce your skin. Is that only in direct sunlight, or does indirect sun affect you as well?"

"It's hard to say." I explained. "I know I am weaker in the full sunlight and can be hurt easier. The indirect sunlight definitely affects me as well, just not to the same extent."

"I see." Jarvis said, his mind appearing distracted suddenly. "And lastly. We know the Verdorben all have the ability to compel others to do what they say. Have you used this ability?"

"Yes." I paused thoughtfully. "But only once. It was on a police officer. I used it to get him to leave us alone after I fought with and captured the tainted one Tobias. We were all bloody and there were smashed cars and a whole big mess. Knowing from my father's job how that's not something cops are just gonna give you a warning for, I used it so we could escape." I motioned towards Tobias with my head as I finished explaining. He was sitting on a chair in the corner of the room, reading a book. I didn't doubt he was merely attempting to avoid conversation with anyone else. The man was strange in normal situations.

"Have you ever tried using it on another member of the bloodline?" Jarvis followed up.

"No." I replied. "I didn't think it worked on members of the bloodline. Does it?"

"Thank you, Elizabeth." Jarvis suddenly seemed disinterested in the conversation.

"No problem." I said, smiling again. Luke had told me it would help them see that I was not evil, but it still felt forced. "Oh, and you can just call me Liz. Elizabeth is only what my father calls me when I am in trouble."

"As you wish, Liz." Jarvis added before turning back towards Jacob. Jacob had not said a word the whole time, but he did half smile before turning and walking away with the English sounding Australian man.

We finally made it out of the room and into the hallway, and I pulled Luke down the short hallway and out the side exit to the building. I had the same thing on my mind the whole night before, and it wasn't until now that I had worked up the courage to talk about it. On the side of the hotel, there was a bench made from large tree logs. A small path led up a slight hill from the bench into the forest about ten yards away. I stopped at the bench but was too nervous to sit down.

"Hey." Luke said as I stopped and turned to face him. "What are we doing out here?"

"Well, I needed to talk to you about something important." I reached up and ran my hand across his cheek and through the hair above his ear. I was glad he had shaved his face, but his hair probably needed to be cut too. Not that it made him any less hot, I just wasn't a fan of long hair. "And I didn't want to talk in there with all these strange new people I just met in a crowded room."

"What is it..." He paused mid-sentence, dipping his head down to kiss me briefly. "That you wanted to talk about Elizabeth?" He smiled teasingly.

"Stop." I replied playfully, gently smacking his chest with my left hand. I had to be very gentle so as not to knock him backwards as I had the last time I tried to lightheartedly tap him. "Am I in trouble or something?"

"No." He answered. "I just think you have a beautiful name, and I like saying it. Is that okay?"

"Actually..." I paused thoughtfully. "When you say it, I don't mind. But I am bias. I happen to love listening to you talk no matter what you say."

"Well good." He added. "Because even though I have never been as much of a talker as Ben or Jazmine are, I do like talking to you." He leaned down and kissed me again.

This time I got a little carried away as our lips met. It was another minute or two, and I had just slid my hands in his shirt, slowly caressing up his ab muscles and chest, before he reluctantly pulled back.

"Liz!" He said smiling, as I reached my hands back under his shirt. "I can't resist you when you do that, and I am trying to respect you. But it is really hard." His smile turned to a sheepish grin.

"Well, that is actually what I wanted to talk to you about." I added, finding the perfect Segway. "What if I don't want you to resist me anymore."

"Liz, I really don't think..." He started.

"Let me finish." I interrupted. "I have every intention of keeping my promise to my mom. But... when I thought I had lost you, I had a lot of time to think." I paused again, looking into the forest at our side as I thought of how to phrase my thoughts. "And when you magically survived and I have you back in my life now, my perspective on things has really changed."

"What do you mean?" Luke asked.

"What I mean is. I want to marry you Leuken Bennett." I said nervously, looking down at my feet before forcing my eyes back to his face to see his response. His face did look surprised at first. But that surprise quickly morphed into a smile.

"Are you asking me to marry you?" He said, his eyes beginning to water. I wasn't sure why he all the sudden looked like he might cry, and for a split second I worried that he didn't want to marry me.

"Well…I mean." I scrambled to find the right words to back pedal. "I wasn't asking you to marry me. Not that I don't want to marry you. I do. It's just… when you talked before about marriage, a few weeks back, I wasn't at a place where I could even think about it. But now, knowing that each day may be our last together, it just feels so right… and… I know what I want. With us going on this trip to Brazil. There is a chance that one or both of us might die, and I want to spend the rest of my life with you. No matter how long or short that is. And… I want to spend it as your wife." I looked back up, and was surprised to see he was smiling now, with tears slowly dripping down his cheeks. "That is, if you still want me."

Luke suddenly picked me up and spun me around in circles a couple of times. As he set me back down, he kissed me. It was a short kiss, and I lightly tasted salt as a tear from one of his cheeks hit my mouth, but it didn't bother me at all. "Sorry." He said, wiping his cheeks quickly before hugging me again. "I just can't think of a time that I have ever been as happy as I am right now."

"Oh really?" I asked and noticed that my eyes were starting to water too. I didn't know why because I was utterly happy. I guess this was what my mom used to refer to as happy tears. "Well, I can't think of one either. So does that mean you do still want to marry me?"

"Of course, I do." He smiled again. "But I would be remiss if I let this stand as a proposal."

"And why is that?" I asked.

"Liz, that's not how a proposal should go." Luke chided. "And besides, I still haven't asked your father, and I need to get you a ring. Plus, we would need your father's permission, since you aren't eighteen for two more days. And I promised my mom I would never propose without asking the dad first."

"You know I don't care about all that sentimental stuff." I added. "Don't get me wrong, I love that you are so thoughtful and so sweet. It's just I am not high maintenance. You could grab a ring out of those cracker jack boxes they had near the front desk, and I would be more than happy. As long as it comes from you, I am good."

"Hold on a second." Luke held his hand in front of me with his index finger up, motioning for me to wait. "I have an idea. I will be right back." He turned as he finished talking, running quickly back into the Motel.

Is he really gonna get a ring out of a cracker jack box? I thought to myself as I waited. The notion should have bothered me as cheesy, but it didn't. I was too excited at the thought of marrying the kid. Looking up into the forest, I could hear the birds chirping. In the distance, I heard a wolf howl ominously. Right after it did, another one howled from a distance in the opposite direction. The sky was just starting to darken as the sun had recently set. Scattered clouds were visible directly overhead and above the tree line. As I turned back towards the door that Luke had vanished into moments before, I was surprised to see him re-emerge already, walking up to me with a nervous smile on his face.

"If I do this now..." He started as he got close to me. "You have to promise not to tell your dad or anyone until I get a chance to at least pretend like I did it right. Okay?"

"What are you talking about?" I was somewhat disappointed when I didn't see a cracker jack box in his hands, but he had definitely not been in there long enough to buy one from the front desk. Had he swiped one without paying?

"Close your eyes, Liz." He said, still smiling.

"Okay..." I was somewhat confused at why he wanted my eyes closed, but I obliged him.

Less than three seconds later he spoke again. "Now open them."

I was completely shocked when I opened my eyes. Luke was down on one knee in front of me. He was smiling broadly, but it was what he held that caught my attention. Inside of a small black ring case, which was popped open in his right hand, was a shiny object. As I looked more closely, I could see a large squarish diamond, set on top of a white gold ring. I was so surprised that I felt completely speechless. There was no way he had time to buy this during our trip, which means he must have bought it before.

"Elizabeth Scott. I have loved you since the moment I first met you, and I will keep loving you forever." He swallowed before finishing. "Will you marry me?"

I could feel my eyes watering again, but it was impossible to keep the smile off my face as I cried. "Oh Luke." The words sounded more like a cry than excited, but I didn't care. "Of course, I will. I would absolutely love to marry you." I grabbed his face in both hands and bent down to kiss him again.

He stood and pulled the ring from the case, slipping it onto the ring finger on my left hand. It slid on nicely and fit perfectly. I looked at the ring again, the princess cut diamond looked huge on my small fingers. It was beautiful and shiny. After he slipped it on, I kissed him again. He picked me up and spun me around one more time, while we kissed. Without thinking, I wrapped my legs around his waist, losing myself in his warm embrace.

"Ahem." I was startled to suddenly hear someone clearing their throat, and I hurriedly dropped back to the ground, letting go of Luke while looking around him to see who it was. "Sorry to startle you two." Jazmine said, looking awkwardly between us and the ground.

"All good." Luke replied, his cheeks flushing as he tried to play it cool. "We were just uh… talking. What's up?"

Jazmine laughed at Luke's reply. "You mean making out? Look I just came to let you know that they are starting to take dinner orders. I know Liz hardly ever eats, but I'm sure you are starving." I noticed that Jazmine trailed off at the end of her sentence as her eyes were staring at my left hand. Instinctively I turned slightly and hid the ring behind my back, hoping that she had not seen it.

"Oh my gosh!" Jazmine shouted excitedly. "Is that what I think it is? Did you guys just get engaged?" She smiled and was almost jumping up and down as she came closer to us.

"Jazmine please." Luke sounded almost panicked. "You can't say anything. Please. I still need to ask Daniel for permission. He would kill me if he knew I proposed without asking him first."

"Don't be silly." Jazmine said as Luke was still finishing speaking. She lunged forward and gave me a big hug. "I am so excited for you Liz. Congratulations!"

"Thanks Jazmine." I replied, hugging her back.

"Please Jazmine." Luke continued as Jazmine let me go and turned to hug him. "Promise you won't say anything? At least not for a couple of days while I figure out a good time to ask."

"Oh Luke." She replied as they embraced. "Like I said, don't be silly. You are marrying my favorite teenager alive. Why would I do anything to mess things up? Yes, I think you are too young, and should probably say I am opposed, but after all we have been through the last few weeks, I think it's fantastic!" She finished hugging him and stepped back, keeping one hand on his elbow. "But just a word of advice, he would kill you if he saw that ring before you ask, so you might not want to keep such a giant rock on her ring finger unless you are trying to shout it from the rooftops that you are engaged."

"Thanks Jaz." Luke sounded mildly relieved by her response.

"We are gonna be sisters!" Jazmine grabbed and squeezed my hand excitedly. This time her voice was more of a loud excited whisper than a yell, which I was grateful for.

"I am excited for that." I said, squeezing back. "I have actually always wanted a sister."

Just then a thought came to me. I pulled the silver necklace my mother had given me out of my shirt, and then pulled my hair together so that I could slip the necklace off. "I have an idea." I said to Luke as he looked at me quizzically. "Hold this." I handed him the necklace after unhooking the clasp on the rear.

"Okay…" He said, grabbing the necklace with both hands.

I reluctantly slid the ring from my finger and threaded it onto the necklace that Luke was holding. The ring settled at the bottom where the star pendant was at, resting on top of it. "Can you put it back on me now?" I asked as I turned, again pulling my hair up and to the side so it would be out of the way.

"Sure." He replied. I could feel him put the necklace back around my neck. "Okay, Its on." I tucked the front of the necklace back down the front of my sweater so that only the thin chain portion around my neck was visible. Even with the V-neck sweater on, this put the ring right in front of my bra. I would have to be doing something pretty crazy for the ring to show now.

"Is that better?" I asked.

"Looks good." Jazmine said, turning to face Luke again. "You better ask him soon though."

"I will." Luke replied nervously. He kissed me one more time before we all went back inside.

CHAPTER X

"Are you sure you don't want me to pull the others from the offsite farm?" Silas asked Priscilla. "If they are coming here to kill us, we stand a better chance with the others to help."

"Don't you think it's a little too late for that." Priscilla replied scathingly. "If they are just landing, they will be here in minutes. By the time the help showed up, we would already be dead." She finished with a scowl at Silas. It was beyond obnoxious how angry she got when she was scared, he thought to himself.

"I only have 21 here who can fight, and many of them are too young or early in their training to be of use against the experienced fighters." Silas cautioned. "If they are coming to kill us, we are as good as dead."

"What if we use the kill switch?" Priscilla said slowly.

"If we do that, we could probably kill the party." Silas replied thoughtfully. "But that would bring out Alastair and his witch. With them in the fight, we wouldn't stand a chance."

"Do you have it programmed to only wipe out the supply we have given them?" Priscilla asked.

"Yes. It is a different button to wipe them out. The emergency kill button affects everyone within about 100 feet, but I programmed a separate one specifically to kill the bloodlines we supplied to Alastair."

"Very well. If they attack, I will move to block while you execute the kill code. Bring in our four best fighters. Any more than that, and they will see it as an act of aggression. Have two of them wear servant clothes to conceal that they are fighters."

"As you wish." Silas sped from the antechamber, hurrying to summon those Priscilla had requested. He had some of his servants run to gather clothes for the two shorter fighters. Once they were dressed and back in the room with Priscilla, Silas gave them clear instructions to intercede should things turn violent, but only if told by one of them. He could feel the other two Auserwhalt approaching as he finished the instructions. A minute later one of his servants knocked at the door.

"My lady, I have Lord Reuben and Lord Vincent of the Chosen here to see you." The elderly serving man said with feigned reverence through a cracked door. "Should I let them in?"

"But of course. Hurry now, don't keep them waiting." Priscilla said loudly, obviously wanting to ensure those outside the door could hear the deference in her voice.

The servant opened the door fully, before turning and speaking to someone in the hallway. "Lady Priscilla and Lord Silas will see you now my Lords."

He was only halfway through his sentence when Reuben strode quickly into the room. His wavy light brown hair was somewhat long, with deep blue eyes and pale skin. Silas had always seen him as a pompous pretty boy who was infatuated with his own supposed greatness, but he knew only a fool would underestimate the man. Reuben, in spite of his many faults, was deadly fast with a sword, and always had a terralium blade sheathed on his hip. As Alastair's henchman, he was the only Auserwhalt besides Alastair and Emmaline that was allowed to make important decisions. He may have come to merely warn Silas and Priscilla, but Silas had no doubt that if they angered him enough, the man would not hesitate to kill them both.

Vincent was shorter than Reuben, by almost a full head. That still left him about the same height as Silas, who was just shy of six feet. Vincent had darker hair, though cut shorter and shaved on the sides. His Persian skin was tan for one of the chosen, and he carried himself with a confident but collected gait. A long scar ran half the length of the front of his neck. The silver bracelet on his right wrist ensured that he would do whatever the taller Auserwhalt told him to do. The bracelet was in every way identical to the one Silas had on his own wrist. A constant reminder that Priscilla owned him in every way imaginable.

"Greetings Silas and Priscilla." Reuben said as he stopped about ten feet shy of the two, standing in the middle of the polished marble floor. His long sleeve silk shirt and black leather pants were both tight on his slender but muscular physique. "I see you are staying cool in the summer heat, while your failures are all over international news!" He raised his voice gradually while he spoke, anger filling his eyes as he finished loudly.

Behind him, Vincent had stopped short, and another twelve bloodlines, clad in all silver-colored clothes, with matching curved blades sheathed at their sides followed the pair into the room. They moved slowly, but purposefully, forming two lines of six behind the men, before standing at ease, their feet shoulder width apart. Their hands were clasped in front of them, resting on their belts. While they varied in height and facial features, most of them were Latino, though from different regions of south and central America. A couple of them in the back row appeared of Nordic descent, as they stood several inches taller than any of the others. Silas recognized the two nearest him in the front row. They were brothers, Brazilian, and had been his best fighters and trainers, about twenty years ago. That was before Aurelia had come with Vincent one visit, to harvest a crop of two bloodlines that were to be sent to Alastair as tribute. Aurelia, who was Alastair's sister, had insisted on taking their two best swordsmen, who were also their trainers, instead of the two youngest from the group.

Silas realized if Reuben gave the order to strike, they would kill him long before he could execute any kill codes from the phone in his front pocket. His only option would be electronic kill switch hanging from his neck, which would also kill his own men. That would leave he and Priscilla alone with the two men. While he might stand a chance against Vincent, he knew Reuben could kill him. Priscilla would not be much help in a fight, which meant regardless of what he did, they would not survive a confrontation tonight. Silas hated being in lose/lose situations, which is all he had been in since Priscilla captured and bonded him with the bracelet.

"We are aware of the bloodlines who killed my crew, Lord Reuben" Priscilla said, trying to sound calm but the fear being somewhat obvious in her voice. "We also killed some of them in the fighting, and I have sent two crews to dispatch those who survived."

"Two crews huh?" Reuben walked closer to Priscilla, towering over her until he was about a foot away, looking down at her with obvious disdain on his face. "Well for your sake, I hope you do not fail again. Alastair's patience for your sloppiness grows thin."

"We will not fail the great Lord, I assure you." Priscilla bowed her head, again in deference, as she spoke.

"While I do believe you, I think we will need assurances." Reuben turned to glance around the room and settled with his eyes on Silas. "Tell me Silas. How many bloodlines are there in this rag tag group that bested twelve of your best fighters?"

"We believe there are about six of them my Lord." Silas replied politely but did not bow.

"So, they have skilled fighters then." Reuben mused thoughtfully, his voice sounded calmer. "And just how do you plan on finding and killing them?"

"We have our ways." Silas added. "Technology allows us to do many things. We believe we will have their heads within a matter of days."

"Very well then." Reuben turned and motioned to the silver clad bloodlines formed in rows near the entrance to the great room. The men turned and filed out, two at a time in synchronized fashion. Reuben started for the door, before turning a few feet short of it, as Vincent walked out.

"Just to be sure we are clear though." He said, looking directly at Priscilla as he spoke. "You have seven days to have their heads. If you do not send proof to us by then, we will be back. And I assure that for you… it will not be pleasant." He turned and walked from the room as quickly as he had entered.

*   *   *

"I do think it is quite incredible that a beauty such as yourself is still unwed." Aurush was saying as he moved slightly closer to Jazmine. She instinctively took a slight step back, but the man didn't seem to notice as he continued. "In my culture, it is not uncommon for the more attractive girls to wed within months of turning sixteen. I find it hard to believe you are already twenty when you are so pretty." He laughed awkwardly as he finished.

Jazmine could not bring herself to laugh, not even for the sake of pity. The boy seemed mostly nice, but between his arrogance and being overly forward, she had already had more interaction than she wanted to with him. "Yeah well, I appreciate the complement, but here in the US, girls don't usually marry until their early to late twenties."

"That is fascinating." Aurush replied. "I mean I myself am turning twenty-five in a few months, but our men usually wed older than our women do."

"Oh. So, is that why you aren't married yourself? Because you aren't old or mature enough yet." Jazmine couldn't help herself from teasing the obnoxious boy. She knew he was a man, but he acted more like a boy. Jazmine heard deep laughter and turned to see Metemba was standing right behind her. He was facing his sister and three of the Asian clan members, but with his side to Jazmine, and the way he looked at her as he laughed, she could tell he must have heard some of their conversation.

Jazmine had been impressed by the man's strong jaw and the way he carried himself. Few men could exhibit cool confidence without coming across as downright arrogant, but Metemba seemed to have mastered this art. He obviously had a sense of humor as well, as he had laughed at her joke.

"Pardon my eavesdropping." The clan chief said as he turned and held a handout to Jazmine. "I know we were introduced earlier, Jazmine of the Bennett clan, but it is a pleasure to meet you face to face." Metemba smiled as he spoke, revealing small dimples on the sides of his mouth, and extremely white teeth. Jazmine had always been picky when it came to teeth, and she liked what she saw. She extended her hand to shake his, and he twisted her palm upwards, resting his other hand gently on top of hers as he shook with both hands.

She couldn't help but notice how big and strong his hands were as she shook. "The pleasure is all mine Chief Abedayo." Jazmine smiled broadly.

"Please, just call me Metemba." The man said as he let go of her hand. "I am only chief because my father passed away with my two older brothers years ago, leaving me as the oldest child. I am no better than anyone else in this room."

"You say you are the oldest in your family?" Aurush cut in. "Well, that must make you pretty old then huh? What are you, like one-hundred or something? Probably old enough to be her grandpa." He giggled awkwardly as he finished speaking, looking around as if he expected others to laugh at his insult.

"I am old enough to have been taught manners, Aurush son of Devansh." Metemba smiled politely at the insult. "If you must know, I am thirty-nine years old. And the light be willing, I consider that pretty young still."

"Oh." Aurush seemed to not even comprehend the dig as he continued. "So that would make you about twice as old as Jazmine then. Sounds pretty old if you ask me."

"Tell me Metemba, what part of Africa are you from again?" Jazmine turned so that Aurush was mostly to her back as she faced the clan chief.

"My family hails from the Namakwa region of South Africa." Metemba said. He read the blank expression on Jazmine's face when he said the name and smiled again. "It is the coastal province that goes inland about a hundred miles North of Cape Town on the western coast of the country. What about you Jazmine? Where are you from?"

"I was born in Hong Kong, before China took it over." Jazmine explained. "My mother had fled mainland China after meeting my American father. We lived there until my parents and little sister were all killed by the Verdorben when I was ten. Isaac found me and took me to the Bennetts. Sara officially adopted me a few years later, and I have been part of their family ever since."

"I am sorry for your loss Jazmine Bennett. May your birth family ever be in the light, until you are with them again." He bowed his head in respect as he spoke, his kind words sounding quite sincere to Jazmine. "And may the light ever shine on the Bennett family for their hospitality and care of you from childhood."

"Thank you." Jazmine replied, suppressing the deep sadness that she tried to keep hidden at the sting she felt from mentioning her parents. Though her memories of them were few, she still held them both with fond views and affection to this day. She didn't know why she had opened up somewhat to this man who she had only just met, but for some reason she felt as though she could trust him. She couldn't discern if it was the mild physical attraction she felt for the man, his strong positivity, or the fact that he seemed especially wise, even if he was only twice her age.

*   *   *

"Okay kid." Daniel Scott said impatiently as he and Luke Bennett stood awkwardly near the walking path on the side of the hotel. "What is it that was so urgent you needed to talk to me alone?" The young man was fidgeting nervously with his hands clasped in front of him. The dim moonlight that shone down on his face illuminated a nervous expression as he seemed to want to look anywhere but at Daniel.

"Well Mr. Scott." The boy began while clearing his throat and glancing up at him. "I know this might come as a bit of a surprise... but... I wanted to talk to you about Liz."

"Okay…" Daniel trailed off, not hiding the confusion he felt. "Spit it out kid. You want my permission to date her or something? I know you two are already a thing, and I'm good with it. She's almost an adult, and I couldn't really control my stubborn girl even if I wanted to."

"About that sir…" Luke paused again, looking down before continuing. "I probably should have asked your permission to court her weeks ago. Sorry for not doing that."

"What do you mean court her?" Daniel raised his voice slightly without thinking. Courting sounded too much like trying to get married, and he wasn't in a place mentally where he could entertain that thought about his baby girl, even if she was about to be an adult. He did have to be somewhat careful though, because in the short time he had been able to spend with Sara, he was already starting to have thoughts about wanting to make long term plans with her. Could he be completely honest with his girlfriend's son, or whatever he and Sara were, with her kid if it meant telling him to cool his jets about his daughter? Something about it did seem almost hypocritical as he thought about it.

"I'm sorry sir. That probably sounded strange." Luke paused for a long moment before continuing. "I know we do not know each other that well, and you thought I was dead until yesterday, so this whole thing will probably sound crazy… but."

"Come on." Daniel interrupted. "Listen guy. I was a cop for over twenty years. I can tell you wanna say something you're scared to say. The sooner you spit it out, the sooner it will be over."

"Very well sir." Luke seemed to stand up straighter this time as he spoke. *The kid must have found some courage.* Daniel thought to himself. "You probably already know this, but I care for your daughter very much. In fact… I would do anything for her. Even give my own life for her if I had to. When I almost died in that explosion,

I had a lot of thoughts as I lay there, my body half squished by the rubble from the building. During that time, I realized, that between the other tainted ones and the other bloodlines that are hunting us, I'm not sure how many days I have left. Not sure how many days any of us have left. All of this got me thinking that I want to spend the rest of my life, however long that is, with your daughter Elizabeth. And now I am coming to you as a man." Luke paused momentarily before continuing. "I know I'm young. Probably too young in your eyes, just like Liz is, but I would like to ask for your blessing to marry your daughter... sir."

Daniel was completely shocked. He felt a mix of emotions, from surprised to angry, and everything in between. It all hit him at once. Just a few months ago, when the demon inside had been controlling him, he was ready to kill this kid for kissing Liz on the front porch. And now *he had the audacity to ask him for his blessing to marry his baby girl?* Seventeen or not, she was the only daughter he had, and there was no part of him that thought that either one of them were old enough or mature enough to get married.

"Wow... that's... not what I was expecting." Daniel was at a momentary loss for words, so he sat down on the bench that was next to where they were standing. Looking off into the trees, he took a long deep breath attempting to gather his thoughts.

"I'm sorry sir." Luke began explaining. "I don't mean to stress you out, but I really do love you daughter."

Daniel held up a hand, not looking up as he tried to absorb what the kid had just asked for. "Just stop." He said quickly. "I need a minute, okay?"

Luke stood there awkwardly, eventually turning to look out into the trees, as Daniel contemplated how to shoot him down.

"Listen kid. I'm not gonna say no." Luke's expression turned almost instantaneously excited. Like a fat kid eyeballing chocolate cake at the end of a salad diet. "But I'm also not gonna say yes." The young man's expression instantly changed, and he hung his head, looking down at the ground.

"I understand sir." Luke said quietly after a moment passed in silence.

"I just really do think you two are a little young." Daniel thought out loud, trying to stay patient with the kid who may very well be his future son in law. He knew if he was too rude Liz would never forgive him. More importantly, he didn't want to do anything to upset Sara. "At the same time though, I do think you are a nice kid. You seem to care about her and treat her with respect, which is important to me. But I'm not sure if you understand something else that is equally important to me." He paused to make sure the words came out right as he formed his thoughts again.

"Before someone can even think about marrying my daughter." He began. "They need to know that if they ever hurt or abandoned my baby girl, after committing to be her husband till death, I would kill them. So, you need to think about that. Are you committed enough to Liz, that you can promise me you would always be faithful, always protect her, and never leave her?"

"Yes sir, you have my word." Luke actually seemed to mean it as he answered him.

"Very well." Daniel replied. "Then you have my word that I will think about it."

"Okay…" The boy trailed off as he stood there, looking at Daniel confused.

"Look, she's not even eighteen for two more days. Give me a couple days to think about it and you'll have my answer. Capeesh? Even if you get engaged, it's not like you would actually get married for a long time."

"Sounds more than fair to me sir." Luke responded. "Thank you for your consideration, Mr. Scott."

"No problem kid." Daniel replied, happy to be done with the conversation. "Just don't go eloping or nothing on me, okay?"

*   *   *

"That is the seventh person with either the mark or the scar that I have counted." The young man clad in all black said with a thick Brazilian accent. He had binoculars up to his eyes and was watching the two men talking on the side of the motel. "And that is just in the two hours since we have been watching. There could be as many as ten or more bloodlines in that motel."

"That is why we should wait to strike." An older man, also with a thick accent, was standing next to the younger man, wearing the same attire. "I have counted five boys and two girls. Unless one or two of them pull off alone so that we can take them out, we will wait for nightfall. Let them be sleeping when we strike. If we kill half of them before the others even know we are there, it will be a piece of cake overpowering the others, even if they fight as fiercely as our masters described. They were dumb enough to leave the satellite phone powered on for us to track, so they probably aren't that strong."

"Even if they are, with two and a half full crews, no one stands a chance against us." The younger man smiled as he put the binoculars back up to his eyes.

CHAPTER XI

Luke woke quickly, startled by the sound of screams coming from another room. It sounded like a young girl screaming. *Trinity,* he thought to himself as the screaming suddenly stopped. He opened his eyes to look around and sat up startled as an unknown man dressed in all black was standing over him next to the bed. Without warning, he swung a sword right at Luke's neck. Rolling sideways as he put an arm up to soften the blow, he felt the blade slice through his arm and just cut the skin on the side of his neck.

He jumped up and to the side as the man with the sword moved to strike him again. "Ben!" He yelled instinctively, hoping to wake his brother and increase his odds of surviving this ambush. As he turned and jumped into the corner of the room away from the man in black, he noticed that Ben was not moving. "Ben wake up!" He shouted as he pulled on Ben's blanket and leg. The movement of the sheets pulled them down just enough for Luke to gasp in disbelief.

As the blanket slid down, Luke noticed that Ben's head was sitting sideways on the pillow, with blood covering the area that separated his decapitated head from his lifeless body. The man wielding the sword moved slowly to the middle of the room with a sinister smile on his lips. "If you don't fight, this will go much easier on you." His accent sounded south American, but Luke couldn't decipher exactly what country.

Luke noticed that the door to his room was open, and he heard screaming coming from the hallway. This time it was a man's scream, followed by shrieks from a voice he recognized as Jazmine in the room next to his. In the hallway, he saw two more men in black running past towards Jazmine's room. *Liz!* He thought to himself as he remembered that Liz and Jazmine were sharing the room two doors down. The man in front of Luke lunged quickly at him without warning.

Luke had been waiting for the man to move. With one arm already missing, he knew his only chance was to end the man quickly. When the man's sword flashed at the only arm he had left, he quickly ducked as the blade just missed his head. Grabbing the man's wrist, Luke kicked hard at the outside of his closest knee, snapping it sideways while simultaneously twisting the man's grip on his sword. He wrenched it from him while spinning away from the attacker's free arm. The man moved to grab Luke, but he moved faster, cutting the man's other leg clean through the thigh. As the man screamed in pain and fell, Luke quickly swung his blade down at an angle, cutting off his head.

Before the corpse had even come to rest, he saw Jazmine running in front of his room, being chased by two men. As he ran to the hallway, he saw absolute chaos. To the right were several men in black, appearing to be surrounding someone on the ground. Looking left, the two men who were chasing Jazmine caught up to her, as two other men blocked her from reaching the exit door at the end of the hall. She turned to defend herself with her glowing white hot terralium dagger. She blocked one strike and then another, but as she moved to slide in between the two attackers back towards Luke, one of the men struck her from behind, slicing his sword down through her shoulder, severing her left arm as she fell forward to the ground. She rolled, slicing the calf of one attacker, as the man on the other side of her cut off her other arm just below her elbow. This caused the dagger to drop from her severed hand.

Luke moved as quick as he could to close the distance as they cut his sister down, with two people in black hacking her to pieces as he moved. Rage filled his veins with each step. Swinging high, he brought his sword down through the closest attacker's neck, who was pre-occupied while striking as Jazmine. The next man looked up just as Luke sliced at his neck, ducking quickly. His duck caused the sword to cut halfway into the man's head, but the blade stopped as it got lodged in the man's skull. As the man's body fell to the ground, Luke pulled hard to wrench his blade free, but as he did so another of the men struck his sword arm at the wrist, slicing through it.

"Ugh!" Luke grunted in pain as he jumped sideways, barely dodging another swing from another black clad attacker who was aiming for his head. He used what was left of his right arm to push off the wall, running down the hallway towards his room. His only chance to survive would be if others could kill these men and heal him. He needed to get back to his other arm and re-attach it. A door opened suddenly to his left, and Shawnee appeared, jumping into the hallway. The African girl had a bloody stump where her left arm should have been and was bleeding from one side of her neck. As she turned to run towards Luke, a man sliced at her from inside the room, cutting into her back as she fell to the ground.

Luke knew he couldn't help her, so he jumped over her attacker as he ran. He lost his balance as he landed, falling, and rolling on the ground. Pushing off the ground with his nub, he spotted Liz. Her hands were covered in blood, as was her face and the front of her baby blue sweater. Judging by the way she held her sword as she ran towards him, Luke didn't think she was hurt.

"Luke!" Liz shouted as she ran, stretching out her free hand at him. The look on her bloody face was one of pure desperation and dread. She seemed to be warning him about something, as she looked past him. He turned just in time to see the sword as it sliced into the center of his head… and darkness engulfed him.

*   *   *

Gasping for air, Luke sat up in bed. It took a moment for his eyes to focus, but when they did, he realized that he was still in his hotel room. He felt a strange warm sensation in his chest and mind. He realized that he had just had a foretelling from the light. The dream had felt so real… because it was a reality that had not yet happened. His special gift from the bloodline was his ability to see the future when the light was willing. At that moment he knew that what he saw would soon happen if he didn't act quickly. He jumped out of bed, moving quickly to Ben's bed to shake him awake.

"What the…" Ben began as he woke, but Luke held a finger to his mouth as he loudly whispered himself.

"There's no time to explain Ben, so I need you to listen, and do exactly as I ask. In a few minutes, dozens of those men in black are going to attack and try to kill everyone in this hotel. Our best chance is if we wake everyone quickly, have them grab their weapons, and ambush the attackers."

"You had a vision?" Ben interrupted.

"Yes." Luke continued. "You wake Mom, Jazmine, the Romany clan, Daniel and the Indians. I will wake the Africans, Australians and Japanese. Have them grab their weapons and meet immediately in the large conference room. Bring the kids as well, even if they are still asleep."

"Okay." Ben grabbed his terralium dagger from the stand next to his bed, as Luke quickly pulled his pants on, grabbing his terralium sword and throwing the carrying case over his back. Ben turned as he was about to walk out the door. "Wait, what if they don't answer the door when I knock?" He asked.

"Then kick it in and wake them up. We probably only have a couple of minutes." Luke explained. He walked past Ben and turned left down the hallway. Just before he knocked on the African's door, he heard Ben knock on his mother's room.

"Who's there?" Luke heard a female voice ask from inside.

"It's me. Luke Bennett. There are men coming to ambush us. I need you to get up immediately. Please hurry and wake your family. They will be here any minute, we are meeting in the conference room now."

Luke was startled when he turned to the door across the hall, as Metemba was standing in the doorway to his room, with the door already open.

"Did you have the vision too?" Metemba asked quickly in his deep voice. "Of the traitors in black ambushing us?"

"Yes." Luke replied. "Do you get the visions too?"

"Not me, but Kwame does." Metemba nodded over his shoulder, and Luke could see the shorter African man walking up behind him. He had a sword in one hand, ready to fight, while his other handheld an even larger blade by the sheath. Kwame handed the larger sword to Metemba, who slung it over his back.

"Can you wake the Japanese, and I will get the Aussies?" Luke asked.

"With pleasure." Metemba said.

"I remember the time on the clock, they will attack in three minutes." Kwame warned as Luke turned to wake the others.

About sixty seconds later, they were mostly gathered in the conference room. Luke gave Liz a hug as she approached him.

"What did you see?" She asked quietly as he held her close.

"The men in black." He replied. "A lot of them. In my dream they killed most of us, including the children, but that was with them ambushing us in our sleep. With us being ready for them, I think we have a fighting chance." Liz shook her head in disbelief as the African clan chief began speaking.

"We need to be in our places in sixty seconds, so everyone listen closely. We will wait and ambush them at the entrances. This should give us the best advantage." Metemba seemed entirely calm as he briefed out his plan. Luke was impressed. "Non bloodlines and children will wait in the center room of the hotel off of the main hallway. Shawnee and Zane will protect them. If we fight them off at the entrances, hopefully the other civilians will sleep through the skirmish."

"I will help protect the kids." Liz interrupted. "Their swords do not work on me or my father."

"Very well." Metemba continued. "Mr. Scott and the Aussies will cover the main entrance with Kwame and Haysom. The Indian Clan will cover the entrance to this conference room with Tobias. The Bennett's will cover the south entrance with me, and the Japanese clan is to cover the north entrance. In Kwame's vision, no one came in the north, but he was killed about two minutes in, so it is hard to say what might happen when we fight back. Does everyone understand their role?"

"Yes." Isaac, Hinata and Devansh answered almost in unison, while others nodded.

"Let them enter a ways in before killing them, as there are at least twenty attackers. We must work together and fight smart to survive. If any of them get a terralium weapon, focus on killing them to get it back. Without our Verdorben friends helping us fight, many of us will likely die tonight." He paused before finishing, looking around the room. "Now everyone take your positions and be silent until you strike. May the light give us strength."

*   *   *

"Be careful, okay?" I told Luke as I kissed him one last time. "I'm not losing you again."

"How could I not be?" He replied. I was impressed by how calm he sounded, considering the situation. "I've got a beautiful fiancé to marry soon. Nothing is getting in the way of that." He winked before turning and running towards the entrance he was covering. Isaac, Jazmine and Metemba had already headed that direction, but Ben was still standing in the room behind me.

"Trust me." Ben said reassuringly to Kezia, who was holding his arm with a scared expression on her face. "These friends have been trained to fight. The safest place for you to be is in this room with Liz and the others. She might not look intimidating, but when Liz gets her crazy on, no one else will stand a chance. I've seen her fight, and the damage is legit."

"I'm not worried about me." The Romany girl replied. "I'm worried about you. I don't want anything to happen to you. I've already lost everything else in my life, but at least I found you. I couldn't bare it if I lost you too." Her eyes were watering as she looked up at Ben.

Just then I realized something. The girl didn't just see Ben as a safety blanket because he had saved her and her niece from her attackers back in Nevada. She had strong feelings for the silly boy.

"You have my word, Kezia." I said reassuringly. "I will keep you safe. And his family will keep him safe. The Bennett's have trained every day for years, just for these types of things."

"Promise me you'll come back?" Kezia said as she hugged Ben close. He wrapped his arms around her too, lifting her gently off the ground.

"Of course, I will." Ben replied smiling as he set her down. "Does a pig like slop? Anyways, I haven't even told you a third of my cheesy jokes yet."

Kezia nodded as Ben let her go. He turned to walk past me. "Be careful." I said to him as he ran down the hall to join the others.

It grew suddenly silent as I looked around the room. The light was off with the door cracked just enough so I could see into the hallway. Shawnee stood next to me at the doorway, while Zane stood at the back window. In the dim light I could see Kezia was a few feet away from me, standing over Trinity, who was laying in the bed next to Alex. She had woken for a brief moment while she was being carried, but Alex had stayed asleep even when my father ran with him down the hallway. Sara was sitting on the nightstand between the two beds, her hand gently resting on Alex's back.

While I thought it was sweet that Sara wanted to look out for my little brother, I knew she could do little to protect him against what was coming. Luckily Shawnee and Zane could help. Both held swords clutched in their hands as we waited and looked ready to use them. I noticed that Shawnee's blade still had the sheath on it, and there was a faint glow at the edge of the sheath. I did not have a weapon but was planning on taking one from the first attacker to burst into our room, that is if any of them made it that far.

"Is that Terralium?" I asked the girl softly.

"Yes." She replied in a quiet whisper. "But don't worry. No one will take this from me."

"Sounds good." I replied, my nerves beginning to settle as the anticipation of fighting sent adrenaline through me. "I just wanted to know in case…" I decided not to finish the statement, as I didn't want to insult the girl by saying she might die.

"Do not worry my pretty American Verdorben friend." She smiled broadly. "I will not die tonight. And I will not let anyone kill you either."

I chuckled softly without thinking. This girl looked not a day older than sixteen, despite how tall she was, but spoke like a stubborn old man. I loved it. "Please, just call me Liz." I replied. Shawnee put a finger quickly to her mouth, shushing me.

Just then I realized why. Outside the window, I could hear the sound of footsteps crunching something on the ground. I held very still and noticed Zane looking at Shawnee. He held one hand up slowly, with three fingers raised on it. The footsteps had just passed outside of our window and appeared to be heading towards the south.

I hope Luke will be okay. I thought to myself as I waited quietly.

*   *   *

Luke was standing just inside the doorway to the room, with the door open, facing the hallway. Jazmine was right behind him, with Metemba in front of him. While Luke considered himself good with a sword, he still lost to Isaac about half of the time when they sparred during practice, so he was happy to allow the older clan chief to be closest to the hallway. As Luke looked past Metemba, across the hall he could barely make out the silhouette of Isaac and Ben.

They were also just behind the open doorway of the room straight across.

As the door to outside opened, Luke could barely hear the men as they came through the doorway and into the hall. Walking quickly, the first two men passed by their doorways without even looking sideways. It was as if they knew the end three rooms were empty by the way they moved, their dark curved blades held in front of them as they walked. As the third man came past the doorway, he glanced to the side, but it was too late. Metemba moved in a flash, slashing the man's head off while making almost no noise. At the same time, Isaac jumped into the hallway as he cut the leg of the fourth man just above the knee, causing him to fall forward as Isaac sliced his head off. The entire hallway lit up from the glow of the bright Terralium blade.

Luke moved fast, throwing himself towards the front two men as he brushed past Metemba into the hallway. Both men turned, likely because of the sudden flashes of light, as Luke also pulled his terralium blade free from the sheath as he cut the closest man's sword arm off at the shoulder. The man was too slow to raise it to defend himself. Luke flashed his blade back around to sever the man's leg, but the other attacker, a short Hispanic man with a mustache in all black, blocked Luke's strike with his sword. In a blink the man flashed his blade towards Luke's head. Luke barely ducked the blow as he summersaulted forwards, cutting the man's calf as he rolled past him on the ground.

Luke stood back up, now on the other side of the men, as the first man whose arm he had sliced off reach down to retrieve his weapon from the ground. Luke struck quickly, flashing his sword first at the man's head, then arm, then leg. The clanging of metal was loud as the man blocked the first two blows, and Isaac and Metemba were fighting several more people near the entrance. There must have been at least eight of the men with swords in the hallway, including the two that were already killed. As Luke and the one-armed man fought, he saw Jazmine had picked up one of the dead men's swords and was fighting the man whose leg Luke had cut.

Jazmine appeared to be winning that fight, while Luke was surprised at the skill level of the one-armed attacker he dueled. The man did not attack very well but was exceptionally good at deflecting. Luke struck quickly, trying to finish the man off so he could help the others, but was only able to land every third or fourth strike. The blows he landed were all shallow cuts or gashes, and he struggled to do lasting damage. After each landed strike, the man's body quickly healed itself. As Luke went hard at the man's leg, the man twisted strangely, allowing his leg to be cut as he slashed at Luke's arm.

Luke ducked just in time to prevent his arm from being chopped off but felt stabbing pain as the man's blade cut through the top of his shoulder and into his collar bone. The man fell sideways from the missing half of his leg, as Luke jumped back, avoiding another slash at his own leg. Shifting the sword to his other arm, Luke slashed at the man's arm again, cutting through the wrist as his sword dropped. He quickly flashed a follow through strike that took off the man's head.

When Luke turned to help his family, he saw Jazmine was standing over the headless corpse of the man she had been fighting, when one of the men in black kicked Ben backwards, knocking both Ben and Jazmine to the ground. Luke jumped over them as he felt his shoulder finish healing, shifting the sword back to his good arm. From far down the hallway, he could also hear the clash of metal and shouts coming from the other side of the hotel.

The man who had kicked Ben was surprisingly pale and was taller than the other men they were fighting. The pale man had raised his sword to strike at Ben and seemed surprised when Luke slashed the man's knee after bringing his sword up to block the strike meant for Ben.

"Thanks." He heard Ben say from behind as Luke twisted to parry another strike aimed at his ribs, and another slash at his neck. Luke quickly noticed that this man swung harder and less careful than the other man had, so he quickly stabbed his sword up through the man's chin and into his head, feeling it stop as it struck the inside top of the man's skull, lifting him slightly off the ground.

The man's body went instantly limp, and Luke dropped the corpse to the ground as he pulled his blade free. Looking back up, Luke saw Isaac cut the head off of the last attacker standing, while Metemba was slashing a body on the ground until it stopped moving. Ben stood and moved to Luke's side, while Jazmine had moved up next to the African clan chief. Both of them now clutched one of the curved blades. As Luke looked past Isaac, Metemba and the dead bodies on the ground, he noticed two more men in black, standing just outside the open door at the end of the hallway.

It was too late by the time Luke noticed that one of the men was holding an assault rifle, as he heard Metemba shout. "Look out!" Metemba jumped in front of Jazmine with his sword out, grabbing her with his free hand and tucking her body in behind him as bullets flashed. Luke felt the pain as instantly as he heard the rounds being fired. Stabbing pain in his leg, torso and chest caused him to fall backwards, and he saw Ben drop as well as the man in black fired his automatic weapon at everyone in the hallway.

Luke quickly jumped back up, ignoring the pain, as he saw Isaac was charging directly at the shooter. He could see that several rounds hit his uncle as he moved, but Isaac seemed almost completely unphased by the shots. Luke ran to help him.

As Isaac swung his sword towards the shooter, the other man in black lunged forward, blocking Isaac's strike with his own sword. This man, who was shorter with a thick mustache and tan skin, snarled as he fought with Isaac. Metemba had fallen to the ground, and Jazmine ran just in front of Luke to Isaac's aid. The sword wielding man in black lashed repeatedly at Isaac, who managed to barely block each strike, as some cut partway into Isaac's flesh. More gunshots sounded from the other side of the hotel.

Jazmine ran past Isaac and the other swordsman, raising her arms high to slash at the man with the gun, who was in the process of changing out his gun magazine as her sword slashed down through his neck and into his shoulder. He had obviously not expected those he had shot to immediately go on the offensive.

Luke reached the man attacking Isaac just as Jazmine felled the shooter. Striking quickly at the man's arm, he slashed through the elbow. Not enough to completely sever the arm, but enough that the man dropped the sword. As he bent to pick it back up, Luke slashed through one leg, swinging his sword up through part of the man's neck, and then back down to finish taking off his head. Before the man's body had finished settling, Jazmine ran past Luke, back into the hotel.

Luke reached out to Isaac's shoulder, seeing that his uncle was covered in blood. "You okay?" He asked.

"Yeah. Just flesh wounds." Isaac replied, as Luke saw the gash on one side of his neck stop bleeding and heal shut. "I'll be fine, let's get back inside before someone else shoots us."

Just as they turned to walk in the motel, as if on cue, gunshots rang out from the outside corner of the building near the woods. As they rushed inside, Luke noticed he had been shot in the lower back one time. Jazmine was crouched down over Metemba, her hand resting on his shoulder.

"I thought you were dead." She sounded very concerned about the man, in spite of Ben leaning against the wall close by, holding his chest as his body finished healing. Luke was surprised to see more concern for the clan chief than her own brother.

"It will take more than bullets to kill me." Metemba said as he sat up. "But your concern is appreciated." He smiled before standing all the way up. "Let's get out of this hallway before they start shooting again. I do not like bullet showers."

*   *   *

Daniel Scott waited patiently, as the men in black filed through the front door to the hotel. He counted six in total as the men entered the room, moving quickly towards the hallway leading to the rooms where Sara, Liz and Alex were hiding. As the front door shut behind the last black clad person, a tall thin man with lightly tan skin and no facial hair, he saw the others jump out from behind the concession area and the bush decoration near the front door.

Jacob and Jarvis reached the attackers first, cutting one's head off as the other man ducked what would otherwise have been a fatal blow from Jarvis. Kwame struck at the same time, slicing one leg from the rear attacker as Daniel jumped at the middle man closest to him.

The man turned as Daniel tackled him, slamming the man into the wall near the front desk counter. As he turned to swing his sword at Daniel, he punched the man quickly in the face, hearing his nose break as the man fell backwards to the ground. Daniel reached down quickly, picking up the man's fallen sword as he felt something hit the back of his neck. As he turned to see what had hit him, another man in black, this one shorter and slightly stockier, with a full goatee, was staring at him in disbelief. Daniel swung his sword at the man, who quickly blocked, swinging his blade back around to strike Daniel's wrist.

While the strike to his arm knocked Daniel's arm back, it did not have the effect the man had intended. Daniel seized on his momentary shock to kick him square in the chest, knocking him into the man behind him who was fighting with the older Australian, causing both to fall to the ground. Jacob took the opportunity to strike his man's head off, while Daniel jumped and brought his sword up, hacking it down into the man's body. His first strike cut through the man's ribs as he struck Daniel again in the side of the head. The impact barely phased Daniel, who cut the man's sword arm. Several more strikes made quick work of the man, until he finally stopped moving after Daniel smashed his sword down through the top of his head, splitting his skull.

When Daniel looked back up, he could see that the other attackers had all been killed. Kwame was holding a large gash on his side that was bleeding, but it quickly healed while Daniel watched. The others were breathing heavily but appeared uninjured.

"Well, that was anti climatic." Haysom Fitch said loudly, as gunshots sounded from the other end of the hotel. "Perhaps the others need…" He was cut short as gunshots rang out from the front door, several striking him in the chest as Haysom fell down.

"Look out!" Kwame yelled as shots continued to sound through the foyer area and into the men surrounding Daniel. One at a time the men fell as they were shot. Jarvis and Kwame were shot down next, while Jacob jumped to the side.

Daniel saw the man at the entrance, another shorter Hispanic man with a short beard, shooting at everyone with an assault rifle. He felt pressure on his chest and stomach as the man shot him last, but he barely noticed as the bullets bounced off. The man with the gun wore surprise on his face, as he saw the rounds had no impact as they struck Daniel. He ran at the man with the gun, and just before he got to the shooter, another man in black lunged at Daniel.

This man was also pale, and looked more European than Latino, he gave a slight yell as he swung the sword at Daniel. Daniel put his free hand up to block the strike, as he swung his sword hard at the man's torso. He was surprised when his blade cut the man entirely in half through the midsection, just below the chest.

The shooter turned and ran when he saw that the gun had no impact on Daniel. He quickly disappeared into the forest as he ran to the South from the hotel. Daniel didn't see a need to chase the man, as he still heard screams and shouts coming from inside the hotel. He also didn't want to take a chance that one or more of these men in black had a terralium weapon. While he considered himself handy in a fight, he had never trained with edged weapons before. All of his training through his years as an officer had been limited to firearms, hand to hand defensive police tactics, kickboxing, and Jiu Jitsu.

Stepping back inside, he was glad to see that all the others were back on their feet. Their blood-soaked clothes made them look like they were all on the verge of death besides Jacob, but Daniel knew that underneath, their bodies had healed. He was about to suggest that they go and reinforce the other entrances, where sounds of fighting were still going on, when he heard a blood curdling scream from the middle of the main hallway. He recognized Sara's voice in spite of the tumult taking place on the other sides of the hotel. Without thinking, and without saying a word, he ran towards her.

CHAPTER XII

It was hard for me to stay put, especially when I could hear shouting and the sound of metal striking metal from both sides of the hotel. When gunshots began sounding off, from the front and right side of the hotel, I grew even more anxious. Luke had told me on at least one occasion that it was nearly impossible for members of the bloodline to be killed by gunfire, but it still made me nervous to hear so much of it.

"Look out!" Zane said suddenly as the loud sound of breaking glass filled the room. I turned to see two men flying through the broken window. Both were covered entirely in black attire, besides their faces which were exposed. The first man landed in a roll, bouncing onto his feet quickly a few feet behind Shawnee. The second man, who looked almost identical to the first, landed on his feet, standing on the bed next to Alex as Sara screamed loudly.

Light illuminated the room as Shawnee drew her terralium sword, swinging it at the first attacker. That man blocked her strike, as the one on the bed swung his blade right at Sara. I jumped to tackle this man but knew I would not hit him in time to protect her. Instant relief hit me when I saw Zane jump and block the strike just before it struck Sara. The force of the attacker's blade pushed the back of Zane's sword into Sara's face, knocking her backwards and into the wall.

It all happened so fast, that I didn't have time to adjust as my body was already hurling towards the man, and I wrapped my arms around him as I struck, knocking both of us off the bed and into the corner of the wall. The man grunted as he pushed on my ribs to force me off of him, but I instinctively hooked my legs around him in a top mount as I punched him several times in the face. Each strike pushed his head further into the wall, with the drywall cracking and a large wooden stud in the wall breaking with my last punch. It was hard to distinguish which cracking sounds were the wall, and which were the bones in the man's face.

The man was clearly unconscious, so I stood to help Shawnee. She was standing over the body of the other attacker, whose arm and head lay separately on the ground from the rest of him. Zane was looking at me with shock on his face, but it quickly faded when I noticed the man I had knocked out was beginning to stir. Zane gently nudged me to the side, while he swung hard with his other arm, driving his sword into the face of the attacker as he finished the man off.

Trinity had begun crying at some point as we fought, but I only just noticed her after it was over. Scanning the room, I could see that Sara was holding Alex on one lap, with Trinity on the other. She was bleeding slightly from what looked like a broken nose and had bruising at the top of her nose from where the back of Zane's blade had struck her. She was speaking softly to the children as she held them close.

"It's okay." She reassured soothingly. "Our friends will keep us safe." Alex had a terrified look on his face, his eyes wide in disbelief, but surprisingly he was not crying. He looked completely freaked out though. I moved quickly to his side and put my hand on the side of his face.

"It's okay buddy." I told him. "We are stopping the bad men, so they don't hurt any of us." Alex nodded but didn't say a word as I stood back up.

"Sara are you okay?" My father said suddenly as he appeared in the doorway. It was a good thing he spoke as he opened the door, because Shawnee quickly raised her blade to strike before she realized who it was.

"I'm fine." Sara said as she saw my father. I could see the relief on her face. "The kids are fine... we are all okay." My dad quickly walked over to her.

"Oh no." He said as he reached her. "What happened to your face?"

"One of the men almost killed me." She explained as she touched her face. She looked surprised to see the blood on her fingers, even though it was running down her face to her chin. "Luckily Zane was here to protect me. He and Liz saved my life."

I saw Zane smile, before turning and going back to the window. I was happy to see he was watching for more attackers. I heard more glass break from both sides down the hallway, but it was hard to say exactly where it came from. If they were jumping into other empty rooms, that would allow them to sneak up on the teams positioned at the entrances.

"Help!" The sound was faint as I heard an unknown voice call from down the hallway. Loud gunshots were going off again from the same direction. It sounded like it was coming from the area of the banquet room.

I moved instinctively for the door, as Shawnee moved out of my way. "Stay with them Dad. I'll be fine!" I called over my shoulder as I left the room. I turned left down the hallway, running towards where the newest shots had come from to help. I could smell the lead and gunpowder in the air as I approached the banquet area. More shots rang out from the room, but a noise from behind caused me to turn.

As I did, a tall man wearing all black emerged from the last room in the hallway, just behind me. He was wielding a curved sword and flashed it at my neck as I ducked to avoid the blow. I reached up instinctively, grabbing the hand and wrist that clutched the sword while kicking the man's stomach. The force of the kick knocked me backwards and into the wall, as I heard the man's wrist snap from the force of his body slamming into the other side of the hallway. His shoulder seemed to crack loudly, and his wrist broke sideways.

The man screamed in pain as I pulled the sword from his now limp hand, but before I had a chance to adjust it right in my hand, another man emerged from the room, swinging his blade at me. With the sword still sideways in my hand, I swung it up to deflect the strike at my free arm, but the man's sword bounced off my arm before my blade struck his. Adjusting my grip, I blocked another strike intended for my head, then one at my leg as I kicked the man in the chest. The force of this knocked him at least twenty feet down the hallway. He fell backwards and slid on the ground. I turned back to the first attacker, who was standing back up from the wall, and snapped his wrist back into place as I faced him.

Without giving him time to react, I sliced at his good arm, hacking it off just above the elbow as the man screamed again in pain. I swung back up in a sweeping motion aiming for his head, but he ducked just in time for the blade to only take off a large piece of his scalp, with hair and flesh falling to the floor as he turned to run in the direction of the banquet hall.

I quickly slashed his rear calf when he turned, causing him to fall forward to the ground. Before he had a chance to get back up, I slammed the sword down at the center of his head. It cracked most of the way through his skull as the back of his head split open, and he lay still.

As I turned to face the other attacker, I felt pressure on the back of my neck, and saw the other man's blade bounce off my neck. *That was close.* I thought to myself as I realized the only reason I wasn't dead was the curse that protected me. I really did need to be more careful. Had that blade been terralium, it would have been over for me.

The attacker seemed surprised when his sword didn't cut me, and I seized on the opportunity to slice at his free arm. He raised his sword to block, but mine cut halfway through his bicep before his blade prevented a full dismemberment. He countered by slicing at my waist, but I blocked this strike with my sword while kicking his ribs. I heard them crack, but he barely seemed phased as he swung time and time again at me. I blocked each blow with my sword, until I finally realized the man was much better with a blade than me.

The next time he swung at me, instead of blocking with my sword, I let his blade land on my free arm, while slicing through his leg just above the knee. He fell down sideways as I struck, and I followed up with multiple strikes to his body and arms. At first, he blocked them as he turned and rolled onto his back, but then I hacked his other leg off.

"Aghh!" The man wailed as the pain hit him. With one leg missing and the other hanging by a thread, he struggled to shift his body to defend, and it only took a few more swings to finish him off. I almost felt bad ending this man's life, as it felt like cheating when I knew I could not be killed. As I thought about the fact that these men traveled the world killing innocent people simply because they had abilities though, the little guilt I had felt faded as quickly as it had come.

More gunshots rang out from the banquet room a few feet away, so I quickly ran to it and opened the door. When I got into the large room, I was surprised by what I saw. Tobias was standing in the corner of the room, with one of the Indian clan members huddled behind him in the corner, as a man in black was shooting Tobias repeatedly with a black rifle. Tobias held his terralium sword glowing in one hand, the light from the white-hot blade slightly illuminated the room.

Near the glass door to the room, I saw the clan chief Devansh's lifeless body lying on the ground, his head and one arm lay several feet away. Another man in black, curved sword in hand, was moving towards where Aurush was lying motionless on the floor, with blood pooled on the ground from his chest and one arm. His body stirred slightly as the man approached, and I realized that the younger Indian clan member must still be alive.

I moved as fast as I could, running a few steps before jumping at the attacker. He was raising his sword to finish off Aurush, but turned as he saw me, instead swinging his sword at me as I hurled towards him in the air. As his sword bounced off my left arm, I pushed my sword into his torso with my right. My body crashed into his just after the sword did, and we both fell tumbling to the ground and into the wall. I stood quickly, ripping my sword free that had lodged in his stomach as the man moaned in pain. He swung his blade at me, and it bounced off my leg as I sliced through the wrist on his sword arm.

Adjusting myself to his side, I swung hard at his neck. He put an arm up to block the blade, but it sliced through his hand and neck, severing his head and lodging in the wood flooring on the ground. More gunshots rang out as the shooter fired repeatedly at me, but Tobias was already running at the man as I turned to face him. The impact of the bullets into my body without feeling any pain was a strange sensation to say the least, but it didn't really bother me. Tobias in a single blow sliced through the man's gun barrel and his left arm. In a sweeping motion back up he hacked sideways through the man's neck to finish him off. It was amazing to me how polished it looked when Tobias and the other bloodline members used their swords. They made it seem easy and were so smooth it reminded me of a choreographed dance of some sort.

I turned to check on Aurush, who was slowly opening his eyes as I watched the wound on his arm heal shut. Were it not for all the blood covering most of the same arm and his torso, you couldn't even tell he had been shot. I extended an arm to help him to his feet, and he took it while smiling sheepishly. "Thanks, Elizabeth." The man said, seeming embarrassed for some reason. "While I would much rather be the one saving the damsel than being saved by her, I would be wrong not to thank you for saving my life." He glanced around the room, and his expression turned to instant shock when he noticed his father's corpse lying near the exit door.

"Papa!" Aurush shouted as he walked to his father's body. "No… how could this…" The man trailed off without finishing, as his older brother Darsh moved up and put an arm around his shoulders.

Something hit my chest as more gunshots sounded off through the window on the door, and I turned to see another man in black firing repeatedly at us. Darsh and Aurush quickly moved to the side, with fresh blood coming from Darsh's back as he was hit at least once. Everything about the situation, with sons being shot at as they grieved the death of their father, filled me with instant rage. This was so wrong!

Without thinking, I ran at the attacker. He fired several more shots at me through the window, but I barely even felt them as I dove through the shattered glass in the doorframe. As I crashed into the gunman, I wrapped my arms around him, causing him to tumble with me as we fell and rolled over on the ground. The man, who smelled of body odor, whipped the butt of his gun into my face, and the butt stock broke as it hit my forehead. I twisted my body to get him in a side mount, and began striking him in the face, ignoring his attempt to strike me again with the gun.

I punched him repeatedly in the face, hearing more than feeling the bones cracking as I broke through his skull and felt my hands stick in wetness with the last hard punch. The disgusting texture and iron rich smell of blood made me stop, as I saw movement to my side. Two men in black were running towards me. One held a sword, while the other began firing at me with an assault rifle. I looked to make sure the sword was the same black metal as the others, and immediately charged at the sword wielding man as bullets repeatedly struck me, tearing through my sweater and bouncing off my neck and legs.

The man with the sword swung hard at my neck, so I ducked under his swipe, striking him in the legs as I wrapped around them and took him down. The man fell backwards but had enough training to keep me in his guard as he wrapped his legs around my torso. My first few strikes at his head connected with his elbow and hands as I heard bones crunch, until finally I struck and cracked his nose. Seeing that this knocked him unconscious, I quickly retrieved his sword from the grass and chopped his head off.

Turning to the shooter, who had dropped his gun and was drawing his own sword, I could see the fear in the man's brown eyes. So, it was no surprise when he turned to run. I ran at him as he turned, and sliced him hard in the upper leg, causing him to fall forward into the dirt. As he raised up on his hands to jump back up, I sliced hard through his upper torso, completely cutting him in half as he fell, screaming briefly in agony before lying still.

Flashes of gunfire at the edge of the woods gave away the position of another black clad assassin, so I ran as quickly as I could towards the flashes, feeling driven by the rage of the grief these evil men had caused to the sons of the Indian clan. Though I barely knew these men, I remembered all the sadness, emptiness and bitterness that had consumed me when my mother was killed. Adding to that the sadness Luke had described when he opened up about wishing he had been able to spend more time with his father, and the grief that Kezia and Trinity were going through from their family being entirely annihilated, it fueled the fire inside of me. That anyone could dedicate themselves to this kind of evil and pain causing was beyond the pale. It had to end... and I was going to end it now.

My anger turned to steel resolve, as I quickly ran to and killed the man who was shooting at me from the woods. No sooner had I dispatched him than another charged towards me with a sword. I was lost in the mission of stopping these men and felt nothing but determination, so I systematically did just that. With each man that came at me, I took them out as quickly as I could. Sometimes with my bare fists, and other times with a sword. Another short Latino with a gun who fired from the side of the building. The darker complected tall man next to him with a dark curved blade. Another gunman in the trees at the opposite corner behind the motel, and then two men who jumped out of the motel through a window, trying to run away. The first I killed quickly, and the other I chased into the forest, running for nearly a minute before I finally caught him as he circled around to some cars that were parked on the other side of a hill from the motel.

After cutting off one leg and an arm from this man, who looked old so must have been ancient, I felt myself coming out of the resolve that had consumed me. I wasn't sure if it was the emotionless look on his face as I prepared to cut off his head, or the fact that he had barely grunted when I sliced off his limbs, but just before I ended his life, I stopped. I didn't know if all the men had been killed or not, but I realized that if this was the last one, there may be value in questioning him. This thought caused the fiery rage inside of me to dull somewhat.

And so instead of killing the man, I awkwardly picked him up and threw him over my shoulder, running with what was left of his body back to the others at the motel. As I approached the building, I saw Luke outside with Isaac, Jazmine, Tobias and Metemba.

"Liz!" I could hear several of them shouting my name from a distance as I approached, but Jazmine spotted me first.

"There she is," I heard Jazmine call to the others. "Oh my gosh, what happened? Are you okay Liz?" The look on Jazmine's face was a mix of shock and worry as she watched me roughly drop the man to the earth in front of me, his maimed body landing clumsily as he grunted.

When I let him go, I looked down at my body, realizing that I was spattered in blood from almost head to toe, with my hands and forearms drenched. Only a few small sections of my sweater still showed the baby blue color it had been before the fighting started, and I realized that I probably looked like some kind of villain from a horror movie. Luke ran up to me, looking me over as he put his hands on my shoulders.

"Are you hurt?" He asked, the worry unmasked from his voice. "Is any of that your blood?"

"No." I reassured him. "Sorry I'm so gross. I just had to stop them all so they wouldn't hurt anyone else." Luke didn't look as grossed out as I thought he should be, which made me feel slightly less bad about all the blood on me. I noticed that everyone but Tobias and Jazmine also had a fair amount of blood, including Luke in several spots on his shirt and pants. "Are you okay?"

"Yeah." He replied calmly, looking down at the man on the ground who was stirring slightly with a confused look on his face. "I got shot a few times, but nothing major."

Isaac walked up and joined in examining the injured man in black. "Thanks for leaving one alive Liz." He said casually, eyeing the man. The wound to the man's leg and arm had healed up, and his healed skin barely even had blood around the nub shaped edges.

"What do you want?" The man asked, his voice had a heavy accent, and his blue eyes were striking with his tan skin. I had never seen a Latino with such deep blue eyes.

"Oh, I don't think you have the right to do the questioning." Isaac said, crouching down so that his face was only a couple feet from the man's head as he spoke. "What I want to know is, who sent you?"

"It doesn't matter." The man spit in my direction, clearly disgusted by me. "Your witch is just as evil as the one that sent me."

"Your accent, it sounds Brazilian." Isaac continued. "Did Silas or Priscilla send you?"

"If I talk. They will kill what little family I have left." The man replied. "You already killed my boys. The twins and my youngest boy. Don't get my wife and daughters killed too."

"So, they did send you then." Isaac said it more as a statement than a question. "Listen, I know that they are holding your family hostage, at the compound in Brazil near their mansion. And you know that in a matter of seconds, perhaps minutes, you will likely be killed by them."

The man did not reply, but his furrowed brow and silence let up that Isaac had spoken true. "The reason we came together as clans, was because after the first group attacked us back in Oregon, one of your men, a man named Royce, told us about your situation. How you are bred and trained to kill other bloodlines, and that your cruel masters use your women and children as hostages to keep you in line. We are going to find and kill Silas and Priscilla, and free your people."

"You cannot." The man replied, pointing at Isaac. "If you even try, they will use their magic. They can kill you instantly, just by thinking it. Even from across the world, their magic knows no bounds." The man paused, before turning his eyes on me, and pointing in my direction. "Only she can kill the witch and her husband. I don't think their magic works on each other."

"This magic you speak of it makes their heads explode right?" Isaac asked.

"Yes, I have seen it before. More than once." He replied, seeming surprised that Isaac knew so much.

"And what if I told you it wasn't magic at all?" Isaac mused aloud. "What if I told you that they have implanted chips in your brains, with an explosive inside that they can activate with the simple push of a button, causing your heads to explode. What would you say then?" Isaac paused, but the man did not reply as he contemplated Isaac's words. "Would you help us find and free your family?"

"It is not at their mansion." The man replied suddenly after another long pause. "They do have a farm there, where they raise and train us, to give to the other tainted ones, but that is not the main compound."

"Go on." Isaac replied, sounding surprised that the man suddenly wanted to talk.

"If I tell you more, do you promise you will try and save them?" The man asked.

"You have my word." Isaac assured the man. "By the light I will use whatever information you give me to free your family."

"There are two compounds." The man continued. "The first is on the outskirts of northern Pirapora. This is where Silas and

Priscilla have their mansion and raise the bloodlines that are sacrificed to the tainted ones from Europe. Every few years they come and take two new fighters for their small army. The other farm, hidden on an actual farm with multiple buildings and barns, has twice as many bloodlines. This is where they are raising an army to fight the European bloodlines. My family is kept there, on the south end of Pirapora, closer to the river. There are over one hundred bloodlines there. Many more than the main one."

"I hate to interrupt this awkward interrogation of a gimpy murderer." Haysom said loudly as he approached from inside the building. The man also had blood on his clothes and seemed shorter than normal as he clutched one of the large black swords in his short stubby arms. "But one of the older guests from the other rooms finally stepped outside. After a loud scream when she saw the fun, we were having without her, she got on the phone to call police. Unless you think we can somehow explain and good feelings this entire mess away, we need to go now. The light itself couldn't make sense of this to even the most rational sort." I noticed that Haysom's eyes had a bit of crazy wideness to them as he spoke. It was the first time I noticed it about the man.

"Haysom's right." Luke said, looking around at the group. "We do need to go. I gave everyone coordinates to the Mansion in Idaho. I say we spread out and meet back there."

A sudden pop sounded off to my left, and I felt moisture in the air as I realized the man we had captured had just been killed. The smell of burnt flesh hit my nostrils as I looked down to see that the man's head was gone. It reminded me of the other who had been killed the same way.

"Well, that's unfortunate." Isaac replied, looking at the man on the ground. "Everyone hurry and grab your things. We need to leave now."

CHAPTER XIII

I was excited when Luke turned into the small opening in the woods that led towards the Idaho mansion. Unlike when we had left just a few days before, the snow was completely melted, making the trees and forest shrubbery a beautiful green color as I took in the mountainside around us. I reached over and put my hand on Luke's leg just above the knee as he drove, gently squeezing it as I smiled at him. The ring on my left ring finger shining brightly as the light touched it.

After my dad had agreed to let us get engaged, Luke had pretended to propose to me in the woods at a rest stop in northern Utah the day before. I had acted surprised and excited, while most of those traveling with us had seemed genuinely surprised. A lot of hugs and congratulations had followed, in addition to some suspicious and mistrusting looks and comments from Jarvis and a couple members of the Japanese clan.

"What is it?" Luke glanced briefly at me, a curious smile creeping onto his full lips as my mind returned to the present. The way the light was shining on him through his window gave a brief glow to his face. His eyes almost seemed to twinkle in the sun as I marveled at how ridiculously good looking the boy was.

"Nothing." I replied smiling. "Do I have to have a reason to check out the man of my dreams?"

"Man of your dreams huh?" Luke teased back. "You sure it's not a nightmare?"

"Oh please. You know how handsome you are." I gently caressed the side of his face with one hand. "Thanks for driving, by the way. You know it's not my favorite."

I had driven for the first 12 hours straight after the Arizona battle, but once everyone rested up, Luke had driven most of the rest of the way. We had stopped at a town in Utah to switch the license plates out on all of the cars. Isaac had a point of contact there who helped to facilitate that, and he had also met another man to give the Satellite phone to for examination. He was fairly certain that it had been used to track us all to the hotel in Arizona, so the man had removed the tracking chip in the radio when they first met up. Isaac explained that while he had removed the SIM card from the satellite phone, this model also had a GPS chip in it to track the device. He had said it was a mistake he wouldn't make again.

"Someone needs to thank me for not throwing up in my mouth just now." Ben teased from the back seat. "Seriously guys. Get a room." He shook his head while smiling.

"Like you can talk." I glanced back at Ben as I spoke. He was sitting directly behind Luke, with Kezia in the middle seat, and Trinity in a car seat next to her. "You think I didn't notice all the hand holding and soft whispering going on back there for the last ten hours?"

"I don't know what you're talking about." Ben replied incredulously. "If my hand slipped while we were sleeping, you can't

HOLD that against me." He smiled again, grabbing Kezia's hand and holding it close with both hands as he emphasized the word hold.

Kezia laughed softly but said nothing as she looked down. Her cheeks flushed. Trinity smiled but didn't speak. The girl had barely spoken at all since Arizona, and when she did, it was only in a whisper to her big cousin.

We pulled into the opening in the trees, with the large grayish mansion coming into view. Many of the trees behind the large building towered over it, with the wooded hill behind it rising towards the looming Selkirk mountains to the north. About halfway up the mountains, I could see the snowline, with more white than green showing above it. Luke parked the car and we stepped out. I wasn't sure why I stretched as I got out, other than instinct. In spite of how long we had been in the car, my body didn't even feel stiff. Another advantage to my newfound curse was not having to worry about aches and pains. In fact, since being shot, I had only felt minor pain when I had sparred with Ben during the day, and even then, it wasn't too bad.

Isaac pulled up in his truck, with my father right behind him in the Tahoe. Several other vehicles bearing the other clans pulled in shortly behind them, and the cars ended up filling the entire front pull through driveway once everyone had parked. Isaac and Tobias led everyone inside. I couldn't help but notice Metemba holding the front door to the mansion open for some time as everyone filed in. It wasn't until Jazmine passed him that he smiled big, and followed her inside before Luke or I even went in. I had asked Luke to stay outside, but I waited until the door closed and everyone was in before I started.

"So…" I took a deep breath, trying to find the words. "When were you wanting to do this?"

"Do what?" Luke asked, looking perplexed.

"Get married." I clarified, lifting my left hand in front of his face to display the ring. The very thought of actually marrying the boy had me so excited that I didn't even pretend to hide it. I was in love. Ridiculously so, and I was determined to marry him as soon as possible... while also trying not come off as some kind of desperate psychopath.

"Oh, I don't know. I kind of thought we would figure that out after the mission in Brazil." Luke said slowly. "Unless you had something else in mind?"

"Actually, I did." I smiled up at him, turning to rest my hands on his hips. "How about tonight?"

"Tonight?!" Luke asked incredulously. "But you don't even have a dress, and your dad only just told me he was good with it as long as we didn't rush."

"I can run into town this afternoon and pick up a white dress." I said reassuringly. "I don't need anything fancy, and this mansion is nice enough to have the wedding right here in the great hall area. Both of our families are already here."

"But Liz" Luke objected. "Your dad would never go for it. He would kill us." He put his hand up on both sides of his head, looking woefully uncomfortable.

"Remember this morning." I decided to try a different angle. "When you bought me that chocolate chip chocolate muffin with orange juice and told me happy birthday." He looked at me without speaking, so I continued. "I thought it was so sweet, and you asked what I wanted for my birthday today. Well, I thought about it, and I want you for my birthday."

"But Liz..." Luke began.

"I'm not finished." I interrupted, putting my finger to his lips to hush him. "I am eighteen years old today, which means I am an adult, so I don't really care what my father thinks to be honest with you. I know I told you that I was good with the ring being my birthday present… but I lied. I want to marry you tonight Leuken Bennett. Because tomorrow we are leaving for Brazil, and there is a decent chance that one or both of us might die. You might not care, but I have things I want to do before I die, including you." I felt my cheeks blush slightly, and it felt odd to be so forward, but I had made up my mind. Now I just needed to convince him why we shouldn't wait.

"I know you care about respecting me, and I made a promise to my mom." I continued. "But if I die tomorrow, or the day after, or whenever that is, I want that to happen as your wife. The only way to guarantee that is if we get married tonight. Our only options are to elope, which you already promised my father we wouldn't do, or to get married here in front of everyone, so that you don't have to break your word. So… what do you say?" I bit my lip as I looked up at him imploringly.

"Uh…I just don't know." Luke took a deep breath as he looked down at me and then back up at the forest. "I don't want to start our marriage with your dad wanting to kill me."

"What don't you know?" I replied, suddenly worrying that maybe he had changed his mind. "Do you not want to marry me anymore?"

"Goodness no." He replied. "I mean of course I do. I want nothing more in the world than to be your husband, but…"

"Then marry me." I cut him off again. "Tonight… and I promise you I will make it worth your while." I smiled mischievously as I pulled him down for a kiss. It was long and sweet, and I pressed myself against him for good measure as we kissed.

"You think he will go along?" Luke asked as we stopped kissing. He looked less nervous and more excited than before.

"Honestly Luke. I don't really care what he thinks." A thought came to me. "You already asked for his permission, so I will tell him right now. He will probably freak out and say I'm too young, and blah, blah, blah or whatever… but at the end of the day, we will be married, and at the end of the night…" I trailed off, my lips lingering against his for a long moment as our noses touched before kissing him again.

"Okay." He said about a minute later when we stopped kissing. "Tonight, it is."

"Are you worried?" I asked, unable to keep the smile from my face. I had never felt so exhilarated and happy.

"Not worried." He replied. "Just excited."

"Me too." I kissed him one more time, before turning towards the house. I shifted my mind to focus on the daunting task ahead. It was time to rip off the emotional band-aid. "Now for the hard part. I'm gonna let my dad know."

*　　　*　　　*

"This is beyond crazy." Special Agent Valdez said to Detective Jimenti as they stood on the grass just outside the motel, surveying the outskirts of the carnage that appeared straight out of some horror movie. "This guy had his face smashed in by something. It's like if they ain't chopping your head or limbs off, they're smashing your skull in."

"Yeah, it didn't make sense before." Jimenti thought out loud as his brain churned, trying to make sense of everything. "But have you noticed one thing in common with all of the scenes?"

"Yeah." Valdez replied. "A lot of people are getting killed, and most of them are dressed in all black with nothing but fake IDs on them. And we got way too many people carrying swords. I don't know what's up with all the swords, but I'm done with swords." His frustration was bleeding through his sarcasm.

"I was thinking the same thing." Jimenti said, chuckling. "But then I noticed that there is one thing in common with almost every single victim from all three scenes with the men in black. Every one of them has had their head decapitated or smashed in." Valdez stood silent, his mouth hanging open as he stared at the corpse, obviously deep in thought.

"Isn't that pretty much what I just said?" Valdez finally spoke. "Everyone cutting stuff off with swords."

"Look." Jimenti looked around to make sure no one else was close before continuing "I know you laughed before when I mentioned the whole super-human powers thing, but after seeing the video of that girl jumping, the boy healing, and all the other crazy stuff going on, I think not admitting the obvious would be a mistake. I'm not pretending to understand exactly what is happening, but there is some supernatural stuff going on here. I think these men in black are superhuman as well, and the only way to kill them is by taking out their heads."

"You know a few weeks ago I would have laughed and told you to see a shrink or something." Valdez said slowly. "But now… I think you might be on to something. Even if it makes me sound like I need a tinfoil hat myself."

"Look at these skull fractures in the forehead here." Jimenti continued. "See how the bone breaks have patterned break points? Unless this man was killed with a strangely shaped cudgel of some sort, I would say it looks like someone literally punch through their skull to smash in their brains. There is nothing natural about that."

Jimenti and Valdez had already looked at the various entrances to the motels and surveyed the carnage there. Two other people appeared to have been killed by head smashing, but the rest had all been cut up, most with the heads missing. A lot of rounds had been fired as well at each of the entrances, but there was a lot more blood than there were bodies, making Jimenti think that others had bled and fled.

"Can you do me a favor?" Jimenti asked. "Have your techs compare all of the different blood samples from here against the samples from the crime scenes in Harrisburg, Las Vegas, and Overton. I want to see if we get any blood matches."

"Yeah, I'll go and tell them." Valdez walked back over to the South entrance to the motel, where forensic technicians with gloves were processing the scene.

Jimenti thought back to the interview he had conducted a few minutes earlier with the female front office employee. He had asked about and shown pictures of the Bennetts and Scotts from Harrisburg when they talked to her about everyone who had checked in the day before. She had only recognized the one who went by Isaac as the one who used his card to rent out most of the motel. Elizabeth Scott and Luke Bennett's pictures looked familiar to her, but she was only certain on Isaac. *Who knows what the man's real name is.* Jimenti thought to himself. She had described a few of them as black, and several of them had "funny accents", but the group was larger than just the two original families from Harrisburg.

The credit card used for the transaction came back to an LLC with a PO box in Washington State, but everything for the account was handled electronically. Jimenti had a feeling that when they pulled on all the strings from the credit card leads, it would probably hit a dead end.

"Those girls from the Phoenix office are on point." Valdez said as he walked back over. "They already got approval to expedite all the DNA workups on the blood. This might get a little bit interesting though."

"Why is that?" Jimenti asked.

"They said that DOD is sending some of their people out." Valdez explained.

"Don't tell me those bastards are taking over our investigation?" Jimenti was instantly annoyed at hearing the military was getting involved. They had a habit of refusing to cooperate with the FBI, let alone task force officers like himself.

"No, surprisingly they aren't" Valdez continued. "Said they are sending a couple of their investigators out to observe and share intel. Whatever that means. Wouldn't surprise me if they snake it from us later, but for now FBI is still primary. You and I both know you are better than any of our agents, so for now we are still good. Even with us escaping the media attention because of how remote this location is, headquarters is sending agents from four additional field offices to assist with this case."

"That does beg the question though." Jimenti added. "With all these men in black, who appear to be some kind of assassins, obviously being the aggressors, yet simultaneously getting their butts kicked by the Bennetts, Scotts, and whoever all these other foreigners are. What are we going to do once we catch up to them?"

"Beats me." Valdez mused. "Maybe arrest them... maybe give them a high five for self-defense. Either way this is already one heck of a case. I'm glad you are primary case agent."

*　　*　　*

"What do you mean you want to get married tonight?" My father said incredulously as he turned to look directly at me. "Are you out of your mind? You two have only been engaged for a day. One day!" He raised his voice more and more as he spoke.

I was sitting on the couch next to him at the edge of the sitting room portion of the main entryway. The other clans were spread throughout the house, with only the two of us in the front room, but I was certain that those in the nearby den and dining area could hear my father with his voice so loud. He had seemed annoyed when I asked him to talk alone, but with others in the back yard and on the front porch, this room seemed the closest to alone that we were going to get. Having the better part of six clans in one house, even if it was a mansion, made things a bit more crowded.

"I know dad. And I completely understand why you would be upset." I tried to keep my voice calm, as I had assumed that he would overreact to some extent when I delivered the news. "But I would like you to hear me out for just one minute. Please."

"Oh, this better be good." He said sarcastically. "Go ahead. I'm listening."

"I know that you think I am young, but I have already been pretty much raising Alex, and taking care of most things around the house for over a year since mom passed. You might think that I am not ready or immature, or whatever excuse you have concocted in your head to justify the fact that you are opposed to this idea. But I think if you are being honest with yourself, what it really comes down to is that you don't want to lose me. Well guess what? You might lose me tomorrow, or the next day, or a week from now. So maybe you should be supportive of letting me do what will make me happy."

"Don't you play the guilt game with me young lady. When I told that kid yes, he didn't say the wedding would be the next day." My father took a deep breath before continuing. He lowered his voice slightly, but he was still talking loudly. "I'm not the one who is being unreasonable here. You want to marry a boy that you have only known for a few months, on the day you turn eighteen, and you expect me to give my permission for something as crazy as this?"

"This wasn't Luke's idea to have the wedding today, it was mine, and I wasn't asking for your permission." I said as I turned to face my father again. Though I could feel my eyes watering, and a tear roll slowly down one cheek, my jaw was clenched. I had never felt more resolved to do something before in my life, and as saddening as his stubborn lack of support was, it didn't sway me an inch. "I was just asking if you would walk me down the aisle. But... obviously you think being stubborn is more important than supporting me on the most important day of my life." I turned and walked away, slamming the large front door behind me as I stepped out onto the porch. The words had come out harsher than I intended, but I couldn't take them back.

CHAPTER XIV

Daniel was pacing back and forth in the woods behind the mansion. He could see one of the Japanese clan members looking out from an upstairs bedroom window at him, but he was too upset to care about who watched him. The audacity of Elizabeth, thinking that she could make her own life changing decisions, when she had only been eighteen for a day, was infuriating to him. *Getting married at her age was insane. If she is so worried about being killed on this mission*, he thought to himself, *then I just won't let her go.*

Daniel was surprised to see Sara walking out of the house towards him. Normally he got excited when he saw the pretty lady, but in his current state of mind, he didn't think that even she could calm him down. He continued pacing as she approached, running his hand through his hair as he walked and turned.

"I was going to ask what happened back there." She began. "But with how loud that argument got, I think half the house heard. I'm guessing Liz talked to you about marrying Luke sooner rather than later?" She stopped about five feet away, right in the middle of the path he had been pacing on. He stopped when he was still a few feet away from her, pausing to look down at her near perfect face.

Her long blonde hair was blowing slightly in the cool breeze, pushing strands of her hair across her blue eyes as she looked up at him. The concern and worry were obvious on her face.

Daniel moved to walk around her but stopped when she put a hand on his forearm. "I can tell you are upset." Sara continued, moving her hand up to gently rest on his cheek and temple. "I probably would be too if I were in your shoes, but please don't shut me out." Daniel could feel the anger dissipating inside of him as she touched his face. Somehow, she had a way of calming him that no one else besides his late wife had been able to do.

"I'm sorry Sara." Daniel replied slowly, looking down into her eyes. "I'm not upset with you. It's just... I don't think they are old enough to get married. When I told Luke that I was okay with it, as long as they didn't run off and elope, I didn't think they would want a shotgun wedding a day later." Sara kept looking at him and ran her hand across the side of his head and on the back of his neck, caressing his head.

"You don't think..." Daniel trailed off without finishing. He didn't think it would be wise to say out loud what he was thinking in that moment.

"Don't think what?" Sara asked.

Daniel stared into the trees above Sara's head for several seconds before continuing. "You don't think that she is pregnant, do you?"

Sara laughed softly. "Oh Dan. I raised Luke better than that. And I'm pretty sure you did the same with Liz. I really don't think that they have been that kind of intimate."

"This was probably your son's idea." Daniel said. "When did he tell you about his plan?"

"Actually, he only just told me after Liz slammed the door at the end of your argument." Sara clarified. "We were chatting with

Jazmine until we heard you get worked up, so I asked Luke what that was all about, and he told me that Liz wants to get married tonight. He tried talking her out of it because he doesn't want you to hate him."

Daniel paused for a long moment before replying. "And what do you think about this crazy idea?"

"I think that you are so upset right now that it is hard to think straight." Sara added. "But I also think you should consider that when you are a member of the bloodline, always being hunted, and always hiding in the shadows, hoping to survive another day, month, or year, you have a different perspective on life and what is truly important. When Nathan first proposed to me, I was only seventeen years old. He was nineteen, and we met because my uncle was friends with his dad, and they had come to a barbeque we were at. It was a week before my eighteenth birthday, and I fell completely in love with the boy."

Daniel had actually never heard the full story about Sara and her husband meeting, so he was minorly interested, in spite of the fact that he had no intention of changing his mind. "And do you think you were old enough to get married?"

"Absolutely. Nathan made me smile every day, and always put me, and eventually the kids, before himself." She paused to smile up at Daniel again. "In a lot of ways, he was similar to you. I have absolutely no regrets about marrying him when I did, a week after I turned eighteen. We were completely happy with two amazing young boys until that monster took him from us."

"Whoa hold on a second." Daniel couldn't help himself. "So, you knew this guy for like a few weeks before you got married? And you don't think that's a little nuts?"

"We spent a lot of time together for those few weeks." Sara said defensively, and Daniel realized it was probably not good to insult her and her husband who had been killed. "And besides, Nathan had said that it felt right with the light, and I felt good about it too. If we hadn't married when we did, I probably wouldn't have my amazing boys, or all the fond memories that I do."

"But didn't you two struggle getting married so young?" Daniel asked.

"Oh of course we did. But you know that getting through challenges together only makes a marriage stronger. We had to move on the fly several times, and Nathan was always looking over his shoulder. But that had more to do with him being bloodline than anything else." Sara explained.

"What did your dad say?" Daniel added. "When he proposed to you at seventeen?"

"Well..." She hesitated before answering. "He actually said no and told me I couldn't see Nathan ever again."

"Seriously?" Daniel asked.

"Oh yes. I lived on a farm and my older sister had already gotten married to a guy who was an alcoholic, so he was completely against me getting married young. So, I ran away with Nathan, and we got married a state away by some random priest in front of two complete strangers. Nathan's father had been so upset when we ran off together, that he refused to come to the wedding, even though I talked Nathan into calling and inviting him."

"Geez." Daniel sat down on a large tree stump resting between several trees. "I wasn't expecting you to go there. I thought your encouraging story about how happy you were was pretty good but then you go and drop that on me."

Sara chuckled lightheartedly. "I'll admit I wasn't planning on talking about that part right now. But you asked." She shrugged her shoulders and stepped closer to him, putting her hand on his chin so that he was looking up at her. Her lips touched his, however briefly, and she pulled away smiling again. It wasn't the first time they had kissed, but before it had always been when no one could see them. "Look, I'm not trying to talk you into letting them get married. If I were in your shoes, I might think it is crazy too. But I do know that they are both adults now, and your daughter can be stubborn like a mule."

"I wonder where she gets that from." Daniel interjected sarcastically.

"Which is actually a great quality... in good people." Sara continued. "We need more people standing for what is right. The point I am trying to make is, if she wants to marry Luke, and he wants to marry her, there is nothing either one of us can do to stop it. You can tell they are both head over heels in love with each other. So, the choice is really, do I want my daughter to know how much I love her and will always be there for her or not?" She gently grabbed both sides of his head. "Or do I want her to think that I don't trust her or her judgment, and damage my relationship with my only daughter on what should be the happiest day of her life? And if I do that... will she ever forgive me for it?"

Daniel let out a heavy sigh. He wanted to argue with the beautiful woman and continue being stubborn. Deep down though, he knew what he needed to do. That didn't mean he had to like it though.

* * *

"The fact that they have not already come is a good sign." Silas was attempting to calm Priscilla down, as she paced back and forth in front of her ornate chair, pulling at the end of her hair occasionally in between wringing her fingers. "The news from Arizona does not give any indication of what happened there."

"But what if one of them talked?" Priscilla was so angry that her voice almost shrieked as she spoke. "I know we killed the survivor when it became obvious that he had been captured, but if these savages are capable of taking out thirty of our best fighters in a matter of minutes, I'm not sure we can stand against them."

"Well, we have more than thirty fighters if we pull from the offsite, but I'm not confident it will be enough." Silas explained. "From the last report before the slaughter, our team leader assured that there were only a dozen or so bloodlines at the motel. I can only assume that some of them were killed as well, which means their forces have been depleted."

"Unless more came after your failure of a leader checked in." Priscilla chided. "There could have been dozens for all we know."

"That is certainly possible." Silas mused. "It is equally possible that they had Auserwhalt with them. Attacking at night without Terralium blades against other chosen would be an almost certain death sentence."

"Wait…you might be on to something." Priscilla said, acting as though she had just had a good idea.

"What is it?" Silas asked.

"What if we set a trap." Priscilla continued. "You said that they had taken one of our satellite phones. Which we used to track them to Arizona. What if we somehow made them think that we were hiding out in Alastair's palace? If we could get them to go, there… Alastair could kill them. And who knows, maybe we would get lucky, and they kill Rueben or Vincent."

"I don't think that will work." Silas began.

"Well why not!?" Priscilla interrupted, shouting.

"Because they disabled the satellite phone yesterday, somewhere in Utah to the north. The likelihood of picking up their signal is slim." Silas tried to keep his tone neutral, so that it was less obvious how stupid he thought the woman was. The bracelet on his wrist was a constant reminder that while she pretended he was her husband, he was forced to be her slave. "Even if we could lead them there, Alastair would dispatch of them easily. His best fighters and the other chosen all have terralium blades. Not to mention, we still have the problem of only having four more days to kill those bloodlines and send their heads to Reuben."

"Do we have any leads?" Priscilla said after a long pause. "Any clues as to where they might be?"

"Unfortunately, no." Silas answered. "I think that our best bet is to wait and lay a trap. When Reuben comes back, he will almost definitely bring Vincent and Aurelia with some of their best fighters. I think if we pull everyone from the farm and have them lay in wait… we might be able to survive this. If we can kill those three, that would only leave Alastair and the other three. We would have to go into hiding for a while and build up our army. We could use their ring and bracelet to control another Auserwhalt and teach them to fight."

"But they will bring their best fighters as well, and we are likely not a match for Reuben and Vincent. Do you think we could overwhelm and kill them?" Priscilla asked.

"We would have to play it just right, as we only have the one terralium sword and dagger." Silas replied. "But if we get them close enough for me to detonate and take out their troops, while ours lie a way off… perhaps we could have a few of ours all attack at once. If we get Vincent and Aurelia's weapons away, we could overpower and kill Reuben."

"Or we could go into hiding now?" Priscilla said cautiously. "They won't be coming for a few days. Perhaps it will give us time to move everyone."

"I surmise that they are already surveilling us now." Silas added. "Our best bet is to identify their spies if they have any and kill them at the same time we ambush them. I highly doubt that they know we have the means to destroy their bloodline guards in an instant."

*   *   *

I was surprised when the other clans showed up at the mansion in Idaho. Luckily, they were staying at a hotel about an hour away because the space was already getting somewhat crowded. As predicted, the French clan had contacted Isaac to let him know that they would not be coming to assist, as they thought it was too dangerous. They did say that if we managed to free to captive bloodlines in Brazil, they would be willing to help if there were others. They said that their main reservations were me, my father and Tobias. The Verdorben were known for being crafty and deceiving people so that they could kill them, and they didn't trust that we had real control over ourselves.

The Danish clan had showed up first, in the early afternoon, as I was just about to leave to go dress shopping. Elias was the clan chief, and he had brought his son Erik and his grandchildren Mikkel and Anna. The younger two appeared close to my age, but they could have been ten or twenty years older for all I knew. Anna at least seemed young, and her brother had made a comment about her snapping recently, but in bloodline time recently could mean a month or several years. She was almost as tall as Ben, with fair skin and long golden blonde hair. Her blue eyes almost made me jealous, but Luke barely spared her a glance before I caught him staring at me again, so I didn't really feel threatened.

Kezia on the other hand, had shot Ben the look of death when he smiled and shook Anna's hand. Judging by the way Anna had seemed to smile more for him than when anyone else was introduced, my guess was that Kezia was simply jealous of the taller girl. I wasn't sure why though, as Kezia was just a pretty in her own way, even if she seemed less confident in her looks. Mikkel had smiled almost too warmly at me when we were introduced, until I had introduced Luke as my fiancé. His expression had immediately changed to just friendly when he congratulated us both.

Elias, who was balding on top with grayish hair on the sides, as well as his son Erik, had both been polite when introduced. But... I couldn't help but notice that they both looked at me and my father with more distrust than the younger generation of Danes had. At least they were not openly hostile towards me.

It was when the Boston clan showed up that my mind had truly been blown. When the two first walked in, I had been almost speechless. The first man, short and stocky, introduced himself simply as Vinny from the Boston clan. It was his companion, who walked in the door just behind him, that completely blew my mind.

"Uncle Tommy?" I said excitedly when the second member of the Boston clan stepped forward to introduce himself. Thomas Barrett was my mom's older brother. With dark hair and blue eyes like my mom, he was skinny but toned, and had a large Adams apple that I remembered poking fun at when I was just a young girl. I hadn't seen him in several years, but I remembered his face, with the large dimples like he had right now as he smiled at me. Without thinking I ran up to him and gave him a big hug.

"Izzie!?" My uncle sounded completely surprised as I picked him up in the air. I think I startled him, as his next words came out rushed and gasping for air. "Too tight."

"Oh sorry." I said as I set him down and let go. "Sometimes I forget about how strong I am."

"No worries sweetie." Tommy replied. "Although, I guess I shouldn't call you that anymore since you're all grown and stuff... I can't believe how big you are now. I swear the last time I saw you; you were about yeah high." He held a hand up to his chest, several inches below my current height. "And you weren't snapped and stuff." He looked down awkwardly as he finished talking.

"Oh my gosh Tommy." I added. "It is so good to see you. My father joked that he thought you might be dead after you didn't make it to mom's funeral." I was confused by his comment about being snapped but decided to ignore it.

"Yeah… about that." Tommy seemed to struggle to know what to say. "Sorry kid, I actually didn't find out until a few months later when I dropped in to check on the parents. By then I was honestly too embarrassed to come see ya."

"That's okay uncle Tommy." Suddenly the fact that he had showed up with the other Boston clan member hit me. "Wait a second… are you a member of the bloodline?"

"Surprise." He said, holding his arms out with a bashful expression on his face. "I guess now you know why I was always on the move huh?"

"I always just assumed you loved to travel and didn't care much for family." I explained. "I actually don't understand. How can you be from the bloodline? Neither grandma or grandpa had superpowers."

"You really didn't know?" Tommy asked incredulously. Now that I thought about it, he only looked a few years older than me, even though my mom had said he was nine years older than her. "Great grandpa Jack was from the bloodline."

"You mean it can pass down without even one parent being from the bloodline?" I asked.

"Yeah silly." Tommy explained. "It is not nearly as common, but the gene can be carried without being manifested. It's all complicated DNA stuff, but if anyone on either side of the family has it in their blood, anyone could be bloodline. Even some of those with both bloodline parents don't get the abilities for some reason, but that's just the way genetics work, I guess. That's why the tainted ones always kill the women and children, even if their abilities haven't manifested yet. How else do you think you got your bloodline abilities?"

"My bloodline abilities?" I wasn't sure how to respond to what he had said. *Oh my gosh! He doesn't know!* I thought to myself.

"Hey Thomas." I was surprised to see my father had stepped up to join us, and he interrupted before I had a chance to explain that I wasn't from the bloodline. Vinny was walking around the room shaking other people's hands. Judging by the sound of my father's voice, he sounded less excited to see my uncle than I had been. He shook Tommy's hand, and he grunted slightly in pain as my father squeezed his hand.

"Wait a second..." Tommy said suddenly, looking at my father in disbelief. "There's no way you are bloodline. I remember you breaking your arm at work in that wreck when Izzie was just a baby..."

"You really don't know?" My father added. He paused for a brief moment before continuing. "We were both cursed by the tainted ones. Both Liz and I are Verdorben now."

"No, no, no..." Tommy was shaking his head in disbelief, distraught at the thought. "Are you freaking kidding me?" He buried his forehead in both hands in disbelief.

"What did you think Tommy?" I interrupted, seeing that my father was still upset. "Did you really think that I was from the bloodline?"

"Well, when you squeezed me yeah." Tommy responded. "What was I supposed to think? You've got it in your blood to be changed. I mean Vinny told me that you guys had Verdorben here, but I didn't think it was my baby niece for crying out loud! Or my brother-in-law. This is nuts." I could tell he was not a fan of our transformation.

"Wait a minute." Isaac interrupted as he came and stood next to me. "Are you Elizabeth's blood uncle? How exactly are you related?"

"Well yeah." Tommy replied, looking confused. "Liz is my sister's daughter."

"You mean your stepsister or half-sister?" Isaac asked.

"No. I mean my blood sister." Tommy explained. "We both had the same mom and dad."

"That is not possible." Isaac sounded adamant as he spoke. "Offspring of the bloodline are immune from the curse of the tainted ones. You must have had a different father or something. Perhaps your mother didn't tell you because she didn't want you to think less of her."

"Listen guy." Tommy got angry as his New York accent became stronger. "I don't even know your name, but if you are gonna accuse my mother of being some kinda slut we can step outside and settle this right now. I don't care if you are old enough to be my grandpa. I got no problem kicking your... "

"Whoa, whoa, whoa!" Vinny stepped in between Isaac and my uncle, putting his hands out. "Let's everybody just calm down and we can talk about this real civilized. Okay Tommy?"

"I'm not the one calling someone else's mom an adulterating whore!" Tommy said gesturing at Isaac. "Maybe someone should teach this old man some manners."

"I'm sorry for giving offense." Isaac said apologetically with his hands out. "That was not my intent. But it is impossible for someone with blood from the bloodline to be transformed."

"Well even if my mom was a slut, and she was not!" Tommy said emphatically. "It wouldn't have made a difference because Uncle Jack was her father. So, I got it from my maternal grandfather. Considering my mom carried both me and Liz's mom, I'm gonna say there is no way Liz wouldn't have the genes."

"And you are sure you are not adopted?" Isaac suddenly turned to me.

"Listen Isaac." My dad turned with obvious frustration on his face. "I watched Liz be born. Before you start hurling out insults and accusations, you might want to think twice. I actually like you, but you are starting to piss me off."

"Please understand." Isaac spoke in an apologetic fashion. "I am not trying to be rude or dramatic. It's just that, Liz couldn't have been turned if she has our blood in her veins. Even if she only carries the gene, the light protects us all from the curse of the Verdorben." Isaac explained.

"Unless." Jacob strode quietly into the room. I was surprised by how heavy his accent was, while somehow sounding very similar to Isaac in every other way as he spoke. "Unless the prophecy is true." He stared at me intently as he finished speaking. It was a little unsettling how he almost seemed to be looking through me when he spoke.

Murmurs erupted from most of the bloodlines in the room as what Jacob said sunk in. I looked at Luke, I'm sure not doing a good job of hiding the utter confusion I felt. "What prophecy?" I asked quietly, looking back and forth between Isaac and Jacob after Luke shrugged. He had appeared equally confused.

"I'm sure it is probably nothing." Isaac said suddenly, his eyes locked on Jacob's for a brief moment before he continued. It reminded me of the look my dad used to give my mom when he didn't want to talk about something in front of the kids.

"Okay… well that wasn't awkward at all." Tommy said sarcastically before smiling again. "It really is good to see you, Liz. And you too Dan. Even if you guys are somehow tainted ones now. Oh and… please tell me baby Alex didn't get possessed by some kinda demon too?"

CHAPTER XV

"Come on it will be fun." Benjamin Bennett said as he motioned for some of the other clan members that were gathered nearby to join them. He had tied a rope between two large trees in the rear lawn of the mansion and placed large rocks on opposite ends of the rope, forming giant squares on the ground for each side. "It might not be beach volleyball, but it's definitely the next best thing. Besides, tonight is gonna be a boring wedding, so let's have fun while we can."

So far only the younger Japanese clan member, his father, Haysom, Benjamin and Kezia were standing on the makeshift volleyball court. They needed one more for even teams. Since Jazmine, Liz and his mom were all in town getting some makeshift supplies for the wedding tonight, Ben thought it would be fun to surprise Kezia. She had mentioned that she loved playing volleyball.

"Why are you looking at me like that?" Ben asked when he noticed that Kezia was giving him a confused look.

"Oh, nothing." Kezia replied, looking down at her feet.

"No what is it?" He pressed.

"I don't know why you called the wedding boring. I actually think it's romantic that they are getting married. Aren't you excited for them?" Kezia asked, smiling as she spoke.

"Oh yeah." Ben instantly felt stupid for downplaying the whole wedding. He actually was happy for his brother and Liz. Since he had met Kezia, his old feelings for Liz were completely gone. "Of course, I do. I just thought it might be fun to play a bit first. You said you love volleyball, right?" He squeezed her shoulder affectionately while looking at her. He actually couldn't remember anyone making him feel so happy like he did around Kezia, and he had no shortage of crushes growing up.

"Yeah, I love it." Kezia reassured smiling at him again.

"I'll play." The tall Danish girl said as she walked over to where they were gathered on the grass. "I'm not very good, but I will give it a try."

"That's what I am talking about." Haysom said excitedly. "I'm glad to see not all you Danes are stuck up. Even if you are way too tall." While Ben thought he meant for it to sound jovial, it came across as completely rude and barely sarcastic.

"Don't worry about him." Ben tried to soften the awkwardness. "It was Anna, right?"

"Yes." The tall girl replied, smiling broadly. "Your memory is obviously as good as your looks Benjamin Bennett."

"Thanks. Please, just call me Ben." Ben replied and smiled back politely. "What should we do for teams?"

"How about me, Anna and Haysom against you three?" Hiroshi asked.

"Works for me." Ben replied. "Get ready to get wrecked!" He teased.

"Well unless you stop incessantly ogling my cousin, baby face." Haysom chided. "I'm not really that worried. I might be midget sized, but I can jump out the gym."

"You guys can serve." Ben said as he threw the volleyball across the makeshift net to Anna. Chuckling softly at Haysom's taunting, he turned to get in position. "You guys want to play two up and one back?" he asked. For some reason, Kezia just nodded without saying anything.

"That works for me." Hiroshi replied, stepping back to cover the rear half of the square.

"You want the right or left side?" Ben asked Kezia.

"This side is fine." Kezia replied, still not looking at Ben. He couldn't tell if she was upset, or just competitive, so he decided not to press the issue.

"Who is serving first?" Anna asked from across the net as she held the ball up.

"Ladies first, by all means." Haysom replied loudly. Ben was beginning to realize that Kezia's older cousin only had one volume, and it was loud. "I want to spike on baby face here." Haysom grinned lightly as he taunted Ben.

Baby face? Ben thought to himself. He didn't bother responding, as he didn't want the short man to think he was getting under Ben's skin. He knew he looked somewhat young, but at sixteen years old, he thought that was kind of normal.

"I'm aiming for you Ben." Anna teased, smiling again as she served. The volley went back and forth several times over a couple of serves before Ben was able to score and get the ball. He was impressed by how deceptively fast Haysom was, and both Anna and Hiroshi were good for having claimed they hadn't played much.

Kezia was also very good and gave perfect set ups whenever she hit the ball. He tried to high five her for her set after he scored, but she completely ignored him. She must have been in the zone, Ben thought to himself.

It wasn't until a few plays later, that Ben realized what was going on with her. He dug a shot from Haysom that almost hit the ground, then Akira set the ball up at the net for Kezia to shoot. When she jumped up to hit the ball, she elevated a couple of feet above the net, as Haysom jumped to challenge her at the net. For some reason, instead of shooting at the open grass in between Haysom and Anna in the front row, she spiked the ball as fast as she could right at Anna's head, striking her in the side of the face so hard that she fell over.

Ben was completely shocked when he saw Anna get hit and go down. Instinctively he crossed over the rope to help her up. "Are you okay?" He asked as he held a hand out.

"Yeah, I am fine." She smiled at Ben again as she took his hand and he helped her to her feet. She smiled at Kezia understandingly. "I'm sure it was an accident."

"That didn't look like an accident!" Haysom said, making an incredulous look at Kezia as he spoke. "What gives cousin? You got beef with the pretty tall one?" Kezia glared at Haysom but didn't say a word.

"It's really fine." Anna said gracefully. "It's all in good fun. The ball must have caught the side of her hand is all, I'm sure."

Ben turned and crossed back over to his side of the court, looking at Kezia confused. She didn't make eye contact, so he walked over to her to ask what caused her to target Anna like that.

"Hey what's going on?" He said quietly under his breath as he rested a hand on her shoulder.

"Nothing." Kezia said, refusing to look at him. "I am fine."

"That didn't look like nothing…" Ben began, but Kezia cut him off.

"I said I'm fine!" She snapped. "Sorry Anna!" She called across the net, before turning and walking angrily off the court.

"That's okay." Anna replied, shrugging at Ben and her teammates.

Ben wasn't sure what to do. He felt bad that Kezia had been rude to Anna, but also didn't want the girl he was crazy for to be mad at him. "Sorry guys, I'm done too." Ben said quickly as he followed after Kezia.

"Okay then!" He heard Haysom say from behind. "Looks like two on two now. Us oldies are gonna destroy you younglings."

Ben followed Kezia through the trees towards the side of the mansion, where she was walking away from the others. He could tell that she was obviously upset, but he wasn't sure if she was mad at the tall Danish girl, or simply taking her anger out on Anna. She had cried in his arms that morning when they went for a walk through the woods, which was the first time she had opened up about her family since her sister and parents had been killed a few days before, but after that she had actually seemed like she was doing a little better. This sudden outburst was completely uncharacteristic for her. She had stopped and was leaning against a tall tree, just out of sight of the rear yard.

"Hey." Ben said as he stopped a few feet short of her. "What is wrong?"

Kezia turned to look at him, nearly scowling her face was so clenched. It was the first time that Ben had ever seen her upset, and it was a little bit scary for him. "You really don't know Benjamin?" She asked.

The way she had said Benjamin made him feel like he was in some serious trouble. "I wouldn't be asking if I did." He said nonchalantly, trying not to show how nervous he was. As instantly as the words came out, he wished that he could take them back.

"Your observation skills are obviously not as good as your looks." Kezia said sarcastically. "Please, call me Ben." She added, grabbing and caressing his hand affectionately. There was nothing but mockery in her expression. "I'm aiming for you Ben." She made her voice sound prissy with a pretend Danish accent as she finished the last part.

Her impersonation of Anna's accent was not very good, but Ben decided against commenting on that part. He had already stuck his foot in his mouth once in the last few seconds. *So, she was jealous of Anna?* He thought to himself. Suddenly it all made sense. The quiet rage and lack of eye contact, the ruthless spike at the girl. "Oh my gosh. You think I have feelings for Anna?" He sounded as surprised as he felt. He had to admit the girl wasn't hard on the eyes, but he only had feelings for Kezia. In fact, he was so smitten with Kezia, that he felt like a part of him was missing whenever he wasn't near her.

Kezia nodded, still looking upset, but didn't speak.

"Goodness no." Ben explained. "I fell for you the second I laid eyes on you back in the desert Kezia Shaw. You are the only girl I care for in that way. Honestly it is almost scary how much I like you already considering we've only known each other for a few days. Besides, Anna is not even my type, even if I wasn't already kinda whooped on you." Kezia's face seemed to soften slightly as he spoke, but she was just looking at him silently with her arms folded. "I mean, honestly I didn't even notice she was flirting with me if that's what you think happened."

"What I think happened?" She raised one eyebrow incredulously. "She practically made out with you with her words for crying out loud. That dirty slut!"

"Oh my gosh Kezia. I've never seen you so upset." Ben exclaimed, he chuckled softly before catching himself. "I promise I don't care for the girl, but if it will make you feel better, I'll be less friendly. Would that make you less worried?"

"Maybe…" She said, looking back down at the ground.

"I know what you need." He said as he thought of a way to break up the mood. "What did the fish say when he swam into the wall?"

"What?" She asked softly.

"Dam!" He finished with a smile. She chuckled softly for a brief moment, and then went back to her half sad, half somber face.

Ben stepped closer to her and put his arms around her, hugging her close. At first, she kept her arms folded, but then she slowly wrapped her arms around him and hugged him back. "So… it might be too soon, but judging by the fact that you got jealous when you didn't need to, you must really care about me huh?" He pulled back just enough to see her face.

"Don't push your luck." Kezia replied, unsuccessfully holding back a small grin. "But yes… you know I care about you. Probably more than I should." He noticed her eyes starting to water slightly as she got emotional. "I just don't want to lose you too."

"Do you think it is because I saved you?" Ben asked. He had always dreamed of saving a beautiful damsel in distress but didn't think it would actually happen for him until it had with Kezia. The tragic circumstances before the save had made it less romantic, but he was so glad he had gotten to her before that bloodline hunter had been able to kill her.

"No silly." Kezia replied. "I thought you were cute when I first saw you back at the meeting. Although, I do appreciate you saving my niece and me. But that is not why I am crazy about you."

"Oh, you are crazy about me, are you?" Ben smiled again, putting two fingers on the bottom of her chin so that he could look her in the eyes.

"Well don't let it get to your…" Kezia began, but Ben cut her off as he leaned in and kissed her. For a split second, she pulled back, and he worried that he had been too forward. But then she leaned back up and continued kissing him. He didn't hate it.

*   *   *

"Luke!" Isaac called after him from the top of the stairs as Luke was walking down them towards the main room.

"What is it?" Luke stopped and turned on the middle landing.

"Can we talk for a moment?" Isaac motioned for Luke to come back to him, so he made his way back up the stairs. The top of the stairs had a large loft, with a couple of chairs that sat facing the large glass windows. The snowcapped mountains behind the window provided a breathtaking view.

Isaac moved past the chairs to a small decorative bench against the wall next to the windows. It faced the stairs, so they would be able to see if anyone walked up on them while they spoke. Luke walked over and sat next to Isaac.

"Look Isaac." Luke decided to try and head off what he thought was coming. "If this is about the whole wedding night topic… I already had the most awkward conversation of my life with my future father-in-law about an hour ago, so I am good. Really, it was so weird… I'd rather not do that again with you."

"Dear goodness boy!" Isaac said, his face flushing. "I had no plan of discussing intimacy with you. Why on earth would you think that?"

"Well, I didn't think Liz's dad would either, but pulled me aside a little while ago trying to explain how to not hurt Liz, so I don't know…" Luke trailed off. He was relieved that Isaac wasn't trying to cover that topic.

"Well, it's certainly not that. Now I know you have already made up your mind." Isaac began, wringing his hands slightly as he spoke. "But I need you to re-consider marrying Elizabeth."

"What?" Luke exclaimed, surprised. "Are you out of your mind? She is in town getting a dress as we speak, and we leave tomorrow afternoon for Brazil. If we don't do this tonight, it might never happen." Isaac had been like a father to him in many ways throughout his life, but he had never really talked to Luke about relationships before. Why would he try to ruin what was about to be the best day of his life? Luke wondered.

"Now please, at least hear me out." Isaac said defensively. "I know you love the girl, and I do not doubt that she loves you too, but there is something you should know…"

"What is it?" Luke asked.

"Have you ever heard about the ancient prophecy?" Isaac asked.

"I've heard several, but none that I recall being called ancient." Luke replied.

"This one predates the Verdorben. It is from a time before the tainted ones even existed, a time when demons wreaked havoc throughout the world. The light created the bloodlines, to be able to defeat the demons, once and for all." Isaac explained.

"Okay…" Luke was confused what this had to do with him marrying Liz, but he owed it to Isaac to at least hear the man out.

"You know that Alastair is the evil leader of the Verdorben. But what I have not yet told you, is that Alastair once belonged to the bloodline, and the light was strong with him. Like you, he was gifted with multiple skills from the light. But where you have two skills, speed and foreseeing, Alastair also had emotional skills like Ben, strength like my brother Jacob, and healing like Jazmine. All these abilities were enhanced in him. The prophecy that had been foretold before Alastair was that one day, someone from the light would be turned to darkness. This person, would eventually turn back to the light, and sacrifice themselves to defeat the last of the demons, once and for all."

"So do you think that prophecy is about Alastair?" Luke asked.

"I did." Isaac explained. "Alastair's wife was killed by one of the last demons, before he could destroy her. The grief crushed him, which many blamed for why he turned away from the light. But it has been centuries now since Alastair became Verdorben, and I hear he is more ruthless now than ever. Before he turned to darkness, he had actually hunted down and destroyed nearly all of the demons. In fact, it was when he went to kill the last demon, an evil monstrous witch, who was the most powerful of all, that he turned to darkness. When he killed that woman, she cursed him with her dying breath, turning him into Verdorben, along with others around him. I and others had always surmised that he was the one mentioned in the prophecy, but I have a feeling we were all wrong."

"Okay…" Luke was still confused.

"When I found out that Elizabeth is from the bloodline though, it made me realize something." Isaac turned to face Luke, putting a hand on his shoulder. "I think that she is the one spoken of in the prophecy."

"That's crazy." Luke said. "She wasn't actually a member of the bloodline though. Before she turned, she was completely normal. Whether or not she has the bloodline genes inside her somewhere, she only carried the gene. She didn't manifest it, right? And she would have, when she was attacked, had it been inside of her."

"I understand why you don't want to believe this." Isaac continued. "But someone from the bloodline has never been turned, no one with even a drop of the bloodline in their blood has become Verdorben."

"But that could just be happenstance." Luke stood up, shaking his head in disbelief. "I appreciate you sharing your theory Isaac, but I think you are wrong."

"Look at her Luke." Isaac persisted, and Luke could feel himself getting more upset. "She is faster and stronger than the other Verdorben. You saw the way she handled those bloodline hunters with ease. She killed well over a dozen of them by herself, in a matter of minutes."

"Yes, but that is just because they didn't have terralium blades." Luke explained.

"Say what you will." Isaac continued. "I am only warning you, because I truly believe that Elizabeth will sacrifice herself to destroy the Verdorben. I don't want you to suffer how I have suffered." Isaac's eyes watered slightly as he finished talking, and Luke realized why.

Isaac's wife and small child had been killed by the Verdorben immediately after the great battle. He had been so devastated, that he had never remarried. Luke felt bad for the man, as he knew he still missed his wife very much, even if it had been decades since she had passed.

"I appreciate your concern." Luke said after a long pause. "And I am truly sorry for your loss. But if I am being honest Isaac, I do not expect to survive the coming battles. I am not sure if Liz will or not. But if I get to spend even one day, or one week as her husband, I will count that as the greatest honor and blessing I could ever wish for."

"You don't know the pain that comes with losing your soulmate Luke." Isaac said somberly. "It is more than any man should ever have to bear."

"But if I don't marry Liz." Luke explained. "Then I have already lost her without even trying. That is something I cannot bear."

"So… then you won't at least consider what I said?" Isaac asked.

"Oh, I have considered it." Luke said, as he turned to walk away. "But my mind is set. I am marrying Liz tonight, and nothing will change that. However long or short our lives last, I will be her husband."

"Very well." Isaac said as Luke walked back towards the stairs. "But I do not envy you the heartache that is coming."

CHAPTER XVI

"Are you sure it's not too much makeup?" I asked Jazmine. I was sitting backwards with a chair between my legs so that I could lean against it without messing up my hair. Jazmine had spent the prior hour doing my hair and makeup, and the only mirror was on the wall across the room, so I had no idea how ridiculous I might look. Not that I didn't trust Jazmine, as her makeup was always perfect. But my idea of makeup was putting on some mascara and maybe eye shadow if I was feeling fancy. Jazmine had brushed on or applied at least ten different types of makeup in the last few minutes. I didn't even know what most of them were called.

"Don't be silly Liz. You look absolutely stunning." Jazmine reassured me. "I'm just applying some finishing touches... and you will be all set." She was putting on something just above my eyes with a brush. As she did my makeup, it made me think of Nikki. I missed my Latina friend from Harrisburg so much and had wanted to invite her to the wedding. Jazmine had insisted that it would be a mistake, as contacting her would likely put us all in danger. Even still, she was the only person not here for this moment that I really wish could have been. But... I knew it would probably be a while before I could see my best friend again... if I ever even got to.

The door opened slowly behind Jazmine, and Sara walked in behind her. "That better not be you, Luke!" Jazmine chided without looking away from the task at hand. "It's bad luck to see your bride before she's walking down the aisle."

"It's just me Jazzy." Sara said as she closed the door behind her. "I wouldn't let Luke s..." She stopped talking mid-sentence and froze when she looked at me.

"Oh no. Does it look bad?" I asked, pointing at my face as I suddenly felt overly self-conscious. I was wearing a thin white slip, with the new silver and sapphire necklace that Sara had bought me dangling around my neck, and my new wedding dress hanging up in the corner of the room.

"Oh no dear." Sara said, her gaze still stuck on me. "You look breathtaking. I can't believe my son is marrying the most beautiful eighteen-year-old alive. If I am being honest, he really doesn't deserve you."

"Oh please. Your son is perfect in every way." I reassured Sara. "He could do a lot better than me. But I'm not complaining."

"No Liz, really." Jazmine cut in. "My brother is a good kid, and he will treat you right. But... he is really stubborn and sometimes gets mad about stupid things. With your looks, you could have any guy you want."

I started to blush. For some reason I had never been good at taking compliments, especially when I didn't think I looked nearly as good as they were making me out to be. "You guys are too nice." I replied. "I am grateful that you are all so awesome. Even though it's definitely not why I am marrying him, that fact that you are all so gracious and kind really does mean a lot to me."

"Well, we already love you like family, so we are happy to make it official." Jazmine said as she finished my make up. "Okay, you are all set Liz."

"Thank you so much for getting me all ready." I replied, standing to walk towards the mirror. "I really am just not good with makeup."

"Wait." Jazmine said as she grabbed my arm just before I got to the mirror. "Not yet, you need to put the dress on first. I want you to be wowed by yourself."

I chuckled without thinking but did as Jazmine instructed. The dress was beautiful, I had to admit as I pulled it from the hanger. It was solid white with modern embroidery, to include some silver threaded designs that ran down the front of the dress. The short sleeves were a white lacey material, and also had the silver threads on the rounded edges that rested just below my shoulder bone. I stepped into the dress and pulled it over my arms. Jazmine helped me zip up the back, and I was relieved when the dress seemed to fit perfectly on my hips. My weight had actually not fluctuated at all since I had been changed, but that had more to do with having a small appetite than anything else.

"Oh my gosh Liz!" Jazmine said excitedly. "There are not words for how amazing you look in that dress. See for yourself though." She smiled and grabbed me gently by the wrist, quickly guiding me over to the mirror. I noticed that the back half of my flowing dress just touched the ground and trialed behind me as I walked.

When I stopped in front of the mirror, I was shocked. I barely recognized myself in the reflection looking back at me. The white dress looked even more beautiful with my shiny necklace and matching earrings, but it was my face and hair that surprised me the most. Whatever combination of various makeups that Jazmine had applied seemed to completely hide the features I wasn't fond of, while somehow making others look even better than they ever had. It reminded me of the makeover shows I had seen on TV where some fashion person took an ugly or plain person and made them look beautiful. The elaborate ringlets that hung down from the pulled up and sideways designs in my hair only made everything look even better. I hadn't even noticed Jazmine slip in the small shiny silver hair clamps that tied it all together.

I guess even plain people can look like models. I thought to myself. "Oh, my goodness Jazmine." I managed to say out loud, relieved that I would at least look the part of the beautiful bride. "I don't know how you pulled it off. But I actually feel pretty. I think even Luke will like it. Don't you?"

"Listen my soon to be sister. He won't be able to keep his hands off you." Jazmine reassured me.

"Well after the ceremony he won't have to." Sara said smiling mischievously. I felt instantly weirded out that my soon to be mother in law was making risqué comments. But at the same time... it was also nice that I would have a mom again. And I couldn't ask for anyone more thoughtful and kinder than Sara. I noticed my eyes were starting to water slightly.

"I just hope you both know how grateful I am to be a part of this amazing family." I said, trying to hold back the tears. "And how I'm having a really hard time holding these tears back because I am so happy right now. I really don't want to mess up this awesome makeup though."

Sara leaned over and hugged me, and Jazmine jumped in to hug me from the side. "Don't worry Liz. I did all the waterproof stuff, so you won't have to worry about tears or anything else messing it up."

"We are happy for you Liz. You and Leuken." Sara added. "After everything you have both been through throughout your lives, and especially in the last few weeks, you deserve this."

There was a tapping noise at the door. "Who is it?" Jazmine asked.

"It's me Daniel." I heard my father's voice coming through the door. "Liz's dad."

"Come on in." Sara said, my father opened the door, and Sara hurried and kissed him before he could even step inside. She was laughing as she pulled away.

"What's so funny?" He asked.

"The fact that you had to say you were Liz's dad." Sara laughed again. "As if there are any other Daniels in the mansion, or that any of us don't already recognize your voice you silly man."

"Okay, I guess I kinda earned that. Glad you could laugh at my expense." My father said, as he turned to look at me. "Holy Crap!" He said suddenly. "Liz, you look amazing!"

"Thanks dad." I replied smiling.

"I still can't believe my baby girl is a grown woman now." He said, smiling back at me. "You don't even look like a teenager anymore. You could seriously pass for mid-twenties with your makeup like that."

"I'll take that as a compliment." Jazmine said. "You don't look so bad yourself." Jazmine said, as she reached over to straighten out my father's tie. He was wearing a black suit with a silver tie that matched the bridesmaid dress we had bought for Jazmine. Ben also got a matching suit and tie, since he was the best man.

A couple of minutes later, after Jazmine got her dress on and her and Sara went downstairs to join the others, I was standing just back from the top of the stairs. My father was next to me, nodding his head slowly as he stared ahead blankly. It was something he only did when he got nervous and was deep in thought.

"What is it dad?" I asked.

"Oh nothing." He replied. "I am fine."

He was such a bad liar. "You're doing that thing you do with your head when you get really nervous. What is it?"

"I just don't want to mess this up that's all." He shrugged.

"It's simple dad." I explained just in case he hadn't paid attention when Sara had told him what to do two minutes before. "Once the music starts, you will grab my left arm, and walk me slowly down the stairs. Wait for the flower girl to do her thing, and escort me up the gap in between the chairs to Luke. You will let go, and Luke will take my arm. After that, you sit in the open chair in the front row and enjoy the ceremony."

"Yeah, I know, it's just…" My father paused looking down at me. "I really do feel bad for being a jerk earlier. I hope you can forgive me baby girl?"

My father hadn't called me baby girl since before my mom had passed. A part of me felt a little old to be called that, now that I was an adult and getting married and all. But I also knew it was my dad's way of showing his affection for me. So, I put my arms around him and gave him a big hug. Deep down, it was nice to hear him say that again.

"I love you daddy." I said softly. "Just cause I am getting married doesn't change that."

"I love you too Liz." He replied, gently lifting me off the ground as he squeezed back.

The music suddenly started playing from the speakers downstairs, and the dull sound of chatter stopped quickly, so only the sound of *Canon in D* could be heard echoing through the large hall and up the stairs.

"You ready?" I asked my dad.

"Let's do this." He replied, linking my arm as we slowly made our way down the stairs. About halfway down I could see the room, with everyone from the clans, in addition to our families, standing in front of their chairs as they looked back towards us. Most of them smiled at me as my eyes glanced over the crowd. Shawnee was smiling the biggest, and even gave me a thumbs up when our eyes briefly met.

I laughed when Alex suddenly blurted out "You look so pretty Izzie!" as loud as he could. But it was the man standing in the front middle of the room, wearing a silver-colored suit with a white tie, who captured my attention as I stepped onto the hall floor.

Luke's blue eyes were wide and seemed surprised when he looked at me. The broad smile that instantly followed the shock calmed my nerves though, as I was trusting he was as impressed with Jazmine's makeup job as I had been. Well... at least I hoped that he was. Either way, I was too happy to let anything ruin this moment. The entire hall had been decorated. Where all the flowers and white decorative cloth streamers that had been hung throughout the room had come from, I didn't know, but it looked amazing. Sara must have enlisted some help to get those hung so quickly while I was getting ready. It was another reason I loved this family I was marrying into.

Trinity was in front of us, holding a basket with rose petals, but appeared to have frozen as she stared at her cousin Kezia, who was seated next to the aisle where she stood. I felt bad for even agreeing to the suggestion that she be the flower girl, as the poor girl had just lost most of her family. I was about to lean down and tell her she could just sit down, when Kezia stood up and grabbed her by the hand, encouraging her to start. Kezia picked up some flowers and threw them in the aisle in front of us, between the folding chairs that were set out with five neat rows on each side. "See how pretty they are." I heard Kezia say to the girl. "Now it's your turn. Can you throw the pretty flowers while we walk?"

Trinity nodded without speaking, grabbing a handful of flowers and throwing them in front of her. "Great job!" Kezia whispered encouragingly to the girl as they walked, and Trinity threw several more handfuls of flowers as the few women in the room "Awed" her cuteness. Alex walked behind her with the ring box held open. Sara and Jazmine had lamented forgetting to buy the small pillows they had at the wedding store, but with Alex's little shirt and tie, it was adorable enough for me.

As I walked up the aisle, everyone was smiling at me, even the clan members whose names I could not remember. It felt surreal. Not only did I feel like I was dreaming, because I was getting married much younger than I had ever imagined. But I also had so much love and support from family and my newly made friends. As I reached Luke in the front of the room, he smiled broadly and leaned down to kiss me. I held one finger up to his lips. "Not till Metemba says sweetheart." I teased, smiling.

"Oh, sorry." Luke replied, kissing my finger before pulling back slightly as he took me from my father by the arm. "You just look so amazing, it's hard not to kiss you." He whispered. My father stepped back to take his seat.

I took a step forward so that we were both facing Metemba, side by side. He was wearing a gray button up shirt and black slacks, showing his extraordinarily white teeth as he smiled. I had been both surprised and impressed when I learned that Metemba was an official priest. I had already forgotten the name of the religion he had his license from in South Africa, but he had already performed several weddings, both for people from his clan, and at several small villages throughout various parts of southern Africa. His sister had said it made it easier for him to travel to war torn parts of the continent without drawing attention. Where he and his fellow clanmates had stopped more than a few cruel and oppressive war lords throughout the years.

The music suddenly stopped. "Beloved friends and family." Metemba began, his deep voice filling the emptiness in the room as he spoke slowly. "Today we are gathered to witness the sacred union of two people who are in love. These joyous occasions remind and inspire us, that there is nothing more important in this life than family. May the light shine and smile upon these two, as they make vows and promises this day. Today they begin their lives together as a new family."

I looked over at Luke, unable to wipe the incredible smile from my face. He was smiling as well, and I was surprised to see a small tear running down his cheek. *So, I'm not the only one feeling overwhelmed with emotion,* I thought to myself.

"You see." Metemba continued cheerfully. "When two people commit to be married, they are promising that they will put each other before all else. The good book even says that when a man and woman are married, they should cleave unto each other, and forsake father, mother, and all else, if necessary, to give themselves completely to one another, and fulfil the bonds of matrimony.

"Leuken Bennett" Metemba paused briefly, focusing his eyes on Luke as he continued. "Do you promise to love and protect Elizabeth Scott, be faithful to her, cherish her, and always put her needs before your own, so long as the light gives you breath?"

Luke looked at me, still smiling, and still watery eyed. "I do." He said.

"Elizabeth Scott." Metemba turned to face me directly. "Do you promise to love and protect Leuken Bennett, be faithful to him, cherish him, and always put his needs before your own, as long as the light gives you breath?"

"I do." I replied, and I felt the tears coming from my eyes. I would say I didn't know why I was crying, but I did know. I had never been so happy in my entire life. The words Metemba spoke were so beautiful. I had every intention of keeping every word of them. Already I felt like my love for Leuken was more powerful than I could have even imagined possible. There was nothing I wouldn't do for the ridiculously handsome boy.

"Then by the power vested in me by the light, and by the Republic of South Africa, I now pronounce you husband and wife." Metemba smiled broadly. "Now you may kiss your beautiful bride Leuken. Congratulations!"

Luke leaned down to kiss me tenderly, but as soon as our lips met, I jumped up and threw my arms around him, kissing him passionately. The kiss only lasted a few seconds, as cheers and screams erupted from the crowd while clapping. When I finally pulled away enough to look in Luke's eyes, I saw the same overwhelming happiness that I felt inside. We were complete now.

Within a few seconds, the music began to play, from a boombox that was sitting on top of the baby grand piano at the edge of the hall. It seemed somewhat out of place on top of such a fancy piano, but it lightened the mood as people relaxed. A few of the men and boys quickly moved the chairs from the center of the room. The first slow song was with my father, who surprisingly got a touch emotional himself as we danced. Next, I got my first married dance with Leuken, *Don't Stop Believing* by Journey. It was the first song we had ever listened to together. I still remembered sitting next to him in the car a few months earlier while we were waiting for Alex to come out of kindergarten. While it had only been a few months, it felt like almost a lifetime ago, so much had happened since then. At the time I had thought the boy was too good to be true, but now, as I held my arms around his neck and we danced as husband and wife, I was living my dream come true.

The rest of the wedding reception seemed to fly by. There was a lot of dancing, laughing, talking, and mingling that happened. When Luke cut the three-tiered double chocolate cake with white frosting, he was pretty careful feeding me my piece, only getting a little smudge on my cheek. He was probably worried about messing up my makeup. Honestly so was I, in spite of Jazmine assuring me it was waterproof. When it was my turn to feed him a slice, I couldn't help but smear a good portion of his face with cake and frosting. I also enjoyed licking off the couple spots he missed wiping by his mouth afterwards.

I didn't let Luke leave my side the entire night. When we finally went outside to the Hummer, everyone had lined up in front of the house, and they threw flower petals, so many flower petals that I didn't know where they had all come from, as we made our way to the Hummer with Luke carrying me in his arms. He gently set me in the passenger side of the car, and we drove off into the dark forest towards the main highway.

About ten minutes later, Luke pulled into the driveway of a small cabin in a clearing in the woods. It was only about five miles from the mansion. Sara had rented it using a credit card she got from Isaac on Airbnb. Luke walked around the front of the car and opened my door. "Mrs. Bennett." He smiled at me as he held his hand out to help me from the car. "Let me carry you, so you don't ruin that amazing dress."

"Well, aren't you charming?" I replied smiling, wrapping one arm around his neck for support as he scooped me up into his arms. "Elizabeth Bennett... I like the sound of that."

"Do you now?" He asked as he walked me slowly up to the front door of the cabin.

"I actually do." I added. "Because it means I'm yours now." Luke stopped on the porch and gave me a long, sweet kiss. "And more importantly, it means you are mine." I probably sounded a bit possessive, but with how happy we were, I didn't think he would care.

Luke set me down gently, punching a code into the keypad for the front door lock. It beeped and I could hear the latch slide open. Luke opened the door, taking my hand as he pulled me inside. The light was on my side of the door, so I clicked it on. The cabin was actually decent size. Rounded wooden logs formed the interior wall, with some hunting and animal décor hanging on each wall. There was a small kitchen to the right, with a door that appeared to lead into a bathroom behind that. To the left was a small sitting area with a couch, and a large king size bed behind that. It had a dark oak wooden frame, with black and white sheets and blankets to make it look somewhat modern.

I couldn't help but get excited when I saw the bed, knowing that there were no more rules keeping me from the smoking hot man I was married to.

"I'll go and grab the suitcase." Luke said as he turned to step back outside.

"Not so fast." I said, gently grabbing his arm with one hand, while I pushed the door shut with the other.

"What is…" He turned to ask as the door clicked shut, but I cut him off as I pulled his face down to kiss him again. While we kissed, I jumped up, trying to wrap my legs around his hips, but the dress made it too hard to hook my legs, so I landed back on my feet, almost falling over backwards. We both laughed, but only for a brief second before kissing again. While we kissed, I pulled his suit jacket off, and then his tie. All the sudden Luke was all I wanted. I couldn't think about anything else. An intense flame seemed to have been lit inside of me, and I didn't want to calm it.

"Wait." I said, catching my breath as I turned away from him. "Unzip me."

"If you insist." Luke teased as he unzipped the back of my dress. I slipped my arms out and stepped out of the dress. With just my slip on, I was able to move better. I turned and jumped up, wrapping myself around Leuken as we began kissing again. My legs were wrapped around the top of his hips to support my wait as he carried me.

I noticed Luke walking me towards the bed, and I couldn't get enough of his lips. A few seconds later he set me down on the bed, leaning over me as we made out. I tried unbuttoning his shirt, but it wasn't coming off fast enough for me. I accidentally broke a button as I tried to pull one open, ripping the shirt slightly.

"Careful baby." He said as he pulled his lips away, smiling.

"No." I teased defiantly, quickly ripping his shirt open all the way and sliding my hands inside the large opening I had created. His skin felt smooth over the tight muscles on his chest and shoulders. This time there were no inhibitions holding either one of us back. No fan to hit my head on, as I had back in Harrisburg. It was just me and Luke, and I had every intention of enjoying him completely. So, I did.

*   *   *

"I still can't believe you woke me up at three in the morning for this." Valdez said grouchily from the passenger seat as Det. Jimenti pulled onto the freeway heading East. "I sure hope your lead pans out."

"Sorry about that, but I do think it will." Jimenti replied, glancing over at his friend and partner.

"You sure you don't want me to call this in?" Valdez asked. He seemed half tired, half nervous as he asked. "You know I could get suspended for doing unsanctioned field work without clearing it with my supervisor. Especially across state lines."

"Oh, I know. I probably will too." Jimenti answered, pausing to carefully craft his next words. "And you know I wouldn't ask this of you if I didn't think it was important. But… I gotta be honest with you, we are in deep over our heads here. I don't think we are trying to catch the right people. FBI and the AUSA seem mostly interested in identifying and catching these black clad assassin dudes, but DOD only seems interested in the teenagers. Personally, I think they are the good guys. They are already being hunted by these crazy South Americans. The last thing they need is our government to turn them into guinea pigs."

"I'm with ya there Mike." Valdez replied. "But with the trail of bodies piling up wherever these kids go, I don't think DOD will see it the same way."

"Which is why we need to keep this little drive between us." Jimenti replied. "With all the lives these kids already saved between Harrisburg and Vegas, we owe it to them to try and figure out what is going on without ruining their lives. Besides, there are some supernatural freaky things going on that I can't explain. I think if we go in with tactical teams and try to capture these kids, we will probably fail, and a lot of good men and women might lose their lives. Kelly would find a way to come to heaven and kill me again if I die and leave her with the four kids all by herself. She's mad enough that I have to work so much when these big cases come up. She only puts up with it because the call out and OT helps pay the bills. I don't want to leave her a widow."

"You know I was with you on wanting to protect the kids, cause they did save some lives." Valdez was nodding slowly as he thought out loud. "I just didn't think that far ahead. But you're probably right. The way they took out those tactical teams of super humans, they likely would make short work of us if we tried to catch them."

"I'm telling you Gil." Jimenti replied. "You might get in trouble for this drive, but it's the right thing to do. I don't think they'll hurt us if they know we just have questions and aren't trying to hook up or lock up anyone."

"I sure hope you are right." Valdez responded. "For both our sakes." He pulled the gold chain up that was tucked in his shirt, kissing the cross that dangled from the end.

CHAPTER XVII

"Oh shoot." Luke's voice woke me up, and I turned to see him standing on the side of the bed, looking at the back patio. "I didn't realize those were see through." He turned to look at me, blushing slightly. The light coming through the windows illuminated behind him as he turned, making his ripped physique almost shine as I admired his stomach and chest muscles.

"Are you even listening?" Luke asked, obviously noticing that I was checking him out instead of paying attention. "Hey Liz." He smiled, pointing to his face. "I'm up here."

"Oh sorry." The pre-married me might have felt embarrassed, but I didn't even care that he had caught me. After everything that had happened the night before, which was definitely the best night of my life, there was really nothing left to hide from one another. "I just got busted checking you out, didn't I?" I focused on Luke's face, trying to remember and process what he had said. Through the sheer curtains behind him, you could see the forest clearly. On the top of the next hill over were a few more cabins, all built near each other. A couple of them had smoke coming from the small chimneys, indicating that they were clearly occupied.

"Oops." I said, standing to wrap my arms around him. "Hopefully no one was looking. If they were, I guess they got a free show."

"Oh my gosh." Luke raised one eyebrow as he looked down at me. "You don't even seem bothered by it."

"Well, it wasn't on purpose." I replied, shrugging my shoulders. "If I had known the curtains were see through, I would have closed the blackout ones too.

"I know it's just." Luke paused thoughtfully, leaning down for a quick kiss. "I don't want anyone else seeing you like that. You're mine. No one else's."

"Don't worry sweetheart. I am yours, and from now on we will make sure the curtains aren't see through before having special time, okay?" I reassured him. "Besides it wasn't just me they could have seen." I smile back at him. "I don't need no other girls checking out my man. My husband." I kissed him again. Leading to more kissing and other good things. About an hour later, we had finished showering and getting dressed, and were sitting at the table. While eating the breakfast Sara had packed for us the night before, there was a sudden knock at the door.

For a split second, I panicked, thinking that perhaps the bloodline hunters had caught up with us. In the sunlight, I was not invincible, meaning we might not be able to fight our way out of this ambush if that's what it was. Luke jumped to his feet, running to the long duffle bag near the bed and pulling out his terralium sword. He held it by the sheath just below the hilt of the blade. I stood up as Luke walked quickly and quietly to the front door, peeping out the hole.

"It's not the bloodline hunters." Luke whispered just loud enough for me to hear. "Looks like cops." He shrugged, seeming to relax a little, as they knocked again loudly on the door.

I relaxed too. Not that I wasn't concerned there were police at the door, but at least I wasn't worried about getting killed. "Just don't answer." I whispered back, walking over to stand near him. These police couldn't possibly be related to any of the incidents that had happened in other states. There was no way. Or at least that was my initial thought.

"Either no one is home, or they aren't coming to the door." I heard a man say from outside. "Let's go Mike." I looked at Luke, and he appeared as confused as I felt.

"Do you think they aren't really police?" I whispered. "Maybe it's more of those guys…"

"I don't know, he's got a badge." Luke replied, moving over to the front window where the blinds were closed. There was a tiny gap on the end of the blinds, so I moved to join him and peaked out the window. Outside, on the front step, I could see a pale bald-headed man standing just in front of the door, a couple of feet back. He had a gold badge sticking out on the front of his belt line and wore a lanyard around his neck with his picture and a blue background. He didn't look anything like the bloodline hunters we had fought.

"We didn't drive all this way just to leave." I could see the bald man was speaking now, his voice muffled through the wall. Without my enhanced hearing, I probably wouldn't have been able to understand what he was saying. The man looked over suddenly, and I stepped back so he couldn't see me through the slit.

"This is the police." The bald man's voice said loudly through the closed door. "I can see you are in there. We just want to talk. Please open the door. No one is in any kind of trouble." The man reassured.

Luke walked over to the front door, leaning his terralium sword against the wall next to the door, but just where it couldn't be seen from outside. He looked at me questioningly.

"Let's just see what they want." I whispered.

Luke unlocked the deadbolt, and slowly opened the door about halfway. The bald man seemed surprised, turning as the door opened, with one hand behind his back. Remembering all of the stories my dad had told about when he would knock on doors as a cop, I was pretty sure he had his hand on his gun. I wasn't too worried about that. Behind him, was another chubbier Hispanic man. He also wore a badge, but his was smaller and shaped more like an oval shield instead of a star. This man stood a little taller than the pale bald one and looked noticeably more nervous. His hand was gripping his gun, though it was still in the holster on his hip.

"Hey guys. I'm detective Jimenti and this is special agent Valdez." The detective looked at me, suddenly putting both hands up in front of his face with the palms facing us. I hadn't realized it, but without thinking I had bladed my body and was clenching one fist at my side, ready to pounce if either of them started shooting. "Look we don't want any trouble. We know there's some bad people after you and we just want to talk. I promise."

Luke had reached for and had his hand on the hilt of his terralium blade. Luckily the cops couldn't see that. I thought it strange that there would be a Detective from southern Idaho with an FBI Agent knocking on our cabin rental door. It didn't make sense. Although lately… almost nothing seemed to, so I guess I should think it was normal.

"If you're a local cop, why is he with you?" I asked, pointing at the agent behind the man. "And if you mean us no harm, why is your partner gripping his gun like he expects trouble?"

The Detective, Jimenti, turned to his partner, with both hands still up. "Agent Valdez, can you please relax?" He asked the other man before turning back to us. "I'm not a local cop. I'm on the Joint

Terrorism Task Force out of Oregon. We aren't going to try and hurt you in any way, as long as you don't hurt us. You have my word."

Luke turned and smiled at me briefly, pulling his hand back from the sword and seemed to relax slightly. "What do you need sir?" He asked calmly.

"I just had a few questions I was hoping you could answer. I don't know if anyone else is inside, but do you mind if we come in?" Jimenti asked, eyeing us both warily.

"We would rather just talk right here." Luke said cautiously. "We are the only ones here. What can we do for you Detective?"

"That's just fine." The Detective replied. "I appreciate you two talking to me. Listen, I'm gonna just cut to the chase. I know why you guys are nervous, because I saw what happened at your house in Harrisburg, and at the school, and in Nevada, at both places. Heck, I even went to the scene in Arizona." I noticed my anxiety growing slightly as the man rattled off nearly every scene we had been at in the last few weeks.

"Wait." I cut in. "How do I know we aren't being recorded?" I stepped to the open doorway and peeked past the men, scanning the tree line for signs of anyone else.

"You aren't. Trust me." Jimenti replied. "We came here by ourselves, and my audio recorder is sitting in my car. This is not a sanctioned visit from the higher ups, if you catch my drift?" The detective raised his eyebrows as he spoke. Why was the man insinuating that they were working alone, when he just explained he was part of a task force?

"Why would you do that?" I asked.

"Because Miss Scott." Jimenti began. "We know you guys have some kind of superpowers, and we think the people in all black who are chasing you do too. I mainly just want to know who these guys are and where they are operating out of so we can stop them before anyone else has to get hurt."

"Look detective." Luke cut in. "I appreciate that you want to help, and we are grateful you came alone, but if we told you what is actually going on, you wouldn't believe us. And then the military or other feds would want to take us and subject us to all kind of human testing in some government lab. In the meantime, the real bad guys, these bloodline hunters, would continue to kill everyone else like us, until only they would be left. If that happens, there is nothing you or your military could do to stop them."

"Why don't you try me? You might be surprised. I really mean you no harm and plan on leaving here, and not even mentioning that we talked if you tell me the truth. No one from the military or the feds would even know we were here." Jimenti stated. "Besides, something tells me you wouldn't go quietly if the military did try and take you."

"Would you sir?" Luke asked. "Let the military, or anyone for that matter take you and imprison you and your family when you hadn't done anything but run and defend yourself?"

"No." Jimenti replied. "I've got four kids, and I would fight to the death protecting them."

"Well, we might not have kids yet." Luke said, smiling briefly at me. "But if you don't let us do what has to be done, there's a good chance we never will."

"Those don't sound like the words of someone who's running. The last scene also didn't look like someone running." Jimenti turned and glanced briefly at his partner. "If you guys don't lay low and stay out of the news, our government is going to have no choice but to apprehend you. You know that right?"

"Detective Jimenti." I cut Luke off before he could talk. "You know my father was a detective, and several of my great uncles and grandparents fought in the military for this great country, so I have the utmost respect for law enforcement and the military. I thank you for your service and the risk you all put yourselves in every day. The last thing I want to do is hurt any law enforcement. That being said, if you came in heavy to try and capture us, we would do our best not to kill anyone, but there could be no guarantees. The only guarantee would be that you would fail, and good people would get hurt in the process. I don't think that either of us want that."

"I appreciate that, and I even believe you." Jimenti replied. "But I do need to know where these guys are hiding so we can stop them. If you keep having bloody battles all over the western United States, some good people are going to get hurt."

"I can tell you this." I continued. "The people who are hunting us, they aren't from the United States, and we don't plan on fighting them here. We are going, very soon, to stop them once and for all. Once we do that, I promise you won't see us or them on the news at all. Hopefully ever again."

"And I'm to believe we won't be filling any more body bags after you stop this group of... what did you call them... bloodline hunters?" Agent Valdez suddenly spoke up from behind Jimenti. "No more decapitations of men wearing all black?"

"I would say that's a safe bet." Luke replied calmly.

"Look Mr. Bennett, you've got skills. I'll give you that." Jimenti cut back into the conversation. "And you've got heart, and guts. But if these guys are from the cartels, there is no way the two of you can take down an entire criminal army."

"I appreciate your concern Detective." Luke replied. "But it isn't just the two of us. We have a lot of people willing to help us where these bad guys are. We will put an end to these ruthless murderers, and then we promise not to make any headlines. Okay?"

"If you don't mind me asking, how did you get your abilities?" Valdez asked.

"I think we have answered enough questions for now." I decided to ignore the man's last question, so I smiled politely. "Do you have a card Detective Jimenti? We have to get going soon, so I'll make you a deal. You promise not to follow us, and I promise I will let you know when we have finished taking out the evil people who are trying to kill us. Do we have a deal?"

"Does this mean you aren't going to answer any more questions?" Jimenti asked, raising one eyebrow. Luke and I both nodded without speaking. "Okay then, we have a deal." He said as he pulled a business card from his back pocket and held it out to me. "By the way, congratulations on the wedding! You two be careful now, you hear?"

*　　*　　*

"This is incredible!" Jazmine said smiling at me as we stepped onto the plane from the ramp. The private jet looked much bigger from the inside then it had when we had first pulled up to the small airport. To the left was a small door with a unisex bathroom sign on it, flanked by a narrow hallway that led to the front cockpit of the plane. To my right, I could see about ten rows, each with two chairs on either side of the aisle. The spacing between the seats was much wider than anything I had seen on a commercial flight. Luke held my hand from behind as I made my way down the aisle to the third row. Jazmine had stopped and stuck her small duffle bag in a storage compartment above one of the seats, so I pulled Luke into the seats across the way from Jazmine. Luke stowed our bags above our seats while I sat in the aisle chair.

I was surprised by how comfortable the chair was, and it even reclined slightly. I turned to look back, as other clan members filed down the rows towards the back of the plane. My father took the seat directly in front of me, while Isaac and the pilot spoke at the front entrance to the plane. I had counted just a minute before when we were all walking across the tarmac to the small steps that led up to the main seating portion of the plane. Besides me, my father, Tobias, Jazmine, Luke and Isaac, were Jacob, Jarvis, Haysom, Metemba, Zane, two of the Danes, all four Japanese bloodlines, my uncle and his companion and all three Indian clan members. Twenty-two of us... to deal with over one hundred bloodlines between the two sites. I wasn't sure if it would be enough, but we had to try. No one should have to live in fear, and until we freed these people, all bloodlines would have to. Not only of the Verdorben, but also of their own kind.

Kwame and Shawnee had stayed behind with Ben, Kezia and the other two Danish clan members to protect the remaining family who were not from the bloodline. Just in case another group of them attacked. After Isaac had confirmed that it was the satellite phone that had been used to track them to Arizona, he was somewhat less concerned about the family being found. But... I felt better knowing that there were six bloodlines still there to help protect the house.

Haysom was the last one on the plane. As he made his way down the aisle with his usual sullen expression, he paused right in front of me. "I don't normally like to get all sentimental about stuff." The man was speaking in a much lower tone than his normal boisterous self. "But I do have to say Liz. Your wedding last night was absolutely perfect. Not only do you two make the most adorable couple ever, but that dress you wore was amazing! Not everyone can be an olive-skinned dream boat like me, but you two really pulled off something special. Congratulations again." He smiled sincerely before making his way further down the aisle.

"Aww... Thanks Haysom." I said as the man walked away. It was the first time I had seen the kind and considerate side of Haysom. He was always talking and joking with others, but usually at their expense and in a cutting way. Some of the other clan members had even called him a "mean girl" behind his back. I had wondered why he was so rude to others, but also felt pity for the little man. He had lost his parents, and most of his relatives. My guess had been that he was just naturally a jerk to others, but that one interaction, however slight, had set my mind to wondering. Perhaps under the gruff exterior, the man did have a kind heart. I could only imagine how much he was probably mocked for his minimal stature all growing up. Maybe his cutting humor was more of a defensive thing than anything else. The man was obviously tough physically, as he had fought off numerous bloodline hunters to survive when almost everyone else from his clan had perished in the ambush.

"Did he just call himself an olive-skinned dream boat?" Luke whispered in my ear as he kissed the side of my face. He started chuckling softly.

"He sure did." I couldn't help but laugh too as I replied. I also couldn't help but think how good it felt when he kissed me by the ear like that. It made me wish we were not on a plane with a bunch of random people and our families. "You know what though? I think he was actually sincere there with his compliment. I don't know about you, but that's the nicest thing I have heard the man say."

"You are right." Luke said, smiling thoughtfully at me. "He usually is kinda grumpy, but that was nice. Maybe he is turning over a new leaf."

"Looks like we are all set." Isaac interrupted as he stood directly in front of us, hovering over the seat next to my dad one row ahead. I had been so sidetracked adoring my handsome husband, that I hadn't even noticed Isaac approaching us. "Our pilot said we will stop for fuel near Ft. Lauderdale, and then land at the private airport just north of Montes Claros, Brazil. That should put us a modest drive from the property they are enslaved at in Pirapora. In flying from Florida, our flight path will also be further from them, hopefully avoiding any advanced notice."

"How confident are you in the location?" My father asked. "Are we even sure these people are being held at the coordinates you got from the first guy whose head exploded?"

"I am pretty certain." Isaac replied. "My friend tracked the satellite phone calls back to the same area, several hours north of Rio De Jannero. The triangulation is not perfect, but the estimated location of call is within a mile of where Royce said the camp was."

"Wait a second." My father continued. "Who's this Royce guy?"

"That was the name of the man who gave us the coordinates after our house was attacked in Harrisburg." Isaac explained. "Right before he was killed."

"Oh, that guy." My father turned to look at me and shrugged apologetically.

"I also just got word that the man my friend hired for recon." Isaac added. "He checked out the coordinates and confirmed there are a lot of people working on what the locals called a farm. He said he didn't get too many pictures, because the people working the farm and the large warehouses seemed to have guards patrolling the perimeter. He didn't want to be too obvious, but he said he did complete a tactical work up which he will have for us when we land. So far, it looks highly probable that we are heading to the right place."

"Are you confident that Silas and Priscilla will be alone?" Luke asked.

"I am not confident of anything at this point." Isaac replied thoughtfully. "But Tobias is bound by that bracelet to speak the truth, and he said he is at least 90% sure that only those two are in South America. He said the main group with Alastair is in Europe, and there is another psychopath in one of the former soviet states in Eastern Europe. Between the six with Alastair, crazy guy, our three, and the two down there, that does account for all twelve Verdorben."

"For our sakes I hope you are right." Luke said, grinning sideways at me. "I've got a lot worth living for."

"We all do." My father said somberly, not looking amused by Luke's comment. "What kind of defenses do we expect at the compound?"

"The Brazilian recon said minimal defenses, but there were a handful of guards on the perimeter of the property, each with rifles slung." Isaac continued. "The bloodline that Liz captured in Arizona implied that there are far more at the offsite then the main location where Silas and Priscilla stay in their mansion. Hopefully by killing the Verdorben first, we can free the rest of the bloodlines without having to kill too many more. We just have to hope that once the tainted ones are dispatched, the others will no longer wish to fight. I do so wish we could have got more information from the maimed captive before he was killed. He was quite liberal with sharing important information once he knew our intent was to free his people."

"How confident are you that we can beat the other Verdorben?" My father asked. "I can barely use a sword, and no firearms I could use would kill them."

"We have enough terralium blades that I am not overly concerned with them." Isaac replied. "Tobias seems convinced that Priscilla is unskilled with combat, and they probably only have one or two Terralium weapons. I think if we strike quickly and kill those two, we shouldn't have to kill many of the bloodlines."

"I hope not." I thought out loud. "It just feels wrong killing them when I know they are all being controlled against their will."

"Sadly, this is not the first time that evil men have used otherwise good people to do horrific things." Isaac added. "Too many people do not understand the importance of freedom, or why you can't allow any person or government to have too much control over people. If the light is willing, we will free as many bloodlines as we can from these oppressive monsters very soon."

*   *   *

Detective Jimenti was thinking quietly while Valdez dozed off in the reclined passenger seat of their sedan. They were only about an hour from their office, and the green countryside off the side of the highway was beginning to have more houses and small towns as they drove. Jimenti was slightly startled when Valdez's cell phone suddenly rang loudly. His partner flinched as he sat up, before pulling out the phone to answer it.

"Hello." Valdez said as he answered the phone. "Okay… where?" There were small pauses between him speaking as someone on the other side of the phone relayed more information. "In Idaho?" Valdez feigned confusion.

Jimenti realized that someone else in the FBI must have chased down the credit card expenses in Idaho being related to the same shell company that had rented the motel in Arizona. "No problem at all." Valdez continued speaking. "Yes, I'll grab my partner and start driving. Can you e-mail me the address? Thanks."

"They caught on to the lead?" Jimenti asked as Valdez hung up the phone.

"Yeah. They actually mentioned the charges at the wedding place in the nearby town though but said nothing about the cabin rental." Valdez explained. "I told them we would head that way, but you have to remember we are already an hour closer than we should be. You know what that means?" Valdez smiled.

"Knowing you buddy, I'm guessing you want some chow first to make the time more believable?" Jimenti asked.

"You know me too well my friend." Valdez replied. "On a serious note though, are you sure we did the right thing back there by letting them go?"

"I'm not sure of anything." Jimenti replied. "This whole thing is crazy. But... I did get the vibe that the kids are good, and they are clearly being hunted by these other people. You know as well as I do that if we had called it in, those kids would already be getting poked and prodded in some military lab."

"Yeah..." Valdez sighed loudly before continuing. "Or we would have a lot of dead feds and they would still be on the run. Either way I know it was the right decision... just helps to hear you confirm what I was already thinking. You know we could both lose our badges for this."

"We could." Jimenti replied. "But it was the right thing to do. This tip is actually perfect."

"Why is that?" Valdez asked.

"Because now we can head out there, see what other information we can find, and no one will be the wiser about our earlier trip." Jimenti added. "Now, what's for lunch?"

"That burger place half an hour back looked delicious." Valdez replied.

"So... more slop, eh?" Jimenti preferred to eat healthy when possible. Early on in his career he had gone from ultra-fit to pretty fat when he worked graveyard shift. Since then, he was much more health conscious and rarely ate anything fried or too unhealthy. His wife teased him for being "too OCD" about food sometimes, but he knew she liked him better this size, so it was worth it.

"It's not slop. It's deliciousness." Valdez smirked. "Burgers and fries are an American meal. Your rabbit hippie food is not. But I still love ya man… just not your food."

CHAPTER XVIII

The only thing I didn't like about being a newlywed, was being stuck on a plane with friends, family, and a bunch of random people for several hours. The night before and morning after our wedding had been absolutely amazing. I loved being held in Leuken's arms and becoming one with the man. And so, it was not easy, finding myself on a private jet with people from both our families on board, to keep my hands off of my ridiculously gorgeous husband. Normally I considered myself a somewhat reserved person, trying to limit any public displays of affection. But as I caressed the inner part of his muscular arms while we flew, I couldn't help but want more.

When we finally landed in Brazil, I was surprised to find the air was warm as we stepped off the plane. Idaho had been just above freezing, but the air was much hotter here. Even with a light breeze, it was probably 30-40 degrees warmer. I was reminded of the time in school years before that I had learned about the tilt of the earth during summer and winter, and it suddenly made sense.

"I almost forgot about summer and winter being flopped in the southern hemisphere." Luke said casually as we walked down the small stairs onto the runway at the small airfield. He was holding my hand as we walked, and I squeezed his affectionately as he glanced back at me.

"It's like you read my mind." I said smiling. "I was seriously just thinking about the same thing."

"Oh, were you now?" Luke pulled me to the side so others could walk past us, wrapping his arms around me and lifting me slightly off the ground. We kissed tenderly, and for a split second, I almost forgot everyone else was still not gone. Without thinking, I wrapped my legs around his waist. "Liz come on." He said instantly as he pushed my legs down with one hand. "Not in public."

"What?" I asked, smiling innocently. "I was just kissing you sweetheart."

"Is that all? That's what you call that?" Luke's face was flushed with redness, as he was obviously embarrassed. Somehow his chagrin made him even more adorable.

"Sorry. I guess I did almost get a bit carried away." I kissed him quickly one more time, before turning to follow the group as I pulled him along. "I'll try to wait till we're alone before I do that again."

"It's not that I don't love it." Luke clarified as we walked. "I just think we should save certain things for private, that's all."

"Yeah, I know. You are probably right." I admitted, smiling mischievously. "But if you weren't so hot it would be a lot easier to control myself."

"Says the girl who looks like a supermodel." Luke chuckled softly. "Like you have room to talk."

Everyone else was filing into a large air hanger across from the end of the runway. Roll up doors wide enough to fit a small car or truck through them were mostly open, and we followed everyone else into the hanger. Inside, there were a few service vehicles parked along the far wall, and a small single engine plane parked near them. The space left in the middle of the hanger was big enough for either one large, or two small planes.

Isaac was speaking in another language to a couple of men who were huddled next to the wall closest to them. On the wall hung a couple of maps printed on large paper. Each map was several feet wide and tall. The first one looked to be a map of some properties and streets. The other appeared to be a close up of a particular property. This second map had several large structures on it, including one building that looked big enough to house a large factory of some sort.

As Isaac spoke, I couldn't help but notice how similar the language was to Spanish. From the Rosetta Stone program, I had done months before when I was having restless nights and couldn't sleep, my Spanish had actually become decent. Nikki would have been proud, even if she barely spoke it herself. I felt a small pain as I thought about the girl who had quickly become my best friend. I missed our early morning conversations, and how ridiculously excited she got about new clothes, shoes, or purses. Deep down, I had really wanted to have her come to the wedding, but I knew it would have been too big of a risk. The feds who were hunting us were almost definitely waiting and hoping that I would contact her, as I was certain most people interviewed would have mentioned how we were best friends.

"What language are they speaking?" I whispered to Luke. "Some of the words sound almost Spanish, but I can tell it is not Spanish."

"My guess would be Portuguese." Luke replied. "I think that is what most people speak in Brazil." He shrugged as he finished speaking.

One of the men was shorter, with very tan skin and surprisingly blue eyes for a Latino. The other man was tall and slender, with a short beard and hardened face. His hair was dirty blonde, with reddish tan skin and more of an American look. His accent also sounded much closer to Isaacs, even while the men were speaking Portuguese.

"Okay everyone." Isaac said loudly as he turned to face our group. "This is Alonzo and Skip. Skip's father is a very close friend of mine, and he is helping us with recon and logistics for this mission." Skip nodded as Isaac spoke, but the serious expression on his face made me think that the man had seen and been through many hard things throughout his life. He scanned over the crowd slowly, spending a second or two sizing up each person as he went around the room. Judging by the expression on his face looking more quizzically skeptical with each person he studied, he did not seem at all impressed by what he saw.

"They have arranged for lodging about halfway between here and the compound, that way everyone can rest up before tomorrow night when we go in. It is almost ten o'clock Brazilian time, which is probably about when we will strike tomorrow night. I am going with Alonzo tonight to do additional recon, and we can confirm what time is best after that. I know it is late, but there will be plenty of time to sleep throughout the morning. Liz, can you sense the other Verdorben?" Isaac turned to look at me as he finished speaking.

"Yes." I replied, feeling the slight tugging sensation in the back of my mind. "They are quite a way to the west." I suddenly realized that I did not sense both of the Verdorben, but only one. My father and Tobias were clear in my mind, as they were only a few feet away, but for some reason, I could only sense one other. I could have sworn that a few minutes before when we had first come in range, there were two of them. "But you must know, only one of them is there right now. I can only sense one now, not two."

"Really?" Isaac seemed somewhat alarmed by this revelation. "What about you Tobias, how many Verdorben do you sense?"

"I sense three actually." Tobias replied, a hint of sarcasm in his voice. A few of the other clan members began to murmur quietly to each other. "Elizabeth and Daniel have stronger signals since they are right in front of me, but I can only sense one of the others from the direction of the compound."

"Do you think one of them left?" Isaac asked.

"No." Tobias added casually. "I think one of them is a fade."

"A fade?" My father asked. "What's a fade?"

"It is one of the Auserwhalt with the ability to hide themselves. It essentially makes it impossible to be sensed by other Verdorben, they simply fade away from our senses. Only a seeker like me or Elizabeth would be able to sense them, and only then if we were within a hundred feet or so." He explained. "When we first landed, I felt two, but judging by the way the other one suddenly vanished, they were either killed, or they are a fade."

"There are other Verdorben that can hide from being sensed?" I asked, surprised by this new revelation. I was minorly annoyed that the man had kept this information from us until now. *What else was he not telling us?* I wondered to myself.

"Let's discuss this more later." Isaac cautioned while giving me a look that suggested he didn't want us discussing the matter in too much detail in front of these men. "I will go with Alonzo now. Skip will show everyone to your vehicles and get you checked into the hotel we are staying at. Jacob, I trust you can coordinate with Skip and get everyone settled at the hotel?"

"That is no problem at all." Jacob replied. I couldn't tell if his accent sounded more British or Aussie, but either way I liked it. He didn't sound as proper or pompous as Jarvis did whenever he spoke.

"Be safe brother." Skip said to Isaac before extending his hand to shake Jacob's. "If you'll follow me sir, I'll show you to your cars. Isaac said you guys didn't mind driving to keep the personnel who knew about this mission down?"

"Yes of course." Jacob replied as he walked towards the opposite side of the hanger from where we had entered. My father, Jazmine, Metemba and the others followed slowly behind them, so Luke and I did the same. As we filed out of the hanger, there were several large SUVs, a car and a truck waiting in the front parking lot. Each vehicle was slightly different, but between the six vehicles, we would all fit without having to be more than four deep in any one car.

"Isaac really had everything set up in advance huh?" I asked Luke as we stood there.

"Yeah." Luke replied, putting his arm around my shoulders as he kissed me quickly on the cheek. "He has always been meticulously organized. His back up plans have back up plans." He smiled again as he finished talking.

"Nice." I replied

It was nearly an hour drive to the hotel, a decently modern looking building that was three stories high and shaped like a long L. Isaac had rented out the entire top floor for us, so just about everyone had their own room. Many people still decided to pair up, and it was then I realized that several in our party were quite nervous about this trip. Since the ambushes that had happened in Nevada and Arizona, I really couldn't blame them. I was also glad that we had not told anyone besides Isaac about the Detective and FBI agent who had shown up at our cabin. I wasn't too worried, as Isaac stated he hadn't used that card for anything else after the wedding things, assuming it was potentially compromised.

He said a different business with its own credit cards and a different PO Box had been used for all of the expenses here in Brazil. He also assured us that nothing could be tied back to him in any way, and that there must have been some advanced analysts working at the Feds to be able to tie the card Sara had used back to the other business card he had used at the Arizona hotel. I was grateful, as the last thing I wanted to do was ever hurt any law enforcement or military personnel. I had too much respect for the sacrifices they made, especially since my father had served in the Marine Corps before becoming a cop.

When we were heading down the hall to the room Luke and I were sharing, and after saying our good nights to the rest of the clanmates who were staying nearby, I was surprised to see that Metemba was talking quietly to Jazmine in the hallway in front of her room as she stood in the doorway.

"You have my word, Jazmine Bennett." Metemba was saying softly to her. "If Kwame has any foretelling, I will knock on your door first. I could not live with myself if anything happened to you."

I didn't catch the rest of the conversation, as I wasn't about to awkwardly stop in the middle of the hallway. Plus, I was pulling Luke quickly down the hallway. While the idea of Jazmine and Metemba becoming a thing was exciting for her, I wasn't about to waste any time in getting Luke alone again. If tonight was possibly going to be my last night with the man, I had every intention of making the most of it. I was also fairly confident he wouldn't mind one bit.

*   *   *

Isaac put the binoculars up to his eyes as he surveyed the back side of the property, closest to where the large factory-like building was located. He and Alonzo were standing behind some thick bushes, which concealed them perfectly from the two sentries that were stationed on both back corners of the large building. They were both armed with assault rifles, and both wore the curved swords in sheaths hanging from their backs. Isaac could also see small cameras on both back corners of the building. Strangely, they were all facing towards the doors of the building rather than out at the yard.

"Those cameras on the corners." Isaac said quietly. "They look angled to see anyone coming out, rather than surveilling the yard outside the factory."

"Yes." Alonzo nodded slowly as he spoke. "The guards too, you can see they watch each side of building for people to come out, not to watch for people come in. I think the guns are more to scare outsiders, and keep people in."

Isaac was impressed by Alonzo's English, in spite of his heavy Brazilian accent. During the drive out, Alonzo had opened up about how Skip had saved his life once. After his military service, Skip had joined the CIA, and worked to train up Alonzo and others from his Brazilian unit on modern military equipment, since the gangs from the favela's had become increasingly violent over the years. This had necessitated intervention from Brazilian military. One day during a transport, their convoy had been ambushed by one of the largest gangs, and Alonzo had been shot in the upper thigh. Skip had killed the attackers, applied a tourniquet to Alonza, and carried him on his back to the one Humvee that had not been destroyed, along with another soldier. Skip had saved both of their lives, and Alonzo had been his trusted source ever since.

Isaac had actually only known Skip as a child before he went into the military and later the Central Intelligence Agency. Skip's father, Douglas Matthews, who retired as a full bird Colonel, had served in Vietnam with Isaac. Isaac had carried him over a mile on his back, behind enemy lines after shrapnel from a claymore mine had lodged in his chest and head. Isaac never told his friend Doug that he had healed him just enough to keep him alive until years later when he found out about the bloodlines, but he was one of Isaac's most trusted friends and had helped him numerous times throughout the years. Even since he retired, Doug had been great for providing contacts and military grade equipment when needed. Much of that was now done through Skip, since the CIA had very little tracking with what happened to the military equipment they supplied to countries that helped the United States.

"During the day I have seen lots of them come out from the inside part and work the farmland to the South and East, but they always come back before dark. Most of those workers are women or older children though. The men stay inside the warehouse for the most part." Alonzo explained.

"Very well." Isaac said, thinking about the best way to handle their operation the next night. "If we want to come in from this way, it will be nearly impossible not to be spotted on approach. Let's take a look at that mansion. From what we know, our best bet is to take out the ones in charge. The others may very well stop fighting once they realize they are free."

*   *   *

"What's wrong sweetheart?" Luke asked as he sat up in the bed. He reached over and gently caressed my cheek as he looked at me. I had been laying there adoring the man for the last half hour or more while he was sleeping, thinking about how lucky and grateful I was that he had chosen me. Of all the girls out there, and he could have had any of them, he had picked me, plain old Elizabeth Scott. Or should I say Elizabeth Bennett. My new name was definitely going to take some getting used to, even if I did already love it. I couldn't help but think that no matter what happened tomorrow night, I would die a happy girl, because I was married to Leuken Bennett. A few days ago, I might have felt embarrassed for being caught checking him out, but after how close we had been the last couple of days, I felt like I didn't need to hide anything from Luke.

"Oh nothing." I said calmly. "I'm not allowed to check out my hot husband?"

"Well, there's not much to check out." He chuckled. "But I'll never complain about those perfect eyes resting on me." Luke leaned over and kissed me gently on the forehead. I smiled at him. His hair was a little disheveled from sleeping, his lightly tannish white skin contrasted only slightly with the sheets that were pulled up to his stomach. Without his shirt on, I couldn't decide where to focus my eyes as he spoke. I wanted to focus on his gorgeous face, but those arms and shoulders…

"It doesn't bother you that they aren't blue like yours?" I asked, forcing myself to focus on the conversation at hand.

"How many times do I have to tell you Liz?" He asked smiling. "Green has always been my favorite color. I wouldn't change a single thing about you even if I could. You can't top perfection, and every inch of you is exactly how I want it."

"Every inch huh?" My smile turned mischievous, as I caressed his arm just above his elbow, tracing the bulging definition of his triceps. Even though he wasn't built like a body builder or overly muscular, the muscles he did have seemed more defined and larger because he didn't really have any fat on him at all.

"Come on." He smiled again, rubbing his eyes with the back of his hand as he yawned. "Don't you ever sleep?"

"Uh… not really." I said, trying my best to make puppy dog eyes at him. "I mean I guess I do for a couple hours a night, but after that I'm just not that tired. Sorry… another bad side effect of the curse I guess." I shrugged.

"You know." He kissed me tenderly on the lips, before pulling away reluctantly. "I would love to stay up with you, but I probably should be at full strength for tomorrow's mission. Don't you think?"

"Ugh." I teased, feigning crankiness but smiling in spite of my best efforts. "I know, but that doesn't mean I can't throw a little fit about it." I pretended to stomp my arms in the air while stomping my legs against the bed, trying to simulate a small child tantrum. Luke laughed loudly.

"You know it really isn't fair Liz?" Luke added as he finished laughing, grinning broadly.

"What?" I asked, switching back to my innocent face.

"Looking that good when you want to get your way. I'm so glad the light led me to you."

"Do you really think I look good?" I asked as he nodded. "Then prove it." I pushed him down against the bed as I leaned over him, bending down to kiss him passionately. I held one of his arms down with my outside hand, supporting my weight with the other. There would be time for sleep later.

CHAPTER XIX

Special Agent Valdez was standing just outside the formal shop in the small Idaho town of Sandpoint, speaking to the DOD liaison who had arrived at the shop long before they had. The population of the city was only a few thousand people, and both the store owner and the other female employee who worked there had viewed Detective Jimenti and the others with sneaking suspicion from when they had first introduced themselves.

"I really appreciate your time Misses Belt." Detective Jimenti said to the store owner as he held out a business card for her to take. "Like I said, these two are not in any kind of trouble, and we don't think that they are dangerous. But they are important witnesses in a homicide investigation that we really do need to get a hold of. If they come back, can you please call me on my cell?"

"Sure, Detective Gemini. Whatever you need." The woman grabbed the card from him and studied it skeptically. "Oh sorry, did I pronounce that wrong?"

"That's okay ma'am. Jimenti isn't exactly a common name." He could tell she had said it wrong on purpose but wasn't about to let this lady get under his skin. "You have a great day now." He forced a smile and nodded at the other girl working the register before turning to exit.

"Well, that wasn't much use." Jimenti said as he stepped outside and walked up to where Valdez was talking to the Army Captain, who had told them he preferred to be called only by Captain Fucille when they had asked him what his first name was. The man reminded Jimenti of his crotchety old uncle, who had the personality of a stone. His chubby rounded face and pale shaved head didn't fit the stereotype of an Army Captain either.

"You didn't get anything else?" Valdez asked.

Before Jimenti could answer, Captain Fucille's phone rang. "Excuse me gentlemen." He said as he stepped away from them and answered the phone.

"No." Jimenti replied. "She only recognized Elizabeth, Sara and Luke's stepsister Jazmine. Said that there were no men with them, but that the women had all been beautiful. She described Elizabeth as "just the prettiest thing you ever did see". Once I mentioned I was a task force officer with the FBI, she had turned a little more standoffish."

"Big surprise. It's funny how these small-town folks only want to talk to the local cops, while big city people seem to trust us feds more. Doesn't really make sense to me, but whatever. I figured this might be a dead end. Any vehicle description?"

"No. She said they had walked off down the street, and she didn't follow them outside to see what they were driving because that would have been rude. According to the store owner, most of their business is from tourists either heading up to see the Selkirk mountains or passing through to or from Canada."

"What do you mean there was nothing!?" Captain Fucille had raised his voice so loud that they could hear him clearly now. "They just rented it two days ago and had a three-day reservation. You keep troops on it, out of sight, and I need to be called the instant they return. I don't care where your tactical teams were pulled from. They need to stay on standby until further notice. This is a matter of national security for crying out loud!"

"Wow…" Jimenti said quietly to Valdez. "Sounds like our hunch was right. They must have sent a tactical team to hit the cabin. Good thing the kids were already gone huh?"

"Yeah, no kidding." Valdez replied shaking his head lightly. "I wasn't sure they would mobilize so quickly, but I guess you were right."

"I just hope that the rest of them were careful. If they can tie anything back to wherever they are hiding, things could get very ugly in a hurry."

*　　*　　*

"Are you sure you don't want one of the Terralium blades. Even just a dagger?" Luke asked. We were seated in chairs in the large open hangar, spaced just slightly apart with everyone else from our party chatting quietly while we waited for the briefing from Isaac.

"Well that just depends on if you want someone to be able to kill me with one." I replied. "The further I am from the Terralium weapons, the less likely I am to be killed right?"

"That's a good point." Luke replied sheepishly, seeming to have not considered how dangerous the weapons were if someone was able to get one from me. "Sorry, I guess I didn't think that one through very well."

"Listen. If the entire point of this mission is to free these other bloodlines from the other Verdorben, then I think you should let me, my father and Tobias deal with the bloodlines while the rest of you focus on killing those two. Once they are gone, and we tell the others that they are free, I have a feeling the fighting should be over." I explained. "I don't have to kill them while we fight, just incapacitate them until their masters are dead. We can save several dozen more lives if we just don't kill anyone else that we don't have to."

"You know, I actually think that is a great idea." Luke sounded excited now. "I will run it by Isaac before he starts his brief." Luke stood and walked over to the corner of the room where Isaac was speaking quietly with Jacob, Alonzo and my father.

"You know I can't make up my mind." Haysom said loudly from the other side of me where he was seated. I turned to look at him, and he was thoughtfully staring at me with a confused expression on his face.

"About what?" I asked.

"About which one of you I want to try and help protect during the fighting tonight." He added. Before I even had a chance to say anything, he continued, speaking quickly. "I mean there is absolutely no way that I'm not going to let you have the Romeo and Juliet ending that I fear may be in store for you. What with how adorable your fledgling little marriage is and all. And while the small spark of chivalry that is still left in me would be inclined to protect you... I can't help but think, after hearing about you in action back in Arizona, that between the two of you, it is likely he more than you that needs the help." He raised one eyebrow thoughtfully as he spoke.

"Oh Haysom. You seriously crack me up." I replied, grinning. "How about you just focus on helping kill the bad guys and protect yourself. I really think that Luke and I will be okay."
It was almost strange how nice the man was being to me.

"Oh, I do plan on doing some killing." Haysom grinned, his eyes taking on an almost crazy look again. He paused briefly before continuing, appearing deep in thought. "But just in case bad things happen tonight, I want you to know something."

"What is that?" I asked. My curiosity was peaked.

"You remind me of my cousin Hazel." His eyes started to water slightly as he spoke, but no tears came. "We were best friends all throughout childhood, and even into our early twenties. So, when she was taken from me by that tall, bearded monster all those years ago, I was devastated. I tried fighting him off, but after several large gashes that almost chopped me in half. She had told me to run away. So... I did. I ran away. To the sound of her screams that have been burned into my memory ever since. When I had begun running, I thought that she would escape too. Instead, she sacrificed herself for me... so that I could get away. It's crazy because you look like a prettier version of her."

"Oh no." I struggled to find the right words to say. "I'm so sorry Haysom. I had no idea."

"Oh, don't be sorry Liz." Haysom continued. "It's been almost twenty years since she was killed. I haven't spoken to anyone about it in years, but for some reason, I felt like the light wanted me to tell you now. Anyways, when I heard that you had helped Isaac kill the evil man responsible for her death. It made me like you all the more."

"Well thank you for sharing that, Haysom." I noticed my eyes were moist as well. His story, while sad, had been deeply moving. "I will try to live up to Hazel's memory."

"You already are Liz." Haysom said, gently patting my wrist as he spoke. "Helping these complete strangers is nice. Even if I personally think that they don't deserve it. Most teenagers couldn't care less about things like this. And besides, Luke also helped save my life from those men in black back in Nevada. So, he's on my good list too." Haysom shrugged and grinned as he finished speaking.

"Hey Haysom." Luke said as he walked back up to join us. He sat down next to me. "Isaac is getting ready to start the briefing."

"Luke." Haysom nodded at him politely but didn't say more.

"Everyone here." Isaac began loudly as everyone else's speaking quickly died down. "Is here because you want to make a difference. And whether your motivation is fear of your family being continually hunted, revenge for those who have already lost loved ones to the monsters that are using these other bloodlines as weapons, or you are motivated by wanting to free the families of these people. Regardless of why you are here, I thank you for joining our clan on this mission.

"Our mission for tonight, is to kill or capture the tainted ones living in this mansion." Isaac paused and pointed at a smaller building near the north side of the map. "And thereby free the bloodlines that are being used as both assassins and slave laborers. Most of the bloodlines, including the women and children, live in this large structure on the far south side of the property. From what Alonzo and I could tell, during the night, there are only about four that stay in the main mansion, and another four that act as sentries. Two are posted outside at the mansion, while two are posted outside the factory.

"In order to limit the number of bloodlines that we have to kill, we need to get in as quickly as possible, striking fast and going straight for the tainted ones. We will stop any bloodlines who get in our way, but the goal there is to incapacitate and not to kill when possible. Is that clear to everyone?"

"Yes." Metemba said as the rest of the clansmen nodded. His deep voice echoed slightly in the mostly empty hangar.

"Liz." Isaac continued. "Can you still sense the tainted ones?"

"Yes." I replied. "Well, the one anyways. I believe they are still in the same spot as yesterday."

- 275 -

"Very good." Isaac added. "The plan is to strike at eleven o'clock since that is when the other Verdorben was able to be sensed. If one is a fade, it would be best to try and catch them both sleeping. According to Tobias, when they sleep is the only time they are not shielded from the senses of other tainted ones. Judging from Liz and our other tainted allies, we cannot count on more than an hour or two of sleep. So, we will stage here." Isaac pointed to a spot on the larger map, a little over a mile from the compound.

"Will they be able to sense our Verdorben from there?" Metemba asked.

"No." Isaac replied. "We are quite confident in that."

"How can we be sure?" Metemba pressed. He obviously wanted to be convinced. I couldn't blame him. The African clan chief seemed wise and mature for his age and was intelligently questioning everything. I was actually surprised that for some reason he seemed to trust me, even though it didn't make logical sense. At least, he didn't look at me with the same obvious mistrust that he had when looking at Tobias. There was no feigning the contempt Metemba had for that man.

"There are very few seekers amongst the Auserwhalt." Tobias explained as I was opening my mouth to speak. "Even Alastair does not possess one. If he did... I would have been killed a long time ago."

"Very good." Isaac nodded at Tobias before continuing. "We will wait at the staging area until Elizabeth confirms that they are both able to be sensed. To strike without either one of them could be catastrophic, as the only way to ensure the enslaved bloodlines are safe from their explosive implants is to take both of them out at the same time. While we do not know the triggering mechanism for the devices, we should assume they have some type of kill switch on them. Do not let them stall, and do not let them escape once the fighting begins. We are hoping to strike at eleven, but it may be hours before we have any confirmation. We will not move until I give the signal on the coms, after Liz and Tobias confirm that the other one can be sensed."

"What coms are we using?" My uncle Tommy asked.

"We have a full complement of coms and tactical gear on the table against that wall. Once we complete the individual assignments and back briefs, we will make sure everyone has what they need." Isaac replied.

"Why do you say not to kill the men in black?" Darsh asked, an angry grimace on his face as he spoke. "If we hold back during the fighting, more of us could be killed. Those animals killed my father!" The rage in his voice was also unmasked.

"That is why I said try. Remember that the men who killed your father are already dead. The ones responsible for sending them, however, are the tainted ones. Save your righteous anger for them." Isaac explained. "If re-enforcements come from the factory before we can kill the tainted ones, we probably won't have a choice. If it comes down to kill or be killed, do what you must. I am mainly saying for Liz, Tobias and Daniel, that the more we can stop without killing them the better. Once we have taken out the Verdorben, we will tell the other bloodline hunters. If they continue to fight, we will kill them. If they lay down their arms, we will of course help them. Does that make sense?"

Darsh and many of the others nodded, but I could still see a wild ferociousness in the man's eyes.

*   *   *

"So?" Reuben asked, sitting up in the gilded chair he had been lounging on while he waited for Aurelia to return. Aurelia turned and closed the door before speaking, her wavy long blonde hair perfectly framing her pretty face. "What did he say?"

"He said we should go a day early." She replied, excitement flashing in her deep blueish black eyes. It made her look both more beautiful and more reckless when she got that expression. "He thinks if we do not, they will likely move everything and clear out the farm."

"Okay. When you say we, I presume this means you will be accompanying us as well?" Reuben clarified. "So, you did ask to come with us?" He smiled. Even though he loved to make Aurelia happy, he also wasn't oblivious to the fact that at times she could be reckless.

"I did and he said I could. He did say that he wants us to take two dozen from the blood guard instead of just one like last time. And he wants us to bring three of the apprentices, to ensure those gifted after Silas and Priscilla's death will be loyal to us, and already well trained."

"Very good." Reuben replied. "Vincent, tell the attendants to ready the supplies and prepare the jet. We will leave at first light."

"Oh, I'm so excited!" Aurelia stated. "I have wanted to kill Priscilla for so long, and now she has finally given us an excuse to." She smiled and walked over to Reuben, kissing him lightly on the lips.

"Don't be too excited my dear." Reuben said thoughtfully. "We might be going twenty-seven deep, but they do have about the same amount of people as we do. Even if many of them are less trained than our blood guards."

"Oh Reuben." Aurelia replied, still smiling. "You do worry too much. What could possibly go wrong?" Her smile turned more sinister than it had been just moments before. "We will get there, kill them, take the rest of the tainted ones, and increase the number of Auserwhalt that work directly for Alastair. If they dare to try and fight us, we cracked the code for the implants and can incapacitate their bloodlines before the fighting even starts. There is no world where this is not going to be a huge win for us."

CHAPTER XX

"Are you sure they aren't sleeping yet?" Luke asked as he gently raised my hand up to his lips and kissed it. He was sitting in the driver's seat of the Chevy Tahoe, which was backed into a parking space at the small park everyone had staged at. Large trees towered over us, and various green vegetation surrounded the small parking lot. I looked at my watch without thinking and was not surprised when it only read 11:53PM. I had updated it to Brazilian time during the earlier meeting, so I knew it was right.

"Be patient sweetheart." I said, smiling as I gently squeezed his hand. I almost felt old calling him that, as I remember my mom using the term of endearment with my father throughout my childhood, but it didn't bother me enough to stop. He was my sweetheart… and so many other wonderful things.

Jazmine and Haysom were seated in the back seat of our car. In the black colored four door sedan parked next to us were Tobias, Metemba, Zane and my father. The three Indian bloodlines were parked on the other side of them. The plan was for the other group of cars, parked a half mile closer, to move in first once the fade was sleeping. They would neutralize the bloodline sentries, while we began moving in from just outside the range where the Verdorben could sense us from.

This way if the tainted ones were not both sleeping, and attempted to flee, the advanced team could intercept them. It all seemed overly tactical to me, but after seeing the plan drawn out on the map back at the hangar a few hours before, I had to admit it seemed brilliant. At least, it seemed like it would give us our best chance at success. Our best chance at freeing these people. Even though I hadn't spoken to anyone besides Leuken about it... I felt terrible about killing all of the other bloodlines back in Arizona. The terrorists in Las Vegas had been a different story, because I knew they were evil men actively trying to kill as many people as they could for whatever sick reason they had concocted to justify their vile deeds. These bloodline hunters, on the other hand, were a whole different story.

Yes, they had done terrible things, and they were actively trying to kill us when I had ended them. The difference was that they themselves were being held against their will. Their lives and the lives of their loved ones were being used as ransom to force them into serving these evil masters. Masters whose main purpose seemed to be the destruction of any and all bloodlines that they could find. It certainly was a sick situation... and while I wanted to believe that I would never allow myself to commit such atrocious acts of violence against innocent people... I had done bad things before myself. Not by choice, but I had done them, nonetheless.

I could also see my father, if Alex and I had been taken prisoner, doing anything to keep us safe. And I knew that he was not alone. The man Royce, who had first told us about these people just a few short weeks before, he too had been a father. He had not seemed like a monster... but more like a father desperate to protect and eventually even free his family. He had even sacrificed his own life trying to save them. Had it not been for his bravery by confiding in us, we would have never known about the plight of his family and the other bloodlines.

Which is why I found myself torn. Could you blame a man and judge him guilty, if he only did evil because he thought he had no other choice? Because he had to choose, between his own life and the life of his family… or the life of complete strangers. The very thought of it made me hate these tainted masters all the more. That rage fueled the fire inside of me that kept me motivated. A fire I now couldn't wait to quench. Without thinking I gently traced my wrist, remembering when Jareth, that monster of a man, had put the cursed bracelet on me. The same bracelet that Tobias now wore. The actions I had done against Luke, while under the control of that evil man because of the relic he used to control me, had filled me with such unimaginable dread, as I had been powerless to stop myself from hurting the man I loved. I shuttered lightly at the very thought of what I had almost done.

"Are you okay Liz?" Luke grabbed my one hand gently, his eyes filled with concern as he looked over at me. I had been so consumed with my thoughts, that I didn't realize I had actually shuttered until his words brought me back to the present. Back to the task at hand.

We needed to free these people. Whatever it took.

"I am fine. Sorry." I said, smiling reassuringly at him.

"You sure?" He didn't seem convinced. "What is it. Are they moving?"

"No, they are still in the same spot. I was just thinking about when Jareth had used that bracelet to force me to hurt you back in Harrisburg. That was the most awful feeling ever. I never want to go through that again." I squeezed his hand gently as I finished speaking.

"Don't worry." Luke reassured. "We won't let anything happen to you. Now that we know what to look for, if we even see one of those bracelets, we will keep them from you."

"Okay. What in the light are you talking about?" Haysom asked from the back seat.

"The bracelet that Tobias wears." Jazmine explained. "We took that from Jareth after he was killed, but before he died, he had used it on Liz to control her. She was beating him in combat until he slipped it on her wrist. After that, he used the ring to control her, and forced her to hurt and almost kill Luke. It was absolutely terrible."

"Oh no!" Haysom seemed surprised. "That's awful. I knew he had almost killed Luke, but I didn't realize he had controlled Liz."

"Had Isaac not showed up when he did." Jazmine continued. "Luke would not be with us today. And who knows... with how powerful she is, we might all be dead."

"And that monster would still be alive." Haysom almost spat as he spoke, the disdain was so strong.

"But thank the light he is not." Jazmine said coolly. "Isaac sent him where the light will never shine on him again."

"I'm sorry Liz." Haysom said, seeming to calm down slightly. "That must have been terrible to lose control like that."

"Yeah... it was pretty bad." I managed to say, suddenly hoping for a subject change. Just then I noticed something, another Verdorben in the distance, almost touching the other tainted one who hadn't seemed to move for the last few minutes.

"You sense that, Liz?" I heard Tobias' voice come through the tiny speaker in my right ear.

"I do." I replied, lightly touching my wrist piece so that my voice would transmit.

"Are we a go then?" Isaac's voice sounded in my ear now.

"Just a minute." I said, focusing closely on the two Verdorben, who felt not too distant from just over a mile away. My mind seemed to wander closer to them as I focused, and I could sense two dark auras. As my mind seemed to literally move, I could sense that they were very close, even in the same room. The sensation of my mind having left my body was disconcerting, yet I could sense that the presences were inside. Suddenly my mind snapped back to where I was in the car, and for a split second I felt a wave of dizziness come over me. "Okay, they aren't moving. We are good to go." I managed to say as the dizzy feeling dissipated almost as quickly as it had come.

"Let's go." Isaac's voice sounded through the coms again. "Advance team only, move up."

Luke shifted the SUV into drive but kept his foot on the brake.

"Not yet brother." Jazmine said politely from the back seat.

"Oh, I know." Luke replied, turning to give Jazmine a quick grin. "I am just getting ready. Too many people's lives are at stake to mess this one up.

"Once we arrive at the mansion, I want silence on Coms until the sentries have been dispatched." Isaac's voice rang slightly in my ear, and I adjusted the volume down slightly from my wrist piece. Excitement and nervousness began to course through me simultaneously. I was excited to stop these monsters, but nervous that someone might get hurt on our side.

*   *   *

The man on the front west side of the mansion was looking down as Isaac slowly approached. He could hear some type of video playing from the phone held in the man's hand. Though the volume was too low to make out what was being said, Isaac was grateful for the distraction. It allowed him to approach from the side, slightly behind the man, who was facing diagonally offset with his body half facing the front of the mansion and half facing the field.

As Isaac got closer, the lad appeared to be not a day older than twenty... which meant he was certainly under forty. Once Isaac was about twenty feet away, he sprang into quick motion. The young man barely had time to look up from his phone and start to turn towards Isaac as his blade whisked from its sheath and tore clean through the man's neck. A faint grunt or scream had just started to form on the man's lips as his head was severed from the body. While it gave Isaac no pleasure to kill this man, he knew it had to be done. They had discussed trying to subdue them alive or simply maim them, but the likelihood of them sounding an alarm and waking all of the others was too great without immediately killing these sentries. The death of these four men, would possibly save dozens of lives. Lives that would be saved on both sides.

Looking across the front of the mansion, Isaac could see that Hinata Chen had also dropped the sentry on the Northern front corner of the mansion

Isaac quickly sheathed his sword, even though it severely bothered him to put it away while still so bloody. *That sheath would take hours to clean properly now.* He thought to himself. Isaac quickly moved the chair from five feet out to right at the corner of the mansion. Reaching down, he grabbed the body up from the ground, setting it back in the chair. He adjusted the headless corpse so that it was leaning up against the wall, with only the shoulder sticking out to be visible from behind. This would provide the appearance of the sentry still being there if someone approached from behind, as the missing head would only be visible from the front of the mansion.

He began walking quickly towards the front door, as the other members of the Hinata clan, Elias and Jacob came from the bushes to meet him near the front entrance. Jarvis, Erik and the Boston clan were staged off to the side of the mansion still. Lying in wait to take out the rear sentries if any alarm was sprung or they tried to give warning to others. That decision had been Isaac's as the sentries on the back of the mansion hadn't been there the night before. He was still trying to limit bloodline losses as much as possible. Elias pulled a small black leather case from his pocket, opening it and quickly inserting several random metal objects into the front door.

"That's strange." Elias whispered quietly, seeming frustrated. "There is no…" He paused mid-sentence, before suddenly pulling down on the silver lever above the ornate handle on the large brown door. The door clicked open, making very little noise. "Should have checked the handle first I guess." He mumbled to himself.

Isaac held back a chuckle as he followed the balding man into the house. The others fell in behind Isaac as they stepped quietly into a large entryway. *Of course, the front door would be unlocked. With supernatural guards and being nearly indestructible themselves, why would the Verdorben need to lock their doors?* Isaac thought to himself. A single light was on at the top of a wide spiraling staircase that led up to a second-floor landing. The floor was a light-colored marble with dark veins running sporadically through it. In the dim light, Isaac could see that the paint on the walls was light, with dark contrasting curtains covering the large windows.

No one was in sight inside the house, and they all paused quietly for a moment after Hiroshi gently closed the door, and it clicked shut. "We are in." Isaac said softly into his watch piece. "Second team, move up quickly." As he finished speaking, he motioned to the stairs, and the others followed Isaac to them.

Alonzo had told Isaac the night before, that the only light staying on for most of the night, came from the Southwestern rear window to the mansion. Once Isaac and the others reached the top of the stairs, they turned right and started slowly down that hallway. Isaac hoped that they could move quietly enough to surprise the Verdorben. His goal was to try and kill them in their sleep, but he wasn't sure if that was realistic or not. He hoped that Liz and the others would arrive quickly enough to help, as his fear was the rest of the bloodlines would come to help if an alarm was sounded.

*   *   *

Silas sat up in bed quickly, started by a faint metallic clanking sound that had come from outside. Instinctively, he reached for the terralium blade at the side of his bed, fearing it was Alastair's men coming to kill them. A quick search with his mind, however, reassured him that there were no other Auserwhalt nearby. He gently set the sword back down, resting it in between his bed and the nightstand. Turning his head, he noticed that Priscilla was still asleep next to him. Her soft breathing barely audible as she lay on the pillow facing the other way.

Silas took a deep breath to calm his nerves, before laying back down himself. While there were things he absolutely despised about his wife, mainly that she controlled him with the bracelet on his wrist, he couldn't deny that she had some redeeming qualities. She was pretty, in spite of the hawkish nose. He found himself less miserable when he just pretended he was only her husband and not her servant, but there was little solace in pretending. Outside of her random emotional outbursts and utter selfishness, she wasn't too unpleasant as a person. She had a decent sense of humor and was mostly intelligent. She had been smart enough to broker the deal with

Alastair over a century ago to both farm and hunt bloodlines for the man. That arrangement had kept them alive thus far.

Silas knew that some of his anxiety was from the looming fact that their arrangement would likely come to an end in two days. This meant they would have to leave their farm and abandon everything they had built, if their seekers were not able to find the bloodlines they had promised Reuben to kill. The odds were especially bleak, since that group had wiped out two and a half of their hunting parties and vanished immediately afterwards. Priscilla had told him if the others were located, he would take two more crews himself, join with the seekers and make sure they laid a proper ambush for the others. But they were running out of time.

As Silas lay there, thinking with his eyes closed, he suddenly noticed something. His mind felt the presence of the other Auserwhalt just as his heart began to race. In his mind it was clear as day. There were three of the chosen closing in on the mansion, and they were moving fast. For a brief moment, he thought about trying to flee, but he knew the bracelet compelled him to stay.

He quickly grabbed Priscilla's arm and shook her awake. "Priscilla!" He said her name loud and urgently. She mumbled softly as she startled awake, opening her eyes to look at him.

"What is it? Why are you waking…" Priscilla stopped herself mid-sentence, as she must have felt the others as well. A panicked expression washed across her face.

"They are coming!" Silas said as he jumped to his feet, grabbing the terralium blade once more. "And they will be here in seconds."

*　　*　　*

The speed limit on the small highway road was 80 kilometers per hour, but Luke was doing half again more than that as the SUV bounced and rocked while we drove. The road curved slightly around small hills, with mostly farmland around them. Without my enhanced vision, I probably wouldn't have been able to make out the rows and rows of various crops that filled the countryside around us in the pale moonlight.

I was about to make a comment on Luke's driving being too crazy, when I felt something disappear from my mind. One of the Verdorben was gone suddenly, and I realized that they must have woken up. I focused on the other tainted one, who I could still feel. As my mind zoomed in on that one, I could tell they were still in the same room from where I had sensed them just moments before.

"One is gone again." I said quickly. "They must have woken up, and the other is moving quickly inside the room."

"What's your ETA?" I heard Isaac whisper through the earpiece.

"About twenty seconds to park." Luke replied. "Another ten seconds on foot to reach the mansion from there."

"Okay. We will hold short. Tell us the instant they move if they try to flee." Isaac replied. As he finished speaking, I heard a strange siren sound coming through the earpiece as well. It cut off just as he stopped transmitting. Less than two seconds later I noticed the Verdorben begin to move. Focusing quickly on that one, I could sense them move quickly to the South.

"Hurry Luke!" I said quickly before speaking into the coms. "At least one is on the move. They are heading south, towards the compound."

*   *   *

A loud siren noise went off just as Isaac finished speaking into the comm unit on his wrist. He motioned for the others with him to move, and they quickly closed the distance to the large door leading to the back room of the hallway. Pulling it open, Isaac could see a small sitting area, with an opening behind the couch that led into another large room. This one had a large bed with nightstands on either end. As he came around the corner in site of the larger room, he saw a man and a woman standing in the back corner, near a window. The man looked mostly normal, with tan skin and dark eyes that appeared surprised to see Isaac and the others appear. The woman with dark hair and even darker eyes wore a scowl of contempt on her face, which quickly turned to panic as Isaac's companions also appeared.

"To the compound. Jump!" The man said quickly, as he jumped through the large glass window, appearing unphased by the breaking glass, or the height he was jumping from. The female seemed surprised for a split second before she quickly followed him and jumped from the window. Most of the broken glass fell out the window, but a few small fragments landed inside.

"Don't let them escape." Isaac said as he sprang into motion, quickly closing the gap and jumping through the window headfirst. As he fell through the air, he could see the girl was collecting herself from the ground, while the male had begun running towards the complex several hundred yards away. The woman shouted something in Portuguese, but her accent was so heavy he could not understand the words.

Isaac landed, rolling to his feet on the grass. The female, who was wearing a silver-colored nightgown with a sword sheath attached to her belt, began to run, but he was quickly catching her. Just as he was about to lunge at her with his sword, the man, who had turned around without Isaac noticing, sprang at Isaac, flashing his own bright terralium sword. Isaac was able to parry the strike, but the force of it made him lose balance as he hit the ground and rolled sideways. The man jumped again to strike at him, and Isaac had to roll sideways to avoid being struck, as the man slashed downwards, hitting the grass and earth where Isaac had been a moment before.

Isaac jumped to his feet, just in time to parry a stroke at his legs, then another at his neck. The speed with which this tainted one moved was impressive, and Isaac instantly realized he was dealing with a master swordsman, on top of being a Verdorben. The man's strikes did not slow, and it was a dancing, whirling four more blocks before Isaac was able to mount a strike at the other man's shoulder, one which the man blocked just in time. Isaac could see that the female had been intercepted by the Japanese clan, and they were fighting on the grass not far from where Isaac was pre-occupied.

He noticed two bloodline hunters, clad in all black, approaching him from the side. With relief, Isaac saw Jacob and Jarvis move to intercept them. Had he been forced to take any attention off this tainted one he was already fighting; he knew he would have been killed by him. He was surprised to hear one of the Chen's suddenly say loudly through the mic in his ear. "Team two hurry, there are dozens coming out of the factory!" The urgency in his voice was unnerving.

Isaac had managed to land a small gash on the man's non-sword arm, and another on the Verdorben's thigh, but he couldn't deny the man's skill. Glancing to his side as he parried another blow at his own head, Isaac noticed a flood of people coming out of the factory to the south. They were all running this way. Towards where they fought with the two Verdorben. *Luke and Liz had better hurry.* He thought to himself. *Or we will all be dead before this night is over.*

CHAPTER XXI

As the car quickly jolted to a stop, I jumped from the passenger seat, already running without looking to see who was following. I didn't need to look in order to know they were coming. I just knew we needed to hurry. "They are in the field area behind the mansion." I called over my shoulder. "Both of them!" I had just noticed that the female Verdorben could be sensed as well. I wasn't sure what had caused her to drop her cloak, but I was too busy running as fast as I could to worry about that. I could hear footsteps behind me as the others followed, but they grew more distant as I ran.

In a few seconds I had cleared the rear corner of the mansion, and I slowed almost to a stop while I assessed the chaotic mess that was unfolding before me. "So much for not waking the others." I thought out loud, as I noticed several dozen bloodline members, most in what appeared to be sleeping garments, yet still armed with swords, running towards where the fighting was at from the south. They were closing in quickly on the six bloodline members who had formed a skirmish line of sorts to protect the others who were fighting. Isaac was closer to me, but he appeared to be holding his own against the tainted one he fought, and I could see Jacob and

Jarvis moving to his aid. Three others fought with the female tainted one on the grass as well. I knew where I needed to go, so I sprinted again, making for the members of our strike team that appeared on the verge of being overwhelmed. That was where the help was needed.

As I got close, I noticed the female Verdorben fall over, as Hinata sliced her head clean off. She disappeared from my mind at the same time that her lifeless body hit the grass. Hinata began moving towards Isaac to help him, while the other two Japanese clan members moved to help the other six on the skirmish line. I sensed Tobias right behind me and turned to bark directions at him.

"Tobias, with me. Do not kill them unless they are armed with Terralium weapons." I almost shouted as I ran.

Approaching the skirmish line from behind, I spoke into the watch piece to ensure I would be heard over all the commotion. "We are here. Leave the bloodlines to us. Stop the other Verdorben."

I ran past the line, as I could see at least forty or fifty bloodlines, most appearing to be young men, charging towards us. Luke shouted something at me from behind, but I could barely hear him over the cries of the charging bloodline hunters and couldn't make out what he said. Catching them off guard seemed the most logical thing to do, and of the few dozen blades that I could see, all of them appeared made form the same black metal that the other hunting parties had wielded when they attacked us. So, I wasn't worried about being hurt in the moonlight.

I tackled the closest bloodline hunter I could see, a shorter middle-aged man who seemed to be leading the charge. The force of my momentum knocked him backwards into several others, with all of us tumbling to the ground in a clumsy heap. I jumped quickly to my feet, just in time to sidestep a swipe at my right arm. As I shifted,

I grabbed the attacker by the wrist, twisting his sword arm into my body while pushing down on his wrist as hard as I could.

I barely noticed the man's painful groan as his arm bones snapped. Pulling his sword from his now limp hand, I swung back around and sliced his other arm off at the shoulder. He swung his limp arm to strike me, but I pivoted and brought my leg up, kicking him across the chest. The force of this strike knocked him backwards into another bloodline hunter who had been about to slice at me, knocking both of them to the ground. I turned to see another sword slashing at my head and noticed Tobias hack that attackers arm off at the elbow, resulting in both the sword and half of an arm flying just past me in the air.

Movement to my other side caught my attention, and I moved to dodge a sword strike that was blocked by a glowing blade before it reached me. Out of nowhere, Luke and Tobias had each taken positions by my side. They were both engaged in blocking strikes from additional attackers. There were three hunters facing Tobias, and four near Luke, so I turned to help my husband. As he blocked one attacker, I sliced off the arm of another that swung his blade at Luke, while simultaneously kicking my leg up to block another strike at him. The man's blade bounced off my leg, but the shock had barely registered on the man's face before I punched him hard in the jaw. Bones cracked as his body crumpled sideways.

Before he even hit the ground, there were two more attackers striking at Luke. He was able to slash one of them in the leg, as I cut the other one through the shoulder of his sword arm. As that one reached to collect his dropped sword, I saw four more men charging at Luke. There was no way I could block all four of them at once, so I quickly grabbed the man who was leaning over by the arm, and violently swung his body away from Luke. He spun in almost a full circle, just in time to swing back around and smash into the four attackers, all of whom seemed surprised that one of their own men's bodies was used as a weapon against them. As they fell, I quickly began slashing at them before they could get up. Taking off a leg at the knee on one, another I slashed through the elbow, and a third I cut clean through the triceps, causing him to drop his sword.

The fourth man I had plowed down with the human baseball bat was already back on his feet before I reached him, but Luke made quick work of him, slashing repeatedly until he took off the man's hand at the wrist. A follow up blow from Luke cut through his calf and the man fell. I turned to see three more attackers charging at Luke. Panic struck me when I realized I could not jump around him fast enough to block all three attackers. Instinctively, I dove at the one closest to me who was slashing at him. I felt something hard bounce off my back as I knocked the man down. Wasting no time, I jumped back to my feet, turning to strike at another attacker. The two other men were both slashing at Luke, who was now bleeding from the neck and one leg had a large gash in it. Whirling in from the other side, suddenly Metemba was there, hacking one of the men attacking Luke through the upper thigh so the man fell hard. Jazmine also came from around Metemba and cut through the shoulder of the other who was about to strike at Luke again.

As that man fell, I turned expecting more attackers to emerge. Instead, I saw at least a dozen bloodline hunters watching us from nearby, swords drawn. They appeared ready to pounce, but one of them was shouting something to the others in Portuguese, while pointing behind me. It was the same middle-aged man I had first tackled. Just then I noticed that I could no longer sense the other Verdorben. Isaac must have finished him off.

I turned to see what they were pointing at, and I noticed Isaac walking towards us, with a large round object in each hand. He was shouting at the top of his lungs in Portuguese, but at first, I didn't recognize what he was saying. It wasn't until he got closer, shouting "Stop!" In English that I realized what he was holding. It was the heads of the male and female Verdorben we had just killed.

I quickly set down my sword, putting both hands up in a peaceful gesture towards the hunters who were watching, but not fighting. To my left, I heard more fighting, and could see that the Japanese and Indian clans were still fighting several bloodlines, even though everyone else had stopped.

"Enough! Stop!" I shouted to my bloodlines as I sprang into motion. I reached the closest bloodline hunters first, grabbing them from behind and throwing them towards the others. I was surprised to see them fly so far through the air before tumbling to a stop. As soon as I grabbed the third hunter and threw him towards the group, I noticed the others, who included at least twenty or more that had been injured, were beginning to shout at their companions. They were telling them to stop fighting.

A small gap quickly formed between the bloodline hunters, and the clans who had come with us. Jacob and Jarvis had joined the line on our side, making the two sides almost even if you didn't count the injured hunters. I moved back over towards Isaac, who was talking to the group in Portuguese. Most of them seemed to be listening, but a few of them looked confused.

"In English, please." The short man who I had first tackled and thrown said loudly to Isaac. "Not all of us speak Portuguese. Some are from central America, and we even have a few from Haiti who speak French. English is best. We all learned that." The man still held his sword in one hand but had lowered it down to his side.

"Listen my fellow bloodlines. We mean you no harm. My name is Isaac Bennett, and we are all from the bloodline, blessed by the light the same as you are." Isaac was speaking loud enough to be almost shouting, his voice carrying clearly through the night, in spite of several injured bloodlines who were sitting or lying in pain, a few even moaning from broken bones that needed to be set to heal properly.

"As you can see, we have killed the demons who had you enslaved." Several women and even a few younger children had emerged from the factory building and were walking cautiously up to join the men. "Silas and Priscilla will rule over you no more. You no longer have to do wrong just to keep your families safe."

"Are you saying we are free?" The shorter man, who appeared to be a leader of some sort. "We are free to leave?" The man looked at Isaac skeptically, but his frequent glancing at the heads of the Verdorben we had killed seemed at least somewhat convincing.

"No quite yet." Isaac explained, setting the heads down on the grass behind him before continuing. "The demons, who we call tainted ones, put implants in your heads. These have bombs inside of them that allowed them to kill you whenever they wanted, in an instant."

"You mean their magic?" The same man asked. "I thought they used magic to kill us?"

"No." Isaac explained. "Not magic. They put chips inside of your heads. It is implanted near the brain stem at the bottom part of your skulls. The explosives attached to the chips allow them to kill you remotely using technology. While the creatures were magic in that they have superhuman strength and are nearly indestructible, they could not use magic to kill you. They had tricked you all so that you would do what they ask."

"Do you have proof of this?" Another taller darker skinned man asked. His accent sounded different from the others. "How do we know you are not trying to trick us as well? How did you know where we were?"

"I do. One of your friends, a man named Royce who was killed a few weeks ago, he is the one who gave us coordinates for where you were. He asked us to come and free his wife, his children, and the rest of you. After his head exploded, I noticed the metallic pieces in the back of where his head had been, and saw the residue left over from the explosion." Isaac explained. "I can show you all. Pick any one of you, and we can operate to remove the device. I have a doctor on call who can be here within the hour. Are there any volunteers?"

"I will do it." The tall man replied without hesitation. "But if you truly mean us no harm, why don't you put your weapons down first?"

"That won't work for us." Isaac continued. "You see several dozen of your kind have already hunted us and killed some of our family members, so forgive us if we are not comfortable disarming in front of you. I will however, as a show of good will, give you time to heal your wounded."

"Some of them cannot heal." The shorter leader said. "You cut their arms and legs off, and they have already healed over."

"They can still heal." Isaac explained. "You simply need to cut the wound again and place the severed flesh against it immediately after. Make sure the cut is close so the tissue will heal completely."

I noticed that Hiroshi was missing part of his left arm. A bloody stump was all that protruded past his elbow. His young face seemed barely bothered by the injury. I walked over to him, just as he leaned down to retrieve the portion of his arm that was missing from the grass. He walked over to stand near Isaac.

"I can show you." He said loudly. Hinata walked up with his sword drawn, nodding at Hiroshi who held his arm stub out directly perpendicular to his side. Without speaking, Hinata sliced down quickly, cutting just the slightest edge of the nub. No sooner had the small sliver of flesh fallen to the earth, than Hiroshi quickly placed his arm piece against the nub. He winced slightly as the arm began to heal itself over. In a matter of seconds, the arm had reattached itself. Hiroshi slowly began to move his fingers.

"The nerves will take another minute to finish healing, but as you can see, it's not so bad." Hiroshi made his hand almost into a fist, with only two fingers not closing completely.

For the next few minutes, Hiroshi, who had set down the sword he was wielding before healing himself, walked amongst the other bloodline hunters, showing them where to cut for the healing process to work. Hinata, Jazmine and Metemba followed him through the crowd. I also walked just behind the group, smiling awkwardly at the bloodline hunters who viewed us all skeptically. Only those who we helped to heal seemed to soften up slightly afterwards.

Two of the bloodline hunters had been killed, and a woman ran up to one of them, crying loudly as she said something undiscernible in a language I did not recognize. The two dead bodies lay near where the Indian clan had been fighting. With the adrenaline still coursing through my veins from the fighting, I couldn't bring myself to blame the men from that clan. They had just had their father killed a few days before by people from this same group. There was no room for judgement or condemnation for the loss of life. Especially when these men had risked everything to help my clan and family.

I hadn't thought about it until that instant, but I was a part of the Bennett clan now. No, I might not be a member of the bloodline, but with my Verdorben abilities, I could still be a contributing member of the team. A team whose purpose seemed to have been fulfilled today. As Isaac and Jacob engaged the informal leader from the bloodline hunters in conversation, I couldn't help but stare at the face of the male Verdorben who had been killed. Unlike the female, his eyes remained open. If I didn't know better, he seemed to almost have a look of relief on them. *What would make another tainted one seem happy about being killed?* I thought to myself.

It bothered me so much, that I found myself walking over to where their bodies lay on the grass. I reached the female first. Her body was mostly pale with a slight tan to it. Skinny arms with even more slender looking fingers were all that protruded from the corpse's nightgown. It was the ring finger on the left hand that drew my attention. A darkened silver ring was on that finger, and I instantly recognized it. The small inscriptions on the metal were only barely visible, even with my enhanced vision. I recognized the object as familiar, because it was identical to the one I wore on my own hand. Mine was on the index finger of my left hand, next to the wedding ring on the finger two from it.

It was the ring that I used to control Tobias. Without thinking, I bent over and slowly slid the ring from the finger of the dead woman. It felt somewhat wrong, pulling it from the corpse like that, but the last thing I wanted was Tobias or another Tainted one having access to that cursed relic. I slipped the ring on my index finger on my right hand and was not surprised that it seemed to adjust to a perfect fit as I slid it on.

My father had started walking towards me from where the two groups still stood in a mostly awkward standstill. Only a few of them had engaged in conversation, while the rest of the hunters seemed completely confused about what to expect next. It was sad that the people had been enslaved for so long, that they almost seemed afraid of real freedom. My sadness was lessened by the rage I felt at how these people had not only been enslaved, but also forced to hunt down and kill innocent people.

Walking over to the other Verdorben's corpse, I grabbed the similarly marked bracelet off of his wrist. The metal it was made from perfectly matched the rings. The engravings looked much smaller on the bracelet, even though they were about the same size. The larger artifact made the small print seem tiny relative to the bracelet's larger size. I slid the bracelet into my jacket pocket, just as my father reached me.

"So, he was being controlled huh?" My father asked.

"It certainly looks that way." I replied. "I'll give you the extra ring and bracelet later. Once people aren't watching." I nodded towards the crowds a little way off.

"You can keep it for all I care." My father said, shaking his head slightly.

"No. I've already got Tobias to control. Why don't you hold onto this one in case we run into any more Verdorben." I explained. "After what happened last time I wore one of those, I'd rather not keep it anyways."

"I'm good either way." My father replied. "At the end of the day, I'd rather you feel safe. If holding on to that makes my baby girl happy, I don't mind." He smiled at me as he finished talking.

I raised an eyebrow at him but couldn't help but smile back. "Your baby girl huh?"

"Yeah, so what?" He chuckled sheepishly. "Just cause you're all grown and married, don't mean I'm not always gonna be your daddy. Or that you'll always be my baby girl. Even if you are strong enough to kill me with your tiny bare hands."

"Sounds good Dad."

"I really am glad you are okay." He said, putting one hand on my shoulder and squeezing it affectionately. "I'm not gonna lie... I was a little worried as we were driving here."

"My Dad, the retired cop was worried?" I asked.

"Not for me." He explained. "I was worried about you and Luke. The last thing I want is anything to happen to you. The way you charged headfirst into that group didn't help either."

"Well, that's silly." I said, smiling as I quickly wrapped both arms around him and hugged him. "I'm more worried about you than me." I teased.

"Hey Liz." Luke said as he walked up to join us. "You okay?"

"Yeah." I grinned and winked at him. "My dad was just worried, so I was letting him know he doesn't have to do that anymore."

My father shrugged at Luke, then turned to walk towards where Isaac and the others were still speaking. "You know, speaking of being worried." I said, glancing up so our eyes were locked. "When you jumped into that throng with me, and we got surrounded, I was terrified that something might happen to you."

"You were terrified?" He asked, appearing slightly incredulous. "I watched my wife dive into a crowd of dozens of bloodline hunters who were all armed with swords. What was I supposed to do, let them hurt you?"

"Honey, we talked about this beforehand. They couldn't hurt me. Not a single one of them had any terralium. That's why the plan was for me, Tobias and my father to hold them off, so that no one else from our side would have to die. Did you forget?" I didn't do a good job of keeping the chastising tone out of my voice as I spoke, but I was still upset that he had put himself in harm's way unnecessarily.

"But I…" Luke started to object, but then he got that look like he realized he was being dumb. "Oh shoot."

"What is it?" I asked.

"You are right." He put a hand to his forehead, shaking his head slightly from side to side as he spoke. "Without thinking, I placed you in great danger. By rushing in to your side, I almost gave them the very weapon they needed to hurt or even kill you. I am so sorry Liz."

"It's okay." I said, putting a hand gently on one side of his face, I pulled his head down slightly so our foreheads touched. "I am fine, and everything worked out. Just promise me one thing please?"

"What is that?" I could see the shame in his eyes.

"Promise me next time we have a plan. You will stick to it. That way, hopefully neither of us get killed." I was staring straight into his eyes.

"You have my word." He looked like he wanted to look away from my gaze, but he kept his eyes on mine.

"Good." I gave him a quick kiss, before turning to survey the others. "When is this doctor Isaac spoke of supposed to be here?"

CHAPTER XXII

The doctor arrived about thirty minutes later. He was a short, squat man with messy, curly hair that was thin on top but thick on the sides. His accent was heavy, but he spoke decent enough English. The truck he drove had a large, silver, enclosed trailer attached. Inside the trailer was a large gurney, and all sorts of medical devices and machinery. The whole setup was quite impressive, and the condition of the interior was immaculate. It took him only a few minutes to get everything set up.

The Haitian bloodline hunter who had volunteered followed the doctor into the medical trailer, along with Isaac and the short informal leader of the group, who I learned was called Gustavo. I stood just outside the trailer with Luke, trying to watch what was happening. Before operating, the doctor used an ultrasound wand on the Haitian, and showed on a large flatscreen television hanging from the wall where the implant was attached at the base of the skull.

He gave the Haitian a shot to knock him out, before using a scalpel and some other medical tools to operate. All in all, the doctor finished the entire process in about 10 minutes. Once done, he held a small metal device with surgical pliers. The device was a little smaller than a golf ball and was covered in blood.

"That would have been much easier." The doctor said as he studied the object. "If the man didn't heal so fast while I operated. This nasty thing needs to be destroyed, but for now please just set it away from everyone."

"If that blows up, will it kill us?" Gustavo asked, eyeing the object suspiciously.

"No." The doctor replied, gently setting it down on a metal tray at the side of the operating table. "The explosion, if not contained inside the head, would probably not be enough to kill anyone. It is the pressure from being inside the brain when it explodes, that makes the device so dangerous."

"Okay good. Can you take mine out next?" Gustavo seemed anxious to have the device removed from his own head, after seeing the other out. I could only imagine how I would feel if I knew there were a device inside me that could put a crater in my brain. Probably the same as he did. I would want that thing out like yesterday.

The Haitian man sat up suddenly and reached back to touch the back of his head. From where I was standing, I couldn't even see a scar on the man's neck. That must have been how the Tainted ones did it. With the way the bloodlines healed, no one would ever even know they had been operated on, let alone that a remote explosive had been placed inside of them. Isaac picked up the small tray and walked over to the middle of the field, a good hundred feet away from anything and anyone besides the grass.

When he came back a minute later, the doctor had just finished switching out the plastic blended lining on the gurney.

"Thank you Doctor." The Haitian man said as he bowed appreciatively to the doctor, who was now changing out his gloves and washing his hands in a small makeshift sink.

"Don't mention it." The doctor said as he nodded back at the man.

"Can you please tell the others, and get a couple more volunteers?" Isaac told the man. "If you want you can show them the explosive on the tray, just be very careful with it please. I don't know what sets it off, but we shouldn't take any chances."

"Of course." The man hurried off towards the large factory building, where several others walked out to meet him. From this far away, I couldn't make out the conversation, but it seemed to be very positive. I also noticed, sitting a little way off from the bloodline hunters, under a large tree, that Metemba and Jazmine were talking. From this distance I could not make out what they were saying, but Metemba appeared to be laughing at something Jazmine had said, as she pushed playfully on his chest. It made me happy to see those two growing closer. While their personalities seemed quite different, Metemba seemed like an absolute stud. Hopefully Jazmine wouldn't have her heart broken by the older man, as she seemed to be very selective in what men she would give the time of day.

A few minutes later the Haitian man returned with two other volunteers, one man looked to be in his mid-twenties, while the other didn't look a day older than fifteen. Both were average height with slender build. The older man had brown eyes, while the younger boy had blue eyes that contrasted nicely with his otherwise dark features.

"My lady." The older of the two said, bowing respectfully to Luke and me. "I want to say thank you all for freeing us. My son Felipe and I are forever in your debt."

"Yes, thank you." The younger boy echoed his father, who in no way looked old enough to be a dad. Although, considering Isaac's age, the older one who looked mid-twenties could realistically have been over fifty for all I knew.

I heard a soft clanking sound and looked over to see the doctor setting another metal chip on a tray. "I will say." The doctor said loudly, looking over at us. "While the quick healing makes it harder to operate fast enough on you guys. I must admit it is nice not having to do any stitches." He smiled slightly as he finished speaking, before turning to start disinfecting the scalpel and pliers he had used.

A couple minutes later, Gustavo slowly exited the trailer, while the younger man, Felipe, went and sat down on the gurney. The doctor pulled out the ultrasound wand and applied some lubricating jelly substance to the back of the boy's neck. As he began manipulating the medical device on the back of Felipe's neck, he suddenly stopped.

"That's odd." He mused aloud. I stepped into the trailer at the same time as the boy's father moved anxiously closer.

"What is it?" The man asked, obviously fearing for his son.

"He doesn't have one." The doctor explained.

"Has he snapped yet?" Luke asked the man.

"Snapped?" The man looked at Luke confused.

"Has the light found him yet?" Luke said it another way, which sounded strange to me. It was probably just because I had never heard him say it that way before. It sounded more like something I would expect Metemba to say. "Does your son have abilities?"

"Oh!" The man said suddenly. "You mean the awakening? No not yet, but he will not be sixteen for another month, so my guess is he will awaken soon after that."

"The awakening huh?" Luke said. "It is interesting the many names the bloodlines have for the changes that happen to many of us."

"They must have been waiting until after the change to put in the implant." Isaac surmised. "Which makes sense if they were trying to keep it a secret from their captives. After snapping, you could knock them out, put the chip in, and they would heal before they ever even knew what had happened. It's quite clever, in an utterly evil sort of way that is." Gustavo was eyeing Isaac questioningly at the clever comment, but just shook his head slightly without commenting.

"Once the doctor finishes removing these bombs from our brains." Gustavo said, turning to look at Isaac and me. "Is he able to do the same for the other bloodlines?"

"Of course." Isaac reassured. "He won't leave until everyone's have been removed."

"I am not talking about just everyone here." Gustavo explained. "There is another factory, about ten miles from here. Twice as many of our kin are at that location. They will need to be freed as well."

"Just a second." Isaac replied. "You know where the others are being kept?"

"Oh yeah." Gustavo added. "I would say at least double the people are at the offsite."

"Well, that's fantastic." Isaac smiled as he spoke. "Are they your family as well?"

"Oh no." Gustavo answered. "I am actually the only one here who even knows about the others. Our masters… I mean, the tainted ones you killed, they kept the other location a secret, so that some other tainted one they feared would never find out about it. The only way to prevent the tributes from telling the others about us, was to make sure that none of them knew."

"What do you mean tributes?" I asked, confused by his comments.

"Every five years, two of our kind were sent away with these other tainted ones who occasionally came. Silas and Priscilla had some kind of agreement that our sons would be sacrificed to serve them. It seemed like some kind of peace offering, at the expense of our own children!" Gustavo's voice grew angrier as he spoke, and he spat at the end.

"You seem quite upset by this. Did you lose someone you cared for as a tribute?" Isaac asked.

"Yes. Two of my sons have been lost to these others, and one of my nephews." He was keeping his emotions mostly in check now, but I still noticed his eyes watering slightly.

"Perhaps we will be able to find them for you someday soon." Luke said optimistically. "Would you like to help us look for them? Maybe we could free them as well."

"Yes." The man's eyes seemed to shift slightly, a glimmer of hope brightening them. "I would like that very much."

*   *   *

"Take him to the doctor." Rico heard someone say, as he felt himself being picked up and carried. He opened his eyes slowly, unsure what to expect after he had become so violently ill before passing out. He wasn't sure how long he had been unconscious for, but judging by the moonlight, it must not have been too long. Morning still hadn't arrived. The last thing he could remember before being sick was the screaming and all the strange people fighting with his group from the compound.

Rico had been adopted a year before. He had stumbled on the compound at the time after running away from home. The Lord of the compound had wanted him killed, but the clan had vouched for him and said that he would work and mind himself if they didn't kill him. One lady, Renae, had even lied and said that Rico was her nephew, to prevent him from being killed. Renae had claimed he was from the bloodline. That had been over a year ago, just after Rico's seventeenth birthday. Since then, Renae had become his informal mother. She was much kinder than the woman his father had married prior to him running away. During the fighting tonight, Renae had told him to run into the forest and hide, but halfway to the forest he had collapsed and started vomiting before passing out. He had never felt an illness come on so quickly before.

Someone was carrying him and running towards a large trailer that was parked on the driveway with a big truck attached to the front of it. A beautiful dark-haired girl he didn't recognize was standing just outside the trailer with some men he also didn't recognize and Gustavo. When he saw Gustavo, the man appeared relaxed, so the fighting must have stopped. This confused Rico, as it appeared the strangers who had attacked them were no longer trying to hurt anyone.

"You can lay him here on the gurney." A man's voice said, and Rico was set down on a padded makeshift bed on top of a metal frame. Glancing around, he recognized the older man who had carried him, but the man worked a different shift, so Rico couldn't remember his name. "What happened to him?" Rico noticed the man speaking was wearing a white coat. *He must be some kind of doctor.* Rico thought to himself.

"I don't know." The older man who had carried him replied. "I found him lying on the ground, in his own vomit. He doesn't appear injured, but I don't know if he hit his head or something. He is not from the bloodline, so I don't think he was fighting.

Rico moved to sit up, but the doctor put a hand gently on his chest. "Not so fast." The doctor said. "Let's take a look at you first." The Doctor proceeded to check Rico's temperature, then his eyes and lungs before letting him sit up. He then checked the back of Rico's neck after putting some cold gel on. Surprisingly to Rico, he felt almost nothing during the process. His nausea and lightheadedness were completely gone. If anything, he felt better than he ever had. Even without his glasses, his vision was completely crisp, and he felt strong with clear thinking. It really was remarkable. For a minute, he thought he was dreaming, until he heard the girl's voice who was standing just outside the trailer.

"I am absolutely certain." The girl was saying. "He is Verdorben now."

"That is not possible." A man with dark hair spoke. He was standing next to Gustavo, just in Rico's view. "Bloodlines cannot be turned."

"Ricardo is not from the bloodline. He was adopted by one of our women a year ago." Gustavo explained. "How can we know for sure?"

"Have you always had this tattoo?" The doctor asked Rico, while rubbing a device on the back of his neck and head.

"I don't have any tattoos sir." Rico explained. "Maybe I got dirt on my neck or something."

The dark-haired man walked into the trailer and walked behind Rico. "Well, that is one way to know. He is definitely one of us now."

Rico was thoroughly confused. *One of them now?* He thought to himself. *Can someone become bloodline without being born into it?* He had no idea what was going on or what it meant for him, but he did know one thing. He liked the way he felt now.

*   *   *

"Are you sure you don't want to come with us Liz?" My father asked as I gave him one last hug. We were standing on the edge of the runway, as the former bloodline hunters were filing onto the plane behind the Japanese clan who had boarded first. There were about a dozen men from the Brazilian compound getting on the plane. A few of them had wives, and one even had two young children who were boarding the plane with them. We were using the same airport we had flown into to fly them out.

"I am sure." I reassured my father. "I will only be a day behind you and will come with the next group."

"Okay. I hate to leave you here, but I do need to get back to Alex."

"Right dad." I smirked knowingly at him. "I'm sure it's Alex you are anxious to hurry back to, and not a pretty blonde mother-in-law of mine, right?" I couldn't help but tease him a little.

"I don't know what you're talking about." He tried to sound innocent, but his cheeks flushed slightly with color as he sheepishly smiled.

"Oh, please dad." I chuckled softly. "Tell Alex... and Sara... we said hi."

"Listen Liz, I already feel kinda awkward about liking your mother-in-law, but in my defense, I had feelings for her long before you and Luke got married, okay? Cut me some slack."

"I'm not hating dad." I reassured him. "I think it's great you found someone you care about. And I don't even care that it's Luke's mom. Honestly, I've never met a more kind or sincere person than Sara, and she is great with Alex. Now that I'm married, it's great for Alex to have another mom-like figure in his life."

"What's this mom-like nonsense?" My father tried to sound defensive. "I like her a lot, but nobody said anything about getting married or anything."

"Mr. Scott please." Luke said suddenly from beside me. I was slightly startled, as I hadn't heard him come back over. He had been chatting with some of the other bloodlines from our group that were heading back on this plane with the others. "I have never seen my mom as happy as she is with you. You'd be a fool not to marry her."

"You think so huh…?" My father seemed lost in thought for a moment before continuing. "I thought you were the overprotective son?"

"Oh, I am sir." Luke clarified. "To put it in your words on the day of our wedding. If you ever break her heart, I will kill you." Luke smiled briefly before continuing. "But that doesn't mean you don't have my blessing, as long as you always treat her right."

"Wow…" My father shook his head lightly and smiled. "You got some balls kid. I like that. I knew there was a reason I said you could marry Liz." He patted Luke on the shoulder.

"I didn't mean any disrespect sir." Luke added. "I just think honesty is important in a family."

"Oh, stop with the sir stuff." My father teased. "You married my daughter, which means we are family now. And I'm not offended by what you said. I actually like that you stand up for your mom. Anyways… you two lovebirds be careful. I'll see ya tomorrow." He turned and continued walking up the ramp and onto the plane.

While the stairs folded up into the plane and the door closed, I turned to Luke. "Do you care if I call that Detective now?" I asked.

"Right now?" Luke asked. "I guess we did promise we would let him know… and they did let us go instead of calling it in when they could have."

"Yeah, I just wanted to get it over with before things get crazy." I added.

"I understand." Luke replied. "But I don't think we should call him without a burner phone."

"Oh, I know." I replied, pulling a small flip phone from my jacket pocket. "Isaac said I could use this one, and to smash it afterwards."

"Well okay then." Luke added. "If Isaac is good with it then call away."

I pulled out the business card I had received from the Detective and held it in one hand while I dialed with the other. There was a short delay before the phone started ringing.

"Detective Jimenti. How can I help you?" The voice on the other side of the phone picked up after just two rings.

"Hey Detective, this is Liz Bennett." I said casually.

"Oh wow." There was a brief pause before he continued. "I didn't actually think you would call. Is everything okay Mrs. Bennett?" His voice sounded concerned.

"Actually yes. Everything is great Detective." I replied. "I just wanted to call and thank you for not calling us in back in Idaho. And I also wanted to let you know that you shouldn't see us or the men in black in the news anytime soon. Hopefully ever."

"Well, that's good. Are you and Luke and the rest of the family okay?" The Detective asked. "How sure are you that they won't come after you anymore?"

"We are all good thanks for asking." I answered. "None of us are injured, and let's just say the head of the snake has been cut off, so no one else from that group will be chasing us, or anyone else for that matter."

"I think that's good." Jimenti continued. "Am I gonna get a call about a bunch more bodies though?"

I chuckled before responding. I supposed that with the limited information I was giving him, it wasn't far fetched for him to ask the question. "No Detective. There are no major crime scenes, and I'm pretty sure even the FBI doesn't have jurisdiction south of the equator. Anyways, I can't keep talking, but just wanted to say thank you for doing the right thing, and let you know the problem is solved."

"Well thank you Liz. I appreciate the heads up and am glad everything worked out for you. Please don't hesitate to call if you ever need anything." He added.

"Thank you, Detective. Be safe out there." I hung up as I finished talking just in case they were trying to track the call. I doubted he was but figured it didn't hurt to be safe.

Luke gently grabbed the phone from my hand, before throwing it hard at the ground. The phone broke in half, shattering loudly, and he smashed the larger half several times on the ground with his foot to ensure it was completely ruined.

"Well, that's one way to destroy it." I said, raising an eyebrow as he shrugged. We both turned back towards the plane on the runway.

As the plane began its takeoff, I stood watching, holding Luke's hand in mine. He was smiling down at me, with a knowing look on his face.

"What's that look for?" I asked.

"Oh nothing." He looked back at the plane as it sped down the runway. The nose of the plane slowly lifted, followed by the rest of the plane. As it climbed above the tree line, I felt satisfied.

"You can't oh nothing me. I know you better than that." I added, smiling back at him. "Come on."

"I was just thinking how glad I am that this whole thing worked out so well." He added as his grin broadened. "We did it. We actually did it. And without losing anyone from our clans."

"Yeah... I guess we did." I couldn't help but smile back, as he reached down and scooped me up, spinning and hugging me simultaneously. I felt almost weightless in his strong arms. His embrace felt good. Even better, was knowing he belonged to me now.

I knew there was uncertainty with what would come next. The knowledge that Alastair and his Verdorben had additional captives was concerning. While many of those we had just freed seemed enthusiastic about hunting down those tainted ones and freeing the others, I noticed a palpable difference from the other clans on how they viewed Alastair and his crew. They seemed much more hesitant to even consider going after the Verdorben in Europe, and so far, had only agreed to have more discussions once everyone was back in the United States. In spite of the unknown and likely danger we would soon be faced with, I felt... optimistic. While Leuken held me in his arms, the heat from the sunrise warmed my face ever so slightly. It seemed there was nothing we couldn't do, as long as we had each other.

EPILOGUE

"It should only take a few hours. We will be back before dinner. I doubt the second plane Isaac chartered from Florida will arrive before then." Luke reassured me as he hugged me. We kissed again, before I reluctantly pulled my lips from his. He was going with Alonzo to take some of the bloodlines we had freed to the airport. These ones were from Chile, so Isaac had chartered flights for them. Alonzo had arranged for fake passports and other documentation needed to start their lives over in their native country. There were two sisters, one husband, and seven children in this group. The other sister's husband had been killed hunting our clans, though I don't think they knew if he was killed in Nevada or the Arizona ambush. Either way, my heart was saddened for the three small children who would never see their father again, and for the mother who would have to raise those children alone.

In the last eighteen hours I had spoken with several of the freed bloodlines, and seeing their humanity made me wish we could have freed them sooner, before so many had lost their lives. It was tragic to see the emotional damage caused to so many from the ruthless tainted ones enslaving and using them as they had.

"Okay. Be careful please." I added.

"I will be. Just relax. We killed these tainted ones, and all of those that were hunting us have been freed. The doctor is almost finished operating on the ones at the offsite location. After that, the ones Isaac was able to talk into joining us will head back to the states with us, and the others can return to their homes."

"Oh, I know. I'm glad. I didn't even think that there would be so many at the other location. That is a lot of bloodlines." I squeezed him one more time before pulling away. "Now get them on that plane and hurry back to me."

"As you wish." Luke smiled and winked at me, before turning to join the family. Alonzo was already in the driver seat of the front SUV, and the families loaded into both of them as Luke got in the driver seat of the rear car. I watched as the two vehicles drove up the long private drive to the main road.

As I turned back to face the mansion, I noticed Tobias standing not too far off. Haysom Fitch, who stood at least a foot shorter than Tobias, was engaged in heated conversation with the man. I walked towards them as their conversation continued.

"So, you are telling me." Haysom was saying. "That they only leave this crazy molester creep alone because he has a nuclear bomb, and they are worried he will kill himself and them with it?"

"That is my understanding." Tobias replied. "For decades he ran and hid from them, which was easy with him being a fade. After the collapse of the Soviet Union though, he got his hands on a couple of dirty bombs from Ukraine. He uses them as an insurance policy of sorts."

"Someone needs to take that guy out too." Haysom was shaking his head as he spoke.

"Hey guys." I said as I joined them. "Before they left, Alonzo updated that there are only a couple dozen bloodlines left who still need their implants removed. Isaac and Gustavo said that there are about fifteen of them that want to join us in the United States. They want to help fight Alastair to free their brothers. The rest of them are planning on heading their own separate ways."

"So, if we add the ten from this group here, including Gustavo that brings our total to about fifty willing to fight." Tobias said. The man actually had a hint of excitement in his voice. "I suppose if I am to die, at least my death will have purpose trying to stop that man."

"Wow!" Haysom said loudly, shooting an angry look at Tobias. "Well with that much optimism, we are guaranteed to succeed." His voice was dripping with sarcasm.

"Surely you listened to Isaac when he spoke about what happened the last time someone tried to take out Alastair and his crew?" Tobias prodded. "They were slaughtered as soon as…" Tobias cut off suddenly, and I realized why as I felt Verdorben in my mind. There were two of them, coming from far to the North.

"You feel that too?" I asked Tobias.

"Yes." He replied, urgency flooding his voice as he spoke. "We need to warn the others immediately! Somehow Alastair has found us!"

"Calm down Tobias." I replied. "It must be my father and the newly changed one. Isaac said he chartered another Jet. I'm sure it is them. Can't you sense they are coming from the same direction they left in?"

"You don't survive as long as I have by assuming things Elizabeth. Even if there is a chance it is Alastair, we must prepare. We need to evacuate everyone now." Tobias said curtly.

Haysom eyed Tobias suspiciously, while shrugging at me. "Do you think it's the main bad guy tainted one Liz?" He asked.

"No." I replied. "It must be my father and the new Verdorben. Should we get the next group ready and meet them at the airport?"

We were not expecting the other jet until later tonight, but obviously Isaac had worked it out.

"I'm telling you Liz, this is a mistake!" Tobias began.

"That's enough Tobias!" I interrupted. "I don't want to hear another word from you about this subject. You are always acting afraid of your own shadow, and it's embarrassing. First you freaked out about freeing these people, then you didn't want me to stop the shooters in Las Vegas, and now this. Just don't talk till we get to the airport.

"I thought that the plan was for my father to head back and stay in Idaho with the newly changed Verdorben, but the plans must have changed for some reason. Let's send Haysom and the rest of the volunteers besides Gustavo. He can hop on the next flight with the others from the off sight that wanted to help fight. I will call Isaac to make sure my father is on that plain, just to be safe."

We scrambled to warn the other families that they needed to pack more quickly. While they seemed somewhat surprised by the updated timeline, there was also an excitement on most of their faces. My guess was the thought of freedom after being prisoners in this place for so long was the cause of their eagerness to leave. I tried calling Isaac to confirm my theory about the plane, but he didn't answer.

It took five vehicles to load everyone in, with Haysom and Tobias each driving one of the other vehicles. I could sense my father and Rico land, about fifteen minutes after we had left the mansion, and was surprised that they did not land at the same small airport we had a few days before. For some reason they had chosen to land at an even smaller landing strip, about twelve miles north of the compound, instead of at the other airport. We had to change direction and circle back a little to get to that airport.

I tried calling my father while driving but was surprised when he didn't answer the phone. Perhaps the roaming was turned off on his phone or something, as it had gone straight to voicemail. I tried calling Luke, and then Isaac again next but got their voicemails as well. A few minutes later, we pulled up to the small landing strip that was called an airport on google maps. This one had a single runway and was even smaller than the one we had flown into two days before. Just off the edge of the runway, I saw two smaller, older looking planes. My guess was that they were used for crop dusting some of the farms in the area, but I wasn't positive.

We parked in the small dirt parking lot, and everyone started unloading their gear. There was only one jet on the runway, a dark silver one that looked slightly newer and larger than the one we had flown in before. "That's a nicer jet than the last one." I said to Haysom as he looked at the jet sitting on the tarmac. From where we had parked, only the tail of the plane was visible.

"Fine by me." Haysom replied. "The sooner we get this group airborne, the sooner we will be able to leave ourselves."

We started walking over to the small industrial building between the parking lot and the fenced off runway. Dark clouds overhead blocked the sun, causing the air to cool and putting all of us under the shadow of the clouds. Just before we reached the front door, I could sense my father and the other one walking through the building towards the front. As the front door to the building opened, I suddenly sensed another tainted one. It felt faint, and I could barely tell it was there at first, but then it became a little less cloudy. The feeling in my mind almost reminded me of when the female had gone to sleep, and suddenly came into my senses. The only difference was this Verdorben felt somehow hazy still. As I focused closer on the faded one, it was hard to place their exact location, other than close in front of me, near the other two. I thought for a moment that perhaps my mind was playing tricks on me. It had been a while since I had last slept.

Just as I started to freak out inside, my phone rang. Pulling it from my pocket, I saw it was Isaac. "Wait." I said to the others, holding my free hand up as I answered the phone. "Hello." I said.

"Hey Liz. What did you need?" Isaac sounded casual on the phone.

"I didn't know your other jet was coming to this smaller airport." I told Isaac. "I am guessing they found the other tainted one who had changed?" I had surmised that the other one I was sensing must be the other human that had been changed when the two Verdorben had been killed, since we initially only found the one.

"What are you talking about Liz?" Isaac suddenly sounded concerned. "The other jet I chartered just left Florida an hour ago."

My stomach sunk so suddenly that I felt like I was gut punched. "Liz, we need to go now!" Tobias said urgently from behind. His voice was almost a shout. "That's not your father!"

Just then the door to the building opened, and several men clad in all silver flooded quickly out of the building. After the first two, was a shorter Persian looking man with a hardened face, wearing dark colored, fancy, close fitting clothes that didn't match the others. I could sense that he was Verdorben. Two more tainted ones filed out right behind him, in addition to about twenty more of the men clad in all silver.

One Verdorben was a tall, pale skinned man, with broad shoulders but a slender waste. The female next to him had hair just as blonde as the taller man, even if she was much shorter. I could feel that she was the blurry one in my senses. I wanted to disappear so badly, but I knew it was too late for that. Instead, I managed just one word. "Run!" I shouted urgently as I turned to flee myself.

I ran for the car, knowing we would have to move fast, with only about a thirty-yard head start from these silver clad hunters and other Verdorben. I reached the SUV quickly, but as I unlocked the doors and moved to get in, I could see that only Tobias, Haysom and a few others were at the cars. The women, holding their children's hands as they ran, were only halfway to us, and the men in silver, with dark colored swords drawn, were catching them.

"They are already lost Liz. If we don't run, we will die!" Tobias said as he reached the other SUV. I glanced back at the others, the dad, uncle and mother had all been knocked over by the men in silver, and a couple of the larger children had been scooped up by others. They tried to fight back, but it became obvious that these men in silver were bloodlines themselves. *This must have been some from Alastair's group.* I thought to myself. Seeing the children caused something inside of me to break, and I knew what I had to do.

Some of the men from Brazil had formed into a line, between two of the women and two smaller children, with dark colored swords drawn to protect themselves and the young ones, but the others had already been captured without a fight. We had about ten from the compound, in addition to Darsh and the other two from the Indian clan all standing in a defensive position.

"No Tobias. We help them now. Free the children." I said, looking back at the man as I began to move back towards the children. Tobias had a look of frustration and hopelessness, but he sprang into motion as the bracelet compelled him to. Looking past the men in silver, I could see the Verdorben, walking slowly towards us. They looked confused, but not at all worried.

"I guess we are doing this." Haysom said through gritted teeth, as he turned to follow me. I ran past him. I didn't have a weapon on me, so I ran at the closest silver clad man, who was holding the oldest child, a teenage boy in a bear hug. He seemed surprised when I ran at him and didn't let go of the boy until I slammed into him. All three of us fell to the ground, but I grabbed his sword from the sheath on his back as we fell.

Pulling the blade free, I quickly sliced off the man's head. The sword was straight, unlike the bloodline hunters we had freed, and appeared sharp on both sides, with a sharp point at the tip. As the man fell to the earth, the boy stood up, looking first at me in disbelief, and then at the others. He was frozen with panic, so I told him what to do.

"Run!" I said urgently to him, hoping the others would not hear. "You must warn the others. If we are captured, you must tell them, or your family will never be free. Now go, run!"

The boy didn't hesitate but turned and ran towards the forest away from the runway. I turned just in time to see two silver bloodlines running towards me. One was rushing at me, while the other seemed intent on chasing after the boy I had just freed. That one ran almost right past me, his focus solely on the boy running towards the tree line.

Knowing I couldn't let him get the boy, I turned and hurled myself towards him as fast as I could, jumping sideways through the air just as he passed me. As I jumped, I slashed at his rear leg, easily slicing through the calf. This caused the man to fall, and I wasted no time finishing him off with a slash through his neck and shoulder that severed his head and arm from his torso. Turning quickly, I blocked an overhead strike from the other attacker, who was slashing towards my head. I blocked another strike at my knee, then my head. It became immediately obvious that I didn't have the skill with a sword that this man did, so after blocking the next strike I kicked him hard in the groin. He stumbled forward in pain, which gave me the opening I needed to strike at his sword arm. His sword moved to block my strike, but he was a split second too slow, so I cut through his wrist, causing him to drop his weapon. As he turned to flee, I stabbed him through the chest, and he fell forward. Pulling my sword free from the moaning man, I sliced his head off as well. Ben had taught me during our play sword sparing not to consider a bloodline dead unless he was beheaded, since they healed so quickly.

I noticed that there were three men running at Tobias, who had just killed another bloodline and was pulling a small child up off the ground. The child began to run towards the forest, as Tobias turned to face his attackers. To my left, I could hear swords clanging where Haysom had joined the other bloodlines who were protecting the women and children. Our people were outnumbered there, but it looked like fifteen of the gray men against our twelve, so I decided to help Tobias first.

Running quickly, I jumped at the closest of the three just as they were about to attack Tobias. My sword struck his leg, as he turned too late to block me completely. Unfortunately, it only tore halfway through the flesh and didn't sever the leg, but the man still fell forward, groaning loudly. As the man tumbled forward, I did a backswing follow through strike to his right arm, cutting through it at his elbow as he dropped his sword. While the third attacker fought with Tobias and their swords clanged back and forth, the second of these three men turned and lunged at me. I blocked his first two strikes, but his third one cut into my wrist slightly, and the unexpected pain caused me to drop my sword. I almost panicked as he stabbed at my stomach, but I was able to pivot just enough to dodge the strike. Grabbing the man's wrist with both hands, I kicked as hard as I could at his closest knee. Luckily it snapped, as his leg bent sideways. The blow also caused him to loosen his grip on the sword, so I wrenched the hilt free from his hand. He grabbed at the blade as I pulled it free, slicing his hand in the process. While adjusting the sword in one hand, I punched him in the face with my off hand, causing him to fall sideways to the ground. He raised up slightly, preparing to stand, but I quickly beheaded him with his own sword. For a split second I felt proud, as I saw Tobias finish off the man he had been battling with. Screams from behind made me turn my attention to where the others were fighting.

The women and children were running towards the forest, as half of the Brazilians had already been killed. "Split up as you run!" I shouted at the women, as I noticed two men chasing after them. The Verdorben stood slightly off watching, and for some reason had not engaged. I realized why when I saw that it was now seven men in gray against four of our men, including Haysom, who had blood running down the side of his face. Turning to Tobias, I told him to go help the kids, as I ran to help Haysom and the others. It looked like two more of them were about to be struck down, as the Brazilians and Haysom were retreating. They dodged and parried strikes as best they could, but it didn't look good for them. Another fell to the gray men as I moved to help.

I shouted loudly as I ran, trying to draw attention from the others. It worked, as two of them turned to face me. Lunging at the man on the left, who was shorter with tan skin, a dark mustache, and an otherwise baby face, I realized I had made a mistake. As I swung at him, he easily blocked my blow while pivoting to strike back. While this was happening, the other man landed a blow to my right side near my hip, and the stinging pain in my side instantly told me he had cut into my flesh. It also made me realize, that while the blade had cut me, it seemed to have stopped when it hit my hip bone, barely cutting through the skin. *The clouds.* I thought to myself, as I realized the sun being darkened made me less susceptible to injury.

Knowing this, instead of blocking the strike at my leg by the nearer man, I ignored it and instead quickly thrust my sword up through his neck and into his head. Stabbing pain in my leg let me know his sword had struck before I killed him. Pulling my blade free from the man's head, I ducked a strike from the other gray clad attacker, while swiping at his leg. I cut through part of his shin, but his sword struck my left shoulder at the same time, causing more searing pain. The man seemed surprised when his blade didn't cut clear through my shoulder, so I quickly chopped at his sword arm as he moved to strike me again. This time I found my mark, slicing through his elbow as his sword and the lower part of his arm fell to the earth. As he turned to run, I sliced through his ankle, causing him to fall forward.

As I was just about to finish him off, I felt movement behind me and quickly turned to strike. I slashed hard at this attacker and was surprised as I turned to see it was one of the Verdorben. I had been so intent on fighting, that I hadn't even noticed the well-dressed shorter man sneak up behind me. I slashed at his neck but realized he didn't even have his sword out as he blocked my strike with his arm. My sword cut into it, but only barely as he quickly moved to grab my wrist. I pulled back and kicked him in the chest, knocking him backwards through the air before crashing on the dirt.

I thought it strange that he hadn't used his sword, as I had felt pressure on my left wrist. When the female Verdorben suddenly shouted "Stop!" I thought that she was talking to the male I was fighting with. That is… until I realized that my body stopped moving. Panic crushed me to the core as I realized I could not move. I tried moving my arms, my legs, but my body stood still. Desperation made me want to deny what had just happened, but when I glanced at my left wrist and saw the silver bracelet attached, I knew I was doomed.

The Verdorben I had just cut glanced at his wrist where it was bleeding from the side but appeared mostly unphased. I noticed he also wore a silver bracelet, nearly identical to the one he had just placed on me.

"You can move, but you will not hurt anyone unless I tell you to, and you will not in any way attempt to remove that bracelet. You also will not allow anyone else to remove your bracelet unless I say so." The woman was smiling with a smug look on her face as she walked closer to me. Her baby blue blouse looked silk, and she wore tight white pants that appeared fancy but flexible. "You are going to be my new pet. What is your name pet?"

I turned to see that Tobias had killed the other two gray men, and the Brazilian bloodlines had disappeared into the forest. Tobias was walking back towards me but appeared confused. Nearby, Haysom had just killed the last man in gray, but he himself looked like he was missing his left hand at the wrist and was covered in blood. He ran towards me with his sword raised, standing between me and the Persian Verdorben, who had stepped back after putting the bracelet on me.

"If you want the lady, you'll have to go through me." Haysom said as he raised his shiny Terralium blade in my defense.

"Run Haysom!" I said urgently. "They have me…"

"Kill him now!" The female Verdorben said, and instantly I felt my body move against my will.

"No!" I shouted as my arms raised my sword and brought it down in a swiping motion, slicing Haysom's head off at the neck from behind. His body slumped to the ground, dropping the terralium blade, and his head came to rest facing me. His eyes looked cold and lifeless, as they lay open on the ground, seeming to look at me.

"Ahhh!" I shouted as the realization of what I had just done against my will hit me. I could see the feeling of betrayal in Haysom's motionless eyes. I turned to see Tobias, who had stopped about twenty yards away. He looked conflicted, as if he didn't know what to do, and then I realized he was stuck. He had finished the order I gave him to help the kids, so now he was defaulting to protecting me, but no one was actively trying to hurt me. "Run Tobias, until you are out of their range, then go back to the others!" I shouted at him. He instantly sprang into motion.

"Call him back." The girl said, chuckling obnoxiously as she ordered me.

"Come back Tobias!" I shouted after the man, who instantly turned around and began walking back towards me. Turning to face the girl, I couldn't hold back the desperation or the rage I was feeling. "I am going to kill you!" I said coldly, trying to hold back the tears that were already flowing from my face.

"Silence!" The woman said. "You will not speak unless someone asks you a question, and then you will always answer honestly. Are we clear pet?"

"Yes." I answered through gritted teeth.

"You will also address me as Master." She added. "Now what is your name pet?"

"Elizabeth Bennett." I replied, hating that I was now a passenger in the mind of this nightmare I was living.

"Well Elizabeth. You will now answer to pet, or..." The girl paused, smiling mischievously. "Bethy. Yes, I like the sound of that. I will call you Bethy my pet." She laughed in a high-pitched, almost shrill tone. I felt myself die on the inside as the reality of what just happened sank in. I had been enslaved again, only this time Isaac was not coming to save me, and neither was anyone else. The only ones left in the parking lot were Tobias and I, the other three Verdorben, and one gray clad bloodline hunter. Everyone else had either been killed or fled. My only hope now was that the others would go for help, and that somehow, they would be able to find and free me. That is... if I even lived long enough for that to happen. Any hopes of rescue were dashed when the blonde-haired woman spoke again.

"Back to the plane. Once we finish refueling, we will regroup to get more blood guards before we return. I wouldn't want these animals to try and free my newest pets."

# # #

Acknowledgements

I would like to thank everyone who helped support me throughout this series. I appreciate those who provided feedback after reading the original manuscript: Logan, Amber, Jeremiah, and Will. A special thanks to Jessica, who focused on our most important responsibility as parents so that I could finish this book.

About the Author

Lee Larsen lives in Las Vegas with his wife and five children. He graduated from University of Nevada Las Vegas with a B.A. He enjoys reading, basketball, running, swimming, hiking, and spending time with friends and family.

Made in the USA
Las Vegas, NV
10 October 2023

78893731R00184